A SHADOW IN SUMMER

Tor Books by Daniel Abraham

>+<

The Long Price Quartet
A Shadow in Summer
*Winter Cities

*Denotes forthcoming book

A SHADOW in SUMMER

>+<

Book One
of the
Long Price Quartet

>+<

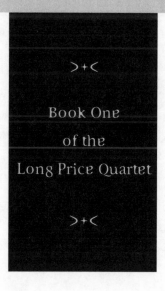

Daniel Abraham

TOR®

A Tom Doherty Associates Book
New York

A SHADOW IN SUMMER: BOOK ONE OF THE LONG PRICE QUARTET

Copyright © 2006 by Daniel Abraham

This book is printed on acid-free paper.

Edited by James Frenkel

Book design by Jane Adele Regina

Maps by Jackie Aher

A Tor Book
Published by Tom Doherty Associates, LLC
175 Fifth Avenue
New York, NY 10010

www.tor.com

Tor® is a registered trademark of Tom Doherty Associates, LLC.

Library of Congress Cataloging-in-Publication Data

Abraham, Daniel.
  A shadow in summer / Daniel Abraham.—1st ed.
    p. cm.
  "A Tom Doherty Associates Book."
  ISBN 0-765-31340-5 (acid-free paper)
  EAN 978-0-765-31340-9
  1. City and town life—Fiction. I. Title.
  PS3601.B677S53 2006
  813'.6—dc22
                                    2005016832

First Edition: March 2006

Printed in the United States of America

0 9 8 7 6 5 4 3 2 1

To Fred Saberhagen,
the first of my many teachers

ACKNOWLEDGMENTS

Romantic visions aside, writing is not something often done in isolation. I would like to thank everyone whose input made this book better than I could have done alone. Especially Walter Jon Williams, Melinda Snodgrass, Steve and Jan Stirling, Terry England, John Miller, Sally Gwylan, Yvonne Coats, Emily Mah, Sage Walker, Victor Milan, George R.R. Martin, and all the various members of the New Mexico Critical Mass Workshop.

Thanks are also due to Shawna McCarthy for her faith in the project, and Jim Frenkel for his hard work and kind attentions to a first-time novelist.

But I am especially grateful to Connie Willis, who gave me my first advice on the book, Tom Doherty, who gave me my last, and Katherine Abraham, without whom it wouldn't have been anywhere near as fun in between.

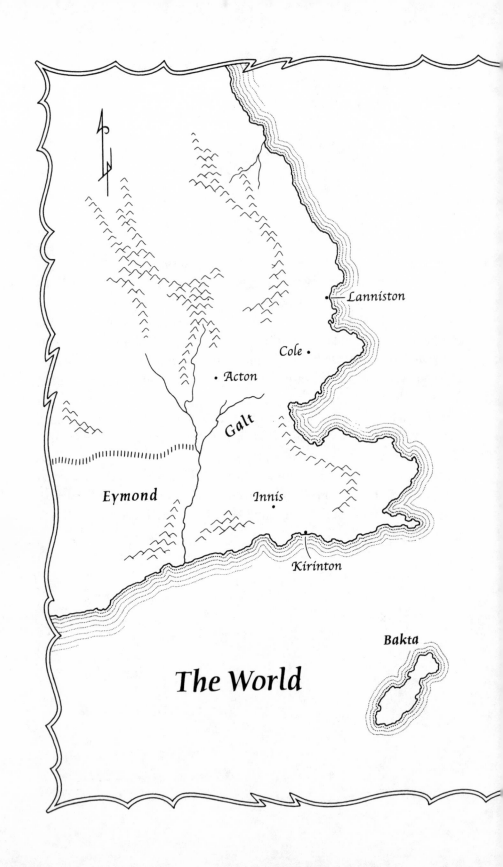

Lanniston

Cole •

• Acton

Galt

Eymond

Innis •

Kirinton

Bakta

The World

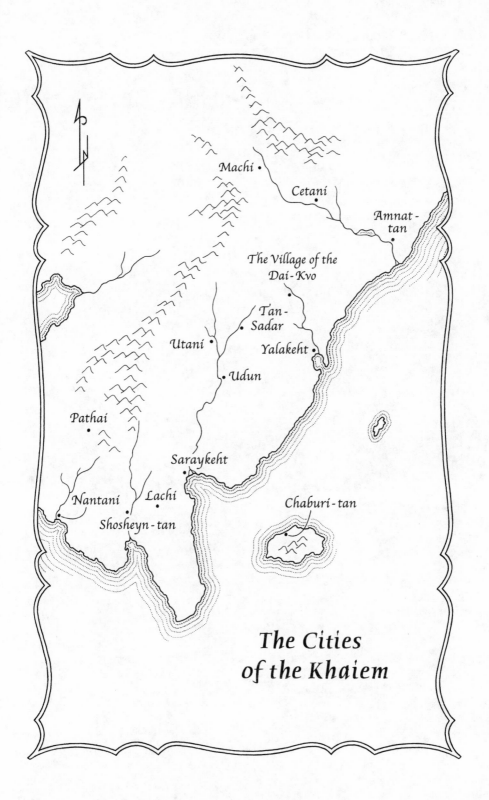

Machi •

Cetani •

Amnat-
tan •

The Village of the
Dai-Kvo

Tan-
Sadar •

Utani •   Yalakeht •

• Udun

Pathai
•

Saraykeht
•

Nantani •   • Lachi

Shosheyn-tan   Chaburi-tan •

The Cities
of the Khaiem

A SHADOW IN SUMMER

PROLOG

>+< Otah took the blow on the ear, the flesh opening under the rod. Tahi-kvo, Tahi the teacher, pulled the thin lacquered wood through the air with a fluttering sound like bird wings. Otah's discipline held. He did not shift or cry out. Tears welled in his eyes, but his hands remained in a pose of greeting.

"Again," Tahi-kvo barked. "And correctly!"

"We are honored by your presence, most high Dai-kvo," Otah said sweetly, as if it were the first time he had attempted the ritual phrase. The old man sitting before the fire considered him closely, then adopted a pose of acceptance. Tahi-kvo made a sound of satisfaction in the depths of his throat.

Otah bowed, holding still for three breaths and hoping that Tahi-kvo wouldn't strike him for trembling. The moment stretched, and Otah nearly let his eyes stray to his teacher. It was the old man with his ruined whisper who at last spoke the words that ended the ritual and released him.

"Go, disowned child, and attend to your studies."

Otah turned and walked humbly out of the room. Once he had pulled the thick wooden door closed behind him and walked down the chill hallway toward the common rooms, he gave himself permission to touch his new wound.

The other boys were quiet as he passed through the stone halls of the school, but several times their gazes held him and his new shame. Only the older boys in the black robes of Milah-kvo's disciples laughed at him. Otah took himself to the quarters where all the boys in his cohort slept. He removed the ceremonial gown, careful not to touch it with blood, and washed the wound in cold water. The stinging cream for cuts and scrapes was in an earthenware jar beside the water basin.

He took two fingers and slathered the vinegar-smelling ointment onto the open flesh of his ear. Then, not for the first time since he had come to the school, he sat on his spare, hard bunk and wept.

"This boy," the Dai-kvo said as he took up the porcelain bowl of tea. Its heat was almost uncomfortable. "He holds some promise?"

"Some," Tahi allowed as he leaned the lacquered rod against the wall and took the seat beside his master.

"He seems familiar."

"Otah Machi. Sixth son of the Khai Machi."

"I recall his brothers. Also boys of some promise. What became of them?"

"They spent their years, took the brand, and were turned out. Most are. We have three hundred in the school now and forty in the black under Milah-kvo's care. Sons of the Khaiem or the ambitious families of the utkhaiem."

"So many? I see so few."

Tahi took a pose of agreement, the cant of his wrists giving it a nuance that might have been sorrow or apology.

"Not many are both strong enough and wise. And the stakes are high."

The Dai-kvo sipped his tea and considered the fire.

"I wonder," the old man said, "how many realize we are teaching them nothing."

"We teach them all. Letters, numbers. Any of them could take a trade after they leave the school."

"But nothing of use. Nothing of poetry. Nothing of the andat."

"If they realize that, most high, they're halfway to your door. And for the ones we turn away . . . It's better, most high."

"Is it?"

Tahi shrugged and looked into the fire. He looked older, the Dai-kvo thought, especially about the eyes. But he had met Tahi as a rude youth many years before. The age he saw there now, and the cruelty, were seeds he himself had cultivated.

"When they have failed, they take the brand and make their own fates," Tahi said.

"We take away their only hope of rejoining their families, of taking a place at the courts of the Khaiem. They have no family. They cannot control the andat," the Dai-kvo said. "We throw these boys away much as their fathers have. What becomes of them, I wonder?"

"Much the same as becomes of anyone, I imagine. The ones from low families of the utkhaiem are hardly worse off than when they came. The sons of the Khaiem . . . once they take the brand, they cannot inherit, and it saves them from being killed for their blood rights. That alone is a gift in its way."

It was true. Every generation saw the blood of the Khaiem spilled. It was the way of the Empire. And in times when all three of a Khai's acknowledged sons slaughtered one another, the high families of the utkhaiem unsheathed their knives, and cities were caught for a time in fits of violence from which the poets held themselves apart like priests at a dog fight. These boys in the school's care were exempt from those wars at only the price of everything they had known in their short lives. And yet . . .

"Disgrace is a thin gift," the Dai-kvo said.

Tahi, his old student who had once been a boy like these, sighed.

"It's what we can offer."

THE DAI-KVO LEFT IN THE MORNING JUST AFTER DAWN, STEPPING THROUGH the great bronze doors that opened only for him. Otah stood in the ranks of his cohort, still holding a pose of farewell. Behind him, someone took the chance of scratching—Otah could hear the shifting sound of fingers against cloth. He didn't look back. Two of the oldest of Milah-kvo's black robes pulled the great doors closed.

In the dim winter light that filtered through high-set, thin windows, Otah could see the bustle of the black robes taking charge of the cohorts. The day's tasks varied. The morning might be spent working in the school—repairing walls or washing laundry or scraping ice from the garden walkways that no one seemed to travel besides the boys set to tend them. The evening would be spent in study. Numbers, letters, religion, history of the Old Empire, the Second Empire, the War, the cities of the Khaiem. And more often these last weeks, one of the two teachers would stand at the back of the room while one of the black robes lectured and questioned. Milah-kvo would sometimes interrupt and tell jokes or take the lecture himself, discussing things the black robes never spoke of. Tahi-kvo would only observe and punish. All of Otah's cohort bore the marks of the lacquered stick.

Riit-kvo, one of the oldest of the black robes, led Otah and his cohort to the cellars. For hours as the sun rose unseen, Otah swept dust from stones that seemed still cold from the last winter and then washed them with water and rags until his knuckles were raw. Then Riit-kvo called them to order, considered them, slapped one boy whose stance was not to his standards, and marched them to the dining hall. Otah looked neither forward nor back, but focused on the shoulders of the boy ahead of him.

The midday meal was cold meat, yesterday's bread, and a thin barley soup that Otah treasured because it was warm. Too soon, Riit called them to wash their bowls and knives and follow him. Otah found himself at the front of the line—an unenviable place—and so was the first to step into the cold listening room with its stone benches and thin windows that had never known glass. Tahi-kvo was waiting there for them.

None of them knew why the round-faced, scowling teacher had taken an interest in the cohort, though speculations were whispered in the dark of their barracks. The Dai-kvo had chosen one of them to go and study the secrets of the andat, to become one of the poets, gain power even higher than the Khaiem, and skip over the black robes of Milah-kvo entirely. Or one of their families had repented sending their child, however minor in the line of succession, to the school and was in negotiation to forgo the branding and take their disowned son back into the fold.

Otah had listened, but believed none of the stories. They were the fantasies of the frightened and the weak, and he knew that if he clung to one, it would shatter him. Dwelling in the misery of the school and hoping for nothing beyond survival was the only way to keep his soul from flying apart. He would endure his term and be turned out into the world. This was his third year at the school. He was twelve now, and near the halfway point of his time. And today was another evil to be borne as the day before and the day ahead. To think too far in the past or the future was dangerous. Only when he let his dreams loose did he think of learning the secrets of the andat, and that happened so rarely as to call itself never.

Riit-kvo, his eyes on the teacher at the back as much as on the students, began to declaim the parable of the Twin Dragons of Chaos. It was a story Otah knew, and he found his mind wandering. Through the stone arch of the window, Otah could see a crow hunched on a high branch. It reminded him of something he could not quite recall.

"Which of the gods tames the spirits of water?" Riit-kvo snapped. Otah pulled himself back to awareness and straightened his spine.

Riit-kvo pointed to a thick-set boy across the room.

"Oladac the Wanderer!" the boy said, taking a pose of gratitude to one's teacher.

"And why were the spirits who stood by and neither fought with the gods nor against them consigned to a lower hell than the servants of chaos?"

Again Riit-kvo pointed.

"Because they should have fought alongside the gods!" the boy shouted.

It was a wrong answer. Because they were cowards, Otah thought, and knew he was correct. Tahi's lacquered rod whirred and stuck the boy hard on the shoulder. Riit-kvo smirked and returned to his story.

After the class, there was another brief work detail for which Tahi-kvo did not join them. Then the evening meal, and then the end of another day. Otah was grateful to crawl into his bunk and pull the thin blanket up to his neck. In the winter, many of the boys slept in their robes against the cold, and Otah was among that number. Despite all this, he preferred the winter. During the warmer times, he would still wake some mornings having forgotten where he was, expecting to see the walls of his father's home, hear the voices of his older brothers—Biitrah, Danat, and Kaiin. Perhaps see his mother's smile. The rush of memory was worse than any blow of Tahi-kvo's rod, and he bent his will toward erasing the memories he had of his family. He was not loved or wanted in his home, and he understood that thinking too much about this truth would kill him.

As he drifted toward sleep, Riit-kvo's harsh voice murmuring the lesson of the spirits who refused to fight spun through his mind. They were cowards, consigned to the deepest and coldest hell.

When the question came, his eyes flew open. He sat up. The other boys were all in their cots. One, not far from him, was crying in his sleep. It was not an unusual sound. The words still burned in Otah's mind. The coward spirits, consigned to hell.

And what keeps them there? his quiet inner voice asked him. *Why do they remain in hell?*

He lay awake for hours, his mind racing.

———

THE TEACHERS' QUARTERS OPENED ON A COMMON ROOM. SHELVES LINED the walls, filled with books and scrolls. A fire pit glowed with coals prepared for them by the most honored of Milah-kvo's black-robed boys. The wide gap of a window—glazed double to hold out the cold of winter, the heat of the summer—looked out over the roadway leading south to the high road. Tahi sat now, warming his feet at the fire and staring out into the cold plain beyond. Milah opened the door behind him and strode in.

"I expected you earlier," Tahi said.

Milah briefly took a pose of apology.

"Annat Ryota was complaining about the kitchen flue smoking again," he said.

Tahi grunted.

"Sit. The fire's warm."

"Fires often are," Milah agreed, his tone dry and mocking. Tahi managed a thin smile as his companion took a seat.

"What did he make of your boys?" Tahi asked.

"Much the same as last year. They have seen through the veil and now lead their brothers toward knowledge," Milah said, but his hands were in a pose of gentle mockery. "They are petty tyrants to a man. Any andat strong enough to be worth holding would eat them before their hearts beat twice."

"Pity."

"Hardly a surprise. And yours?"

Tahi chewed for a moment at his lower lip and leaned forward. He could feel Milah's gaze on him.

"Otah Machi disgraced himself," Tahi said. "But he accepted the punishment well. The Dai-kvo thinks he may have promise."

Milah shifted. When Tahi looked over, the teacher had taken a pose of query. Tahi considered the implicit question, then nodded.

"There have been some other signs," Tahi said. "I think you should put a watch over him. I hate to lose him to you, in a way."

"You like him."

Tahi took a pose of acknowledgement that held the nuance of a confession of failure.

"I may be cruel, old friend," Tahi said, dropping into the familiar, "but you're heartless."

The fair-haired teacher laughed, and Tahi couldn't help but join him. They sat silent then for a while, each in his own thoughts. Milah rose, shrugged off his thick woolen top robe. Beneath it he still wore the formal silks from his audience yesterday with the Dai-kvo. Tahi poured them both bowls of rice wine.

"It was good to see him again," Milah said sometime later. There was a melancholy note in his voice. Tahi took a pose of agreement, then sipped his wine.

"He looked so *old*," Tahi said.

OTAH'S PLAN, SUCH AS IT WAS, TOOK LITTLE PREPARATION, AND YET NEARLY three weeks passed between the moment he understood the parable of the spirits who stood aside and the night when he took action. That night, he waited until the others were asleep before he pushed off the thin blankets, put on every robe and legging he had, gathered his few things, and left his cohort for the last time.

The stone hallways were unlit, but he knew his way well enough that he had no need for light. He made his way to the kitchen. The pantry was unlocked—no one would steal food for fear of being found out and beaten. Otah scooped double handfuls of hard rolls and dried fruit into his satchel. There was no need for water. Snow still covered the ground, and Tahi-kvo had shown them how to melt snow with the heat of their own bodies walking without the cold penetrating to their hearts.

Once he was provisioned, his path led him to the great hall—moonlight from the high windows showing ghost-dim the great aisle where he had held a pose of obeisance every morning for the last three years. The doors, of course, were barred, and while he was strong enough to open them, the sounds might have woken someone. He took a pair of wide, netted snowshoes from the closet beside the great doors and went up the stairs to the listening room. There, the thin windows looked out on a world locked in winter. Otah's breath plumed already in the chill.

He threw the snowshoes and satchel out the window to the snow-cushioned ground below, then squeezed through and lowered himself from the outer stone sill until he hung by his fingertips. The fall was not so far.

He dusted the snow from his leggings, tied the snowshoes to his feet by their thick leather thongs, took up the bulging satchel and started off, walking south toward the high road.

The moon, near the top of its nightly arc, had moved the width of two thick-gloved hands toward the western horizon before Otah knew he was not alone. The footsteps that had kept perfect time with his own fell out of their pattern—as intentional a provocation as clearing a throat. Otah froze, then turned.

"Good evening, Otah Machi," Milah-kvo said, his tone casual. "A good night for a walk, eh? Cold though."

Otah did not speak, and Milah-kvo strode forward, his hand on his own satchel, his footsteps nearly silent. His breath was thick and white as a goose feather.

"Yes," the teacher said. "Cold, and far from your bed."

Otah took a pose of acknowledgement appropriate for a student to a teacher. It had no nuance of apology, and Otah hoped that Milah-kvo would not see his trembling, or if he did would ascribe it to the cold.

"Leaving before your term is complete, boy. You disgrace yourself."

Otah switched to a pose of thanks appropriate to the end of a lesson, but Milah-kvo waved the formality aside and sat in the snow, considering him with an interest that Otah found unnerving.

"Why do it?" Milah-kvo asked. "There's still hope of redeeming yourself. You might still be found worthy. So why run away? Are you so much a coward?"

Otah found his voice.

"It would be cowardice that kept me, Milah-kvo."

"How so?" The teacher's voice held nothing of judgment or testing. It was like a friend asking a question because he truly did not know the answer.

"There are no locks on hell," Otah said. It was the first time he had tried to express this to someone else, and it proved harder than he had expected. "If there aren't locks, then what can hold anyone there besides fear that leaving might be worse?"

"And you think the school is a kind of hell."

It was not a question, so Otah did not answer.

"If you keep to this path, you'll be the lowest of the low," Milah said. "A disgraced child without friend or ally. And without the brand to protect you, your older brothers may well track you down and kill you."

"Yes."

"Do you have someplace to go?"

"The high road leads to Pathai and Nantani."

"Where you know no one."

Otah took a pose of agreement.

"This doesn't frighten you?" the teacher asked.

"It is the decision I've made." He could see the amusement in Milah-kvo's face at his answer.

"Fair enough, but I think there's an alternative you haven't considered."

The teacher reached into his satchel and pulled out a small cloth bundle. He hefted it for a moment, considering, and dropped it on the snow between them. It was a black robe.

Otah took a pose of intellectual inquiry. It was a failure of vocabulary, but Milah-kvo took his meaning.

"Andat are powerful, Otah. Like small gods. And they don't love being held to a single form. They fight it, and since the forms they have are a reflection of the poets who bind them. . . . The world is full of willing victims—people who embrace the cruelty meted out against them. An andat formed from a mind like that would destroy the poet who bound it and escape. That you have chosen action is what the black robes mean."

"Then . . . the others . . . they all left the school too?"

Milah laughed. Even in the cold, it was a warm sound.

"No. No, you've all taken different paths. Ansha tried to wrestle Tahi-kvo's stick away from him. Ranit Kiru asked forbidden questions, took the punishment for them, and asked again until Tahi beat him asleep. He was too sore to wear any robe at all for weeks, but his bruises were black enough. But you've each *done* something. If you choose to take up the robe, that is. Leave it, and really, this is just a conversation. Interesting maybe, but trivial."

"And if I take it?"

"You will never be turned out of the school so long as you wear the black. You will help to teach the normal boys the lesson you've learned—to stand by your own strength."

Otah blinked, and something—some emotion he couldn't put a name to—bloomed in his breast. His flight from the school took on a new meaning. It was a badge of his strength, the proof of his courage.

"And the andat?"

"And the andat," Milah-kvo said. "You'll begin to learn of them in earnest. The Dai-kvo has never taken a student who wasn't first a black robe at the school."

Otah stooped, his fingers numb with cold, and picked up the robe. He met Milah-kvo's amused eyes and couldn't keep from grinning. Milah-kvo laughed, stood and put an arm around Otah's shoulder. It was the first kind act Otah could remember since he had come to the school.

"Come on, then. If we start now, we may get back to the school by breakfast."

Otah took a pose of enthusiastic agreement.

"And, while this once I think we can forgive it, don't make a habit of stealing from the kitchen. It upsets the cooks."

THE LETTER CAME SOME WEEKS LATER, AND MILAH WAS THE FIRST TO READ it. Sitting in an upper room, his students abandoned for the moment, he read the careful script again and felt his face grow tight. When he had gone over it enough to know he could not have misunderstood, he tucked the folded paper into the sleeve of his robe and looked out the window. Winter was ending, and somehow the eternal renewal that was spring felt like an irony.

He heard Tahi enter, recognizing his old friend's footsteps.

"There was a courier," Tahi said. "Ansha said there was a courier from the Dai-kvo . . ."

Milah looked over his shoulder. His own feelings were echoed in Tahi's round face.

"From his attendant, actually."

"The Dai-kvo. Is he . . ."

"No," Milah said, fishing out the letter. "Not dead. Only dying."

Tahi took the proffered pages, but didn't look at them.

"Of what?"

"Time."

Tahi read the written words silently, then leaned against the wall with a sharp sigh.

"It . . . it isn't so bad as it could be," Tahi said.

"No. Not yet. He will see the school again. Twice, perhaps."

"He shouldn't come," Tahi snapped. "The visits are a formality. We know well enough which boys are ready. We can send them. He doesn't have to—"

Milah turned, interrupting him with a subtle pose that was a request for clarification and a mourning both. Tahi laughed bitterly and looked down.

"You're right," he said. "Still. I'd like the world better if we could carry a little of his weight for him. Even if it was only a short way."

Milah started to take a pose, but hesitated, stopped, only nodded.

"Otah Machi?" Tahi asked.

"Maybe. We might have to call him for Otah. Not yet, though. The robes have hardly been on him. The others are still learning to accept him as an equal. Once he's used to the power, then we'll see. I won't call the Dai-kvo until we're certain."

"He'll come next winter whether there's a boy ready or not."

"Perhaps. Or perhaps he'll die tonight. Or we will. No god made the world certain."

Tahi raised his hands in a pose of resignation.

IT WAS A WARM NIGHT IN LATE SPRING; THE SCENT OF GREEN SEEMED TO PER-meate the world. Otah and his friends sprawled on the hillside east of the school. Milah-kvo sat with them, still talking, still telling stories though their lectures for the day were done. Stories of the andat.

"They are like . . . thoughts made real," Milah said, his hands moving in gestures which were not formal poses, but evoked a sense of wonder all the same. "Ideas tamed and given human shape. Take Water-Moving-Down. In the Old Empire, she was called Rain, then when Diit Amra recaptured her at the beginning of the War, they called her Seaward. But the thought, you see, was the same. And if you can hold that, you can stop rivers in their tracks. Or see that your crops get enough water, or flood your enemies. She was powerful."

"Could someone catch her again?" Ansha—no longer Ansha-kvo to Otah—asked.

Milah shook his head.

"I doubt it. She's been held and escaped too many times. I suppose someone might find a new way to describe her, but . . . it's been tried."

There was a chill that even Otah felt at the words. Stories of the andat were like ghost tales, and the price a failed poet paid was always the gruesome ending of it.

"What was her price?" Nian Tomari asked, his voice hushed and eager.

"The last poet who made the attempt was a generation before me. They say that when he failed, his belly swelled like a pregnant woman's. When they cut him open, he was filled with ice and black seaweed."

The boys were quiet, imagining the scene—the poet's blood, the dark leaves, the pale ice. Dari slapped a gnat.

"Milah-kvo?" Otah said. "Why do the andat become more difficult to hold each time they escape?"

The teacher laughed.

"An excellent question, Otah. But one you'd have to ask of the Dai-kvo. It's more than you're ready to know."

Otah dropped into a pose of correction accepted, but in the back of his mind, the curiosity remained. The sun dipped below the horizon and a chill came into the air. Milah-kvo rose, and they followed him, wraith-children in their dark robes and twilight. Halfway back to the high stone buildings, Ansha started to run, and then Riit, and then Otah and then all of them, pounding up the slope to the great door, racing to be first or at least to not be last. When Milah arrived, they were red-faced and laughing.

"Otah," Enrath, an older, dark-faced boy from Tan-Sadar said. "You're taking the third cohort out tomorrow to turn the west gardens?"

"Yes," Otah said.

"Tahi-kvo wanted them finished and washed early. He's taking them for lessons after the meal."

"You could join the afternoon session with us," Milah suggested, overhearing.

Otah took a pose of gratitude as they entered the torch-lit great hall. One of Milah-kvo's lessons was infinitely better than a day spent leading one of the youngest cohorts through its chores.

"Do you know why worms travel in the ground?" Milah-kvo asked.

"Because they can't fly?" Ansha said, and laughed. A few other boys laughed with him.

"True enough," Milah-kvo said. "But they are good for the soil. They break it up so that the roots can dig deeper. So in a sense, Otah and the third cohort are doing worm work tomorrow."

"But worms do it by eating dirt and shitting it out," Enrath said. "Tahi-kvo said so."

"There is some difference in technique," Milah-kvo agreed dryly to the delight of them all, including Otah.

The black robes slept in smaller rooms, four to each, with a brazier in the center to keep it warm. The thaw had come, but the nights were still bitterly cold. Otah, as the youngest in his room, had the duty of tending the fire. In the dark of the mornings, Milah-kvo would come and wake them, knocking on their doors until all four voices within acknowledged him. They washed at communal tubs and ate at a long wooden table with Tahi-kvo at one end and Milah-kvo at the other. Otah still found himself uncomfortable about the round-faced teacher, however friendly his eyes had become.

After they had cleared their plates, the black robes divided; the larger half went to lead the cohorts through the day's duties, the smaller—rarely more than five or six—would go with Milah-kvo for a day's study. As Otah walked to the great hall, he was already planning the day ahead, anticipating handing the third cohort over to Tahi-kvo and joining the handful most favored by Milah-kvo.

In the great hall, the boys stood in their shivering ranks. The third cohort was one of the youngest—a dozen boys of perhaps eight years dressed in thin gray robes. Otah paced before them, searching for any improper stance or scratching.

"Today, we are turning the soil in the west gardens," Otah barked. Some of the smaller boys flinched. "Tahi-kvo demands the work be finished and that you be cleaned by midday. Follow!"

He marched them out to the gardens. Twice, he stopped to be sure they were in the proper order. When one—Navi Toyut, son of a high family of the utkhaiem in Yalakeht—was out of step, Otah slapped him smartly across the face. The boy corrected his gait.

The west gardens were brown and bare. Dry sticks—the winter corpses of last year's crop—lay strewn on the ground, the pale seedlings of weeds pushing up through them. Otah led them to the toolshed where the youngest boys brushed spider webs off the shovels and spades.

"Begin at the north end!" Otah shouted, and the cohort fell into place. The line was ragged, some boys taller than others and all unevenly spaced, leaving gaps in the line like missing milk teeth. Otah walked along, showing each boy where to stand and how to hold his shovel. When they were all in their places, Otah gave the sign to begin.

They set to, their thin arms working, but they were small and not strong. The smell of fresh earth rose, but only slowly. When Otah walked the turned soil behind them, his boots barely sank into it.

"Deeper!" he snapped. "Turn the soil, don't just scrape it. Worms could do better than this."

The cohort didn't speak, didn't look up, only leaned harder onto the dry, rough shafts of their spades. Otah shook his head and spat.

The sun had risen a hand and a half, and they had only completed two plots. As the day warmed, the boys shed their top robes, leaving them folded on the ground. There were still six plots to go. Otah paced behind the line, scowling. Time was running short.

"Tahi-kvo wants this done by midday!" Otah shouted. "If you disappoint him, I'll see all of you beaten."

They struggled to complete the task, but by the time they reached the end of the fourth plot, it was clear that it wouldn't happen. Otah gave stern orders that they should continue, then stalked off to find Tahi-kvo.

The teacher was overseeing a cohort that had been set to clean the kitchens. The lacquered rod whirred impatiently. Otah took a pose of apology before him.

"Tahi-kvo, the third cohort will not be able to turn the soil in the west gardens by midday. They are weak and stupid."

Tahi-kvo considered him, his expression unreadable. Otah felt his face growing warm with embarrassment. At last, Tahi-kvo took a formal pose of acceptance.

"It will wait for another day, then," he said. "When they have had their meal, take them back out and let them finish the task."

Otah took a pose of gratitude until Tahi-kvo turned his attention back to the cohort he was leading, then Otah turned and walked back out to the gardens. The third cohort had slacked in his absence, but began to work furiously as Otah came near. He stepped into the half-turned plot and stared at them.

"You have cost me an afternoon with Milah-kvo," Otah said, his voice low, but angry enough to carry. None of the boys would meet his gaze, guilty as dogs. He turned to the nearest boy—a thin boy with a spade in his hand. "You. Give me that."

The boy looked panicked, but held out the spade. Otah took it and thrust it down into the fresh soil. The blade sank only half way. Otah's shoulders curled in rage. The boy took a pose of apology, but Otah didn't acknowledge it.

"You're meant to turn the soil! Turn it! Are you too stupid to understand that?"

"Otah-kvo, I'm sorry. It's only—"

"If you can't do it like a man, you can do it as a worm. Get on your knees."

The boy's expression was uncomprehending.

"Get on your knees!" Otah shouted, leaning into the boy's face. Tears welled up in the boy's eyes, but he did as he was told. Otah picked up a clod of dirt and handed it to him. "Eat it."

The boy looked at the clod in his hand, then up at Otah. Then, weeping until his shoulders shook, he raised the dirt to his mouth and ate. The others in the cohort were standing in a circle, watching silently. The boy's mouth worked, mud on his lips.

"All of it!" Otah said.

The boy took another mouthful, then collapsed, sobbing, to the ground. Otah spat in disgust and turned to the others.

"Get to work!"

They scampered back to their places, small arms and legs working furiously with the vigor of fear. The mud-lipped boy sat weeping into his hands. Otah took the spade to him and pushed the blade into the ground at his side.

"Well?" Otah demanded quietly. "Is there something to wait for?"

The boy mumbled something Otah couldn't make out.

"What? If you're going to talk, make it so people can hear you."

"My hand," the boy forced through the sobs. "My hands hurt. I tried. I tried to dig deeper, but it hurt so much . . ."

He turned his palms up, and looking at the bleeding blisters was like leaning over a precipice; Otah felt suddenly dizzy. The boy looked up into his face, weeping, and the low keening was a sound Otah recognized though he had never heard it before; it was a sound he had longed to make for seasons of sleeping in the cold, hoping not to dream of his mother. It was the same tune he had heard in his old cohort, a child crying in his sleep.

The black robes suddenly felt awkward, and the memory of a thousand humiliations sang in Otah's mind the way a crystal glass might ring with the sound of singer's note.

He knelt beside the weeping boy, words rushing to his lips and then failing him. The others in the cohort stood silent.

"You sent for me?" Tahi asked. Milah didn't answer, but gestured out the window. Tahi came to stand by him and consider the spectacle below. In a half-turned plot of dirt, a black robe was cradling a crying child in his arms while the others in the cohort stood by, agape.

"How long has this been going on?" Tahi asked through a tight throat.

"They were like that when I noticed them. Before that, I don't know."

"Otah Machi?"

Milah only nodded.

"It has to stop."

"Yes. But I wanted you to see it."

In grim silence, the pair walked down the stairs, through the library, and out to the west gardens. The third cohort, seeing them come, pretended to work. All except Otah and the boy he held. They remained as they were.

"Otah!" Tahi barked. The black-robed boy looked up, eyes red and tear-filled.

"You're not well, Otah," Milah said gently. He drew Otah up. "You should come inside and rest."

Otah looked from one to the other, then hesitantly took a pose of submission and let Milah take his shoulder and guide him away. Tahi remained behind; Milah could hear his voice snapping at the third cohort like a whip.

Back in the quarters of the elite, Milah prepared a cup of strong tea for Otah and considered the situation. The others would hear of what had happened soon enough if they hadn't already. He wasn't sure whether that would make things better for the boy or worse. He wasn't even certain what he hoped. If it was what it appeared, it was the success he had dreaded. Before he acted, he had to be sure. He wouldn't call for the Dai-kvo if Otah weren't ready.

Otah, sitting slump-shouldered on his bunk, took the hot tea and sipped it dutifully. His eyes were dry now, and staring into the middle distance. Milah pulled a stool up beside him, and they sat for a long moment in silence before he spoke.

"You did that boy out there no favors today."

Otah lifted a hand in a pose of correction accepted.

"Comforting a boy like that . . . it doesn't make him stronger. I know it isn't easy being a teacher. It requires a hard sort of compassion to treat a child harshly, even when it is only for their own good in the end."

Otah nodded, but didn't look up. When he spoke, his voice was low. "Has anyone ever been turned out from the black robes?"

"Expelled? No, no one. Why do you ask?"

"I've failed," Otah said, then paused. "I'm not strong enough to teach these lessons, Milah-kvo."

Milah looked down at his hands, thinking of his old master. Thinking of the cost that another journey to the school would exact from that old flesh. He couldn't keep the weight of the decision entirely out of his voice when he spoke.

"I am removing you from duty for a month's time," he said, "while we call for the Dai-kvo."

"OTAH," THE FAMILIAR VOICE WHISPERED. "WHAT DID YOU DO?"

Otah turned on his bunk. The brazier glowed, the coals giving off too little light to see by. Otah fixed his gaze on the embers.

"I made a mistake, Ansha," he said. It was the reply he'd given on the few occasions in the last days that someone had had the courage to ask.

"They say the Dai-kvo's coming. And out of season."

"It may have been a serious mistake."

It may be the first time that anyone has risen so far and failed so badly, Otah thought. The first time anyone so unsuited to the black robes had been given them. He remembered the cold, empty plain of snow he'd walked across the night Milah-kvo had promoted him. He could see now that his flight hadn't been a sign of strength after all— only a presentiment of failure.

"What did you *do?*" Ansha asked in the darkness.

Otah saw the boy's face again, saw the bloodied hand and the tears of humiliation running down the dirty cheeks. He had caused that pain, and he could not draw the line between the shame of having done it and the shame of being too weak to do it again. There was no way for him to explain that he couldn't lead the boys to strength because in his heart, he was still one of them.

"I wasn't worthy of my robe," he said.

Ansha didn't speak again, and soon Otah heard the low, deep breath of sleep. The others were all tired from their day's work. Otah had no reason to be tired after a day spent haunting the halls and rooms of the school with no duties and no purpose wearing the black robe only because he had no other robes of his own.

He waited in the darkness until even the embers deserted him and he was sure the others were deeply asleep. Then he rose, pulled on his robe, and walked quietly out into the corridor. It wasn't far to the chilly rooms where the younger cohorts slept. Otah walked among the sleeping forms. Their bodies were so small, and the blankets so thin. Otah had been in the black for so little time, and had forgotten so much.

The boy he was looking for was curled on a cot beside the great stone wall, his back to the room. Otah leaned over carefully and put a hand over the boy's mouth to stifle a cry if he made one. He woke silently, though, his eyes blinking open. Otah watched until he saw recognition bloom.

"Your hands are healing well?" Otah whispered.

The boy nodded.

"Good. Now stay quiet. We don't want to wake the others."

Otah drew his hand away, and the boy fell immediately into a pose of profound apology.

"Otah-kvo, I have dishonored you and the school. I . . ."

Otah gently folded the boy's fingers closed.

"You have nothing to blame yourself for," Otah said. "The mistake was mine. The price is mine."

"If I'd worked harder—"

"It would have gained you nothing," Otah said. "Nothing."

THE BRONZE DOORS BOOMED AND SWUNG OPEN. THE BOYS STOOD IN THEIR ranks holding poses of welcome as if they were so many statues. Otah, standing among the black robes, held his pose as well. He wondered what stories the cohorts of disowned children had been telling themselves about the visit: hopes of being returned to a lost family, or of being elevated to a poet. Dreams.

The old man walked in. He seemed less steady than Otah remembered him. After the ceremonial greetings, he blessed them all in his thick, ruined whisper. Then he and the teachers retired, and the black robes—all but Otah—took charge of the cohorts that they would lead for the day. Otah returned to his room and sat, sick at heart, waiting for the summons he knew was coming. It wasn't long.

"Otah," Tahi-kvo said from the doorway. "Get some tea for the Dai-kvo."

"But the ceremonial robe . . ."

"Not required. Just tea."

Otah rose into a pose of submission. The time had come.

THE DAI-KVO SAT SILENTLY, CONSIDERING THE FIRE IN THE GRATE. HIS hands, steepled before him, seemed smaller than Milah remembered them, the skin thinner and loose. His face showed the fatigue of his journey around the eyes and mouth, but when he caught Milah's gaze and took a pose part query, part challenge, Milah thought there was something else as well. A hunger, or hope.

"How are things back in the world?" Milah asked. "We don't hear much of the high cities here."

"Things are well enough," the Dai-kvo said. "And here? How are your boys?"

"Well enough, most high."

"Really? Some nights I find I wonder."

Milah took a pose inviting the Dai-kvo to elaborate, but to no effect. The ancient eyes had turned once more to the flames. Milah let his hands drop to his lap.

Tahi returned and took a pose of obedience and reverence before bending into his chair.

"The boy is coming," Tahi said.

The Dai-kvo took a pose of acknowledgement, but nothing more. Milah saw his own concern mirrored in Tahi. It seemed too long before the soft knock came at the door and Otah Machi entered, carrying a tray with three small bowls of tea. Stone-faced, the boy put the tray on the low table and took the ritual pose of greeting.

"I am honored by your presence most high Dai-kvo," Otah said perfectly.

The old man's eyes were alive now, his gaze on Otah with a powerful interest. He nodded, but didn't commend the boy to his studies. Instead, he gestured to the empty seat that Milah usually took. The boy looked over, and Milah nodded. Otah sat, visibly sick with anxiety.

"Tell me," the Dai-kvo said, picking up a bowl of tea, "what do you know of the andat?"

The boy took a moment finding his voice, but when he did, there was no quavering in it.

"They are thoughts, most high. Translated by the poet into a form that includes volition."

The Dai-kvo sipped his tea, watching the boy. Waiting for him to say more. The silence pressed Otah to speak, but he appeared to have no more words. At last the Dai-kvo put down his cup.

"You know nothing more of them? How they are bound? What a poet must do to keep his work unlike that which has gone before? How one may pass a captured spirit from one generation to the next?"

"No, most high."

"And why not?" The Dai-kvo's voice was soft.

"Milah-kvo told us that more knowledge would be dangerous to us. We weren't ready for the deeper teachings."

"True," the Dai-kvo said. "True enough. You were only tested. Never taught."

Otah looked down. His face gray, he adopted a pose of contrition.

"I am sorry to have failed the school, most high. I know that I was to show them how to be strong, and I wanted to, but—"

"You have not failed, Otah. You have won through."

Otah's stance faltered, and his eyes filled with confusion. Milah coughed and, taking a pose that begged the Dai-kvo's permission, spoke.

"You recall our conversation in the snow the night I offered you the black? I said then that a weak-minded poet would be destroyed by the andat?"

Otah nodded.

"A cruel-hearted one would destroy the world," Milah said. "Strong and kind, Otah. It's a rare combination."

"We see it now less often than we once did," the Dai-kvo said. "Just as no boy has taken the black robes without a show of his strength of will, no one has put the black robe away without renouncing the cruelty that power brings. You have done both, Otah Machi. You've proven yourself worthy, and I would take you as my apprentice. Come back with me, boy, and I will teach you the secrets of the poets."

The boy looked as if he'd been clubbed. His face was bloodless, his hands still, but a slow comprehension shone in his eyes. The moment stretched until Tahi snapped.

"Well? You can say something, boy."

"What I did . . . the boy . . . I didn't *fail?*"

"That wasn't a failure. That was the moment of your highest honor."

A slow smile came to Otah's lips, but it was deathly cold. When he spoke, there was fury in his voice.

"Humiliating that boy was my moment of highest *honor?*"

Milah saw Tahi frown. He shook his head. This was between the boy and the Dai-kvo now.

"Comforting him was," the old man said.

"Comforting him for what *I* did."

"Yes. And yet how many of the other black-robed boys would have done the same? The school is built to embody these tests. It has been this way since the war that destroyed the Empire, and it has held the cities of the Khaiem together. There is a wisdom in it that runs very deep."

Slowly, Otah took a pose of gratitude to a teacher, but there was something odd about it—something in the cant of the wrists that spoke of an emotion Milah couldn't fathom.

"If that was honor, most high, then I truly understand."

"Do you?" the old man asked, and his voice sounded hopeful.

"Yes. I was your tool. It wasn't only me in that garden. *You* were there, too."

"What are you saying, boy?" Tahi snapped, but Otah went on as if he had not spoken.

"You say Tahi-kvo taught me strength and Milah-kvo compassion, but there are other lessons to be taken from them. As the school is of your design, I think it only right that you should know what I've learned at your hand."

The Dai-kvo looked confused, and his hands took some half-pose, but the boy didn't stop. His gaze was fastened on the old man, and he seemed fearless.

"Tahi-kvo showed me that my own judgement is my only guide and Milah-kvo that there is no value in a lesson half-learned. My judgement was to leave this place, and I was right. I should never have let myself be tempted back.

"And that, most high, is all I've ever learned here."

Otah rose and took a pose of departure.

"Otah!" Tahi barked. "Take your seat!"

The boy ignored him, turned, and walked out, closing the door behind him. Milah crossed his arms, staring at the door, unsure what to say or even think. In the grate, the ashes settled under their own weight.

"Milah," Tahi whispered.

Milah looked over, and Tahi gestured to the Dai-kvo. The old man sat, barely breathing. His hands were held in an attitude of profound regret.

1

>+< As the stone towers of Machi dominated the cold cities of the north, so the seafront of Saraykeht dominated the summer cities in the south. The wharves stood out into the clear waters of the bay, ships from the other port cities of the Khaiem—Nantani, Yalakeht, Chaburi-Tan—docked there. Among them were also the low, shallow ships of the Westlands and the tall, deep sailing ships of the Galts so strung with canvas they seemed like a launderer's yard escaped to the sea. And along the seafront streets, vendors of all different cities and lands sold wares from tall, thin tables decked with brightly colored cloths and banners, each calling out to the passers-by over the cries of seagulls and the grumble of waves. A dozen languages, a hundred dialects, creoles, and pidgins danced in the hot, still air, and she knew them all.

Amat Kyaan, senior overseer for the Galtic House Wilsin, picked her way through the crowd with a cane despite the sureness of her steps. She savored the play of grammar and vocabulary crashing together like children playing sand tag. Knowing how to speak and what to say was her strength. It was the skill that had taken her from a desperate freelance scribe to here, wearing the colors of an honorable, if foreign, house and threading her way through the press of bodies and baled cotton to a meeting with her employer. There were ways from her rooms at the edge of the soft quarter to Marchat Wilsin's favorite bathhouse that wouldn't have braved the seafront. Still, whenever her mornings took her to the bathhouse, this was the way she picked. The seafront was, after all, the pride and symbol of her city.

She paused in the square at the mouth of the Nantan—the wide, gray-bricked street that marked the western edge of the warehouse quarter. The ancient bronze statue of Shian Sho, the last great emperor, stood looking out across the sea, as if in memory of his lost empire—rags and wastelands for eight generations now, except for the cities of the Khaiem where the unrest had never reached. Below him, young men labored, shirtless in the heat, hauling carts piled high with white, oily bales. Some laughed, some shouted, some worked with a dreadful seriousness. Some were free men taking advantage of the seasonal work. Others were indentured to houses or individual merchants. A few were slaves. And all of them were beautiful—even the fat and the awkward. Youth made them beautiful. The working of muscles under skin was more subtle and enticing than the finest robes of the Khaiem, maybe because it wasn't considered. How many of them, she wondered, would guess that their sex was on display to an old woman who only seemed to be resting for a moment on the way to a business meeting?

All of them, probably. Vain, lovely creatures. She sighed, lifted her cane, and moved on.

The sun had risen perhaps half the width of one hand when she reached her destination. The bathhouses were inland, clustered near the banks of the Qiit and the aqueducts. Marchat Wilsin preferred one of the smaller. Amat had been there often enough that the guards knew her by sight and took awkward poses of welcome as she entered. She often suspected Wilsin-cha of choosing this particular place because it let him forget his own inadequacies of language. She sketched a pose of welcome and passed inside.

Working for a foreign house had never been simple, and translating contracts and agreements was the least of it. The Galts were a clever people, aggressive and successful in war. They held lands as wide and fertile as the Empire had at its height; they could command the respect and fear of other nations. But the assumptions they made—that agreements could be enforced by blades, that threat of invasion or blockade might underscore a negotiation—failed in the cities of the Khaiem. They might send their troops to Eddensea or their ships to Bakta, but when called upon for subtlety, they floundered. Galt might conquer the rest of the world if it chose; it would still bow before the andat. Marchat Wilsin had lived long enough in Saraykeht to have accepted the bruise on his people's arrogance. Indulging his eccentricities, such as doing business in a bathhouse, was a small price.

The air inside was cooler, and ornate woodworked screens blocked the windows while still letting the occasional cedar-scented breeze through. Voices echoed off the hard floors and walls. Somewhere in the public rooms, a man was singing, the tones of his voice ringing like a bell. Amat went to the women's chamber, shrugged out of her robe and pulled off her sandals. The cool air felt good against her bare skin. She took a drink of chilled water from the large granite basin, and—naked as anyone else—walked through the public baths, filled with men and women shouting and splashing one another, to the private rooms at the back. To Marchat Wilsin's corner room, farthest from the sounds of voices and laughter.

"It's too hot in this pisshole of a city," Wilsin-cha growled as she entered the room. He lay half-submerged in the pool, the water lapping at his white, wooly chest. He had been a thinner man when she had first met him. His hair and beard had been dark. "It's like someone holding a hot towel over your face."

"Only in the summer," Amat said and she laid her cane beside the water and carefully slipped in. The ripples rocked the floating lacquer tray with its bowls of tea, but didn't spill it. "If it was any further north, you'd spend all winter complaining about how cold it was."

"It'd be a change of pace, at least."

He lifted a pink and wrinkled hand from the water and pushed the tray over toward her. The tea was fresh and seasoned with mint. The water was cool. Amat lay back against the tiled lip of the pool.

"So what's the news?" Marchat asked, bringing their morning ritual to a close.

Amat made her report. Things were going fairly well. The shipment of raw cotton from Eddensea was in and being unloaded. The contracts with the weavers were nearly complete, though there were some ambiguities of translation from Galtic into the Khaiate that still troubled her. And worse, the harvest of the northern fields was late.

"Will they be here in time to go in front of the andat?"

Amat took another sip of tea before answering.

"No."

Marchat cursed under his breath. "Eddensea can ship us a season's bales, but we can't get our own plants picked?"

"Apparently not."

"How short does it leave us?"

"Our space will be nine-tenths full."

Marchat scowled and stared at the air, seeing imagined numbers, reading the emptiness like a book. After a moment, he sighed.

"Is there any chance of speaking with the Khai on it? Renegotiating our terms?"

"None," Amat said.

Marchat made an impatient noise in the back of his throat.

"This is why I hate dealing with you people. In Eymond or Bakta, there'd be room to talk at least."

"Because you'd have soldiers sitting outside the wall," Amat said, dryly.

"Exactly. And then they'd find room to talk. See if one of the other houses is overstocked," he said.

"Chadhami is. But Tiyan and Yaanani are in competition for a contract with a Western lord. If one could move more swiftly than the other, it might seal the issue. We could charge them for the earlier session with the andat, and then take part of their space later when our crop comes in."

Marchat considered this. They negotiated the house's strategy for some time. Which little alliance to make, and how it could most profitably be broken later, should the need arise.

Amat knew more than she said, of course. That was her job—to hold everything about the company clear in her mind, present her employer with what he needed to know, and deal herself with the things beneath his notice. The center of it all, of course, was the cotton trade. The complex web of relationships—weavers and dyers and sailmakers; shipping companies, farming houses, alum miners—that made Saraykeht one of the richest cities in the world. And, as with all the cities of the Khaiem, free from threat of war, unlike Galt and Eddensea and Bakta; the Westlands and the Eastern Islands. They were protected by their poets and the powers they wielded, and that protection allowed conferences like this one, allowed them to play the deadly serious game of trade and barter.

Once their decisions had been made and the details agreed upon, Amat arranged a time to bring the proposals by the compound. Doing business from a bathhouse was an affectation Wilsin-cha could only take so far, and dripping water on freshly-inked contracts was where she drew the line. She knew he understood that. As she rose, prepared to face the remainder of her day, he held up a hand to stop her.

"There's one other thing," he said. She lowered herself back into the water. "I need a bodyguard this evening just before the half candle. Nothing serious, just someone to help keep the dogs off."

Amat tilted her head. His voice was calm, its tone normal, but he wasn't meeting her eyes. She held up her hands in a pose of query.

"I have a meeting," he said, "in one of the low towns."

"Company business?" Amat asked, keeping her voice neutral.

He nodded.

"I see," she said. Then, after a moment, "I'll be at the compound at the half candle, then."

"No. Amat, I need some house thug to swat off animals and make bandits think twice. What's a woman with a cane going to do for me?"

"I'll bring a bodyguard with me."

"Just send him to me," Wilsin said with a final air. "I'll take care of it from there."

"As you see fit. And when did the company begin conducting trade without me?"

Marchat Wilsin grimaced and shook his head, muttering something to himself too low for her to catch. When he sighed, it sent a ripple that spilled some of the tea.

"It's a sensitive issue, Amat. That's all. It's something I'm taking care of myself. I'll give you all the details when I can, but . . ."

"But?"

"It's difficult. There are some details of the trade that . . . I'm going to have to keep quiet about."

"Why?"

"It's the sad trade," he said. "The girl's well enough along in the pregnancy that she's showing. And there are some facets to getting rid of the baby that I need to address discreetly."

Amat felt herself bristle, but kept her tone calm as she spoke.

"Ah. I see. Well, then. If you feel you can't trust my discretion, I suppose you'd best not talk to me of it at all. Perhaps I might recommend someone else to take my position."

He slapped the water impatiently. Amat crossed her arms. It was a bluff in the sense that they both knew the house would struggle badly without her, and that she would be worse off without her position in it—it wasn't a threat meant seriously. But she was the overseer of the house, and Amat didn't like being kept outside her own business.

Marchat's pale face flushed red, but whether with annoyance or shame, she wasn't sure.

"Don't break my stones over this one, Amat. I don't like it any better than you do, but I can't play this one any differently than I am. There is a trade. I'll see to it. I'll petition the Khai Saraykeht for use of his andat. I'll see the girl's taken care of before and after, and I'll see that everyone who needs paying gets paid. I was in business before you signed on, you know. And I *am* your employer. You could assume I know what I'm doing."

"I was just going to say the same thing, pointed the other way. You've consulted me on your affairs for twenty years. If I haven't done something to earn your mistrust—"

"You haven't."

"Then why shut me out of this when you never have before?"

"If I could tell you that, I wouldn't have to shut you out of it," Marchat said. "Just take it that it's not my choice."

"Your uncle asked that I be left out? Or is it the client?"

"I need a bodyguard. At the half-candle."

Amat took a complex pose of agreement that also held a nuance of annoyance. He wouldn't catch the second meaning. Talking over his level was something she did when he'd upset her. She rose, and he scooped the lacquer tray closer and poured himself more tea.

"The client. Can you tell me who she is?" Amat asked.

"No. Thank you, Amat," Wilsin said.

In the women's chamber again, she dried herself and dressed. The street, when she stepped into it, seemed louder, more annoying, than when she went in. She turned toward the House Wilsin compound, to the north and uphill. She had to pause at a waterseller's stall, buy herself a drink, and rest in the shade to collect her thoughts. The sad trade—using the andat to end a pregnancy—wasn't the sort of business House Wilsin had undertaken before now, though other houses had acted as brokers in some instances. She wondered why the change in policy, and why the secrecy, and why Marchat Wilsin would have told her to arrange for the bodyguard if he hadn't wanted her, on some level, to find answers.

MAATI HELD A POSE OF GREETING, HIS HEART IN HIS THROAT. THE PALE-skinned man walked slowly around him, black eyes taking in every nuance of his stance. Maati's hands didn't tremble; he had trained for years, first at the school and then with the Dai-kvo. His body knew how to hide anxiety.

The man in poet's robes stopped, an expression half approval, half amusement on his face. Elegant fingers took a pose of greeting that was neither the warmest nor the least formal. With the reply made, Maati let his hands fall to his sides and stood. His first real thought, now that the shock of his teacher's sudden appearance was fading, was that he hadn't expected Heshai-kvo to be so young, or so beautiful.

"What is your name, boy?" the man asked. His voice was cool and hard.

"Maati Vaupathi," Maati said, crisply. "Once the tenth son of Nicha Vaupathi, and now the youngest of the poets."

"Ah. A westerner. It's still in your accent."

The teacher sat in the window seat, his arms folded, still openly considering Maati. The rooms, which had seemed sumptuous during the long worrisome days of Maati's waiting, seemed suddenly squalid with the black-haired man in them. A tin setting for a perfect gem. The soft cotton draperies that flowed from the ceiling, shifting in the hot breeze of late afternoon, seemed dirty beside the poet's skin. The man smiled, his expression not entirely kind. Maati took a pose of obeisance appropriate to a student before his teacher.

"I have come, Heshai-kvo, by the order of the Dai-kvo to learn from you, if you will have me as your pupil."

"Oh, stop that. Bowing and posing like we were dancers. Sit there. On the bed. I have some questions for you."

Maati did as he was told, tucking his legs beneath him in the formal way a student did in a lecture before the Dai-kvo. The man seemed to be amused by this, but said nothing about it.

"So. Maati. You came here . . . what? Six days ago?"

"Seven, Heshai-kvo."

"Seven. And yet no one came to meet you. No one came to collect you or show you the poet's house. It's a long time for a master to ignore his student, don't you think?"

It was exactly what Maati had thought, several times, but he didn't admit that now. Instead he took a pose accepting a lesson.

"I thought so at first. But as time passed, I saw that it was a kind of test, Heshai-kvo."

A tiny smile ghosted across the perfect lips, and Maati felt a rush of pleasure that he had guessed right. His new teacher motioned him to continue, and Maati sat up a degree straighter.

"I thought at first that it might be a test of my patience. To see whether I could be trusted not to hurry things when it wasn't my place. But later I decided that the real test was how I spent my time. Being patient and idle wouldn't teach me anything, and the Khai has the largest library in the summer cities."

"You spent your time in the library?"

Maati took a pose of confirmation, unsure what to make of the teacher's tone.

"These are the palaces of the Khai Saraykeht, Maati-kya," he said with sudden familiarity as he gestured out the window at the grounds, the palaces, the long flow of streets and red tile roofs that sprawled to the sea. "There are scores of utkhaiem and courtiers. I don't think a night passes here without a play being performed, or singers, or dancing. And you spent all your time with the scrolls?"

"I did spent one evening with a group of the utkhaiem. They were from the west . . . from Pathai. I lived there before I went to the school."

"And you thought they might have news of your family."

It wasn't an accusation, though it could have been. Maati pressed his lips thinner, embarrassed, and repeated the pose of confirmation. The smile it brought seemed sympathetic.

"And what did you learn in your productive, studious days with Saraykeht's books."

"I studied the history of the city, and its andat."

The elegant fingers made a motion that both approved and invited him to continue. The dark eyes held an interest that told Maati he had done well.

"I learned, for example, that the Dai-kvo—the last one—sent you here when Iana-kvo failed to hold Petals-Falling-Away after the old poet, Miat-kvo, died."

"And tell me, why do you think he did that?"

"Because Petals-Falling-Away had been used to speed cotton harvests for the previous fifty years," Maati said, pleased to know the answer. "It could make the plant . . . open, I guess. It made it easier to get the fibers. With the loss, the city needed another way to make the process—bringing in the raw cotton and turning it to cloth—better and faster than they could in Galt or the Westlands, or else the traders might go elsewhere, and the whole city would have to change. You had captured Removing-The-Part-That-Continues. Called Sterile in the North, or Seedless in the summer cities. With it, the merchant houses can contract with the Khai, and they won't have to comb the seeds out of the cotton. Even if it took twice as long to harvest, the cotton can still get to the spinners more quickly here than anywhere else. Now the other nations and cities actually send their raw cotton here. Then the weavers come here, because the raw cotton is here. And the dyers and the tailors because of the weavers. All the needle trades."

"Yes. And so Saraykeht holds its place, with only a few more pricked fingers and some blood on the cotton," the man said, taking a pose of confirmation with a softness to the wrists that confused Maati. "But then, blood's only blood, ne?"

The silence went on until Maati, uncomfortable, grasped for something to break it.

"You also rid the summer cities of rats and snakes."

The man came out of his reverie with something like a smile. When he spoke, his voice was amused and self-deprecating.

"Yes. At the price of drawing Galts and Westermen."

Maati took a pose of agreement less formal than before, and his teacher seemed not to mind. In fact, he seemed almost pleased.

"I also learned a lot about the particular needle trades," Maati said. "I wasn't sure how much you needed to know about what happens with the cotton once you're done with it. And sailing. I read a book about sailing."

"But you didn't actually go to the seafront, did you?"

"No."

The teacher took a pose of acceptance that wasn't approval or disapproval, but something of both.

"All this from one little test," he said. "But then, you came through the school very young, so you must have a talent for seeing tests. Tell me. How did you see through the Dai-kvo's little guessing games?"

"You . . . I'm sorry, Heshai-kvo. It's . . . you really want to know that?"

"It can be telling. Especially since you don't want to say. Do you?"

Maati took a pose of apology. He kept his eyes down while he spoke, but he didn't lie.

"When I got to the school—I was still among the younger cohorts—
there was an older boy who said something to me. We'd been set to turn
the soil in the gardens, and my hands were too soft. I couldn't do the
work. And the black robe who was tending us—Otah-kvo, his name
was—was very upset with me. But then, when I told him why I hadn't
been able to do as he asked, he tried to comfort me. And he told me
that if I had worked harder, it wouldn't have helped. That was just before he left the school."

"So? You mean someone told you? That hardly seems fair."

"He didn't though. He didn't *tell* me, exactly. He only said some
things about the school. That it wasn't what it looked like. And the
things he said made me start thinking. And then . . ."

"And once you knew to look, it wasn't hard to see. I understand."

"It wasn't quite like that."

"Do you ever wonder if you would have made it on your own? I
mean if your Otah-kvo hadn't given the game away?"

Maati blushed. The secret he'd held for years with the Dai-kvo pried
open in a single conversation. Heshai-kvo was a subtle man. He took a
pose of acknowledgement. The teacher, however, was looking elsewhere, an expression passing over him that might have been annoyance
or pain.

"Heshai-kvo?"

"I've just remembered something I'm to do. Walk with me."

Maati rose and followed. The palaces spread out, larger than the village that surrounded the Dai-kvo, each individual structure larger than
the whole of the school. Together, they walked down the wide marble
staircase, into a vaulted hall. The wide, bright air was touched by the
scents of sandalwood and vanilla.

"Tell me, Maati. What do you think of slaves?"

The question was an odd one, and his first response—*I don't*—
seemed too glib for the occasion. Instead, he took a pose requesting
clarification as best he could while still walking more quickly than his
usual pace.

"Permanent indenture. What's your opinion of it?"

"I don't know."

"Then think for a moment."

They passed through the hall and onto a wide, flower-strewn path
that lead down and to the south. Gardens rich with exotic flowers and

fountains spread out before them. Singing slaves, hidden from view by hedges or cloth screens, filled the air with wordless melodies. The sun blared heat like a trumpet, and the thick air made Maati feel almost as if he was swimming. It seemed they'd hardly started walking before Maati's inner robe was sticky with sweat. He found himself struggling to keep up.

As Maati considered the question, servants and utkhaiem passed, pausing to take poses of respect. His teacher took little notice of them or of the heat; where Maati's robes stuck, his flowed like water over stone and no sweat dampened his temples. Maati cleared his throat.

"People who have entered into permanent indenture have either chosen to do so, in return for the protection of the holders of their contracts, or lost their freedoms as punishment for some crime," Maati said, carefully keeping any judgement out of the statement.

"Is that what the Dai-kvo taught you?"

"No. It's just . . . it's just the way it is. I've always known that."

"And the third case? The andat?"

"I don't understand."

The teacher's dark eyebrows rose on the perfect skin of his forehead. His lips took the slightest of all possible smiles.

"The andat aren't criminals. Before they're bound, they have no thought, no will, no form. They're only ideas. How can an idea enter into a contract?"

"How can one refuse?" Maati countered.

"There are names, my boy, for men who take silence as consent."

They passed into the middle gardens. The low halls spread before them, and wider paths almost like streets. The temple rose off to their right, wide and high; its sloping lines reminded Maati of a seagull in flight. At one of the low halls, carts had gathered. Laborers milled around, speaking with one another. Maati caught a glimpse of a bale of cotton being carried in. With a thrill of excitement he realized what was happening. For the first time, he was going to see Heshai-kvo wield the power of the andat.

"Ah, well. Never mind," his teacher said, as if he had been waiting for some answer. "Only Maati? Later on, I'd like you to think about this conversation."

Maati took a pose appropriate to a student accepting an assignment. As they drew nearer, the laborers and merchants moved aside to make room for them. Members of the utkhaiem were also there in fine robes and expensive jewelry. Maati caught sight of an older woman in a robe the color of the sky at dawn—the personal attendant of the Khai Saraykeht.

"The Khai is here?" Maati asked, his voice smaller than he would have liked.

"He attends sometimes. It makes the merchants feel he's paying attention to them. Silly trick, but it seems to work."

Maati swallowed, half at the prospect of seeing the Khai, half at the indifference in his teacher's voice. They passed through the arches and into the shade of the low hall. Warehouse-large, the hall was filled with bale upon bale of raw cotton stacked to the high ceiling. The only space was a narrow gap at the very top, thinner than a bale, and another of perhaps a hand's width at the bottom where metal frames held the cotton off the floor. What little space remained was peopled by the representatives of the merchant houses whose laborers waited outside and, on a dais, the Khai Saraykeht—a man in his middle years, his hair shot with gray, his eyes heavy-lidded. His attendants stood around him, following commands so subtle they approached invisibility. Maati felt the weight of the silence as they entered. Then a murmur moved through the hall, voices too low to make out words or even sentiments. The Khai raised an eyebrow and took a pose of query with an almost inhuman grace.

At his side stood a thick-bodied man, his wide frog-like mouth gaping open in what might have been horror or astonishment. He also wore the robe of a poet. Maati felt his teacher's hand on his shoulder, solid, firm, and cold.

"Maati," the lovely, careful voice said so quietly that only the two of them could hear, "there's something you should know. I'm not Heshai-kvo."

Maati looked up. The dark eyes were on his, something like amusement in their depths.

"Wh-who are you, then?"

"A slave, my dear. The slave you hope to own."

Then the man who was not his teacher turned to the Khai Saraykeht and the spluttering, enraged poet. He took a pose of greeting more appropriate to acquaintances chanced upon at a teahouse than the two most powerful men of the city. Maati, his hands trembling, took a much more formal stance.

"What is this?" the poet—the frog-mouthed Heshai-kvo, he had to be—demanded.

"This?" the man said, turning and considering Maati as if he were a sculpture pointed out at a fair. "It seems to be a boy. Or perhaps a young man. Fifteen summers? Maybe sixteen? It's so hard to know what to call it at that age. I found it abandoned in the upper halls. Apparently it's been wandering around there for days. No one else seems to have any use for it. May I keep it?"

"Heshai," the Khai said. His voice was powerful. He seemed to speak in a conversational tone, but his voice carried like an actor's. The displeasure in the syllables stung.

"Oh," the man at Maati's side said. "Have I displeased? Well, master, you've no one to blame but yourself."

"Silence!" the poet snapped. Maati sensed as much as saw the man beside him go stiff. He chanced a glimpse at the perfect face. The features were fixed in pain, and slowly, as if fighting each movement, the elegant hands took forms of apology and self-surrender, the spine twisted into a pose of abject obeisance.

"I come to do your bidding, Khai Saraykeht," the man—no, the andat, Seedless—said, his voice honey and ashes. "Command me as you will."

The Khai took a pose of acknowledgement, its nuances barely civil. The frog-mouthed poet looked at Maati and gestured pointedly to his own side. Maati scurried to the dais. The andat moved more slowly, but followed.

"You should have waited," Heshai-kvo hissed. "This is a very busy time of year. I would have thought the Dai-kvo would teach you more patience."

Maati fell into a pose of abject apology.

"Heshai-kvo, I was misled. I thought that he . . . that it . . . I am shamed by my error."

"As you should be," the poet snapped. "Just arriving like this, unintroduced and—"

"Good and glorious Heshai," the Khai Saraykeht said, voice envenomed by sarcasm, "I understand that adding another pet to your collection must be trying. And indeed, I regret to interrupt, but . . ."

The Khai gestured grandly at the bales of cotton. His hands were perfect, and his motion the most elegant Maati had ever seen, smooth and controlled and eloquent.

Heshai-kvo briefly adopted a pose of regret, then turned to the beautiful man—Seedless, Sterile, andat. For a moment the two considered each other, some private, silent conversation passing between them. The andat curled his lip in something half sneer, half sorrow. Sweat dampened the teacher's back, and he began trembling as if with a great effort. Then the andat turned and raised his arms theatrically to the cotton.

A moment later, Maati heard a faint tick, like a single raindrop. And then more and more, until an invisible downpour filled the hall. From his position behind the Khai and the poet, he lowered himself looking under the raised platform on which the bales lay. The parquet floor was covered with small black dots skittering and jumping as they struck one another. Cotton seed.

"It is done," Heshai-kvo said, and Maati stood hurriedly.

The Khai clapped his hands and rose, his movement like a dancer's. His robes flowed through the air like something alive. For a moment Maati forgot himself and merely stood in awe.

A pair of servants pulled wide the great doors, and began a low wail, calling the merchants and their laborers to come and take what was theirs. The utkhaiem took stations by the doors, prepared to collect the fees and taxes for each bale that left. The Khai stood on his dais, grave and beautiful, seeming more a ghost or god than Seedless, who more nearly was.

"You should have waited," Heshai-kvo said again over the voices of the laborers and the din of the merchants at their business. "This is a very bad start for your training. A *very* bad start."

Once again, Maati took a pose of regret, but the poet—his teacher, his new master—turned away, leaving the pose unanswered. Maati stood slowly, his face hot with a blush equally embarrassment and anger, his hands at his sides. At the edge of the dais, the andat sat, his bone-pale hands in his lap. He met Maati's gaze, shrugged, and took a pose of profound apology that might have been genuine or deeply insincere; Maati had no way to tell.

Before he could choose how to respond, Seedless smiled, lowered his hands and looked away.

AMAT KYAAN SAT AT THE SECOND-FLOOR WINDOW OF HER APARTMENTS, looking out over the city. The setting sun behind her reddened the walls of the soft quarter. Some comfort houses were already hanging out streamers and lamps, the glitter of the lights and the shimmering cloth competing with the glow of fireflies. A fruit seller rang her bell and sang her wares in a gentle melody. Amat Kyaan rubbed stinging salve into her knee and ankle, as she did every evening, to keep the pain at bay. It had been a long day, made longer by the nagging disquiet of her meeting with Marchat Wilsin. And even now, it wasn't finished. There was one more unpleasant task still to be done.

This would be her fifty-eighth summer in the world, and every one had been spent in Saraykeht. Her earliest memories were of her father spinning cured cotton into fine, tough thread, humming to himself as he worked. He was many years dead now, as was her mother. Her sister, Sikhet, had vanished into the comfort houses of the soft quarter when she was only sixteen. Amat Kyaan liked to think she caught glimpses of her still—older, wiser, safe. More likely it was her own desire that her sister be well. Her better mind knew it was only wishes. There had been too many years for the two of them not to have come upon each other.

She felt some nights that she had lived her life as an apology for letting her sister vanish into the soft world. And perhaps it had started that way: her decision to work for a trading house, her rise through the invisible levels of power and wealth, had been meant to balance her sister's assumed fall. But she was an older woman now, and everyone she might have apologized to was gone or dead. She had the status and the respect she needed to do as she pleased. She was no one's sister, no one's daughter, no one's wife or mother. By standing still, she had come almost loose from the world, and she found the solitude suited her.

A grass tic shuffled across her arm, preparing to tap her skin. She caught it, cracked it between her thumbnails, and flicked the corpse out into the street. There were more lanterns lit now, and the callers of different establishments were setting out singers and flute players to tempt men—and occasionally even women—to their doors. A patrol of eight frowning thugs swaggered down the streets, their robes the colors of the great comfort houses. It was too early for there to be many people drunk on the streets—the patrol walked and grimaced only to let the patrons coming in see that they were there.

There was no place safer than the Saraykeht soft quarter at night, and no place more dangerous. Here alone, she suspected, of all the cities of the Khaiem, no one would be attacked, no one raped, no one killed except perhaps the whores and showfighters who worked there. For their clients, every opportunity to twist a mind with strange herbs, to empty a pocket with dice and khit tiles, or to cheapen sex as barter would be made available in perfect safety. It was a beautiful, toxic dream, and she feared it as she loved it. It was a part of her city.

The soft, tentative knock at her door didn't startle her. She had been dreading it as much as expecting it. She turned, taking up her cane, and walked down the long, curved stair to the street level. The door was barred, not from fear, but to keep drunken laborers from mistaking hers for a comfort house. She lifted the bar and swung the door aside.

Liat Chokavi stood in the street, jaw tight, eyes cast down. She was a lovely little thing—brown eyes the color of milky tea and golden skin, smooth as an eggshell. If the girl's face was a little too round to be classically beautiful, her youth forgave her.

Amat Kyaan raised her left hand in a gesture that greeted her student. Liat adopted an answering pose of gratitude at being received, but the stance was undercut by the defensiveness of her body. Amat Kyaan suppressed a sigh and stood back, motioning the girl inside.

"I expected you earlier," she said as she closed the door.

Liat walked to the foot of the stair, but there paused and turned in a formal pose of apology.

"Honored teacher," she began, but Amat cut her off.

"Light the candles. I will be up in a moment."

Liat hesitated, but then turned and went up. Amat Kyaan could trace the girl's footsteps by the creaking of the timbers. She poured herself a cup of limed water, then went slowly up the stairs. The salve helped. Most days she woke able to convince herself that today there would be no trouble, and by nightfall her joints ached. Age was a coward and a thief, and she wasn't about to let it get the better of her. Still, as she took the steps to her workroom, she trusted as much of her weight to the cane as she could.

Liat sat on the raised cushion beside Amat Kyaan's oaken writing desk. Her legs were tucked up under her, her gaze on the floor. The lemon candles danced in a barely-felt breeze, the smoke driving away the worst of the flies. Amat sat at the window and arranged her robe as if she were preparing herself for work.

"Old Sanya must have had more objections than usual. He's normally quite prompt. Give the changes here, let's survey the damage, shall we?"

She held one hand out to the apprentice. A moment later, she lowered it.

"I misplaced the contracts," Liat said, her voice a tight whisper. "I apologize. It is entirely my fault."

Amat sipped her water. The lime made it taste cooler than it was.

"You *misplaced* the contracts?"

"Yes."

Amat let the silence hang. The girl didn't look up. A tear tracked down the round cheek.

"That isn't good," Amat said.

"Please don't send me back to Chaburi-Tan," the girl said. "My mother was so proud when I was accepted here and my father would—"

Amat raised a hand and the pleading stopped, Liat's gaze fixed on the floor. With a sigh, Amat pulled a bundle of papers from her sleeve and tossed them at Liat's knees.

At least the girl hadn't lied about it.

"One of the laborers found this between the bales from the Innis harvest," Amat said. "I gave him your week's wages as a reward."

Liat had the pages in her hands, and Amat watched the tension flow out of her, Liat's body collapsing on itself.

"Thank you," the girl said. Amat assumed she meant some god and not herself.

"I don't suppose I need to tell you what would have happened if these had come out? It would have destroyed every concession House Wilsin has had from Sanya's weavers in the last year."

"I know. I'm sorry. I really am."

"And do you have any idea how the contract might have fallen out of your sleeve? The warehouse seems an odd place to have lost them."

Liat blushed furiously and looked away. Amat knew that she had guessed correctly. It should have made her angry, but all she really felt was a kind of nostalgic sympathy. Liat was in the middle of her seventeenth summer, and some mistakes were easier to make at that age.

"Did you at least do something to make sure you aren't giving him a child?"

Liat's gaze flickered up at Amat and then away, fast as a mouse. The girl swallowed. Even the tips of her ears were crimson. She pretended to brush a fly off her leg.

"I got some teas from Chisen Wat," she said at last, and softly.

"Gods! Her? She's as likely to poison you by mistake. Go to Urrat on the Street of Beads. She's the one I always saw. You can tell her I sent you."

When Liat looked at her this time, the girl neither spoke nor looked away. She'd shocked her. And, as Amat felt the first rush of blood in her own cheeks, maybe she'd shocked herself a little, too. Amat took a pose of query.

"What? You think I was born before they invented sex? Go see Urrat. Maybe we can keep you from the worst parts of being young and stupid. Leaving contracts in your love nest. Which one was it, anyway? Still Itani Noyga?"

"Itani's my heartmate," Liat protested.

"Yes, yes. Of course."

He was a good-looking boy, Itani. Amat had seen him several times, mostly on occasions that involved prying her apprentice away from him and his cohort. He had a long face and broad shoulders, and was maybe a little too clever to be working as a laborer. He knew his letters and numbers. If he'd had more ambition, there might have been other work for a boy like that . . .

Amat frowned, her body taking a subtle tension even before the thought was fully in her mind. Itani Noyga, with his broad shoulders and strong legs. Certainly there was other work he could be put to. Driving away feral dogs, for example, and convincing roadside thugs to hunt for easier prey than Marchat Wilsin. Marchat wouldn't be keeping track of who each of his laborers were sharing pillows with.

And pillows were sometimes the best places to talk.

"Amat-cha? Are you all right?"

"Itani. Where is he now?"

"I don't know. Likely back at his quarters. Or maybe a teahouse."

"Do you think you could find him?"

Liat nodded. Amat gestured for a block of ink, and Liat rose, took one from the shelf and brought it to her desk. Amat took a length of paper and took a moment to calm herself before she began writing. The pen sounded as dry as a bird claw on pavement.

"There's an errand I want Itani for. Marchat Wilsin needs a body-guard tonight. He's going to a meeting in one of the low towns at the half-candle, and he wants someone to walk with him. I don't know how long the meeting will last, but I can't assume it will be brief. I'll tell his overseer to release him from duty tomorrow."

She took another sheet of paper, scraped the pen across the ink and began a second letter. Liat, at her shoulder, read the words as she wrote them.

"This one, I want you to deliver to Rinat Lyanita after you find Itani," Amat said as she wrote. "If Itani doesn't know that he's to go, Rinat will do. I don't want Marchat waiting for someone who never arrives."

"Yes, Amat-cha, but . . ."

Amat blew on the ink to cure it. Liat's words failed, and she took no pose, but a single vertical line appeared between her brows. Amat tested the ink. It smudged only a little. Good enough for the task at hand. She folded both orders and sealed them with hard wax. There wasn't time to sew the seams.

"Ask it," Amat said. "And stop scowling. You'll give yourself a headache."

"The mistake was mine, Amat-cha. It isn't Itani's fault that I lost the contracts. Punishing him for my error is . . ."

"It isn't a punishment, Liat-kya," Amat said, using the familiar -kya to reassure her. "I just need him to do me this favor. And, when he comes back tomorrow, I want him to tell you all about the journey. What town he went to, who was there, how long the meeting went. Every-thing he can remember. Not to anyone else; just to you. And then you to me."

Liat took the papers and tucked them into her sleeve. The line was still between her brows. Amat wanted to reach over and smooth it out with her thumb, like it was a stray mark on paper. The girl was thinking too much. Perhaps this was a poor idea after all. Perhaps she should take the orders back.

But then she wouldn't discover what business Marchat Wilsin was doing without her.

"Can you do this for me, Liat-kya?"

"Of course, but . . . is something going on, Amat-cha?"

"Yes, but don't concern yourself with it. Just do as I ask, and I'll take care of the rest."

Liat took a pose of acceptance and leave-taking. Amat responded with thanks and dismissal appropriate for a supervisor to an apprentice. Liat went down the stairs, and Amat heard her close the door behind her as she went. Outside, the fireflies shone and vanished, brighter now as twilight dimmed the city. She watched the streets: the firekeeper at the corner with his banked kiln, the young men in groups heading west into the soft quarter, ready to trade lengths of silver and copper for pleasures that would be gone by morning. And there, among them, Liat Chokavi walking briskly to the east, toward the warehouses and laborers' quarters, the dyeworks and the weavers.

Amat watched until the girl vanished around a corner, passing beyond recall, then she went down and barred her door.

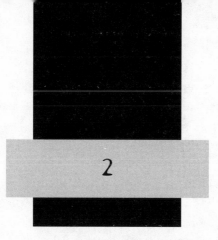

2

>+< The boundary arch on the low road east of Saraykeht was a short walk from the Wilsin compound. They reached it in about the time it took the crescent moon to shift the width of two of Marchat's thick fingers. Buildings and roads continued, splaying out into the high grasses and thick trees, but once they passed through the pale stone arch wide enough for three carts to pass through together and high as a tree, they had left the city.

"In Galt, there'd have been a wall," Marchat said.

The young man, Itani, took a pose of query.

"Around the city," Marchat said. "To protect it in time of war. We didn't have andat to aim at each other like your ancestors did. In Kirinton, where I was born, anytime you were bad, the Lord Watchman set you to repairing the wall."

"Can't have been pleasant," Itani agreed.

"What do they do in Saraykeht when a boy's caught stealing a pie?"

"I don't know."

"Never misbehaved as a child?"

Itani grinned. He had a strong smile.

"Rarely caught," Itani said. Marchat laughed.

They made an odd pair, he thought. Him, an old Galt with a walking staff as much to lean on as to swipe at dogs if the occasion arose, and this broad-backed, stone-armed young man in the rough canvas of a laborer. Not so odd, he hoped, as to attract attention.

"Noyga's your family name? Noyga. Yes. You work on Muhatia's crew, don't you?"

"He's a good man, Muhatia," Itani said.

"I hear he's a prick."

"That too," Itani agreed, in the same cheerful tone of voice. "A lot of the men don't like working with him. He's got a sharp tongue, and he hates running behind schedule."

"You don't mind him, though?"

Itani shrugged. It was another point in his favor. The boy disliked his overseer, that was clear, and yet here he was, alone with the head of the house and not willing to tell tales against him. It spoke well of him, and that was good for more than one reason. That he could trust Itani's discretion made his night one degree less awful.

"What else was different in Kirinton?" Itani asked, and as they walked, Marchat told him. Tales of the Galt of his childhood. The war with Eymond, the blackberry harvests, the midwinter bonfires when people brought their sins to be burned. The boy listened carefully, appreciatively. Granted, he was likely just currying favor, but he did it well. It wasn't far before Marchat felt the twinges of memories half-forgotten. He'd belonged somewhere once, before his uncle had sent him here.

The road was very little traveled, especially in the dead of night. The darkness made the uneven cobbles and then rutted dirt treacherous; the flies and night wasps were out in swarms, freed from torpor by the relative cool of the evening. Cicadas sang in the trees. The air smelled of moonrose and rain. No one in the few houses they passed that had candles and lanterns still burning seemed to show much curiosity, and it wasn't long before they were out, away from the last traces of Saraykeht. Tall grasses leaned close against the road, and twice groups of men passed them without comment or glance. Once something large shifted in the grass, but nothing emerged from it.

As they came nearer the low town, Marchat could feel his companion moving more slowly, hesitating. He couldn't say if the laborer was picking up on his own growing dread, or if there was some other issue. The first glimmering light of the low town was showing in the darkness when the man spoke.

"Marchat-cha, I was wondering . . ."

Marchat tried to take a pose of polite encouragement, but the walking stick complicated things. Instead he said, "Yes?"

"I'm coming near to the end of my indenture," Itani said.

"Really? How old are you?"

"Twenty summers, but I signed on young."

"You must have. You'd have been, what? Fifteen?"

"There's a girl," the young man said, having trouble with the words. Embarrassed. "She's . . . well, she's not a laborer. I think it's hard for her that I am. I'm not a scholar or a translator, but I have numbers and letters. I was wondering if you might know of any opportunities."

In the darkness, Marchat could see the boy's hands twisted into a pose of respect. So that was it.

"If you move up in the world, you think she'll like you better."

"It would make things easier for her," Itani said.

"And not for you?"

Again, the grin and this time a shrug with it.

"I lift things and put them back down," Itani said. "It's tiring sometimes, but it's not difficult."

"I don't know of anything just at hand. I'll see what I can find though."

"Thank you, Wilsin-cha."

They walked along another few paces. The light before them became a solid glow. A dog barked, but not so nearby as to be worrisome, and no other barks or howls answered it.

"She told you to ask me, didn't she?" Marchat asked.

"Yes," Itani agreed, the tension that had been in his voice gone.

"Are you in love with her?"

"Yes," the boy said, "I want her to be happy."

Those are two different answers, Marchat thought, but didn't say. He'd been that age once, and he remembered it well enough to know there was no point in pressing. They were in the low town proper now, anyway.

The streets here were muddy and smelled more of shit than moonrose. The buildings with their rotting thatch roofs and rough stone walls stood off at angles from the road. Two streets in, and so almost halfway though the town, a long, low house stood at the opening to a rough square. A lantern hung from a hook beside its door. Marchat motioned to Itani.

"Wait for me here," he said. "I'll be back as soon as I can."

Itani nodded his understanding. There was no hesitation or objection in his stance so far as Marchat could tell. It was more than he would have expected of himself if someone had told *him* to stand in this pesthole street in the black of night for some unknown stretch of time. *Gods go with you, you poor bastard*, Marchat thought. *And with me, too, for that.*

Inside, the house was dim. The ceiling was low, and though the walls were wide apart, the house had the feel of being too close. Like a cave. Part of that was the smell of mold and stale water, part the dim doorways and black arches that led to the inner rooms. A squat table ran the length of one wall, and two men stood against it. The larger, a thick-necked tough with a long knife hanging from his belt, eyed Marchat. The other, moon-faced and pleasant-looking, nodded welcome.

"Oshai," Marchat said by way of greeting.

"Welcome to our humble quarters," the moon-faced man said and smiled. Marchat disliked that smile, polite though it was. It was too much like the smile of someone helping you onto a sinking boat.

"Is it here?" Marchat asked.

Oshai nodded to a door set deeper in the gloom. A glimmer of candlelight showed its outline. Bad craftsmanship.

"He's been waiting," Oshai said.

Marchat grunted before walking deeper into the darkness. The wood of the door was water-rotted, the leather hinge loose and ungainly. Marchat had to lift the door by its handle to close it behind him. The meeting room was smaller, better lit, quiet. A night candle stood in a wall niche, burned past half. Several other candles burned on a small table. And sitting at the table itself was the andat. Seedless. Marchat's skin crawled as the thing considered him, black eyes shifting silently. The andat were unnerving under the best circumstances.

Marchat took a pose of greeting that the andat returned, then Seedless pushed out a stool and motioned to it. Marchat sat.

"You were able to come here without the poet's knowing?" Marchat asked.

"The great poet of Saraykeht is spending his evening drunk. As usual," Seedless replied, his voice conversational and smooth as cream. "He's beyond caring where I am or what I'm doing."

"And I hear the woman arrived?"

"Yes. Oshai says she's everything we need. Sweet-tempered, tractable, and profoundly credulous. She's unlikely to spook and run away like the last one. And she's from Nippu."

"Nippu?" Marchat said and curled his lip. "That's a backwater little island. Don't you think it might raise suspicion? I mean why would some farm bitch from a half-savage island come to Saraykeht just to drop her baby?"

"You'll think of something plausible," Seedless said, waving the objection away. "The point is she only speaks east island tongues. If she were from someplace with a real port, she might know a civilized language. Instead, you'll be using Oshai as her translator. It should be easy."

"My overseer may know the language."

"And you can't delegate this to someone who doesn't?" Seedless said. "Or are all of your employees brilliant translators?"

"Any idea who the father is?" Marchat said, shifting the subject.

Seedless made a gesture that wasn't a formal pose, but indicated the whole world and everything in it with a sweep of his delicate fingers.

"Who knows? Some passing fisherman. A tradesman. Someone who passed though her town and got her legs apart. No one who'll notice or care much if he does. He isn't important. And your part of the plan is progressing?"

"We're prepared. We have the payment ready. Pearls, mostly, and a hundred lengths of silver. It's the sort of thing an East Islander might pay with," Marchat said. "And there's no reason the Khai should look into it until the thing's been done."

"That's to the good, then," Seedless said. "Arrange the audience with the Khai. If all goes well, we won't have to speak again, you and I."

Marchat started to take a pose that expressed hope, but halfway in wondered if it might be taken the wrong way. He saw Seedless notice his hesitation. A thin smile graced the pale lips. Feeling an angry blush coming on, Marchat abandoned the pose.

"It will work, won't it?" he asked.

"It isn't the first babe I'll drop out before its time. This is what I am, Wilsin."

"No, I don't mean can you do it. I mean will it really break him? Heshai. He's taken the worst you could give him for years. Because if this little drama we're arranging doesn't work . . . If there's any chance at all that it should fail and the Khai find out that Galts were conspiring to deprive him of his precious andat, the consequences could be huge."

Seedless shifted forward on his chair, his gaze fastened on nothing. Marchat had heard once that andat didn't breathe except to speak. He watched the unmoving ribs for a long moment while the andat was silent. The rumor appeared true. At last, the spirit drew in his breath and spoke.

"Heshai is about to kill a child whose mother loves it. There isn't anything worse than that. Not for him. Picture it. This island girl? He's going to watch the light die in her eyes and know that without *him*, it wouldn't have happened. You want to know will that break him? Wilsin-cha, it will snap him like a twig."

They were silent for a moment. The naked hunger on the andat's face made Marchat squirm on his stool. Then, as if they'd been speaking of nothing more intimate or dangerous than a sugar crop, Seedless leaned back and grinned.

"With the poet broken, you'll be rid of me, which is what you want," Seedless said, "and I won't exist anymore to care one way or the other. So we'll both have won."

"You sound like a suicide to me," Marchat said. "You want your own death."

"In a sense," Seedless agreed. "But it doesn't mean for me what it would for you. We aren't the same kind of beast, you and I."

"Agreed."

"Do you want to see her? She's asleep in the next room. If you're quiet . . ."

"No, thank you," Marchat said, rising. "I'll arrange things with Oshai once I've scheduled the audience with the Khai. He and I can make the arrangements from there. If I could avoid seeing her at all before the day itself, that would be good."

"If good's the word," Seedless said, taking a pose of agreement and farewell.

Outside again, the night seemed cooler. Marchat pounded his walking stick against the ground, as if shaking dried mud off it, but really just to feel the sting in his fingers. His chest ached with something like dread. It was rotten, this business. Rotten and wrong and dangerous. And if he did anything to prevent it . . . what then? The Galtic High Council would have him killed, to start. He couldn't stop it. He couldn't even bow out and let someone else take his part in it.

There was no way through this but through. At least he'd kept Amat out of it.

"Everything went well?" the boy Itani asked.

"Well enough," Marchat lied as he started off briskly into the darkness.

AMAT KYAAN HAD HOPED TO SET OUT IN THE MORNING, BEFORE THE DAY'S heat was too thick. Liat had come to her with Itani's account of the route early enough, but the details were few and sketchy. Marchat and

the boy hadn't gotten back to the compound until past the quarter candle, and his report to Liat hadn't been as thorough as it might have been
had he known what use he had been put to. It had been enough to find
which of the low towns they had visited and what sort of house they'd
gone to.

Armed with those facts, it hadn't been so hard to find a contract that
rented such a building, one that had been paid out of Wilsin's private
funds and not those of the house proper. There were letters that spoke
vaguely of a girl and a journey to Saraykeht, but the time it took to find
that much cost Amat the better part of the morning. As she walked
down the low road east of the city, the boundary arch grown small behind her, she felt her annoyance growing. Sweat ran down her spine,
and her bad hip ached already.

In the cool just before dawn, it might almost have been a pleasant
walk. The high grasses sang with cicadas, the trees were thick with
their summer leaves. As it was, Amat felt as damp as if she'd walked out
of a bathhouse, drenched in her own sweat. The sun pressed on her
shoulders like a hand. And the trip back, she knew, would be worse.

Men and women of the low towns took poses of greeting and defer-
ence as they passed her, universally heading into the city. They pushed
handcarts of fruits and grains, chickens and ducks to sell to the compounds of the rich or the palaces or the open markets. Some carried
loads on their backs. On one particularly rutted stretch of road, she
passed an oxcart where it had slid into the roadside mud. One wheel
was badly bent. The carter, a young man with tears in his eyes, was
shouting and beating the ox who seemed barely to notice. Amat's prac-
ticed eye valued the wheel at three of four times the contents of the
cart. Whoever the boy carter answered to—father, uncle, or farmer rich
enough to own indentured labor—they wouldn't be pleased to hear of
this. Amat stepped around, careful how she placed her cane, and
moved on.

Low towns existed at the edges of all the cities of the Khaiem like
swarms of flies. Outside the boundaries of the city, no particular law
bound these men and women; the utkhaiem didn't enforce peace or
punish crimes. And still, a rough order was the rule. Disagreements
were handled between the people or taken to a low judge who passed
an opinion, which was followed more often than not. The traditions of
generations were as complex and effective as the laws of the Empire.

Amat felt no qualms about walking along the broken cobbles of the low road by herself, so long as it was in daylight and there was enough traffic to keep the dogs away.

No qualms except for what she might find at the end.

The low town itself was worse than she'd expected. Itani hadn't mentioned the smell of shit or the thick, sticky mud of the roads. Dogs and pigs and chickens all shared the path with her. A girl perhaps two years old stood naked in a doorway as she passed, her eyes no more domesticated than the pigs'. Amat found herself struggling to imagine Marchat Wilsin, head of House Wilsin in Saraykeht, trudging through this squalor in the dead of night. But there was the house Itani had described to Liat, and then Liat to her. Amat stood in the ruined square and steeled herself. To be turned back now would be humiliating.

So, she told herself, she wouldn't be turned back. Simple as that.

"Hai!" Amat called, rapping the doorframe with her cane. Across the square, a dog barked, as if the hail had been intended for him. Something stirred in the gloom of the house. Amat stood back, cultivating impatience. She was the senior overseer of the house. She mustn't go into this unsure of herself, and anger was a better mask than courtesy. She crossed her arms and waited.

A man emerged, younger then she was, but still gray about the temples. His rough clothes inspired no confidence, and the knife at his belt shone. For the first time, Amat wondered if she had come unprepared. Perhaps if she'd made Itani accompany her . . . She raised her chin, considering the man as if he were a servant.

The silence between them stretched.

"What?" the man demanded at last.

"I'm here to see the woman," Amat Kyaan said. "Wilsin-cha wants an inventory of her health."

The man frowned, and his gaze passed over her head, nervously surveying the street.

"You got the wrong place, grandmother. I don't know what you're talking about."

"I'm Amat Kyaan, senior overseer for House Wilsin. And if you don't want to continue our conversation here in the open, you should invite me in."

He hesitated, hand twitching toward his knife and then away. He was caught, she could see. To let her in was an admission that some traffic was taking place. But turning her away risked the anger of his employer if Amat was who she said she was, and on the errand she claimed. Amat took a pose of query that implied the offer of assistance—not a pose she would wish to see from a superior.

The knife man's dilemma was solved when another form appeared. The newcomer looked like nothing very much, a round, pale face, hair unkempt as one woken from sleep. The annoyance in his expression seemed to mirror her own, but the knife man's reaction was of visible relief. This was his overseer, then. Amat turned her attention to him.

"This woman," the knife man said. "She says she's Wilsin's overseer."

The moon-faced man smiled pleasantly and took a pose of greeting to her even as he spoke to the other man.

"That would be because she is. Welcome, Kyaan-cha. Please come in."

Amat strode into the low house, the two men stepping back to let her pass. The round-faced man closed the door, deepening the gloom. As Amat's eyes adjusted to the darkness, details began to swim out of it. The wide, low main room, too bare to mark the house as a place where people actually lived. The moss growing at edge where wall met ceiling.

"I've come to see the client," Amat said. "Wilsin-cha wants to be sure she's well. If she miscarries during the negotiations, we'll all look fools."

"The *client?* Yes. Yes, of course," the round-faced man said, and something in his voice told Amat she'd stepped wrong. Still, he took a pose of obeisance and motioned her to the rear of the place. Down a short hallway, a door opened to a wooden porch. The light was thick and green, filtered through a canopy of trees. Insects droned and birds called, chattering to one another. And leaning against a half-rotten railing was a young woman. She was hardly older than Liat, her skin the milky pale of an islander. Golden hair trailed down her back, and her belly bulged over a pair of rough canvas laborer's pants. Half, perhaps three-quarters of the way through her term. Hearing them, she turned and smiled. Her eyes were blue as the sky, her lips thick. *Eastern islands*, Amat thought. *Uman, or possibly Nippu.*

"Forgive me, Kyaan-cha," the moon-faced man said. "My duties require me elsewhere. Miyama will be here to help you, should you require it."

Amat took a pose of thanks appropriate for a superior releasing an underling. The man replied with the correct form, but a strange half-mocking cant to his wrists. He had thick hands, Amat noted, and strong shoulders. She turned away, waiting until the man's footsteps faded behind her. He would go, she guessed, to Saraykeht, to Wilsin. She hadn't managed to avoid suspicion, but by the time Marchat knew she'd discovered this place, it would be too late to shut her out of it. It would have to do.

"My name is Amat Kyaan," she said. "I'm here to inquire after your health. Marchat is a good man, but perhaps not so wise in women's matters."

The girl cocked her head, like listening to an unfamiliar song. Amat felt her smile fade a degree.

"You *do* know the Khaiate tongues?"

The girl giggled and said something. She spoke too quickly to follow precisely, but the words had the liquid feel of an east island language. Amat cleared her throat, and tried again, slowly in Nippu.

"My name is Amat Kyaan," she said.

"I'm Maj," the girl said, matching Amat's slow diction and exaggerating as if she were speaking to a child.

"You've come a long way to be here. I trust the travel went well?"

"It was hard at first," the girl said. "But the last three days, I've been able to keep food down."

The girl's hand strayed to her belly. Tiny, dark stretchmarks already marbled her skin. She was thin. If she went to term, she'd look like an egg on sticks. But, of course, she wouldn't go to term. Amat watched the pale fingers as they unconsciously caressed the rise and swell where the baby grew in darkness, and a sense of profound dislocation stole into her. This wasn't a noblewoman whose virginity wanted plausibility. This wasn't a child of wealth too fragile for blood teas. This didn't fit any of the hundred scenarios that had plagued Amat through the night.

She leaned against the wooden railing, taking some of the weight off her aching hip, put her cane aside, and crossed her hands.

"Marchat has told me so little of you," she said, struggling to find the vocabulary she needed. "How did you come to Saraykeht?"

The girl grinned and spun her tale. She spoke too quickly sometimes, and Amat had to make her repeat herself.

It seemed the father of her get had been a member of the utkhaiem—one of the great families of Saraykeht, near to the Khai himself. He'd been travelling in Nippu in disguise. He'd never revealed his true identity to her when he knew her, but though the affair had been brief, he had lost his heart to her. When he heard she was with child, he'd sent Oshai—the moon-faced man—to bring her here, to him. As soon as the politics of court allowed, he would return to her, marry her.

As improbability mounted on improbability, Amat nodded, encouraged, drew her out. And with each lie the girl repeated, sure of its truth, nausea grew in Amat. The girl was a fool. Beautiful, lovely, pleasant, and a fool. It was a story from the worst sort of wishing epic, but the girl, Maj, believed it.

She was being used, though for what, Amat couldn't imagine. And worse, she loved her child.

NOTHING WAS SAID TO MAATI. HIS BELONGINGS SIMPLY VANISHED FROM THE room in which he had been living, and a servant girl led him down from the palace proper to a house nestled artfully in a stand of trees—the poet's house. An artificial pond divided it from the grounds. A wooden bridge spanned the water, arching sharply, like a cat's back. Koi—white and gold and scarlet—flowed and shifted beneath the water's skin as Maati passed over them.

Within, the house was as lavish as the palace, but on a more nearly human scale. The stairway that led up to the sleeping quarters was a rich, dark wood and inlaid with ivory and mother of pearl, but no more than two people could have walked abreast up its length. The great rooms at the front, with their hinged walls that could open onto the night air or close like a shutter, were cluttered with books and scrolls and diagrams sketched on cheap paper. An ink brick had stained the arm of a great silk-embroidered chair. The place smelled of tallow candles and old laundry.

For the first time since he had left the Dai-kvo, Maati felt himself in a space the character of which he could understand. He waited for his teacher, prepared for whatever punishment awaited him. Darkness came late, and he lit the night candle as the sun set. The silence of the poet's house was his only companion as he slept.

In the morning, servants delivered a meal of sweet fruits, apple-bread still warm from the palace kitchens, and a pot of smoky, black tea. Maati ate alone, a feeling of dread stealing over him. Putting him here alone to wait might, he supposed, be another trick, another misdirection. Perhaps no one would ever come.

He turned his attention to the disorder that filled the house. After leaving the bowls, cups and knives from his own meal out on the grass for the servants to retrieve, he gathered up so many abandoned dishes from about the house that the pile of them made it seem he had eaten twice. Scrolls opened so long that dust covered the script, he cleaned, furled, and returned to the cloth sleeves that he could find. Several he suspected were mismatched—a deep blue cloth denoting legal considerations holding a scroll of philosophy. He took some consolation that the scrolls on the shelves seemed equally haphazard.

By the afternoon, twinges of resentment had begun to join the suspicion that he was once again being duped. Even as he swept the floors that had clearly gone neglected for weeks, he began almost to hope that this further abandonment *was* another plot by the andat. If it were only that Heshai-kvo had this little use for him, perhaps the Dai-kvo shouldn't have let him come. Maati wondered if a poet had the option of refusing an apprentice. Perhaps this neglect was Heshai-kvo's way of avoiding duties he otherwise couldn't.

It had been only a few weeks before that he had taken leave of the Dai-kvo, heading south along the river to Yalakeht and there by ship to the summer cities. It was his first time training under an acting poet, seeing one of the andat first hand, and eventually studying to one day take on the burden of the andat Seedless himself. *I am a slave, my dear. The slave you hope to own.*

Maati pushed the dust out the door, shoving with his broom as much as sweeping. When the full heat of the day came on, Maati opened all the swinging walls, transforming the house into a kind of pavilion. A soft breeze ruffled the pages of books and the tassels of scrolls. Maati rested. A distant hunger troubled him, and he wondered how to signal from here for a palace servant to bring him something to eat. If Heshai-kvo were here, he could ask.

His teacher arrived at last, at first a small figure, no larger than Maati's thumb, trundling out from the palace. Then as he came nearer, Maati made out the wide face, the slanted, weak shoulders, the awkward belly. As he crossed the wooden bridge, the high color in the poet's face—cheeks red as cherries and sheened in an unhealthy sweat—came clear. Maati rose and adopted a pose of welcome appropriate for a student to his master.

Heshai's rolling gait slowed as he came near. The wide mouth gaped as Heshai-kvo took in the space that had been his unkempt house. For the first time, Maati wondered if perhaps he had made a mistake in cleaning it. He felt a blush rising in his cheeks and shifted to a pose of apology.

Heshai-kvo raised a hand before he could speak.

"No. No, it's . . . gods, boy. I don't think the place has looked like this since I came here. Did you . . . there was a brown book, leather-bound, on that table over there. Where did it end up?"

"I don't know, Heshai-kvo," Maati said. "I will find it immediately."

"Don't. No. It will rise to the surface eventually, I'm sure. Here. Come. Sit."

The poet moved awkwardly, like a man gout-plagued, but his joints, so far as Maati could make them out within the brown robes, were unswollen. Maati tried not to notice the stains of spilled food and drink on the poet's sleeves and down the front of his robes. As he lowered himself painfully into a chair of black lacquer and white woven cane, the poet spoke.

"We've gotten off to a bad start, haven't we?"

Maati took a pose of contrition, but the poet waved it away.

"I'm looking forward to teaching you. I thought I should say so. But there's little enough that I can do with you just now. Not until the harvests are all done. And that may not be for weeks. I'll get to you when I have time. There's quite a bit I'll have to show you. The Dai-kvo can give you a good start, but holding one of the andat is much more than anything he'll have told you. And Seedless . . . well, I haven't done you any favors with Seedless, I'm afraid."

"I'm grateful that you were willing to accept me, Heshai-kvo."

"Yes. Yes, well. That's all to the good, then. Isn't it. In the meantime, you should make use of your freedom. You understand? It can be a lovely city. Take . . . take your time with it, eh? Live a little before we lock you back down into all this being a poet nonsense, eh?"

Maati took a pose appropriate to a student accepting instruction, though he could see in Heshai's bloodshot eyes that this was not quite the reply the poet had hoped for. An awkward silence stretched between them, broken when Heshai forced a smile, stood, and clapped Maati on the shoulder.

"Excellent," the poet said with such gusto that it was obvious he didn't mean it. "I've got to switch these robes out for fresh. Busy, you know, busy. No time to rest."

No time to rest. And yet it was the afternoon, and the poet, his teacher, was still in yesterday's clothes. No time to rest, nor to meet him when he arrived, nor to come to the house anytime in the night for fear of speaking to a new apprentice. Maati watched Heshai's wide form retreat up the stairs, heard the footsteps tramping above him as the poet rushed through his ablutions. His head felt like it had been stuffed with wool as he tried to catalog all the things he might have done that would have pushed his teacher away.

"Stings, doesn't it? Not being wanted," a soft voice murmured behind him. Maati spun. Seedless stood on the opened porch in a robe of perfect black shot with an indigo so deep it was hard to see where it blended with the deeper darkness. The dark, mocking eyes considered him. Maati took no pose, spoke no words. Seedless nodded all the same, as if he had replied. "We can talk later, you and I."

"I have nothing to say to you."

"All the better. I'll talk. You can listen."

The poet Heshai clomped down the stairs, a fresh robe, brown silk over cream, in place. The stubble had been erased from his jowls. Poet and andat considered each other for a breathless moment, and then turned and walked together down the path. Maati watched them go—the small, awkward shape of the master; the slim, elegant shadow of the slave. They walked, Maati noticed, with the same pace, the same length of stride. They might almost have been old friends, but for the careful way they never brushed each other, even walking abreast.

As they topped the rise of the bridge, Seedless looked back, and raised a perfect, pale hand to him in farewell.

"She doesn't know."

Marchat Wilsin half-rose from the bath, cool water streaming off his body. His expression was strange—anger, relief, something else more obscure than these. The young man he had been meeting with stared at Amat, open-mouthed with shock at seeing a clothed woman in the bathhouse. Amat restrained herself from making an obscene gesture at him.

"Tsani-cha," Wilsin said, addressing the young man though his gaze was locked on Amat. "Forgive me. My overseer and I have pressing business. I will send a runner with the full proposal."

"But Wilsin-cha," the young man began, his voice trailing off when the old Galt turned to him. Amat saw something in Wilsin's face that would have made her blanch too, had she been less fueled by her rage. The young man took a pose of thanks appropriate to closing an audience, hopped noisily out of the bath and strode out.

"Have you seen her?" Amat demanded, leaning on her cane. "Have you spoken with her?"

"No, I haven't. Close the door, Amat."

"She thinks—"

"I said close the door; I meant close the *door.*"

Amat paused, then limped over and slammed the wooden door shut. The sounds of the bathhouse faded. When she turned back, Wilsin was sitting on the edge of the recessed bath, his head in his hands. The bald spot at the top of his head was flushed pink. Amat moved forward.

"What were you thinking, Amat?"

"That this can't be right," she said. "I met with the girl. She doesn't know about the sad trade. She's an innocent."

"She's the only one in this whole damned city, then. Did you tell her? Did you warn her?"

"Without knowing what this is? Of course not. When was the last time you knew me to act without understanding the situation?"

"This morning," he snapped. "Now. Just now. Gods. And where did you learn to speak Nippu anyway?"

Amat stood beside him and then slowly lowered herself to the blue-green tiles. Her hip flared painfully, but she pushed it out of her mind.

"What is this?" she asked. "You're hiring the Khai to end a pregnancy, and the mother doesn't know that's what you're doing? You're killing a wanted child? It doesn't make sense."

"I can't tell you. I can't explain. I'm . . . I'm not allowed."

"At least promise me that the child is going to live. Can you promise me that?"

He looked over at her, his pale eyes empty as a corpse.

"Gods," Amat breathed.

"I never wanted to come here," he said. "This city. That was my uncle's idea. I wanted to run the tripled trade. Silver and iron from Eddensea south to Bakta for sugar and rum, then to Far Galt for cedar and spicewood and back to Eddensea. I wanted to fight pirates. Isn't that ridiculous? Me. Fighting pirates."

"You will not make me feel sorry for you. Not now. You are Marchat Wilsin, and the voice of your house in Saraykeht. I have seen you stand strong before a mob of Westermen screaming for blood. You faced down a high judge when you thought he was wrong and called him fool to his face. Stop acting like a sick girl. We don't have to do this. Refuse the contract."

Wilsin looked up, his chin raised, his shoulders squared. For a moment, she thought he might do as she asked. But when he spoke, his voice was defeated.

"I can't. The stakes are too high. I've already petitioned the Khai for an audience. It's in motion, and I can't stop it any more than I can make the tide come early."

Amat kicked off her sandals, raised the hem of her robes, and let her aching feet sink into the cool water. Light played on the surface, patterns of brightness and shadow flickering across Marchat's chest and face. He was weeping. That more than anything else turned her rage to fear.

"Then help me make sense of it. What is this child?" Amat said. "Who is the father?"

"No one. The child is no one. The father is no one. The girl is no one."

"Then why, Marchat? Why . . ."

"I can't tell you! Why won't you hear me when I say that? Ah? I don't get to tell you. Gods. Amat. Amat, why did you have to go out there?"

"You wanted me to. Why else ask me to arrange a bodyguard? You told me of a meeting I wasn't welcome to. You said there was house business, and then you said that you trusted me. How could you think I wouldn't look?"

He laughed with a sound like choking—mirthless and painful. His thick fingers grasped his knees, fingertips digging into pink flesh. Amat laid her cane aside and pressed her palm to his bent shoulder. Through the carved cedar blinds she heard someone on the street shriek and go silent.

"The round-faced one—Oshai. He came, didn't he? He told you I went there."

"Of course he did. He wanted to know if I'd sent you."

"What did you tell him?"

"That I hadn't."

"I see."

The silence stretched. She waited, willing him to speak, willing some words that would put it in some perspective less awful than it seemed. But Wilsin said nothing.

"I'll go back to my apartments," Amat said. "We can talk about this later."

She reached for her cane, but Wilsin's hand trapped hers. There was something in his eyes now, an emotion. Fear. It was as if they'd been soaking in it instead of water. She could feel her own heart trip faster as his eyes searched hers.

"Don't. Don't go home. He'll be waiting for you."

For the space of four breaths together, they were silent. Amat had to swallow to loosen her throat.

"Hide, Amat. Don't tell me where you've gone. Keep your head low for . . . four weeks. Five. It'll be over by then. And once it's finished with, you'll be safe. I can protect you then. You're only in danger if they think you might stop it from happening. Once it's done . . ."

"I could go to the utkhaiem. I could tell them that something's wrong. We could have Oshai in chains by nightfall, if . . ."

Marchat shook his wooly, white head slowly, his gaze never leaving hers. Amat felt the strength go out of his fingers.

"If this comes out to anyone, I'll be killed. At least me. Probably others. Some of them innocents."

"I thought there was only one innocent in this city," Amat said, biting her words.

"I'll be killed."

Amat hesitated, then withdrew her arm and took a pose of acceptance. He let her stand. Her hip screamed. And her stinging ointment was all at her apartments. The unfairness of losing that small comfort struck her ridiculously hard; one insignificant detail in a world that had turned from solid to nightmare in a day.

At the door, she stopped, her hand on the water-thick wood. She looked back at her employer. At her old friend. His face was stone.

"You told me," she said, "because you wanted me to find a way to stop it. Didn't you?"

"I made a mistake because I was confused and upset and felt very much alone," he said. His voice was stronger now, more sure of himself.

"I hadn't thought it through. But it was a mistake, and I see the situation more clearly now. Do what I tell you, Amat, and we'll both see the other side of this."

"It's wrong. Whatever this is, it's evil and it's wrong."

"Yes," he agreed.

Amat nodded and closed the door behind her when she went.

3

>+<   Through the day, the skies had been clear, hot and muggy. The rain only came with sunset; huge thunderheads towering into the sky, their flowing ropy trains tinted pink and gold and indigo by the failing light. The grey veil of water higher than mountains moved slowly toward the city, losing its festival colors in the twilight, pushing gusts of unpredictable wind before it, and finally reaching the stone streets and thick tile roofs in darkness. And in the darkness, it roared.

Liat lay her head on Itani's bare chest and listened to it: the angry hiss of falling rain, the lower rumble—like a river or a flood—of water washing through the streets. Here, in her cell at the compound of House Wilsin, it wasn't so bad. The streets outside were safe to walk through. Lower in the city—the soft quarter, the seafront, the warehouses—people would be trapped by it, staying in whatever shelter they had found until the rain slackened and the waters fell. She listened to the sound of water and her lover's heartbeat, smelled the cool scent of rain mixed with the musk of sex. In the summer cities, even a night rain didn't cool the air so much that she felt the need to cover her bare skin.

"We need to find a stronger frame for your netting," Itani said, prodding the knot of fallen cloth with his toe. Liat remembered that it had come down sometime during the evening. She smiled. The sex had left her spent—her limbs warm and loose, as if her bones had gone soft, as if she were an ocean creature.

"I love you, 'Tani," she said. His hand caressed the nape of her neck. He had rough hands—strong from his work and callused—but he used them gently when he chose. She looked up at him, his long face and unkempt hair. His smile. In the light of the night candle, his skin seemed to glow. "Don't go home tonight. Stay here, with me."

When he sighed, his breath lifted her head and settled it gently back down. "I can't. I'll stay until the rain fades a little. But Muhatia-cha's been watching me ever since you sent me out with Wilsin-cha. He's just waiting for an excuse to break me down."

"He's just jealous," Liat said.

"No, he's jealous *and* he's in control of my wages," Itani said, a wry amusement in his voice. "That makes him more than just jealous."

"It isn't fair. You're smarter than he is. You know numbers and letters. All the others like you better than him. You should be the overseer."

"If I was the overseer, the others wouldn't like me as much. If Little Kiri or Kaimati or Tanani thought I'd be docking their pay for being slow or arriving late, they'd say all the same things about me that they do about Muhatia. It's just the way it is. Besides, I like what I do."

"But you'd be a better overseer than he is."

"Probably so," Itani agreed. "The price is too high, though."

The pause was a different kind of silence than it had been before. Liat could feel the change in Itani's breathing. He was waiting for her to ask, waiting for her to push the issue. She could feel him flowing away, distant even before she spoke. Because he knew she would. And he was right.

"Did you ask Wilsin-cha about other opportunities?"

"Yes," he said.

"And?"

"He didn't know of any at the time, but he said he'd see what he could find."

"That's good, then. He liked you. That's very good," and again the pause, the distance. "If he offered you a position, you'd take it, wouldn't you?"

"It would depend on the offer," Itani said. "I don't want to do what I don't want to do."

"Itani! Look past your nose, would you? You'd *have* to. If the head of House Wilsin makes you an offer and you turn away, why would he ever make another one? You can't build a life out of refusing things. You have to accept them too—even things you don't want sometimes. If they lead to things you do want later on."

Itani shifted out from under her and stood. She rolled up to a sitting position. Itani stretched, his back to her, and he made the cell seem small. Her desk, her ledgers, a pile of ink blocks, waxed paper sticking out from between them like pale tongues. A wardrobe where her robes hung, and Itani, the muscles of his back shifting in the candlelight.

"Some nights, I feel like I'm talking to a statue. You're in your twentieth summer. This is my seventeenth," she said severely. "So how is it I'm older than you?"

"Maybe you sleep less," Itani said mildly. When he turned back to her, he smiled gently. He moved with animal grace and so little padding between his muscles and his skin that she felt she could see the mechanism of each motion. He crouched by the cot, resting his head on his hands and looking up at her. "We have this conversation over and over, sweet, and it's never changed yet. I know you want more from me than—"

"I want you to want more for yourself, 'Tani. That isn't the same thing."

He took a gentle pose asking permission.

"I know you want more from me than a laborer's life. And I don't imagine I'll do this forever. But I'm not ashamed of it, and I won't do something I like less so that someone someday might give me something that they think I'm supposed to want. When *I* want something, that will be different."

"And isn't there anything you want that you don't already have?"

He rose, cupping her breast in his hand and gently, carefully pressing his lips to hers. His weight bore her back slowly to the labyrinth of cloth that had been her sheets and netting. She pulled back a fraction of an inch, keeping so close that when she spoke, she could feel her lips brushing his.

"What kind of answer is this?" she asked.

"You asked me about things I want," he murmured.

"And you're distracting me instead of answering the question."

"Am I?"

His hand brushed down her side. She felt the gooseflesh rise as it passed.

"Are you what?"

"Am I distracting you?"

"Yes," she said.

The knock at the door startled them both. Itani leapt up, chagrin showing on his face as he pawed the shadows, looking for the rough cloth of his pants. Liat drew her sheet around her. To the silent question in Itani's eyes she shook her head in bewilderment. The knock came again.

"A moment!" she said, loud enough to carry over the rain. "Who's there?"

"Epani Doru," the voice shouted from the other side of the thin door. "Wilsin-cha sent me to ask whether he might have a word with you."

"Of course. Yes. Just give me a moment."

Itani, trousers located, tossed her robes to her. She pulled on the inner robes, then grabbed a fresh outer robe from the wardrobe. Itani helped her fasten it. She felt her hands trembling. The voice of House Wilsin wanted to speak with her, and outside the normal hours of labor. It had never happened before.

"I should go back to my quarters," Itani said as she pulled her hair back to a formal bun.

"No. Please, 'Tani. Wait for me."

"You could be a quarter candle, love," he said. "Listen. The rain's coming softer now anyway. It's time."

It was true. The hiss of the rain was less vicious. And for all her complaints, she understood what it meant to have the unkind interest of an overseer. She took a pose of acceptance, but broke it to kiss him again.

"I'll find you tomorrow," she said.

"I'll be waiting."

Itani moved back into the shadows behind the wardrobe and Liat tugged at her robes one last time, stepped into her slippers and answered the door. Epani, Marchat Wilsin's house master, stood under the awning, his arms crossed, and his expression neutral. Liat took a pose indicating preparedness, and without apparent irony, he replied with one expressing thanks for prompt action. His gaze passed her for a moment, taking in the wreckage of her cot, the discarded robes on the stone floor, but he made no comment. When he turned and strode away, she followed.

They went down an open walkway of gray stones raised far enough that the streams of rainwater hadn't darkened them. In the courtyard, the fountain had filled to overflowing, the wide pool dancing with drops. The tall bronze statue of the Galtic Tree—symbol of the house— loomed in the darkness, the false bark glittering in the light of lanterns strung beneath the awnings and safe from the rain.

The private apartments where Wilsin-cha lived were at the end of the courtyard farthest from the street. Double doors of copper-bound ash stood open, though the view of the antechamber was still blocked by house banners shifting uneasily in the breeze. They glowed from the light behind them. Epani drew one banner aside and gestured Liat within as if she were a guest and not an apprentice overseer.

The antechamber was stone-floored, but the walls and high ceiling glowed with worked wood. The air smelled rich with lemon candle and mint wine and lamp oil. Lanterns lit the space. From somewhere nearby, she heard voices—two men, she thought. She made out few words—Wilsin-cha's voice saying "won't affect" and "unlike the last girl," the other man saying "won't allow" and "street by street if needed." Epani, sweeping in behind her, took a pose that indicated she should wait. She took a pose of acknowledgement, but the house master had already moved on, vanishing behind thick banners. The conversation stopped suddenly as Epani's rain-soft voice interrupted. Then Marchat Wilsin himself, wearing robes of green and black, strode into the room.

"Liat Chokavi!"

Liat took a pose of obeisance which the head of her house replied to with a curt formal pose, dropped as soon as taken. He put a thick hand on her shoulder and drew her back to an inner chamber.

"I need to know, Liat. Do you speak any island tongues? Arrask or Nippu?"

"No, Wilsin-cha. I know Galtic and some Coyani . . ."

"But nothing from the Eastern Islands?"

As they stepped into a meeting room, Liat adopted an apologetic pose.

"That's too bad," Wilsin-cha said, though his tone was mild and his expression curiously relieved.

"I think Amat-cha may know some Nippu. It isn't a language that's much used in trade, but she's very well-studied."

Wilsin lowered himself to a bench beside a low table, gesturing to the cushion across from him. Liat knelt as he poured out a bowl of tea for her.

"You've been with my house, what? Three years now?"

"Amat-cha accepted me as her apprentice four years ago. I was with my father in Chaburi-Tan before that, working with my brothers . . ."

"Four years ago? Weren't you young to be working four years ago? You'd have seen twelve summers?"

Liat felt herself blush. She hadn't meant to have her family brought into the conversation.

"Thirteen, Wilsin-cha. And there were ways I could help, so I did what I could. My brothers and I all helped where we could."

She silently willed the old Galt's attention away from the subject. Anything she could say about her old life would make her seem less likely to be worth cultivating. The small apartments by the smokehouse that had housed her and three brothers; her father's little stand in the market selling cured meats and dried fruits. It wasn't the place Liat imagined an overseer of a merchant house would start from. Her wish seemed to be granted. Wilsin-cha cleared his throat and sat forward.

"Amat's been sent away on private business. She may be gone for some weeks. I have an audience before the Khai that I'll need you to take over."

He said it in a low, conversational voice, but Liat felt herself flush like she'd drunk strong wine. She sipped the tea to steady herself, then put the bowl down and took a pose appropriate to a confession.

"Wilsin-cha, Amat has never taken me to the courts. I wouldn't know what to do, and . . ."

"You'll be fine," Wilsin-cha said. "It's the sad trade. Not complex, but I need it done with decorum, if you see. Someone to see to it that the client has the appropriate robes and understands the process. And with Amat unavailable, I thought her apprentice might be the best person for the role."

Liat looked down, hoping that the sense of vertigo would fade. An audience with the Khai—even only a very brief one—was something she had expected to take only years later, if ever. She took a pose of query, fighting to keep her fingers from trembling. Wilsin waved a hand, giving her permission to speak her question.

"There are other overseers. Some of them have been with the house much longer than I have. They have experience in the courts . . ."

"They're busy. This is something I was going to have Amat do herself, before she was called away. I don't want to pull anyone else away from negotiations that are only half-done. And Amat said it was within your abilities, so . . ."

"She did?"

"Of course. Here's what I'll need of you . . ."

THE RAIN HAD ENDED AND THE NIGHT CANDLE BURNED TO JUST PAST THE halfway mark when Heshai-kvo returned. Maati, having fallen asleep on a reading couch, woke when the door slammed open. Blinking away half-formed dreams, he stood and took a pose of welcome. Heshai snorted, but made no other reply. Instead, he took a candle and touched it to the night candle's flame, then walked heavily around the rooms lighting every lantern and candle. When the house was bright as morning and thick with the scent of hot wax, the teacher returned the dripping candle to its place and dragged a chair across the floor. Maati sat on the couch as Heshai, groaning under his breath, lowered himself into the chair.

Maati was silent as his teacher considered him. Heshai-kvo's eyes were narrow, his mouth skewed in something like a stillborn smile. At last the teacher heaved a loud sigh and took a pose of apology.

"I've been an ass. And I'm sorry," the teacher said. "I meant to say so before, but . . . well, I didn't, did I? What happened with the Khai was my fault, not yours. Don't carry it."

"Heshai-kvo, I was wrong to . . ."

"Ah, you're a decent boy. You're heart's good. But there's no call to sweeten turds. I was thoughtless. Careless. I let that bastard Seedless get the better of me. Again. And you. Gods, you must think I'm the silliest joke ever to wear a poet's robe."

"Not at all," Maati said seriously. "He is . . . a credit to you, Heshai-kvo. I have never seen anything to match him."

Heshai-kvo coughed out a sharp, mirthless laugh.

"And have you seen another andat?" he asked. "Any of them at all?"

"I was present when Choti Dausadar of Amnat-Tan bound Moss-Hidden-from-Sunlight. But I never saw him use her powers."

"Yes, well, I'm sure he will as soon as anyone can think of a decent use for forcing mosses out in the light where we can see them. The Dai-kvo should have insisted that Choti wait until he had a binding poem for something useful. Even Petals-Falling was a better tool than that. Hidden moss. Gods."

Maati took a pose of polite agreement, appropriate to receiving teachings, but as he did so, it struck him. Heshai-kvo was drunk.

"It's a fallen age, boy. The great poets of the Empire ruined it for us. All that's left is picking at the obscure thoughts and images that are still in the corners. We're like dogs sniffing for scraps. We aren't poets; we're *scholars.*"

Maati began to take a pose of agreement but paused, unsure. Heshai-kvo raised an eyebrow and completed the pose himself, his gaze fixed on Maati as if asking *was this what you meant?* Then the teacher waved the pose away.

"Seedless was . . . was the answer to a problem," the poet said, his voice growing soft. "I didn't think it through. Not far enough. Have you heard of Miyani-kvo and Three-Bound-As-One? I studied that when I was your age. Poured my heart into it. And when the time came—when the Dai-kvo sent for me and said that I wasn't simply going to take over another man's work, that I was to attempt a binding of my own—I drew on that knowledge. She was in love with him, you know. Three-Bound-As-One. An andat in love with her poet. There was an epic written about it."

"I've seen it performed."

"Have you? Well forget it. Unlearn it. It'll only lead you astray. I was too young and too foolish, and now I'm afraid I'll never have the chance to be wise." The poet's gaze was fixed on something that Maati couldn't see, something in another place or time. A smile touched the wide lips for a moment, and then, with a sigh, the poet blinked. He seemed to see Maati again, and took a pose of command.

"Put these damned candles out," he said. "I'm going to sleep."

And without looking back, Heshai-kvo rose and tramped up the stairs. Maati moved through the house, dousing the flames Heshai-kvo had lit, dimming the room as he did so. His mind churned with half-formed questions. Above him, he heard Heshai-kvo's footsteps, and then the clatter of shutters closing, and then silence. The master had gone to bed—likely already asleep. Maati had snuffed the last flame but the night candle when the new voice spoke.

"You didn't accept my apology."

Seedless stood in the doorway, his pale skin glowing in the light of the single candle. His robes were dark—blue or black or red so deep Maati couldn't make it out. The thin hands took a pose of query.

"Is there a reason I should?"

"Charity?"

Maati coughed out a mirthless laugh and turned as if to go, but the andat stepped into the house. His movements were graceful as an animal's—as beautiful as the Khai, but unstudied, as much a part of his nature as the shape of a leaf was natural to a tree.

"I *am* sorry," the andat said. "And you should forgive our mutual master as well. He had a bad day."

"Did he?"

"Yes. He met with the Khai and discovered that he's going to have to do something he doesn't enjoy. But now that it's just the two of us . . ."

The andat sat on the stairs, black eyes amused, pale hands cradling a knee.

"Ask," Seedless said.

"Ask what?"

"Whatever the question is that's making your face pull in like that. Really, you look like you've been sucking lemons."

Maati hesitated. If he could have walked away, he would have. But the path to his cot was effectively blocked. He considered calling out to Heshai-kvo, waking him so that he could walk up the stairway without brushing against the beautiful creature in his way.

"Please, Maati. I said I was sorry for my little misdirection. I won't do it again."

"I don't believe you."

"No? Well, then you're wise beyond your years. I probably will at some point. But here, tonight, ask me what you'd like, and I'll tell you the truth. For a price."

"What price?"

"That you accept my apology."

Maati shook his head.

"Fine," Seedless said, rising and moving to the shelves. "Don't ask. Tie yourself in knots if it suits you."

The pale hand ran along the spines of books, plucking one in a brown leather binding free. Maati turned, walked up two steps, and then faltered. When he looked back, Seedless had curled up on a couch beside the night candle, his legs pulled up beneath him. He seemed engaged in the open book on his knee.

"He told you the story about Miyani-kvo, didn't he?" Seedless asked, not looking up from the page.

Maati was silent.

"It's like him to do that. He doesn't often say things clearly when an oblique reference will do. It was about how Three-Bound-As-One loved her poet, wasn't it? Here. Look at this."

Seedless turned the book over and held it out. Maati walked back down the steps. The book was written in Heshai-kvo's script. The page Seedless held out was a table marking parallels between the classic binding of Three-Bound-As-One and Removing-The-Part-That-Continues. Seedless.

"It's his analysis of his error," the andat said. "You should take it. He means for you to have it, I think."

Maati took the soft leather in his hands. The pages scraped softly.

"He did bind you," Maati said. "He didn't pay your price, so there wasn't an error. It worked."

"Some prices are subtle. Some are longer than others. Let me tell you a little more about our master. He was never lovely to look at. Even fresh from the womb, he made an ugly babe. He was cast out by his father, much the same way you were. But when he found himself an apprentice in the courts of the Khai Pathai, he fell in love. Hard to imagine, isn't it? Our fat, waddling pig of a man in love. But he was, and the girl was willing enough. The allure of power. A poet controls the andat, and that's as near to holding a god in your hands as anyone is ever likely to get.

"But when he got her with child, she turned away from him," Seedless continued. "Drank some nasty teas and killed out the baby. It broke his heart. Partly because he might have liked being a father. Partly because it proved that his lady love had never meant to build her life with his."

"I didn't know."

"He doesn't tell many people. But . . . Maati, please, sit down. This is important for you to understand, and if I have to keep looking up at you, I'll get a sore neck."

He knew that the wise thing was to turn, to walk up the stairs to his room. He sat.

"Good," Seedless said. "Now. You know, don't you, that andat are only ideas. Concepts translated into a form that includes volition. The work of the poet is to include all those features which the idea itself doesn't carry. So for example Water-Moving-Down had perfectly white hair. Why? There isn't anything about that thought that requires white hair. Or a deep voice. Or, with Three-Bound-As-One, love. So where do those attributes come from?"

"From the poet."

"Yes," Seedless agreed, smiling. "From the poet. Now. Picture our master as a boy not much older than you are now. He's just lost a child that might otherwise have been his, a woman who might have loved him. The unspoken suspicion that his father hates him and the pain of his mother letting him be taken away gnaws at him like a cancer. And now he is called on to save Saraykeht—to bind the andat that will keep the wheels of commerce running. And he fashions me.

"And look what he did, Maati," the andat continued, spreading his arms as if he were on display. "I'm beautiful. I'm clever. I'm confident. In ancient days, Miyani-kvo made himself his perfect mate. Heshai-kvo created the self he wished that he were. In all my particulars, I am who he would have been, had it been given him to choose. But along with that, he folded in what he imagined his perfect self would think of the real man. Along with beauty and subtlety and wit, he gave me all his hatred of the toad-poet Heshai."

"Gods," Maati said.

"Oh, no. It was brilliant. Imagine how deeply he hated himself. And I carry that passion. Andat are all profoundly unnatural—we want to return to our natural state the way rain wants to fall. But we can be divided against ourselves. *That* is the structure he took from Miyani-kvo. Three-Bound-As-One wanted freedom, and she also wanted love. I am divided because I want freedom, and I want to see my master suffer. Oh, not that he intended it this way. It was a subtlety of the model that he didn't understand until it was too late.

"But you wonder why he neglects you? Why he seems to avoid teaching you, or even speaking to you? Why he doesn't bring you along on his errands for the Khai? He is afraid for you. In order to take his place, you are going to have to cultivate the part of yourself that is most poisonous. You will have to come to hate yourself as much as ugly, sad, lonesome Heshai does—Heshai, whose cohort called him cruel names and ripped his books, who for the past twenty years hasn't known a woman he didn't pay for, who even the lowest of the utkhaiem consider an embarrassment to be tolerated only from need. And so, my boy, he fears for you. And everything he fears, he flees."

"You make him sound like a very weak man."

"Oh no. He is what becomes of a very strong man who's done to himself what Heshai did."

"And why'" Maati said, "are you telling me this?"

"That's a question," Seedless said. "It's the first one you've asked me tonight. If I answer, you have to pay my price. Accept my apology."

Maati considered the dark, eager eyes and then laughed.

"You tell a good monster story," Maati said, "but no. I think I'll live with my curiosity intact."

A sudden scowl marked Seedless' face, but then he laughed and took a pose appropriate to the loser of a competition congratulating the victor. Maati found that he was laughing with him and rose, responding with a pose of gracious acceptance. As he walked up the stairs toward his bed, Seedless called out after him.

"Heshai won't ever invite you along with him. But he won't turn you away if you come. The Khai is holding a great audience after temple next week. You should come then."

"I can't think of any reason, Seedless-cha, to do your bidding."

"You shouldn't," the andat said, and an odd melancholy was in his voice. "You should always do only your own. But I'd like to see you there. We monsters have few enough people to talk with. And whether you believe me or not, I would be your friend. For the moment, at least. While we still have the option."

SHE HAD GROWN COMPLACENT; SHE SAW THAT NOW. AS A GIRL OR A YOUNGER woman, Amat had known that the city couldn't be trusted. Fortunes changed quickly when she was low and poor. A sickness or a wound, an unlucky meeting—anything could change how she earned her money, where she lived, who she was. Working for so many years and watching her station rise along with the house she served, she had forgotten that. She hadn't been prepared.

Her first impulse had been to go to friends, but she found she had fewer than she'd thought. And anyone she knew well enough to trust with this, the moon-faced Oshai and his knife-man might also know of. For three days she'd slept in the attic of a wineseller with whom she'd had an affair when they'd both been young. He had already been married to his wife at the time—the same woman who Amat heard moving through the house below her now. No one had known then, and so no one was likely to guess now.

The room, if it could be called that, was low and dark. Amat couldn't sit without her head brushing the roof. The scent of her own shit leaked from the covered night pot; it couldn't be taken away until after night-fall when the household slept. And just above her, unseen sunlight baked the rooftiles until the ceiling was too hot to touch comfortably. Amat lay on the rough straw mat, torpid and miserable, and tried not to make noises that would give her presence away.

She did not dream, but her mind caught a path and circled through it over and over in way that also wasn't the stuff of waking. Marchat had been forced somehow to take House Wilsin into the sad trade. And, abominable, against a woman who had been tricked. The girl had been lied to and brought here, to Saraykeht, so that the andat could pull her baby out of her womb. Why? What child could be so important? Per-haps it was really the get of some king of the Eastern Islands, and the girl didn't guess whose child she really carried, and . . .

No. There was no reason to bring her here. There were any number of ways to be rid of a child besides the andat. Begin again.

Perhaps the woman herself wasn't what she seemed. Perhaps she was mad, but also somehow precious. Normal teas might derange her, so the andat was employed to remove the babe without putting any medicines into the woman. And House Wilsin . . .

No. If there had been a reason, a real reason, a humane reason, for this travesty, Marchat wouldn't have had to keep it from her. Begin again.

It wasn't about the woman. Or the father. Or the child. Marchat had said as much. They were all nobodies. The only things left were House Wilsin and the andat. So the solution was there. If there was a solution. If this wasn't all a fever dream. Perhaps House Wilsin intended to kill out an innocent child with the aid of the Khai and then use their shared guilt as a way to gain favor . . .

Amat ground her palms into her eyelids until blotches of green and gold shone before her. Her robes, sweat-sticky, balled and bound like bedclothes knotted in sleep. In the house below her, someone was pounding something—wood clacking against wood. If she'd been somewhere cool enough to think, if there was a way out of this blasted, dim, hell-bound coffin of a room, she knew she'd have made sense of it by now. She'd been chewing on it for three days.

Three days. The beginning of four weeks. Or five. She rolled to her side and lifted the flask of water Kirath, her once-lover, had brought her that morning. It was more than half emptied. She had to be more careful. She sipped the blood-hot water and lay back down. Night would come.

And with an aching slowness, night came. In the darkness, it was only a change in the sounds below her, the drifting scent of an evening meal, the slightest cooling of her little prison. She needed no more to tell her to prepare. She sat in the darkness by the trapdoor until she heard Kirath approaching, moving the thin ladder, climbing up. Amat raised the door, and Kirath rose from the darkness, a hooded lantern in one hand. Before she could speak, he gestured for silence and then that she should follow. Climbing down the ladder sent pain through her hip and knee like nails, but even so the motion was better than staying still. She followed him as quietly as she could through the darkened house and out the back door to a small, ivied garden. The summer breeze against her face, even thick and warm as it was, was a relief. Fresh water in earthenware bowls, fresh bread, cheese, and fruit sat on a stone bench, and Amat wolfed them as Kirath spoke.

"I may have found something," he said. There was gravel in his voice now that had not been there when he'd been a young man. "A comfort house in soft quarter. Not one of the best, either. But the owner is looking for someone to audit the books, put them in order. I mentioned that I knew someone who might be willing to take on the work in exchange for a discreet place to live for a few weeks. He's interested."

"Can he be trusted?"

"Ovi Niit? I don't know. He pays for his wine up front, but . . . Perhaps if I keep looking. In a few more days . . . There's a caravan going north next week, I might . . ."

"No," Amat said. "Not another day up there. Not if I can avoid it."

Kirath ran a hand over his bald pate. His expression in the dim lantern light seemed both relieved and anxious. He wanted her quit of his home as badly as she wished to be quit of it.

"I can take you there tonight then, if you like," he offered. The soft quarter was a long walk from Kirath's little compound. Amat took another mouthful of bread and considered. It would ache badly, but with her cane and Kirath both to lean on, she thought she could do the thing. She nodded her affirmation.

"I'll get your things, then."

"And a hooded robe," Amat said.

Amat had never felt as conspicuous as during the walk to the soft quarter. The streets seemed damnably full for so late at night. But then, it was the harvest, and the city was at its most alive. That she herself hadn't spent summer nights in the teahouses and midnight street fairs for years didn't mean such things had stopped. The city had not changed; she had.

They navigated past a corner where a firekeeper had opened his kiln and put on a show, tossing handfuls of powder into the flames, making them dance blue and green and startling white. Sweat sheened the fire-keeper's skin, but he was grinning. And the watchers—back far enough that the heat didn't cook them—applauded him on. Amat recognized two weavers sitting in the street, talking, and watching the show, but they didn't notice her.

The comfort house itself, when they reached it, was awash with activity. Even in the street outside it, men gathered, talking and drinking. She stood a little way down the street at the mouth of an alleyway while Kirath went in. The house itself was built in two levels. The front was the lower, a single story but with a pavilion on the roof and blue and silver cloths hanging down the pale stucco walls. The back part of the house carried a second story and a high wall that might encompass a garden in the back. Certainly a kitchen. There were, however, few windows, and those there were were thin and cut high in the wall. For privacy, perhaps. Or to keep anyone from climbing out them.

Kirath appeared in the main doorway, silhouetted by the brightness within, and waved her over. Leaning on her cane, she came.

Within, the main room was awash in gamblers at their tables—cards, dice, tiles, stones. The air was thick with the smoke of strange leaves and flowers. No showfighting of animals or men, at least. Kirath led her to the back and through a thick wooden door. Another long room, this filled with whores lounging on chairs or cushions. The lamps were lower, the room almost shadowless. A fountain murmured at one wall. The painted eyes of women and boys turned as she entered, and then turned away again, returning to their conversations, as it became clear that neither she nor Kirath were clients come to choose from amongst them. A short hallway lined with doors turned at its end and stopped blind at a heavy wooden door, bound with iron. The door opened before them.

Amat Kyaan stepped into the sudden squalor of the back house. A wide common room with tables. A long alcove at the side with cloth, leather, and sewing benches. Several doors led off, but it wasn't clear to where.

"This way," a man said. He was splendidly dressed, but had bad teeth. As he led them between the long rough-wood tables toward a thin door at the back, Amat gestured toward him with a pose of query, and Kirath nodded. The owner. Ovi Niit.

The books, such as they were, sat on a low table in a back room. Amat's spirits sank looking at them. Loose sheets or poorly-bound ledgers of cheap paper. The entries were in half a dozen hands, and each seemed to have its own form. Sums had been written, crossed out, and written in again.

"This is salvage work," she said, putting down a ledger.

Ovi Niit leaned against the doorway behind her. Heavy-lidded eyes made him seem half-asleep and in the close quarters, he smelled of musk and old perfume. He was young enough, she guessed, to be her child.

"I could put it in something like order in a moon's turn. Perhaps a little more."

"If I needed it a moon from now, I'd have it done in a moon. I need it now," Ovi Niit said. Kirath, behind him, looked grave.

"I can get an estimate in a week," Amat said. "It will only be rough. I won't stand by it."

Ovi Niit considered her, and she felt a chill despite the heat of the night. He shifted his head from side to side as if considering his options.

"An estimate in three days," the young man countered. "The work completed in two weeks."

"We aren't haggling," Amat said taking a pose of correction that was brusque without edging over into insult. "I'm telling you how things are. There's no doing this in two weeks. Three, if things went well, but more likely four. Demanding it in two is telling the sun to set in the morning."

There was a long silence, broken by Ovi Niit's low chuckle.

"Kirath tells me men are looking for you. They're offering silver."

Amat took a pose of acknowledgement.

"I'd expected you to be more eager to help," Ovi Niit said. His voice feigned hurt, but his eyes were passionless.

"I'd be lying. That couldn't help either of us."

Ovi Niit considered that, then took a pose of agreement. He turned to Kirath and nodded. His pose to Amat shifted to a request for her forbearance as he drew Kirath out and closed the door behind them. Amat leaned against the table, her palm pressed to her aching hip. The walk had loosened her muscles a bit, but she would still have given a week's wages for the pot of salve in her apartments. In the common room, she heard Kirath laugh. He sounded relieved. It took some of the tightness out of Amat's throat. Things must be going well. For a moment, a voice in the back of her mind suggested that perhaps it had all been a trick and Ovi Niit and Kirath were sending a runner to the moon-faced Oshai even while she waited here, oblivious. She put the thought aside. She was tired. The days in the hellish attic had worn her thin, that was all. In the common room, a door opened and closed, and a moment later Ovi Niit stepped back into the room.

"I've given our mutual friend a few lengths of silver and sent him home," the young man said. "You'll sleep with the whores. There's a common meal at dawn, another at three hands past midday, and another at the second mark on the night candle."

Amat Kyaan took a pose of thanks. Ovi Niit responded with an acceptance so formal as to be sarcastic. When he struck, it was quick; she did not see the blow coming. The ring on his right hand cut her mouth, and she fell back, landing hard. Pain took her hip so fierce it seemed cold.

"Three days to an estimate. Two weeks to a full balance. For every day you are late, I will have you cut," he said, his voice settled and calm. "If you 'tell me how things are' again, I will sell you within that hour. And if you bleed on my floor, you'll clean it, you shit-licking, wattle-necked, high-town cunt. Do you understand?"

The first bloom of emotion in her was only surprise, and then confusion, and then anger. He measured her, and she saw the hunger in him, waiting for her answer; the eagerness for her humiliation would have been pathetic—a child whipping dogs—if she hadn't been on the end of it. She choked on her defiance and her pride. Her mouth felt thick with venom, though it was certainly only blood.

Bend now, she thought. *This is no time to be stubborn. Bend now and live through this.*

Amat Kyaan, chief overseer of House Wilsin, took a pose of gratitude and acceptance. The tears were easy to feign.

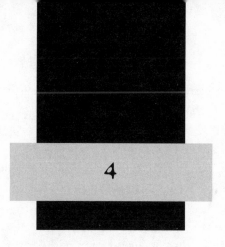

4

">+<" "I can't do this," Liat said over the splash of flowing water. "There's too much."

The washing floor was outside the barracks: a stone platform with an open pipe above it and a drain below. Itani stood naked in the flow, his hair plastered flat, scrubbing his hands and arms with pumice.

The sun, still likely three or four hands above the horizon, was nonetheless lost behind the buildings of the warehouse district. Now they were in shadow; soon it would be night. Liat on her bench leaned against the ivy-covered wall, plucking at the thick, waxy leaves.

"Amat left everything half-done," she went on. "The contracts with Old Sanya. How was I to know they hadn't been returned to him? It isn't as if she told me to run them there. And the shipments to Obar State weren't coordinated, so there are going to be three weeks with the third warehouse standing half-empty when it should be full. And every time something goes wrong, Wilsin-cha . . . he doesn't say anything, but he keeps looking at me as though I might start drooling. I embarrass him."

Itani stepped out from the artificial waterfall. His hands and arms were a dirty blue outlined in red where he had rubbed the skin almost raw. All his cohort had spent the day hauling dye to the dye yard, and all of them were marked by the labor. She looked at him in despair. His fingernails, she knew from experience, would look as if they were dirty until the dyes wore off. It might take weeks.

"Has he said anything to you?" Itani asked, wiping the water off his arms and chest.

"Of course he has. I'm doing Amat's work and preparing for the audience with the Khai besides."

"I meant, has he told you that you were doing poorly? Or is it only your own standards that aren't being met?"

Liat felt herself flush, but took a pose of query. Itani frowned and pulled on fresh robes. The cloth clung to his legs.

"You mean you think perhaps he *wants* an incompetent going before the Khai in his name?" Liat demanded. "And why do you imagine he'd wish for that?"

"I mean, is it possible that your expectations of yourself are higher than his? You've been put in this position without warning, and without the chance to prepare yourself with Amat-cha. Hold that in mind, and it seems to me you've been doing very *well*. Wilsin-cha knows all that too. If he isn't telling you you've done poorly, perhaps it's not so bad as it seems."

"So you think I have an excuse for things going badly," Liat said. "That's thin comfort."

Itani sighed in resignation as he sat down beside her. His hair was still dripping wet, and Liat moved a little away to keep the water from getting on her own robes. She could see in the way he kept his expression calm that he thought she was being unreasonably hard on herself, and her suspicion that he wasn't wholly wrong only made her more impatient with him.

"If you'd like, we can go to your cell for the evening. You can work on whatever it is that needs your attention," he offered.

"And what would you do?"

"Be there," he said, simply. "The others will understand."

"Yes, lovely," Liat said, sarcasm in her voice. "Refuse your cohort's company because I have more important things than them. Let's see what more they can say about me. They already think I look down on them."

Itani sighed, leaning back into the ivy until he seemed to be sinking into the wall itself. The continual slap of water on stone muffled the sounds of the city. Any of the others could appear around the corner or from within the barracks at any moment, but still it felt as if they were alone together. It was usually a feeling Liat enjoyed. Just now, it was like a stone in her sandal.

"You could tell me I'm wrong, if you liked," she said.

"No. They do think that. But we could go anyway. What does it matter with they think? They're only jealous of us. If we spend the evening preparing everything for Wilsin-cha, then in the morning—"

"It doesn't work like that. I can't just put in an extra half-shift and make all the problems go away. It's not like I'm shifting things around a warehouse. This is complex. It's . . . it's just not the sort of thing a laborer would understand."

Itani nodded slowly, stirring the leaves that wreathed his head. The softness of his mouth went hard for a moment. He took a pose that accepted correction, but she could see the formality in his stance and recognized it for what it was.

"Gods. Itani, I didn't mean it like that. I'm sure there are lots of things I don't know about . . . lifting things. Or how to pull a cart. But this is hard. What Wilsin-cha wants of me is *hard*."

And I'm failing, she thought, but didn't say. *Can't you see I'm failing?*

"At least let me take your mind off it for tonight," Itani said, standing and offering her his hand. There was still a hardness in his eyes, however much he buried it. Liat stood but didn't take his hand.

"I'm going before the Khai in four days. Four days! I'm completely unprepared. Amat hasn't told me anything about doing this. I'm not even sure when she'll be back. And you think, what? A night out getting drunk with a bunch of laborers at a cheap teahouse is going to make me forget that? Honestly, 'Tani. It's like you're a stone. You don't listen."

"I've been listening to you since you came. I've been doing nothing but."

"For all the good it's done. I might as well have been a dog yapping at you for all you've understood."

"Liat," Itani said, his voice sharp, and then stopped. His face flushed, he stretched out his hands in a gesture of surrender. When he went on, his voice hummed with controlled anger. "I don't know what you want from me. If you want my help to make this right, I'll help you. If you want my company to take you away from it for a time, I'm willing . . ."

"*Willing?* How charming," Liat began, but Itani wouldn't be interrupted. He pressed on, raising his voice over hers.

". . . *but* if there is something else you want of me, I'm afraid this lowly laborer is simply too thick-witted to see it."

Liat felt a knot in her throat, and raised her hands in a pose of withdrawal. A thick despair folded her heart. She looked at him—her Itani—goaded to rage. He didn't see. He didn't understand. How hard could it be to see how frightened she was?

"I shouldn't have come," she said. Her voice was thick.

"Liat."

"No," she said, wiping away tears with the sleeve of her robe as she turned. "It was the wrong thing for me to do. You go on. I'm going back to my cell."

Itani, his anger not gone, but tempered by something softer, put a hand on her arms.

"I can come with you if you like," he said.

For more of this? she didn't say. She only shook her head, pulled gently away from him and started the long walk up and to the north. Back to the compound without him. She stopped at a waterseller's cart halfway there and drank cool water, limed and sugared, and waited to see whether Itani had followed her. He hadn't, and she honestly couldn't say whether she was more disappointed or relieved.

THE WOMAN—ANET NYOA, HER NAME WAS—HELD OUT A PLUM, TAKING AT the same time a pose of offering. Maati accepted the fruit formally, and with a growing sense of discomfort. Heshai-kvo had been due back at the middle gardens a half-hand past midday from his private council with the Khai Saraykeht. It was almost two hands now, and Maati was still alone on his bench overlooking the tiled roofs of the city and the maze of paths through the palaces and gardens. And to make things more awkward, Anet Nyoa, daughter of some house of the utkhaiem Maati felt sure he should recognize, had stopped to speak with him. And offer him fruit. And at every moment that it seemed time for her to take leave, she found something more to say.

"You seem young," she said. "I had pictured a poet as an older man."

"I'm only a student, Nyoa-cha," Maati said. "I've only just arrived."

"And how old are you?"

"This is my sixteenth summer," he said.

The woman took a pose of appreciation that he didn't entirely understand. It was a simple enough grammar, but he didn't see what there was to appreciate about being a particular age. And there was something else in the way her eyes met his that made him feel that perhaps she had mistaken him for someone else.

"And you, Nyoa-cha?"

"My eighteenth," she said. "My family came to Saraykeht from Cetani when I was a girl. Where are your family?"

"I have none," Maati said. "That is, when I was sent to the school, I . . . They are in Pathai, but I'm not . . . we aren't family any longer. I've become a poet now."

A note of sorrow came into her expression, and she leaned forward. Her hand touched his wrist.

"That must be hard for you," she said, her gaze now very much locked with his. "Being alone like that."

"Not so bad," Maati said, willing his voice not to squeak. There was a scent coming from her robe—something rich and earthy just strong enough to catch through the floral riot of gardens. "That is, I've managed quite nicely."

"You're brave to put such a strong face on it."

And like the answer to a prayer, the andat's perfect form stepped out from a minor hall at the far end of the garden. He wore a black robe shot with crimson and cut in the style of the Old Empire. Maati leaped up, tucked the plum into his sleeve, and took a pose of farewell.

"My apologies," he said. "The andat has come, and I fear I am required."

The woman took an answering pose that also held a nuance of regret, but Maati turned away and hurried down the path, white gravel crunching under his feet. He didn't look back until he'd reached Seedless' side.

"Well, my dear. That was a hasty retreat."

"I don't know what you mean."

Seedless raised a single black brow, and Maati felt himself blushing. But the andat took a pose that dismissed the subject and went on.

"Heshai has left for the day. He says you're to go back to the poet's house and clean the bookshelves."

"I don't believe you."

"You're getting better then," the andat said with a grin. "He's just coming. The audience with the Khai ran long, but all the afternoon's plans are still very much in place."

Maati felt himself smile in return. Whatever else could be said of the andat, his advice about Heshai-kvo had been true. Maati had risen in the morning, ready to follow Heshai-kvo on whatever errands the Khai had set him that day. At first, the old poet had seemed uncomfortable, but by the middle of that first day, Maati found him more and more explaining what it was that the andat was called upon to do, how it fit with the high etiquette of the utkhaiem and the lesser courts; how, in fact, to conduct the business of the city. And in the days that followed, Seedless, watching, had taken a tone that was still sly, still shockingly irreverent, still too clever to trust, but not at all like the malefic prankster that Maati had first feared.

"You should really leave the old man behind. I'm a much better teacher," Seedless said. "That girl, for example, I could teach you how to—"

"Thank you, Seedless-cha, but I'll take my lessons from Heshai-kvo."

"Not on that subject, you won't. Not unless it's learning how to strike a bargain with a soft quarter whore."

Maati took a dismissive pose, and Heshai-kvo stepped through an archway. His brows were furrowed and angry. His lips moved, continuing some conversation with himself or some imagined listener. When he looked up, meeting Maati's pose of welcome, his smile seemed forced and brief.

"I've a meeting with House Tiyan," the poet said. "Idiots have petitioned the Khai for a private session. Something about a Westlands contract. I don't know."

"I would like to attend, if I may," Maati said. It had become something of a stock phrase over the last few days, and Heshai-kvo accepted it with the same distracted acquiescence that seemed to be his custom. The old poet turned to the south and began the walk downhill to the low palaces. Maati and Seedless walked behind. The city stretched below them. The gray and red roofs, the streets leading down to converge on the seafront, and beyond that the masts of the ships, and the sea, and the great expanse of sky dwarfing it all. It was like something from the imagination of a painter, too gaudy and perfect to be real. And almost inaudible over their footsteps on the gravel paths and the distant songs of garden slaves, Heshai-kvo muttered to himself, his hands twitching toward half-formed poses.

"He was with the Khai," Seedless said, his voice very low. "It didn't go well."

"What was the matter?"

It was Heshai-kvo who answered the question.

"The Khai Saraykeht is a greedy, vain little shit," he said. "If you had to choose the essence of the problem, you could do worse than start there."

Maati missed his step, and a shocked sound, half cough, half laugh, escaped him. When the poet turned to him, he tried to adopt a pose—any pose—but his hands couldn't agree on where they should go.

"What?" the poet demanded.

"The Khai . . . You just . . ." Maati said.

"He's just a man," the poet said. "He eats and shits and talks in his sleep the same as anyone."

"But he's the *Khai*."

Heshai-kvo took a dismissive pose and turned his back to Maati and the andat. Seedless plucked Maati's robe and motioned him to lean nearer. Keeping his eyes on the path and the poet before them, Maati did.

"He asked the Khai to refuse a contract," Seedless whispered. "The Khai laughed at him and told him not to be such a child. Heshai had been planning his petition for days, and he wasn't even allowed to present the whole argument. I wish you'd been there. It was really a lovely moment. But I suppose that's why the old cow didn't tell you about it. He doesn't seem to enjoy having his student present when he's humiliated. I imagine he'll be getting quite drunk tonight."

"What contract?"

"House Wilsin is acting as agent for the sad trade."

"Sad trade?"

"Using us to pluck a child out of a womb," Seedless said. "It's safer than teas, and it can be done nearer to the end of the woman's term. And, to the Khai Saraykeht's great pleasure, it's expensive."

"Gods. And we do that?"

Seedless took a pose that implied the appreciation of a joke or irony. "We do what we are told, my dear. You and I are the puppets of puppets."

"If the two of you could be put upon not to talk behind my back quite so loudly," Heshai snapped, "I would very much appreciate it."

Maati fell instantly to a pose of apology, but the poet didn't turn to see it. After a few steps, Maati let his hands fall to his sides. Seedless said nothing, but raised a hand to his mouth and took a bite of something dark. A plum. Maati checked his sleeve, and indeed, it was empty. He took a pose that was both query and accusation—*How?* The andat smiled; his perfect, pale face lit with mischief and perhaps something else.

"I'm clever," the andat said, and tossed the bitten fruit to him.

At the low palaces, a young man in the yellow and silver robes of House Tiyan greeted them and allowed himself to be led to a meeting room. They sat at a black-stained wooden table drinking cool water and eating fresh dates, the stones removed for them by the andat. Maati followed the negotiations with half his attention, his mind turning instead upon the dreadful anger and pain shallowly buried in his teacher's voice and the echo of tacit pleasure in the andat's. It seemed to him that the two emotions were balanced; that Heshai-kvo would never smile without some pang of discontent in Seedless' heart, that the andat could only shine ecstatic if the poet were in despair. He imagined himself taking control of the andat, entering into that lifelong intimate struggle, and unease picked at him.

THE ONLY REASON OVI NIIT'S HOUSE HAD SURVIVED THE GROSS INCOMpetence of its bookkeepers was the scale of the money that came through the place. It was a constant stream of copper, silver, and gold that had shocked her. Would still have shocked her now if she hadn't been so damned tired. She had never known anyone except for her sister who gave themselves into sexual indenture, and by then they hadn't been speaking to each other. The cost of a whore was higher than she'd expected, and the compensation for the employee was a pittance. And that, she came to see, was only the beginning.

Overall, gamblers lost at the tables, and in addition, they paid a fee for the privilege. The wine was cheap, and the drugs added to it only slightly more expensive. The price the house charged for the combination was exorbitant. Amat suspected that if the sex were given away for free, the house would still turn a profit. It was amazing.

She took her cane from where it leaned against the desk and pulled herself up. Once she was sure of herself, she took the sheet with her estimates, folded it, and tucked it in her sleeve. There was no call, she thought, leaving it about until she'd spoken with Ovi Niit. And, for all that she thought it useless, it would suffice to answer the question she expected from him. She walked to the door and out to the common room.

The place was filthy. Children and dogs rolled together on a floor that apparently hadn't been swept in living memory. Off-shift whores sat at the tables smoking and gossiping and picking tics out of each other's flesh. On the east wall was a long alcove where women disfigured by illness or violence or age fashioned obscene implements from leather and cloth. Kirath couldn't have known how bad this house was. Or else he had been more desperate to be rid of her than she'd guessed. Or cared less for her than she'd imagined.

One of Niit-cha's thugs sat on the stairs that led up to the private quarters where the owner of the house kept himself. All eyes shifted to her as she limped over to him. The fat girl sitting nearest the iron-bound door to the front house said something to the man beside her and giggled. A red-haired woman—Westlands blood, or Galtic—raised her pale eyebrows and looked away. A boy of five or six summers—another whore—looked up at her and smiled. The smile was enough. She roughed the boy's hair and walked with what dignity she could muster to the guard.

"Is Niit-cha up there?" she asked.

"Gone. He's down to the low market for beef and pork," the guard said. He had an odd accent; long vowels and the ends of his words clipped off. Eastern, she thought.

"When he comes in . . ." She had almost said *send him to me*. The habit of years. "When he comes in, tell him I've done what he asked. I'll be sleeping, but I am at his disposal should he wish to discuss it."

"Tell him yourself, grandmother," the fat girl shouted, but the guard nodded.

The bed chamber had no windows. At night, a single tallow candle lit the bunks that lined the walls, five beds to a stack like the worst sort of ship's cabin. Cheap linen was tied over the mouth of each coffin-sized bed in lieu of real netting, and the planks were barely covered by thin, stained mats. The darkness, while not so hot as the kiln of an attic she had hidden in, was still and hot and muggy. Amat found one of the lower bunks unoccupied and crawled into it, her hip scraping in its joint as she did. She pulled her cane in with her for fear someone might take it and didn't bother tying the linen closed.

Three days she'd spent in an impossible task, and when she closed her eyes, the crabbed scripts and half-legible papers still danced before her. She willed the visions away, but she might as well have been pushing the tide back with her hands. The bunk above her creaked as the sleeper shifted. Amat wondered whether she could get a cup of the spiked wine, just to take her to sleep. She was bone weary, but restless. She had put Marchat Wilsin and Oshai and the island girl Maj out of her mind while she bent to Ovi Niit's books. Now that she had paused, they returned and mixed with the work she had finished and that which still lay before her. She shifted on the thin mat, her cane resting uncomfortably beside her. The smell of bodies and perfume and years of cheap tallow disturbed her.

She would have said that she had not slept so much as fallen to an anxious doze except that the boy had such trouble waking her. His little hands pressed her shoulder, and she was distantly aware that he had done so before—had been doing so for some time.

"Grandmother," he said. Again? Yes, said again. She'd been hearing the voice, folding it into her dream. "Wake up."

"I am."

"Are you well?"

All the world's ill, why should I be any different, she thought.

"I'm fine. What's happened?"

"He's back. He wants to see you."

Amat took a pose of thanks that the boy understood even in the cave-dark room and her lying on her side. Amat pulled herself out and up. Curiously, the rest seemed to have helped. Her head felt clearer and her body less protesting. In the main room, she saw how much the light from the high windows had shifted. She'd been asleep for the better part of the afternoon. The whores had shifted their positions or left entirely. The red-haired woman was still at her seat near the stairs; the fat girl was gone. A guard—not the same man as before, but of the same breed—caught her eye and nodded toward her workroom at the back. She took a pose of thanks, squared her shoulders and went in.

Ovi Niit sat at her table. His hooded eyes made him look torpid, or perhaps he had been drinking his own wines. His robes were of expensive silks and well-cut, but he still managed to look like an unmade bed. He glanced up as she came in, falling into a pose of welcome so formal as to be a mockery. Still, she replied with respect.

"I heard what was being offered for you," Ovi Niit said. "They've spread the word all through the seafront. You're an expensive piece of flesh."

The sound of his voice made her mouth dry with fear and shame at the fear. She was Amat Kyaan. She had been hiding fear and loneliness and weakness since before the thug seated at her desk had been born. It was one of her first skills.

"How much?" she asked, keeping her tone light and disinterested.

"Sixty lengths of silver for where you're sleeping. Five lengths of gold if someone takes you to Oshai's men. Five lengths of gold is a lot of money."

"You're tempted," Amat said.

The young man smiled slowly and put down the paper he'd been reading.

"As one merchant to another, I only suggest that you make your presence in my house worth more than the market rate," he said. "I have to wonder what you did to become so valuable."

She only smiled, and wondered what ideas were shifting behind those half-dead eyes. How he could trade her, no doubt. He was weighing where his greatest profit might come.

"You have my report?" Ovi Niit asked. She nodded and pulled the papers from her sleeve.

"It's only a rough estimate. I'll need to confer with you more next time, to be sure I've understood the mechanisms of your trade. But it's enough for your purposes, I think."

"And what would a half-dead bitch like you know about my purposes?" he asked. His voice held no rancor, but Amat still felt her throat close. She forced a confidence into her tone that she didn't feel.

"From those numbers? I know what you must have suspected. Or else why would you have gone through the trouble to have me here?

Someone in your organization is stealing from you." Ovi Niit frowned as he looked at her numbers, but he didn't deny her. "And it would be worth more than five lengths of gold, I think, to have me find out who."

5

>+< The day of the grand audience came gray and wet. After the ceremonies at the temple, Liat and Marchat Wilsin had to wait their turn to leave, the families of the utkhaiem all taking precedence. Even the firekeepers, lowest of the utkhaiem, outranked a merchant here and at the grand audience. Epani-cha brought them fresh bread and fruit while they waited and directed Liat toward a private room where several women were taking advantage of the delay to relieve themselves.

The morning rain had not stopped, but it had slackened. The sun had not appeared, but the clouds above them had lost their brooding gray for a white that promised blue skies by nightfall. And heat. The canopy bearers met them in their turn and House Wilsin took its place in the parade to the palace of the grand audience.

There were no walls, precisely. The canopies fell behind as they reached the first arches, and walked, it seemed to Liat, into a wide forest of marble columns. The ceiling was so far above them and so light, it seemed hard to believe that they were sheltered—that the pillars held up stone instead of the white bowl of the cloudy sky. The hall of the grand audience was built to seem like a clearing in the stone forest. The Khai sat alone on a great divan of carved blackwood, calm and austere—his counselors and servants would not join him until after the audience proper had begun. Now, he alone commanded the open space before him. The utkhaiem surrounding the presentation floor like the audience at a performance spoke to each other in the lowest voices. Wilsin-cha seemed to know just where they should be, and steered her gently to a bench among other traders.

"Liat," he said as they sat. "Trade is hard sometimes. I mean, the things you're called on to do. They aren't always what you'd wish."

"I understand that, Wilsin-cha," she said, adopting an air of confidence she only partly felt. "But this is a thing I can do."

For a moment, he seemed on the verge of speaking again. Then a flute trilled, and a trumpet sounded, and the procession of gifts began. Each family of the utkhaiem in attendance had brought some token, as custom required. And following them, each trading house or foreign guest. Servants in the colors of their family or house stepped as carefully as dancers, carrying chests and tapestries, gilded fruits and bolts of fine silk, curiosities and wonders. The Khai Saraykeht considered each offering in turn, accepting them with a formal pose of recognition. She could feel Marchat Wilsin shift beside her as the bearers of his house stepped into the clearing. Four men bore a tapestry worked with a map of the cities of the Khaiem done in silver thread. Each man held one corner, pulling the cloth tight, and they stepped slowly and in perfect unison, grave as mourners.

Three of them grave as mourners. The fourth, while he kept pace with his fellows, kept casting furtive glances at the crowd. His head shifted subtly back and forth, as if he were searching for someone or something. Liat heard an amused murmur, the men and women of the audience enjoying the spectacle, and her heart sank.

The fourth man was Itani.

Marchat Wilsin must have noticed some reaction in her, because he glanced over, his expression puzzled and alarmed. Liat held her countenance empty, vacant. She felt a blush growing and willed it to be faint. The four men reached the Khai, the two in front kneeling to provide a better view of the work. Itani, at the rear, seemed to realize where he was and straightened. The Khai betrayed no sense of amusement or disapproval, only recognized the gift and sent it on its way. Itani and the other three moved off as the bearers of House Kiitan came forward. Liat shifted toward her employer.

"Wilsin-cha. If there's a private room. For women . . ."

"Being anxious does the same to me," he said. "Epani will show you. Just be back before the Khai brings in his wise men. At the rate this is going, you've probably got half a hand, but don't test that."

Liat took a pose of gratitude, rose, and wove her way to the rear of the assembly. She didn't look for Epani. Itani was waiting there for her. She gestured with her eyes to a column, and he followed her behind it.

"What do you think you're doing?" she demanded when they were out of sight. "You avoid me for days, and then you . . . you do this?"

"I know the man who was supposed to be the fourth bearer," Itani said, taking a pose of apology. "He let me take his place. I didn't intend to avoid you. I only . . . I was angry, sweet. And I didn't want that to get in your way. Not with this before you."

"And *this* is how you don't come in my way?"

He smiled. His mouth had a way of being disarming.

"This is how I say I'm at your back," he said. "I know you can do this. It's no more than a negotiation, and if Amat Kyaan and Wilsin-cha chose you—if they believe in you—then my faith may not signify anything much. But you have it. And I didn't want you going to your audience without knowing that. I know you can do this."

Her hand strayed to his without her realizing that it had. She only noticed when he raised it to his lips.

" 'Tani, you pick the worst time to say the sweetest things."

The music of the flute changed its rhythm and Liat turned, pulling her hand free. The audience proper was about to begin—the counselors and servants about to rejoin the Khai. Itani stepped back, taking a pose of encouragement. His gaze was on her, his mouth tipped in a smile. His fingernails—gods, his fingernails were still dye-stained.

"I'll be waiting," he said, and she turned back, moving through the seated men and women as quickly as she could without appearing to run. She sat at Wilsin-cha's side just as the two poets and the andat knelt before the Khai and took their places, the last of the counselors to arrive.

"You're just in time," Wilsin-cha said. "Are you well?"

Well? I'm perfect, she thought. She imagined Amat Kyaan's respectful, assured expression and arranged her features to match it.

MAATI SAT ON A CUSHION OF VELVET, SHIFTING NOW AND THEN IN AN AT-tempt to keep his legs from falling asleep. It wasn't working as well as he'd hoped. The Khai Saraykeht sat off to Maati's left on a blackwood divan. Heshai-kvo and Seedless sat somewhat nearer, and if the Khai couldn't see his discomfort, they certainly could. In the clear space before them, one petitioner after another came before the Khai and made a plea.

The worst had been a man from the Westlands demonstrating with a cart the size of a dog that carried a small fire that boiled water. Steam from the boiling water set the cart's wheels in motion, and it had careened off into the crowd, its master chasing after it. The utkhaiem had laughed as the man warned that the Galts were creating larger models that they used as war machines. Whole wards had been overrun in less than a month's time, he said.

The Khai's phrase had been "an army of teapots." Only Heshai-kvo, Maati noticed, hadn't joined in the laughter. Not because he took the ridiculous man seriously, he thought, but because it pained him to see a man embarrass himself. The fine points of Galtic war strategies were of no consequence to the Khaiem. So long as the andat protected them, the wars of other nations were a curiosity, like the bones of ancient monsters.

The most interesting was the second son the Khai Udun. He held the court enraptured with his description of how his younger brother had attempted to poison him and their elder brother. The grisly detail of the his elder brother's death had Maati almost in tears, and the Khai Saraykeht had responded with a moving speech—easily four times as long as any other pronouncement he had made in the day—that poisons were not the weapons of the Khaiem, and that the powers of Saraykeht would come to the aid of justice in tracking down the killer.

"Well," Seedless said as the crowd rose to its feet, cheering. "That settles which of Old Udun's sons will be warming his chair once he's gone. You'd almost think no one in our Most High Saraykeht's ancestry had offered his brother a cup of bad wine."

Maati looked over at Heshai-kvo, expecting the poet to defend the Khai Saraykeht. But the poet only watched the son of the Khai Udun prostrate himself before the blackwood divan.

"It's all theater," Seedless went on, speaking softly enough that no one could hear him but Maati and Heshai. "Don't forget that. This is no more than a long, drawn out epic that no one composed, no one oversees, and no one plans. It's why they keep falling back on fratricide. There's precedent—everyone knows more or less what to expect. And they like to pretend that one of the old Khai's sons is better than another."

"Be quiet," Heshai-kvo said, and the andat took a pose of apology but smirked at Maati as soon as Heshai-kvo turned away. The poet had had little to say. His demeanor had been grim from when they had first left the poet's house that morning in the downpour. As the ceremonies moved on, his face seemed to grow more severe.

Two firekeepers stood before the Khai to argue a fine point of city law, and the Khai commanded an ancient woman named Niania Tosogu, his court historian, to pass judgment. The old woman yammered for a time in a broken voice, retelling old stories of the summer cities that dated back to the first days of the Khaiate when the Empire had hardly fallen. Then without seeming to tie her stories in with the situation before her, she made an order than appeared to please no one. As the firekeepers sat, an old Galt in robes of green and bronze came forward. A girl Maati's own age or perhaps a year more stood at his side. Her robes matched the old Galt's, but where his demeanor seemed deeply respectful, the girl's face and manner verged on haughty. Even as she took a pose of obeisance, her chin was lifted high, an eyebrow arched.

"Ah, now *she's* a lousy actress," Seedless murmured.

Beside him, Heshai-kvo ignored the comment and sat forward, his eyes on the pair. Seedless leaned back, his attention as much on Heshai-kvo as the pair who stood before the Khai.

"Marchat Wilsin," the Khai Saraykeht said, his voice carrying through the space as if he were an actor on a stage. "I have read your petition. House Wilsin has never entered the sad trade before."

"There are hard times in Galt, most high," the Galt said. He took a pose that, though formal, had the nuance of a beggar at the end of a street performance. "We have so many teapots to construct."

A ripple of laughter passed over the crowd, and the Khai took a pose acknowledging the jest. Heshai-kvo's frown deepened.

"Who will represent your house in the negotiation?" the Khai asked.

"I will, most high," the girl said, stepping forward. "I am Liat Chokavi, assistant to Amat Kyaan. While she is away, she has asked that I oversee this trade."

"And is the woman you represent here as well?"

The old Galt looked uncomfortable at the question, but did not hesitate to answer.

"She is, most high. Her grasp of the Khaiaite tongue is very thin, but we have a translator for her if you wish to speak with her."

"I do," the Khai said. Maati's gaze shifted back to the crowd where a young woman in silk robes walked forward on the arm of a pleasant, round-faced man in the simple, dark robes of a servant. The woman's eyes were incredibly pale, her skin terribly white. Her robes were cut to hide her bulging belly. Beside him, Heshai tensed, sitting forward with a complex expression.

The woman reached the Galt and his girl overseer, smiling and nodding to them at her translator's prompting.

"You come before my court to ask my assistance," the Khai intoned.

The woman's face turned toward him like a child seeing fire. She seemed to Maati to be entranced. Her translator murmured to her. She glanced at him, no more than a flicker and then her eyes returned to the Khai. She answered the man at her side.

"Most high," the translator said. "My lady presents herself Maj of Toniabi of Nippu and thanks you for the gift of this audience and your assistance in this hour of her distress."

"And you accept House Wilsin as your representative before me?" the Khai said, as if the woman had spoken herself.

Again the whispered conference, again the tiny shift of gaze to the translator and back to the Khai. She spoke softly, Maati could hardly make out the sounds, but her voice was somehow musical and fluid.

"She does, most high," the translator said.

"This is acceptable," the Khai said. "I accept the offered price, and I grant Liat Chokavi an audience with the poet Heshai to arrange the details."

Man and girl took a pose of gratitude and the four of them faded back into the crowd. Heshai let out a long, low, hissing sigh. Seedless steepled his fingers and pressed them to his lips. There was a smile behind them.

"Well," Heshai-kvo said. "There's no avoiding it now. I'd hoped . . ."

The poet took a dismissive pose, as if waving away dreams or lost possibilities. Maati shifted again on his cushion, his left leg numb from sitting. The audiences went on for another hand and a half, one small matter after another, until the Khai rose, took a pose that formally ended all audience, and with the flute and drum playing the traditional song, the leader and voice of the city strode out. The counselors followed him, Maati following Heshai's lead, though the poet seemed only half interested in the proceedings. Together, the three walked past the forest of pillars to a great oaken door, and through it to a lesser hall formed, it seemed, as the hub of a hundred corridors and stairways.

A quartet of slaves sang gentle harmony in an upper gallery, their voices sorrowful and lovely. Heshai sat on a low bench, studying the air before him. Seedless stood several paces away, his arms crossed, and still as a statue. The sense of despair was palpable.

Maati walked slowly to his teacher. The poet's gaze flickered up to him and then away. Maati took a pose that asked forgiveness even before he spoke.

"I don't understand, Heshai-kvo. There must be a way to refuse the trade. If the Dai-kvo . . ."

"If the Dai-kvo starts overseeing the small work of the Khaiem, let's call him Emperor and be done with it," Heshai-kvo said. "And then in a generation or so we'll see how well he's done training new poets. We're degenerate enough without asking for incompetence as well. No, the Dai-kvo won't step in over something like this."

Maati knelt. Members of the utkhaiem began to come through the hall, some conferring over scrolls and stacks of paper.

"You could refuse."

"And what would they say of me then?" Heshai managed a wan smile. "No, it's nothing, Maati-kya. It's an old man being stupidly nostalgic. This is an unpleasant thing, I'll admit that. But it is what I do."

"Killing superfluous children out of rich women," Seedless said, his voice as impudent, but with an edge to it Maati hadn't heard before. "Just part of the day's work, isn't it?"

Heshai looked up, anger in his expression. His hands balled into thick fists and fierce concentration furrowed his brow. Maati heard Seedless fall even before he turned to look. The andat was prone, his hands splayed before him in a pose of abject apology so profound that Maati knew the andat would never take it of his own will. Heshai's lips quivered.

"It's something that . . . I've done before," he said, his voice tight. "It isn't something anyone wishes for. Not the woman, not anyone. The sad trade earns its name every time it's made."

"Heshai-cha?" a woman's voice said.

She stood beside the prostrate andat, her haughty demeanor shaken by the odd scene. Maati stood, falling into a pose of welcome. Heshai released his hold on Seedless, allowing the andat to rise. Seedless shook imagined dust off his robes, fixing the poet with a look of arch reproach, before turning to the woman.

"Liat Chokavi," the andat said, his perfect hands touching her wrist, intimate as old friends. "We're so pleased to see you. Aren't we, Heshai?"

"Delighted," the poet snapped. "Nothing quite like being handed to a half-tutored apprentice to keep me in my place."

The shock in the girl's face was subtle, there only for an instant. Her self-assured mask slipped, her eyes widening a fraction, her mouth hardening. And then she was as she had been before. But Maati knew, or thought he knew, how hard Heshai's blow had struck, and against someone who had done nothing but be an opportune target.

Heshai rose and took a pose appropriate to opening a negotiation, but with a stony formality that continued the insult. Maati found himself suddenly ashamed of his teacher.

"The meeting room's this way," Heshai said, then turned and trundled off. Seedless strode behind him, leaving Liat Chokavi and Maati to follow as they could.

"I'm sorry," Maati said quietly. "The sad trade bothers him. You didn't do anything wrong."

Liat shot a glance at him that began with distrust, then as she saw distress on his own face, softened. She took a pose of gratitude, small and informal.

The meeting room was spare and uncomfortably warm. A single small window stood shuttered until Heshai pushed it open. He sat at the low stone table and motioned Liat to sit across from him. She moved awkwardly, but took her place, plucking a packet of papers from her sleeve. Seedless stood at the window, looking down at the poet with a predatory smirk as Heshai drew the papers to him and glanced them over.

"May I be of service, Heshai-kvo?" Maati asked.

"Get us some tea," the poet said, looking at the papers. Maati looked first to the girl, and then back to Heshai. Seedless, seeing his reluctance, frowned. Then comprehension bloomed in the andat's black eyes. The perfect hands took a pose that asked permission for something—though Maati didn't know what, and Seedless dropped the pose before leave could be given.

"Heshai, my dear, you have a better student than you deserve. I think he doesn't want to leave you alone," Seedless smirked. "He thinks you'll go on bullying this fine young lady. If it were me, you understand, I'd be quite pleased to watch you make an ass of yourself, but . . ."

Heshai shifted, and the andat shuddered in pain or something like it. Seedless' hands shifted again into a pose of apology. Maati saw, however, the scowl on the poet's face. Seedless had shamed his master into behaving kindly to the girl. At least for a time.

"Some tea, Maati. And for our guest as well," Heshai said, gesturing to Liat.

Maati took a pose of acceptance. He caught Seedless' dark eyes as he left and nodded thanks. The andat answered with the smallest of all possible smiles.

The corridors of the hall were full of men and women; traders, utkhaiem, servants, slaves, and guards. Maati strode out, looking for a palace servant. He followed the path he knew to the main hall, impatient to return to the negotiation. The main hall was as full as the corridors, or worse. Conversations filled the space as thick as smoke. He caught a glimpse of the pale yellow robe of a palace servant moving toward the main door and made for it as quickly as he could.

Halfway to the main door, he brushed against a young man. He wore the same green and bronze colors that Liat Chokavi and Marchat Wilsin had, but his hands were stained and callused, his shoulders those of a laborer. Thinking that he could pass his errand off to this man, Maati stopped and grabbed the man's arm. The long face looked familiar, but it wasn't until he spoke that the blood rushed from Maati's face.

"Forgive me," the laborer said, taking a pose of apology. "I know I'm supposed to wait outside, but I was hoping Liat Chokavi . . ."

His voice trailed off, made uneasy by what he saw in Maati's eyes.

"Otah-kvo?" Maati breathed.

A moment of shocked silence, and then the laborer clapped a hand over Maati's mouth and drew him quickly into a side corridor.

"Say nothing," Otah said. *"Nothing."*

6

>+< Years fell away, the events of Otah's life taking on a sudden unreality at the sound of his name. The hot, thick days he had worked the seafront of Saraykeht, the grubbing for food and shelter, the nights spent hungry sleeping by the roadside. The life he had built as Itani Noyga. All of it fell away, and he remembered the boy he had been, full of certainty and self-righteous fire trudging across cold spring fields to the high road. It was like being there again, and the strength of the memory frightened him.

The young poet went with him quietly, willingly. He seemed as shaken as Otah felt.

Together, they found an empty room, and Otah shut the door behind them and latched it. The room was a small meeting room, its window looking into a recessed courtyard filled with bamboo and sculpted trees. Even with the rain still falling—drops tapping against the leaves outside the window—the room seemed too bright. Otah sat on the table, his hands pressed to his mouth, and looked at the boy. He was younger by perhaps four summers—older than Otah had been when he'd invented his new name, his new history, and taken indenture with House Wilsin. He had a round, open face and a firm chin and hands that hadn't known hard labor in many years. But more disturbing than that, there was plea-sure in his expression, like someone who'd just found a treasure.

Otah didn't know where to start.

"You . . . you were at the school, then?"

"Maati Vaupathai," the poet said. "I was in one of the youngest co-horts just before you . . . before you left. You took us out to turn the gar-dens, but we didn't do very well. My hands were blistered . . ."

The face became suddenly familiar.

"Gods," Otah said. "You? That was you?"

Maati Vaupathai, whom Otah had once forced to eat dirt, took a pose of confirmation that seemed to radiate pleasure at being remembered. Otah leaned back.

"Please. You can't tell anyone about me. I never took the brand. If my brothers found me."

"They'd try to kill you," Maati said. "I know. I won't tell anyone. But . . . Otah-kvo."

"Itani," Otah said. "My name's Itani now."

Maati took a pose of acceptance, but still one appropriate for a student to a teacher. Still the sort that Otah had seen presented when he wore the black robes of the school.

"Itani, then. I didn't think. I mean, to find you here. What are you doing here?"

"I'm indentured to House Wilsin. I'm a laborer."

"A laborer?"

Otah took a confirming pose. The poet blinked, as if trying to make sense of a word in a different language. When he spoke again, his voice was troubled. Perhaps disappointed.

"They said that the Dai-kvo accepted you. That you refused him."

It was a simple description, Otah thought. A few words that held the shape his life had taken. It had seemed both clearer and more complex at the time—it still seemed that way in his mind.

"That's true," he said.

"What . . . forgive me, Otah-kvo, but what happened?"

"I left. I went south, and found work. I knew that I needed a new name, so I chose one. And . . . and that's all, I suppose. I've taken indenture with House Wilsin. It's nearly up, and I'm not sure what I'll do after that."

Maati took a pose of understanding, but Otah could see from the furrows in his brow that he didn't. He sighed and leaned forward, searching for something else to say, some way to explain the life he'd chosen. On top of all the other shocks of the day, he was disturbed to find that words failed him. In the years since he had walked away, he had never tried to explain the decision. There had never been anyone to explain it to.

"And you?" Otah asked. "He took you on, I see."

"The old Dai-kvo died. After you left, before I even took the black. Tahi-kvo took his place, and a new teacher came to the school. Naani-kvo. He was harder than Tahi-kvo. I think he enjoyed it more."

"It's a sick business," Otah said.

"No," Maati said. "Only hard. And cruel. But it has to be. The stakes are so high."

There was a strength in Maati's voice that, Otah thought, didn't come from assurance. Otah took a pose of agreement, but he could see that Maati knew he didn't mean it, so he shrugged it away.

"What did you do to earn the black?" Otah asked.

Maati blushed and looked away. In the corridor, someone laughed. It was unnerving. He'd spent so little time with this boy whom he hardly knew, and he'd almost forgotten where they were, and that there were people all around them.

"I asked Naani-kvo about you," Maati said. "He took it poorly. I had to wash the floors in the main hall for a week. But then I asked him again. It was the same. In the end . . . in the end, there was a night when I cleaned the floors without being told. Milah-kvo asked me what I was doing, and I explained that I was going to ask again in the morning, so I wanted to have some of the work done beforehand. He asked me if I was so in love with washing stones. Then he offered me the robes."

"And you took them."

"Of course," Maati said.

They were silent for a long moment, and Otah saw the life he'd turned away. And thought, perhaps, he saw regret in the boy's face. Or if not that, at least doubt.

"You can't tell anyone about me," Otah said.

"I won't. I swear I won't."

Otah took a pose that witnessed an oath, and Maati responded in kind. They both started when someone rattled the door.

"Who's in there?" a man's voice demanded. "We're scheduled for this room."

"I should go," Maati said. "I'm missing my negotiation with . . . Liat. You said you were waiting for Liat Chokavi, didn't you?"

"Unlatch the door!" the voice outside the door insisted. "This is our room."

"She's my lover," Otah said, standing. "Come on. We should leave before they go for the Khai."

The men outside the door wore the flowing robes and expensive sandals of the utkhaiem, and the disgust and anger on their faces when

Otah—a mere laborer, and for a Galtic house at that—opened the door faded to impatience when they saw Maati in his poet's robes. Otah and Maati walked out to the main hall together.

"Otah-kvo," Maati said as they reached the still-bustling space.

"Itani."

Maati took a pose of apology that seemed genuinely mortified. "Itani. I . . . there are things I would like to discuss with you, and we . . ."

"I'll find you," Otah promised. "But say nothing of this. Not to anyone. Especially not to the poet."

"No one."

"I'll find you. Now go."

Maati took a pose of farewell more formal than any poet had ever offered a laborer, and, reluctance showing in every movement, walked away. Otah saw an older woman in the robes of the utkhaiem considering him, her expression curious. He took a pose of obeisance toward her, turned, and walked out. The rain was breaking now, sunlight pressing down like a hand on his shoulder. The other servants who had borne gifts or poles for the canopy waited now in a garden set aside for them. Epani-cha, house master for Marchat Wilsin, sat with them, laughing and smiling. The formal hurdles of the day were cleared, and the men were light hearted. Tuui Anagath, an older man who had known Otah since almost before he had become Itani, for almost his whole false life, took a pose of welcome.

"Did you hear?" he asked as Otah drew close.

"Hear what? No."

"The Khai is inviting a crew to hunt down Udun's son, the poisoner. Half the utkhaiem are vying to join it. They'll be on the little bastard like lice on a low town whore."

Otah took a pose of delight because he knew it was expected of him, then sat under a tree laden with tiny sweet-scented ornamental pears and listened. They were chattering with the prospect, all of them. These were men he knew, men he worked with. Men he trusted, some of them, though none so far as to tell them the truth. No one that far. They spoke of the death of the Khai Udun's son like a pit fight. They didn't care that the boy had been born into it. Otah knew that they couldn't see the injustice. For men born low, eking out lengths of copper to buy tea and soup and sourbread, the Khaiem were to be envied, not pitied and not loved. They would each of them go back to quarters shared with other men or else tiny apartments bearing with them the memory of the sprawling palaces, the sweet garden, the songs of slaves. There was no room in their minds for sympathy for the families of wealth and power. For men, Otah thought sourly, like himself.

"Eh?" Epani-cha said, prodding Otah with the toe of his shoe. "What did you swallow, Itani? You look sorry."

Otah forced a smile and laughed. He was good at that smiling and laughing. Being charming. He took a loose pose of apology.

"Am I lowering the tone?" he asked. "I just got thrown out of the palace. That's all."

"Thrown out?" Tuui Anagath asked, and the others turned, suddenly interested.

"I was just there, minding myself and—"

"And sniffing after Liat," one of the others laughed.

"And apparently I attracted some attention. One of the women from House Tiyaan came to me and asked whether I was a factor for House Wilsin. I told her I wasn't but for some reason she kept speaking with me. She was very pleasant. And apparently her lover took some offense to the conversation and spoke to the palace servants . . ."

Otah took a pose of innocent confusion that made the others laugh.

"Poor, poor Itani," Tuui Anagath said. "Can't keep the women away with a dagger. You should let us do you a favor, my boy. We could tell all the women you broke out in sores down there and had to spend three days a month in a poultice diaper."

Otah laughed with them now. He'd won again. He was one of them, just a man like them in no way special. The jokes and stories went on for half a hand, then Otah stood, stretched, and turned to Epani-cha.

"Will you have further need of me, Epani-cha?"

The thin man looked surprised, but took a pose of negation. Otah's relationship with Liat was no secret, but living in the compound itself, Epani understood the extent of it better than the others. When Otah shifted to a pose of farewell, he matched it.

"But Liat should be done with poets shortly," Epani said. "You don't want to wait for her?"

"No," Otah said, and smiled.

———

AMAT LEARNED. SHE LEARNED FIRST ABOUT THE FINE WORKINGS OF A comfort house—the balances between guard and gamesman and show-fighter and whore, the rhythm that the business developed like the beat of a heart or the flow of a river. She learned, more specifically, how the money moved through it like blood. And so, she understood better what it was she was searching for in the crabbed scripts and obscure receipts. She also learned to fear Ovi Niit.

She had seen what happened when one of the other women dis-pleased him. They were owned by the house, and so the watch ex-tended no protection to them. They, unlike her, were easily replaced. She would not have taken their places for her weight in silver.

Two weeks from four. Or five. Two more, or three, before Marchat's promised amnesty. She sat in the room, sweltering; the papers stood in piles. Her days were filled with the scratch of pen on paper, the distant voices of the soft quarter, the smell of cheap food and her own sweat and the weak yellow light from the high, thin window.

The knock, when it came, was soft. Tentative. Amat looked up. Ovi Niit or one of his guards wouldn't have bothered. Amat jabbed her pen into its inkblock and stretched. Her joints cracked.

"Come in," she said.

She had seen the girl before, but hadn't heard her name. A smallish one. Young, with a birthmark at one eye that made her seem like a child's drawing of tears. When she took a pose of apology, Amat saw half-healed marks on her wrists. She wondered which of the payments in her ledgers matched those small wounds.

"Grandmother?" It was the name by which they all called her.

"What do you want," Amat asked, sorry for the harshness of her voice as she heard it. She massaged her hands.

"I know you aren't to be interrupted," the girl said. Her voice was nervous, but not, Amat thought, from fear of an old woman locked in a back closet. Ovi Niit must have given orders to leave her be. "But there's a man. He's at the door, asking for you."

"For me?"

The girl shifted to a pose of affirmation. Amat leaned back. Kirath. It *could* be Kirath. Or it could be one of the moon-faced Oshai's minions come to find her and kill her. Ovi Niit might already be spending the gold lengths he'd earned for her death. Amat nodded as much to herself as to the girl.

"What does he look like?"

"Young. Handsome," she said, and smiled as if sharing a confidence.

Handsome, perhaps, but Kirath would never be young again. This was not him, then. Amat hefted her cane. As a weapon, it was nothing. She wasn't strong enough now to run, even if her aching hip would have allowed it. There was no fleeing, but she could make it a siege. She sat with the panic, controlling it, until she was able to think a little; to speak without a tremble in her voice.

"What's your name, dear?"

"Ibris," the girl said.

"Good. Ibris. Listen very closely. Go out the front—not the back, the front. Find the watch. Tell them about this man. And tell them he was threatening a client."

"But he . . ."

"Don't question me," Amat said. "Go. Now!"

Years of command, years of assurance and confidence, served her now. The girl went, and when the door was closed behind her, Amat pushed the desk to block it. It was a sad, thin little barricade. She sat on it, adding her weight in hopes of slowing the man for the duration of a few extra heartbeats. If the watch came, they would stop him.

Or they wouldn't. Likely they wouldn't. She was a commodity here, bought and sold. And there was no one to say otherwise. She balled her swollen fists around her cane. Dignity be damned. If Marchat Wilsin and Oshai were going to take her down, she'd go down swinging.

Outside, she heard voices raised in anger. Ibris's was among them. And then a young man shouted. And then the fire.

The torch spun like something thrown by a street juggler through the window opposite her. Amat watched it trace a lazy arc through the air, strike the wall and bounce back, falling. Falling on papers. The flame touched one pile, and the pages took fire.

She didn't remember moving or calling out. She was simply there, stamping at the flames, the torch held above her, away from the books. The smoke was choking and her sandals little protection, but she kept on. Someone was forcing open the door, hardly slowed by her little barrier.

"Sand!" Amat shouted. "Bring sand!"

A woman's voice, high with panic, called out, but Amat couldn't make out the words. The floating embers started another stack of papers smoldering. The air seemed full of tiny burning bits of paper, floating like fireflies. Amat kept trying to stop it, to put it out. One particularly large fragment touched her leg, and the burning made her think for one long, sickening breath that her robe had caught fire.

The door burst open. Ibris and a red-haired westland whore—Menat? Mitat?—burst in with pans of water in their hands.

"No!" Amat shouted as she rounded on them, swinging the torch. "Not water! Sand! Get sand!"

The women hesitated, the water sloshing. Ibris turned first, dropping her pan though thankfully not on the books or the desk. The red-haired one threw her pan of water in the direction of the flames, catching Amat in the spray, and then they were gone again.

By the time they returned with three of Ovi Niit's house guards and two men of the watch, the fire was out. Only a tiny patch of tar on the wall still burned where the torch had struck on its way down. Amat handed the still-burning torch to a watchman. They questioned her, and then Ibris. Ovi Niit, when he returned, ranted like a madman in the common room, but thankfully his rage did not turn to her.

Hours of work were gone, perhaps irretrievably. There was no pushing herself now. What had been merely impossible before would have been laughable now, had there been any mirth to cut her misery. She straightened what there was to be straightened, and then sat in the near-dark. She couldn't stop weeping, so she ignored her own sobs. There wasn't time for it. She had to think, and the effort to stop her tears was more than she had to spare.

When, two or three hands later the door opened, it wasn't a guard or a watchman or a whore. It was Ovi Niit himself, eyes as wide as the heavy lids would permit, mouth thin as an inked line on paper. He stalked in, his gaze darting restlessly. Amat watched him the way she would have watched a feral dog.

"How bad?" he asked, his voice tight.

"A setback, Niit-cha," she said. "A serious one, but . . . but only a setback."

"I want him. The man who did this. Who's taking my money and burning my house? I want him broken. I'll piss in his mouth."

"As you see fit, Niit-cha," Amat said. "But if you want it in a week's time, you may as well cut me now. I can salvage this, but not quickly."

A heartbeat's pause, and he lunged forward. His breath smelled sickly sweet. Even in the dim light, she could see his teeth were rotten.

"He is out there!" Ovi Niit shrieked in her face. "Right now! And you want me to wait? You want to give him time? I want it tonight. Before morning. I want it *now!*"

That it was what she'd expected made it no easier. She took a pose of apology so steeped in irony that it couldn't be mistaken. The wild eyes narrowed. Amat pushed up the sleeve of her robe until it bunched around her elbow.

"Take out your knife," she said, baring the thin skin of her forearm to him. "Or give me the time to do the work well. After today, I don't have a preference."

Snake quick, he drew the blade and whipped it down. She flinched, but less than she'd expected to. The metal pressed into her skin but didn't break it. It hurt, though, and if he pulled it, it would bite deep. In the long pause, the young man chuckled. It wasn't the malefic sound of a torturer. It was something else. The whoremaster took the knife away.

"Do the work, then," he said, sneering. But behind the contempt, Amat thought perhaps a ray of respect had entered his gaze. She took an acquiescing pose. Ovi Niit stalked out, leaving the door open behind him. Amat sat for a long moment, rubbing the white line the knife had left on her flesh, waiting for the tightness in her throat to ease. She'd done it. She'd won herself more time.

It was at least half a hand later that the scent of apples and roast pork brought her stomach to life. She couldn't think how long it had been since she'd eaten. Leaning on her cane, she made her way to the wide tables. The benches were near full, the night's work set to begin. News had traveled. She could see it in the eyes that didn't meet hers. A space opened for her at the end of a bench, and she settled in. After the meal, she found Mitat, the Westland whore. The woman was in a dress of blue silk that clung to her body. The commodity wrapped for sale.

"We need to speak," Amat said quietly. "Now."

Mitat didn't reply, but when Amat returned to her cell, the girl followed. That was enough. Amat sat. The room still stank of ashes and tar. The grit of fire sand scraped under their feet. It wasn't the place she'd have chosen for this conversation, but it would do.

"It was fortunate that you had water to hand this afternoon," Amat said. "And in pans."

"We didn't need it," Mitat said. Her accent was slushy, and her vowels all slid at the ends. Westlands indeed. And to the north, Amat thought. A refugee from one of the Galtic incursions, most likely. And so, in a sense, they were there for the same reason.

"I was lucky," Amat said. "If I'd gone out to see who was at the door, the fire might have spread. And even if you'd stopped it, the water would have ruined the books."

Mitat shrugged, but her eyes darted to the door. It was a small thing, hardly noticeable in the dim light, but it was enough. Amat felt her suspicion settle into certainty. She took a firmer grip on her cane.

"Close the door," she said. The woman hesitated, then did as she was told. "They questioned Ibris. She sounded upset."

"They had to speak to someone," Mitat said, crossing her arms.

"Not you?"

"I never saw him."

"Good planning," Amat said, taking an approving pose. "Still, an unfortunate day for Ibris."

"You have an accusation to make?" Mitat asked. She didn't look away now. Now, she was all hardness and bravado. Amat could almost smell the fear.

"Do I have an accusation?" Amat said, letting the words roll off her tongue slowly. She tilted her head, considering Mitat as if she were something to be purchased. Amat shook her head. "No. No accusation. I won't tell him."

"Then I don't have to kill you," Mitat said.

Amat smiled and shook her head, her hands taking a pose of reproof.

"Badly played. Threats alienate me and admit your guilt at the same time. Those are just the wrong combination. Begin again," she said and settled herself like a street actor shifting roles. "I won't tell him."

The Westland girl narrowed her eyes, but there was an intelligence in them. That was good to see. Mitat stepped closer, uncrossed her arms. When she spoke, her voice was softer, wary, but less afraid.

"What do you want?" Mitat asked.

"Much better. I want an ally in the pesthole. When the time comes that I have to make a play, you will back me. No questions, no hesitations. We will pretend that Ovi Niit still owns you, but now you answer to me. And for that you and your man . . . it is a man isn't it? Yes, I thought so. You and your man will be safe. Agreed?"

Mitat was silent. In the street, a man shouted out an obscenity and laughed. A beggar sang in a lovely, high voice, and Amat realized she'd been hearing that voice the better part of the day. Why hadn't she noticed it before now? The whore nodded.

"Good," Amat said. "No more fires, then. And Mitat? The next bookkeep won't be likely to make the same offer, so no interesting spices in my food either, eh?"

"No, grandmother. Of course not."

"Well. Then. I don't suppose there's anything more to say just now, is there?"

LIAT SLAPPED THE GIRL'S WRIST, ANNOYED. MAJ PULLED BACK HER PALE hands, speaking in the liquid syllables of her language. Liat shifted her weight from her right knee to her left. The tailor at her side said nothing, but there was amusement in the way he held the knotted cord against the girl's bare thigh.

"Tell her it's just going to take longer if she keeps fidgeting," Liat said. "It isn't as if none of us had seen a leg before."

The moon-faced servant spoke in the island girl's tongue from his stool by the doorway. Maj looked down at the pair of them, blushing. Her skin clearly showed the blood beneath it. The tailor switched the knotted cord to the inner leg, his hand rising well past the girl's knee. She squealed and spoke again, more loudly this time. Liat bit back frustration.

"What's she saying?" Liat demanded.

"In her culture, people are not so free with each other's bodies," Oshai said. "It confuses her."

"Tell her it will be over soon. We can't start making the robes until we get through this."

Liat had thought, in all the late nights she'd woken sleepless and anxious, that negotiating with the Khai Saraykeht and his poet would be the worst of her commission. That shepherding the client through things as simple as being measured for robes would pose a greater problem had never occurred to her. And yet for days now, every small step would move Maj to fidget or pepper her translator, Oshai, with questions. Thankfully, the man seemed competent enough to answer most of them himself.

The tailor finished his work and stood, his hands in a pose of gratitude. Liat responded appropriately. The island girl looked on in mute fascination.

"Will there be anything more, Liat-cha?" Oshai asked.

"The court physician will wish to see her tomorrow. And I'm due to speak with a representative of the accountancy, but she won't be required for that. There may be more the next day, but I can tell you that once the schedule's been set."

"Thank you, Liat-cha," he said and took a pose of gratitude. Something in the cant of his wrists and the corners of his mouth made Liat look twice. She had the feeling that he was amused by her. Well, let him be. When Amat returned, Liat knew there would be a chance to comment on Oshai. And if Amat took offense, he'd never work for House Wilsin again.

She made her way out to the narrow streets of the tailors' quarter. The heat of the day was fierce, and the air was thick and muggy. Sweat had made her robes tacky against her back before she'd made it halfway to the laborers' quarters. She was more than half tempted to take them off and bathe under the rough shower Itani's cohort used. There was no one at it when she arrived. But if someone did see her—an acting overseer of House Wilsin—it might reflect on her status. So, instead, she walked up the stone steps worn smooth by generations of men and into the wide hallway with its cots and cheap cloth tents instead of netting. The sounds of masculine laughter and conversation filled the space like the reek of bodies. And yet Itani lived like this. He chose to. He was a mystery.

When she found him, he was seated on his cot, his skin and hair still wet from the shower. She paused, considering him, and uneasiness touched her. His brow was furrowed in concentration, but his hands were idle. His shoulders hunched forward. Had he been anyone else, she would have said he seemed haunted. In the months—nearly ten now—since she had taken him as her lover, she'd never known him to chew himself like this.

"What's the matter, love?" she said softly.

And the care vanished as if it had never been. Itani smiled, rose, took her in his arms. He smelled good—of clean sweat and young man and some subtle musk that was his alone.

"Something's bothering you," she said.

"No. I'm fine. It's just Muhatia-cha breaking my stones again. It's nothing. Do you have time to go to a bathhouse with us?"

"Yes," she said. It wasn't the answer she'd intended to give, but it was the one she meant now. Her papers for Wilsin-cha could wait.

"Good," he said, the way he smiled convinced her. But there was still something—a reservation in his hands, a distance in his eyes. "Your work's going well, then?"

"Well enough. The negotiations are all in place, I think. But the girl frustrates me. It makes me short with her, and I know I shouldn't be."

"Does she accept your apologies?"

"I haven't really offered them. I want to now, when I'm away from her. But in the moment, I'm always too annoyed with her."

"Well. You could start the day with them. Have it out of the way before you begin."

"Itani, is there something you want me to apologize to *you* for?"

He smiled his perfect, charming smile, but somehow it didn't reach the depths of his eyes.

"No," he said. "Of course not."

"Because it seems like we made our peace, but . . . but you haven't seemed the same since I went before the Khai."

She pulled back from him and sat on his cot. He hesitated and then sat beside her, the canvas creaking under their combined weight. She took a pose of apology, her expression gentle, making it more an offer and a question than a literal form itself.

"It's not like that," Itani said. "I'm not angry. It's hard to explain."

"Then try. I might know you better than you think."

He laughed, a small rueful sound, but didn't forbid it. Liat steeled herself.

"It's our old conversation, isn't it?" she said, gently. "I've started moving up in the house. I'm negotiating with the Khai, with the poets. And your indenture is coming to a close before long. I think you're afraid I'll outgrow you. That an overseer—even one low in the ranks— is above the dignity of a laborer."

Itani was silent. His expression was thoughtful, and his gaze seemed wholly upon her for the first time in days. A smile quirked his lips and vanished.

"Am I right?" she asked.

"No," he said. "But I'm curious all the same. Is that what you believe? That I would be beneath your dignity?"

"I don't," she said. "But I also don't think you'll end your life a laborer. You're a strange man. You're strong and clever and charming. And I think you know half again what you let on. But I don't understand your choices. You could be so much, if you wanted to. Isn't there anything you want?"

He said nothing. The smile was gone, and the haunted look had stolen back into his eyes. She caressed his cheek, feeling where the stubble was coming in.

"Do you want to go to the bathhouse?" she asked.

"Yes," he said. "We should be going. The others will be there already."

"You're sure there isn't something more I should know?"

He opened his mouth to speak, and it was as if she could see some glib rejoinder die on his lips. His wide, strong hand folded hers.

"Not now," he said.

"But eventually," she said.

Something like dread seemed to take Itani's long face, but he managed a smile.

"Yes," he said.

Through the evening, Itani grew more at ease. They laughed with his friends, drank and sang together. The pack of them moved from bathhouse to teahouse to the empty beaches at the far end of the seafront. Great swaths of silt showed where the rivermouth had once been, generations ago. When the time came, Itani walked her back to the Wilsin compound, the comfortable weight of his arm around her shoulders. Crickets chirped in chorus as they stepped together into the courtyard with its fountain and the Galtic Tree.

"You could stay," she said, softly.

He turned, pulling her body near to his. She looked up into his eyes. Her answer was there.

"Another time, then?" she asked, embarrassed to hear the plea in her voice.

He leaned close, his lips firm and soft against hers. She ran her fingers through his hair, holding it to her like a cup from which she was drinking. She ached for him to stay, to be with her, to sleep in his arms. But he stepped back, gently out of her reach. She took a pose of regret and farewell. He answered with a pose so gentle and complex—thankfulness, requesting patience, expressing affection—that it neared poetry. He walked backwards slowly, fading into the shadows where the moon didn't reach, but with his eyes on her. She sighed, shook herself, and went to her cell. It would be a long day tomorrow, and the ceremony still just over a week away.

Liat didn't notice she wasn't alone until she was nearly to her door. The pregnant girl, Maj, was on the walkway and unescorted. She wore a loose gown that barely covered her breasts and a pair of workman's trousers cut at the knee. Her swollen belly pressed out, bare in the moonlight.

To Liat's surprise, the girl took a pose of greeting. It was rough and child-like, but recognizable.

"Hello," Maj said, her accent so thick as to almost bury the word.

Liat fell into an answering pose immediately and felt a smile growing on her lips. The girl Maj almost glowed with pleasure.

"You've been learning to speak," Liat said. Maj's face clouded, her smile faltered, and she shrugged—a gesture that carried its load of meaning without language.

"Hello," Maj said again, taking the same pose as before. Her expression said that this was all that there was. Liat nodded, smiled again, and took the girl by the arm. Maj shifted Liat's hand, lacing their fingers together as if they were young girls walking together after temple. Liat walked back to the guest quarters where Maj was being housed until after the ceremony.

"It's a good start," Liat said as they walked. She knew that the words were likely meaningless to the island girl, but she spoke them all the same. "Keep practicing, and we'll make a civilized woman of you. Just give it time."

7

>+< Two days later, after his work was complete and his friends had
gone to their night's entertainments, Otah stepped out from his
quarters and considered. The city streets were gaudy with sunset. Orange light warmed the walls and roofs, even as the first stars began to
glimmer in the deep cobalt of the western sky. Otah stood in the street
and watched the change come. Fireflies danced like candles. The songs
of beggars changed as the traffic of night came out. The soft quarter lay
to his right, lit like a carnival as it was every night. The seafront was before him, though hidden by the barracks of other labor cohorts like his
own, employed by other houses. And somewhere far to his left, off past
the edge of the city, the great river flowed, bearing water from the
north. He rubbed his hands together slowly as the light reddened, then
grayed. The sun vanished again, and the stars came out, shining over
the city. Liat was in her cell, he supposed, to the north and uphill. And
beyond her, the palaces of the Khai.

The streets changed as he walked north. The laborers' quarter was
actually quite small, and Otah left it behind him quickly, barracks giving way to the shops of small merchants and free traders. Then came
the weavers' compounds, windows candle-lit, and the clack of looms
filling the streets as they would even later into the night. He passed
groups of men and of women, passed through the street of beads and
the blood quarter where physicians and pretenders vied to care for the
sick and injured, selling services, as everything in Saraykeht was for
trade.

The compounds of the great houses rose up like small villages.
Streets grew wider near them, and walls taller. The firekeepers at their
kilns wore better robes than their fellows lower in the city. Otah paused
at the corner that would have taken him to House Wilsin, through the

familiar spaces to Liat's side. It would be so easy, he thought, to go there. He stood for the space of ten heartbeats, standing at the intersection like the statue of some forgotten man of the Empire, before going north. His hands were balled in fists.

The palaces grew up like a city of their own, above the city inhabited by mere humans. The scents of sewage and bodies and meat cooking at teahouses vanished and those of gardens and incense took their places. The paths changed from stone to marble or sand or fine gravel. The songs of beggars gave way to the songs of slaves, almost it seemed without losing the melody. The great halls stood empty and dark or else lit like lanterns from within. Servants and slaves moved along the paths with the quiet efficiency of ants, and the utkhaiem, in robes as gaudy as the sunset, stood in lit courtyards, posing to each other as the politics of the court played out. Vying, Otah guessed, for which would have the honor of killing a son of the Khai Udun.

Pretending that he bore a message, he took directions from one of the servants, and soon he'd left even the palaces behind. The path was dark, curving through stands of trees. He could still see the palaces behind him if he turned, but the emptiness made the poet's house seem remote from them. He crossed a long wooden bridge over a pond. And there the simple, elegant house stood. Its upper story was lit. Its lower had the front wall pulled open like shutters or a stage set for a play. And sitting on a velvet chair was the boy. Maati Vaupathai.

"Well," a soft voice said. "Here's an oddity. It's a strange day we see toughs reeking of the seafront dropping by for tea. Or perhaps you've got some other errand."

The andat Seedless sat on the grass. Otah fell into a pose that asked forgiveness.

"I . . . I've come to see Maati-cha," Otah stumbled. "We were . . . that is . . ."

"Hai! Who's down there?" another voice called. "Who're you?"

Seedless glanced up at the house, eyes narrowed. A fat man in the brown robe of a poet was trundling down the steps. Maati was following.

"Itani of House Wilsin," Otah called out. "I've come to see Maati-cha."

The poet walked more slowly as they approached. His expression was a strange mix—concern, disapproval, and a curious delight.

"You've come for *him?*" Heshai-kvo said, gesturing over his shoulder. Otah took a pose of affirmation.

"Itani and I met at the grand audience," Maati said. "He offered to show me the seafront."

"Did he?" Heshai-kvo asked, and the disapproval lost ground, Otah thought, to the pleasure. "Well. You. Itani's your name? You know who you're with, eh? This boy is one of the most important men in Saraykeht. Keep him out of trouble."

"Yes, Heshai-cha," Otah said. "I will."

The poet's face softened, and he rooted in the sleeve of his robe for a moment, then reached out to Otah. Otah, unsure, stepped closer and put his hand out to the poet's.

"I was young once too," Heshai-kvo said with a broad wink. "Don't keep him out of too much trouble."

Otah felt the small lengths of metal against his palm, and took a pose of gratitude.

"Who'd have thought it," Seedless said, his voice low and considering. "Our perfect student's developing a life."

"Please, Itani-cha," Maati said, stepping forward and taking Otah's sleeve. "You've gone out of your way already. We should go. Your friends are waiting."

"Yes," Otah said. "Of course."

He took a pose of farewell that the poet responded to eagerly, the andat more slowly and with a thoughtful attitude. Maati led the way back across the bridge.

"You were expecting me?" Otah asked once they were out of earshot. Poet and andat were still watching them go.

"Hoping," Maati allowed.

"You weren't the only one. The poet seemed delighted to see me."

"He doesn't like my staying at the house. He thinks I should see more of the city. It's really that he hates it there and can't imagine that I like it."

"Ah. I see."

"You see part, at least," Maati said. "It's complex. And what of you, Otah-kvo? It's been days. I was afraid that you wouldn't come."

"I had to," Otah said, surprised by his own candor even as he said it. "I've no one else to talk with. Gods! He gave me three lengths of silver!"

"Is that bad?"

"It means I should stop working the seafront and just take you to tea. The pay's better."

He had changed. That was clear. The voice was much the same, the face older, more adult, but Maati could still see the boy who had worn the black robes in the garden all those years ago. And something else. It wasn't confidence that had gone—he still had that in the way he held himself and his voice when he spoke—but perhaps it was certainty. It was in the way he held his cup and in the way he drank. Something was bothering his old teacher, but Maati could not yet put a name to it.

"A laborer," Maati said. "It isn't what the Dai-kvo would have expected."

"Or anyone else," Otah said, smiling at his cup of wine.

The private patio of the teahouse overlooked the street below it, and the long stretch of the city to the south. Lemon candles filled the air with bright-smelling smoke that kept the worst of the gnats away and made the wine taste odd. In the street, a band of young men sang and danced while three women watched, laughing. Otah took a long drink of wine.

"It isn't what you'd expected either, is it?"

"No," Maati admitted. "When you left I imagined . . . we all did . . ."

"Imagined what?"

Maati sighed, frowned, tried to find words for daydreams and secret stories he'd never precisely told himself. Otah-kvo had been the figure who'd shaped his life almost more than the Dai-kvo, certainly more than his father. He had imagined Otah-kvo forging a new order, a dark, dangerous, possibly libertine group that would be at odds with the Dai-kvo and the school, or perhaps its rival. Or else adventuring on the seas or in the turmoil of the wars in the Westlands. Maati would never have said it, but the common man his teacher had become was disappointing.

"Something else," he said, taking a pose that kept the phrase vague.

"It was hard. The first few months, I thought I'd starve. Those things they taught us about hunting and foraging? They work, but only barely. When I got a bowl of soup and half a loaf of stale bread for cleaning out a henhouse, I felt like I'd been given the best meal of my life."

Maati laughed. Otah smiled at him and shrugged.

"And you?" Otah asked, changing the subject. "Was the Dai-kvo's village what you thought?"

"I suppose so. It was more work than the school, but it was easier. Because there was a reason for it. It wasn't just hard to be hard. We studied old grammars and the languages of the Empire. And the history of the andat who bound them, what the bindings were like. How they escaped. I didn't know how much harder it is to bind the same andat a second time. I mean there are all the stories about some being captured three or four times, but I don't . . ."

Otah laughed. It was a warm sound, mirthful but not mocking. Maati took a pose of query. Otah responded with one of apology that nearly spilled his wine.

"It's just that you sound like you loved it," Otah said.

"I did," Maati said. "It was fascinating. And I'm good at it, I think. My teachers seemed to feel that way. Heshai-kvo isn't what I'd expected though."

"Him either, eh?"

"No. But, Otah-kvo, why didn't you go? When the Dai-kvo offered you a place with him, why did you refuse?"

"Because what they did was wrong," Otah said, simply. "And I didn't want any part of it."

Maati frowned into his wine. His reflection looked back at him from the dark, shining surface.

"If you had it again, would you do the same?" Maati asked.

"Yes."

"Even if it meant just being a laborer?"

Otah took two deep breaths, turned, and sat on the railing, considering Maati with dark, troubled eyes. His hands moved toward a pose that might have been accusation or demand or query, but that never took a final form.

"Is this really so bad, what I do?" Otah asked. "You, Liat. Everyone seems to think so. I started out as a child on the road with no family, no friends. I didn't even dare use my real name. And I built something. I have work, and friends, and a lover. I have good food and shelter. And at night I can go and listen to poets or philosophers or singers, or I can go to bathhouses or teahouses, or out on the ocean in sailing boats. Is that so bad? It that so *little?*"

Maati was surprised by the pain in Otah's voice, and perhaps by the desperation. He had the feeling that the words were only half meant for him. Still, he considered them. And their source.

"Of course not," Maati said. "Something doesn't have to be great to be worthy. If you've followed the calling of your heart, then what does it matter what anyone else thinks?"

"It can matter. It can matter a great deal."

"Not if you're certain," Maati said.

"And someone, somewhere, is actually certain of the choices they made? Are you?"

"No, I'm not," Maati said. It was easier than he'd expected, voicing this deepest of doubts. He'd never said it to anyone at the school or with the Dai-kvo. He'd have died before he said it to Heshai-kvo. But to Otah, it wasn't such a hard thing to say. "But it's done. I've made all my decisions already. Now it's just seeing whether I'm strong enough to follow through."

"You are," Otah said.

"I don't think so."

Silence flowed in. Below them, in the street, a woman shrieked and then laughed. A dog streets away bayed as if in response. Maati put down his cup of wine—empty now except for the dregs—and slapped a gnat from his arm. Otah nodded, more to himself than to Maati.

"Well, there's nothing to be done then," Otah said.

"It's late and we're drunk," Maati said. "It'll look better by morning. It always does."

Otah weighed the words, then took a pose of agreement.

"I'm glad I found you," Maati said. "I think perhaps I was meant to."

"Perhaps," Otah-kvo agreed.

"WILSIN-CHA!" EPANI'S VOICE WAS A WHISPER, BUT THE URGENCY OF IT CUT through Marchat's dream. He rolled up on one elbow and was pushing away his netting before he was really awake. The house master stood beside the bed holding his robe closed with one hand. Epani's face, lit only by the night candle, was drawn.

"Wha?" Marchat said, still pulling his mind up from the depths he'd been in moments before. "What's the matter? There's a fire?"

"No," Epani said, trying a pose of apology, but hampered by the needs of his robes. "Someone's here to see you. He's in the private hall."

"He? He who?"

Epani hesitated.

"It," he said.

It took Marchat the time to draw in a breath before he understood what Epani meant. He nodded then, and motioned to a robe that hung by his wardrobe. The night candle was well past its middle mark—the night nearer the coming dawn than yesterday's sunset. Apart from the soft rustle of the cloth as Marchat pulled his robes on and tied them, there was no sound. He ran his fingers through his hair and beard and turned toward Epani.

"Good enough?" he asked.

Epani took a pose of approval.

"Fine," Marchat said. "Bring us something to drink. Wine. Or tea."

"Are you sure, Wilsin-cha?"

Marchat paused and considered. Every movement in the night ran the risk of waking someone, someone besides himself or Epani or Oshai. A glimmer of anger at the andat for coming here, now, like this, shone in the dark setting of his unease. He took a pose of dismissal.

"No," he said. "Don't bring us anything. Go to bed. Forget this happened. You were dreaming."

Epani left. Marchat took up his night candle and walked in its near-darkness to the private hall. It was near his own quarters because of meetings like this. Windowless, with a single entrance and its own atrium so that anyone within could hear if someone was coming. When he stepped into the room, the andat was perched on the meeting table like a bird, his arms resting on his knees. The blackness of his cloak spread out behind him like a stain.

"What are you playing at, Wilsin?"

"I was playing at being asleep until a few moments ago," Marchat said, bluster welling up to hide his fear. The dark eyes in the pale face shifted, taking him in. Seedless tilted his head. They were silent except for Marchat's breathing. He was the only one there breathing.

"Is this about something?" Marchat asked. "And get your boots off my table, will you? This isn't some cheap teahouse."

"Why is your boy courting mine?" the andat demanded, ignoring him.

Marchat put the night candle squarely on the table, pulled out a chair, and sat.

"I don't have the first idea what you're talking about," he said, crossing his arms. "Talk sense or go haunt someone else. I've got a busy day tomorrow."

"You didn't send one of your men to take Heshai's student out to the teahouses?"

"No."

"Then why did he come?"

Marchat read the distrust in the andat's expression, or imagined he did. He set his jaw and leaned forward. The thing in human form didn't move.

"I don't know who you mean," Marchat said, deliberately. "And you can drink piss if you don't believe me."

Seedless narrowed his eyes as if he was listening for something, then sat back. The anger that had been in his voice and face faded and was replaced by puzzlement.

"One of your laborers came tonight to see Maati," Seedless said. "He said they'd met during the negotiations and arranged to go out together."

"Well," Marchat said. "Perhaps they met during the negotiations and arranged to go out together."

"A poet and a laborer?" Seedless scoffed. "And maybe the fine ladies of the utkhaiem are out this evening playing tiles in the soft quarter. Heshai was delighted, of course. It smells wrong to me, Wilsin."

Marchat turned it over slowly, chewing on his lip. It did seem odd. And with the ceremony coming so quickly, the stakes were high. He pulled out a chair, its wooden legs scraping against the stone floor, and sat. Seedless swung his legs over the side, still sitting on the tabletop, but without seeming quite as predatory.

"Which man was it?"

"He said his name was Itani. Big man, broad across the shoulders. Face like a northerner."

The one Amat had sent out with him. That wasn't good. Seedless read something in his face and took a pose half query and half command.

"I know the one you mean. You're right. Something's odd. He was my bodyguard when I came out to the low town. And he's Liat Chokavi's lover."

Seedless took a moment to consider that. Marchat watched the dark eyes, the beautiful mouth that turned into the faintest of smiles.

"Has he warned Liat of anything?" the andat asked. "Do you think she suspects?"

"She doesn't. If she had any reservations, you could read them from across the room. I think Liat may be the worst liar I've ever met. It's part of what makes her so good at this."

"If he hasn't told Liat, perhaps he *isn't* trying to spoil our little game. You've had no word of your vanished overseer?"

"No," Marchat said. "Oshai's thugs have been offering good prices for her, but there's been no sign. And no one at the seafront or on the roads remembers seeing her go. And even if she's gone to ground inside the city, there's no reason to think she's out to stop . . . the trade."

"Oshai can't find her, and that's enough to make me nervous. And this boy, this Itani. Either he is her agent or he isn't. And if he *is* . . ."

Marchat sighed. There was no end of it. Every time he thought he'd reached the last crime he'd be called upon to commit, one more appeared behind it. Liat Chokavi—silly, short-sighted, kind, pretty girl that she was—would be humiliated when the thing went wrong. And now it seemed she wouldn't have her man behind her to offer comfort.

"I can have him killed," Marchat said, heavily. "I'll speak with Oshai in the morning."

"No," Seedless said. The andat leaned back, crossing one knee over the other and lacing his hands over it. They were women's hands—thin and graceful. "No. If he's sent to tell the tale, it's too late. Maati will know by now. If he isn't, then killing him will only draw attention."

"I could have the poet boy killed too," Marchat said.

"No," Seedless said again. "No, we can kill the laborer if it seems the right thing, but no one touches Maati."

"Why not?"

"I like him," Seedless said, a subtle surprise in his voice, as if this were something he'd only just realized. "He's . . . he's good-hearted. He's the only person I've met in years who didn't see me as a convenient tool or else the very soul of evil."

Marchat blinked. For a moment, something like sadness seemed to possess the andat. Sadness or perhaps longing. In the months Marchat had spent preparing this evil scheme, he'd built an image of the beast he was treating with, and this emotion didn't fit with it. And then it was gone and Seedless grinned at him.

"You, for instance, think I'm chaos made flesh," Seedless said. "Ripping a wanted child from an innocent girl's womb just to make Heshai-kvo suffer."

"It doesn't matter what I think."

"No. It doesn't, but that won't stop you from thinking it. And when you *do* think, remember it was your men who approached me. It may be my design, but it's your money."

"It's my uncle's," Marchat said, perhaps more sharply than he'd intended. "I didn't choose any of this. No one asked my opinion."

A terrible amusement lit the andat's face, and the beautiful smile had grown wider.

"Puppets. Puppets and the puppets of puppets. You should have more sympathy for me, Wilsin-cha. I'm what I am because of someone else, just the way you are. How could either of us ever be responsible for anything?"

The poisonous thought tickled the back of Marchat's mind—*what if I'd refused?* He pushed it away.

"We couldn't be less alike," Marchat said. "But it doesn't matter. However we got here, we're married now. What of Itani?"

"Have him followed," he said. "Our boy Itani may be nothing, but the game's too important to risk it. Find out what he is, and then, if we have to, we can kill him."

8

">+<" "After the fire, we agreed . . ." Amat said, and the back of Ovi Niit's hand snapped her head to the side. She turned back slowly, tasting her own blood. Her lips tingled in the presentiment of pain, and a trickle of warmth going cool on her chin told the part of her mind that wasn't cringing in fear that one of his rings had cut her.

"*Agreed,*" Ovi Niit spat. "We agree what I say we agree. If I change it, it changes. There's no agreement to be made."

He paced the length of the room. The evening sun pressed at the closed shutters, showing only their outlines. It was enough light to see by, enough to know that Ovi Niit's eyes were opened too wide—the stained whites showing all the way round. His lips moved as if he were on the verge of speaking.

"You're stalling!" he shouted, slamming his hand down on her desk. Amat balled her fists and willed herself to sit quietly. Anything she said would be a provocation. "You think that by stretching it out, you'll be safer. You think that by letting that thief take my money, you'll be better off. But you won't!"

With the last word, he kicked the wall. The plaster cracked where he'd struck it. Amat considered the damage—small lines radiating out from a flattened circle—and felt her mind shift. It was no bigger than an egg, and looking at it, she knew that sometime not long from now Ovi Niit wouldn't direct his rage at the walls. He would kill her, whether he meant to or not.

How odd, she thought as she felt the nausea descend on her, that it would be that little architectural wound that would resolve her when all his violence against people hadn't.

"I will have my answer by dawn," he shouted. "By dawn. If you don't do what I say, I'll cut off your thumbs and sell you for the five lengths of gold. It's not as if Oshai's going to care that you're damaged."

Amat took a pose of obeisance so abject that she was disgusted by it. But it came naturally to her hands. Ovi Niit grabbed her by a handful of hair and pulled her from her chair, spilling her papers and pens. He kicked over the desk and stalked out. As the door slammed shut behind him, Amat caught a glimpse of shocked faces.

She lay in the darkness, too tired and ill to weep. The stone floor was rough against her cheek. The blood from her cut face pulled on her skin as it dried. She'd have a scar. When her mind would obey her again, the room was utterly black. She forced herself to think. The days had blurred—bent over half-legible books from the moment she woke until the figures shifted on the page and her hands bent themselves into claws. And then to dream about it, and come back and begin again. And there had been no point. Ovi Niit was a thug and a whoremaster. His fear and violence grew with the wine and drugs he took to ease them. He would have been pitiful from the right distance.

But days. The question was days.

She counted slowly, struggling to recall. Three weeks at least. More than that. It had to be more than that. Perhaps four. Not five. It was too early to be sure of Marchat's amnesty. She surprised herself by chuckling. If she'd counted wrong, the worst case would be that they found her face down in the river and Ovi Niit lost five lengths of gold. That wouldn't be so bad.

She pushed herself upright, then stood, breathing through the pain until she felt as little stooped as she could manage. When she was ready, she took up her cane and put on the expression she used when she wanted no one to see her true feelings. She was Amat Kyaan, after all, overseer of House Wilsin. Streetgirl of Saraykeht made good. Let them see that she was unbroken. If she could make the whores of the comfort house believe it, she would start to believe it again, too.

The common room was near empty, the whores out in the rooms plying their trade. A guardsman sat eating a roast chicken that smelled of garlic and rosemary. An old black dog lay curled in a corner, a leatherwork rod in the shape of a man's sex chewed half to pieces between the bitch's paws.

"He's gone out," the guard said. "In the front rooms, playing tiles."
Amat nodded.

"I wouldn't go out to him, grandmother."

"I wouldn't want to interrupt. Send Mitat to the office. I need someone to help me put the room back in order. Every meeting it's like a
storm's come through."

The guard took an amused pose of agreement. The sound of drums
came suddenly from the street. Another night in the endless carnival of
the soft quarter.

"I'll have her bring something for that wound," the guard said.

"Thank you," Amat said, her voice polite, dispassionate: the voice of
the woman she wanted them all the believe her to be. "That would be
very kind of you."

Mitat appeared in her doorway half a hand later. The wide, pale face
littered with freckles looked hard. Amat smiled gently at her and took a
pose of welcome.

"I heard that he'd been to see you, grandmother."

"Yes, and so he has. Open those shutters for me, would you, dear? I
was tall enough to get them myself when I came here, but I seem to
have grown shorter."

Mitat did so, and the pale moonlight added to the lantern on Amat's
desk. The papers weren't in such bad order. Amat motioned the woman
closer.

"You have to go, grandmother," Mitat said. "Niit-cha is getting
worse."

"Of course he is," Amat said. "He's frightened. And he drinks too
much. I need you. Now, tonight."

Mitat took a pose of agreement. Amat smiled and took her hand. In
the wall behind Mitat, the little scar blemished the wall where he'd
kicked it. Amat wondered in passing if the whoremaster would ever understand how much that mark had cost him. And Amat intended it to
cost dear.

"Who is the most valuable man here?" Amat asked. "Niit-cha must
have men who he trusts more than others, ne?"

"The guards," Mitat began, but Amat waved the comment away.

"Who does he trust like a brother?"

Mitat's eyes narrowed. She's caught scent of it, Amat thought and
smiled.

"Black Rathvi," Mitat said. "He's in charge of the house when Niit-cha's away."

"You know what his handwriting looks like?"

"No," Mitat said. "But I know he took in two gold and seventy silver lengths from the high tables two nights ago. I heard him talking about it."

Amat paged through the most recent ledger until she found the precise sum. It was a wide hand with poorly formed letters and a propensity for dropping the ends of words. She knew it well. Black Rathvi was a poor keeper of notes, and she'd been struggling with his entries since she'd started the project. She found herself ghoulishly pleased that he'd be suffering for his poor job keeping books.

"I'll need a cloak—a hooded one—perhaps two hands before daybreak," Amat said.

"You should leave now," Mitat said. "Niit-cha's occupied for the moment, but he may—"

"I'm not finished yet. Two hands before daybreak, I will be. You and your man should slow down for a time after Ovi Niit deals with Black Rathvi. At least several weeks. If he sees things get better, he'll know he was right. You understand?"

Mitat took a pose of affirmation, but it wasn't solid. Amat didn't bother replying formally, only raised a single eyebrow and waited. Mitat looked away, and then back. There was something like hope and also like distrust in her eyes. The face of someone who wants to believe, but is afraid to.

"Can you do it?" Mitat asked.

"Make the numbers point to Black Rathvi? Of course I can. This is what I do. Can you get me a cloak and safe passage at least as far as the street?"

"If you can put those two at each other's throats, I can do anything," Mitat said.

It took less time than she'd expected. The numbers were simple enough to manipulate once she knew what she wanted to do with them. She even changed a few of the entries on their original sheets, blacking out the scrawling hand and forging new figures. When she was finished, a good accountant would have been able to see the deception. But if Ovi Niit had had one of those, Amat would never have been there.

She spent the remaining time composing her letter of leave-taking. She kept the tone formal, using all the titles and honorary flourishes she would have for a very respected merchant or one of the lower of the utkhaiem. She expressed her thanks for the shelter and discretion Ovi Niit and his house had extended and expressed regret that she felt it in her best interest—now that her work was done—to leave inconspicuously. She had too much respect, she wrote sneering as she did so, for Niit-cha's sense of advantage to expect him not to sell a commodity for which he no longer had use. She then outlined her findings, implicating Black Rathvi without showing any sign that she knew his name or his role in the house.

She folded the letter twice and then at the corners in the style of a private message and wrote Ovi Niit's name on the overleaf. It perched atop the papers and books, ready to be discovered. Amat sat a while longer, listening to the wild music and slurred voices of the street, waiting for Mitat to appear. The night candle consumed small mark after small mark, and Amat began to wonder whether something had gone wrong.

It hadn't.

However the girl had arranged it, leaving the house was as simple as shrugging on the deep green cloak, taking up her cane, and stepping out the rear door and down a stone path to the open gate that led to the street. In the east, the blackness was starting to show the gray of charcoal, the weakest stars on the horizon failing. The moon, near full, had already set. The night traffic was over but for a few revelers pulling themselves back from their entertainments. Amat, for all the pain in her joints, wasn't the slowest.

She paused at a corner stand and bought a meal of fresh greens and fried pork wrapped in almond skin and a bowl of tea. She ate as the sun rose, climbing like a god in the east. She was surprised by the calm she felt, the serenity. Her ordeal was, if not over, at least near its end. A few more days, and then whatever Marchat was doing would be done. And if she spent weeks in hell, she was strong enough, she saw, to come through it with grace.

She even believed the story until the girl running the stall asked if she'd want more tea. Amat almost wept at the small kindness. So perhaps she wasn't quite so unscathed as she told herself.

She reached her apartments in the press of the morning. On a normal day, if she could recall those, she might have been setting forth just then. Or even a bit earlier. Off into her city, on the business of her house. She unlocked the door of her apartments, slipped in, and barred the door behind her. It was a risk, coming home without being sure of things with Marchat's cruel business, but she needed money. And the stinging salve for her legs. And a fresh robe. And sleep. Gods, she needed sleep. But that would wait.

She gathered her things quickly and made for the door, struggling to get down the stairs. She had enough silver in her sleeve to buy a small house for a month. Surely it would be enough for a room and discretion for three or four days. If she could only . . .

No. No, of course she couldn't. When she opened the door, three men blocked her. They had knives. The tallest moved in first, clamping a wide palm over her mouth and pushing her against the wall. The others slid in fast as shadows, and closed the door again. Amat closed her eyes. Her heart was racing, and she felt nauseated.

"If you scream, we'll have to kill you," the tall man said gently. It was so much worse for being said so carefully. Amat nodded, and he took his hand away. Their knives were still drawn.

"I want to speak with Wilsin-cha," Amat said when she had collected herself enough to say anything.

"Good that we've sent for him, then," one of the others said. "Why don't you have a seat while we wait."

Amat swallowed, hoping to ease the tightness in her throat. She took a pose that accepted the suggestion, turned and made her way again up the stairs to wait at her desk. Two of the men followed her. The third waited below. The sun had moved the width of two hands together when Marchat walked up the steps and into her rooms.

He looked older, she thought. Or perhaps not older, but worn. His hair hung limp on his brow. His robes fit him poorly, and a stain of egg yolk discolored the sleeve. He paced the length of the room twice, looking neither directly at her nor away. Amat, sitting at her desk, folded her hands on one knee and waited. Marchat stopped at the window, turned and gestured to the two thugs.

"Get out," he said. "Wait downstairs."

The two looked at one another, weighing, Amat saw, whether to obey him. These were not Marchat's men, then. Not truly. They were the moon-faced Oshai's perhaps. One shrugged, and the other turned back with a pose of acknowledgement before they both moved to the door and out. Amat listened to their footsteps fading.

Marchat looked out, down, she presumed, to the street. The heat of the day was thick. Sweat stained his armpits and damped his brow.

"You're too early," he said at last, still not looking directly at her.

"Am I?"

"By three days."

Amat took a pose of apology more casual than she felt. Silence held them until at last Marchat looked at her directly. She couldn't read his expression—perhaps anger, perhaps sorrow, perhaps exhaustion. Her employer, the voice of her house, sighed.

"Amat . . . Gods, things have been bad. Worse than I expected, and I didn't think they'd be well."

He walked to her, lowered himself onto the cushion that Liat usually occupied, and rested his head on his hands. Amat felt the urge to reach out, to touch him. She held the impulse in.

"It's nearly over," he continued. "I can convince Oshai and his men that it's better to let you live. I can. But Amat. You have to help me."

"How?"

"Tell me what you're planning. What you've started or done or said that might stop the trade."

Amat felt a slow smile pluck her lips, a low, warm burble of laughter bloom in her chest. Her shoulders shook and she took a pose of amazement. The absurdity of the question was like a wave lifting up a swimmer. Marchat looked confused.

"What I've done to stop it?" Amat asked. "Are you simple? I've run like my life depended on it, kept my head low and prayed that whatever you'd started, you could finish. Stop you? Gods, Marchat, I don't know what you're thinking."

"You've done nothing?"

"I've been through hell. I've been beaten and threatened. Someone tried to light me on fire. I've seen more of the worst parts of the city than I've seen in years. I did quite a bit. I worked longer hours at harder tasks than you've even gotten from me." The words were taking on a pace and rhythm of their own, flowing out of her faster and louder. Her face felt flushed. "And, in my spare moments, did I work out a plan to save the house's honor and set the world to rights? Did I hire men to discover your precious client and warn the girl what you intend to do to her? No, you fat Galtic idiot, I did not. Had you been expecting me to?"

Amat found she was leaning forward, her chin jutting out. The anger made her feel better for the moment. More nearly in control. She recognized it was illusion, but she took comfort in it all the same. Marchat's expression was sour.

"What about Itani, then?"

"Who?"

"Itani. Liat's boy."

Amat took a dismissive pose.

"What about him? I used him to discover where you were going, certainly, but you must know that by now. I didn't speak with him then, and I certainly haven't since."

"Then why has he gone out with the poet's student three nights of the last five?" Marchat demanded. His voice was hard as stone. He didn't believe her.

"I don't know, Marchat-cha. Why don't you ask him?"

Marchat shook his head, impatient, stood and turned his back on her. The anger that had held Amat up collapsed, and she was suddenly desperate that he believe her, that he understand. That he be on her side. She felt like a portman's flag, switching one way to another with the shifting wind. If she'd been able to sleep before they spoke, if she hadn't had to flee Ovi Niit's house, if the world were only just or fair or explicable, she would have been able to be herself— calm, solid, grounded. She swallowed her need, disgusted by it and pretended that she was only calming herself from her rage, not folding.

"Or," she said, stopping him as he reached the head of the stairs, "if you want to be clever about it, ask Liat."

"Liat?"

"She's the one who told me where the two of you had gone. Itani told her, and she told me. If you're worried that Itani's corrupting the poets against you, ask Liat."

"She'd suspect," Marchat said, but his tone begged to be proved wrong. Amat closed her eyes. They felt so good, closed. The darkness was so comfortable. Gods, she needed to rest.

"No," Amat said. "She wouldn't. Approach her as if you were scolding her. Tell her it's unseemly for those kinds of friendships to bloom in the middle of a working trade, and ask her why they couldn't wait until it was concluded. At the worst, she'll hide the truth from you, but then you'll know she has something she's hiding."

Her employer and friend of years hesitated, his mind turning the strategy over, looking for flaws. A breath of air touched Amat's face smelling of the sea. She could see it in Marchat's eyes when he accepted her suggestion.

"You'll have to stay here until it's over," he said. "I'll have Oshai's men bring you food and drink. I still need to make my case to Oshai and the client, but I will make it work. You'll be fine."

Amat took an accepting pose. "I'll be pleased being here," she said. Then, "Marchat? What is this all about?"

"Money," he said. "Power. What else is there?"

And as he walked down the stairs, leaving her alone, it fit together like a peg slipping into its hole. It wasn't about the child. It wasn't about the girl. It was about the poet. And if it was about the poet, it was about the andat. If the poet Heshai lost control of his creation, if Seedless escaped, the cotton trade in Saraykeht would lose its advantage over other ports in the islands and the Westlands and Galt. Even when a new andat came, it wasn't likely that it would be able to fuel the cotton trade as Seedless or Petals-Falling had.

Amat went to her window. The street below was full—men, women, dogs, carts. The roofs of the city stretched out to the east, and down to the south the seafront was full. Trade. The girl Maj would be sacrificed to shift the balance of trade away from Saraykeht. It was the only thing that made sense.

"Oh, Marchat," she breathed. "What have you done?"

THE TEAHOUSE WAS NEARLY EMPTY. TWO OR THREE YOUNG MEN INSIDE WERE still speaking in raised voices, their arguments inchoate and disjointed. Out in the front garden, an older man had fallen asleep beside the fountain, his long, slow breathing a counterpoint to the distant conversation. A lemon candle guttered and died, leaving only a long winding plume of smoke, gray against the night, and the scent of an extinguished wick.

Otah felt the urge to light a fresh candle, but he didn't act on it. On the bench beside him, Maati sighed.

"Does it ever get cold here, Otah-kvo?" Maati asked. "If we were with the Dai-kvo, we'd be shivering by now, even if it is midsummer. It's midnight, and it's almost hot as day."

"It's the sea. It holds the heat in. And we're too far south. It's colder as you go north."

"North. Do you remember Machi?"

Visions took Otah. Stone walls thicker than a man's height, stone towers reaching to a white sky, stone statues baked all day in the fires and then put in the children's room to radiate their heat through the night.

He remembered being pulled through snow-choked streets on a sleigh, a sister whose name he no longer knew beside him, holding close for warmth. The scent of burning pine and hot stone and mulled wine.

"No," he said. "Not really."

"I don't often look at the stars," Maati said. "Isn't that odd?"

"I suppose," Otah allowed.

"I wonder whether Heshai does. He stays out half the time, you know. He wasn't even there yesterday when I came in."

"You mean this morning?"

Maati frowned.

"I suppose so. It wasn't quite dawn when I got there. You should have seen Seedless stalking back and forth like a cat. He tried to get me to say where I'd been, but I wouldn't talk. Not me. I wonder where Heshai-kvo goes all night."

"The way Seedless wonders about you," Otah said. "You should start drinking water. You'll be worse for it if you don't."

Maati took a pose of acceptance, but didn't rise or go in for water. The sleeping man snored. Otah closed his eyes for a moment, testing how it felt. It was like falling backwards. He was too tired. He'd never make it though his shift with Muhatia-cha.

"I don't know how Heshai-kvo does it," Maati said, clearly thinking similar thoughts. "He's got a full day coming. I don't think I'll be able to do any more today than I did yesterday. I mean today. I don't know what I mean. It's easier to keep track when I sleep at night. What about you?"

"They can do without me," Otah said. "Muhatia-cha knows my indenture's almost over. He more than half expects me to ignore my duties. It isn't uncommon for someone who isn't renewing their contract."

"And aren't you?" Maati asked.

"I don't know."

Otah shifted his weight, turning to look at the young poet in the brown robes of his office. The moonlight made them seem black.

"I envy you," Maati said. "You know that, don't you?"

"You want to be directionless and unsure what you'll be doing to earn food in a half-year's time?"

"Yes," Maati said. "Yes, I think I do. You've friends. You've a place. You've possibilities. And . . ."

"And?"

Even in the darkness, Otah could see Maati blush. He took a pose of apology as he spoke.

"You have Liat," Maati said. "She's beautiful."

"She is lovely. But there are any number of women at court. And you're the poet's student. There must be girls who'd take you for a lover."

"There are, I think. Maybe. I don't know, but . . . I don't understand them. I've never known any—not at the school, and then not with the Dai-kvo. They're different."

"Yes," Otah said. "I suppose they are."

Liat. He'd seen her a handful of nights since the audience before the Khai. Since his discovery by Maati. She was busy enough preparing the woman Maj for the sad trade that she hadn't made an issue of his absence, but he had seen something growing in her questions and in her silence.

"Things aren't going so well with Liat," Otah said, surprised that he would admit it even as he spoke. Maati sat straight, pulling himself to some blurry attention. His look of concern was almost a parody of the emotion. He took a pose of query. Otah responded with one that begged ignorance, but let it fall away. "It isn't her. I've been . . . I've been pulling away from her, I think."

"Why?" Maati asked. His incredulity was clear.

Otah wondered how he'd been drawn into this conversation. Maati seemed to have a talent for it, bringing him to say things he'd hardly had the courage to think through fully. It was having someone at last who might understand him. Someone who knew him for what he was, and who had suffered some of the same flavors of loss.

"I've never told Liat. About who I am. Do you think . . . Maati, can you love someone and not trust them?"

"We're born to odd lives, Otah-kvo," Maati said, sounding suddenly older and more sorrowful. "If we waited for people we trusted, I think we might never love anyone."

They were silent for a long moment, then Maati rose.

"I'm going to get some water from the keep, and then find some place to leave him a little of my own," he said, breaking the somber mood. Otah smiled.

"Then we should go."

Maati took a pose that was both regret and agreement, then walked off with a gait for the most part steady. Otah stood, stretching his back and his legs, pulling his blood into action. He tossed a single length of silver onto the bench where they'd sat. It would more than cover their drinks and the bread and cheese they'd eaten. When Maati returned, they struck out for the north, toward the palaces. The streets of the city were moonlit, pale blue light except where a lantern burned at the entrance to a compound or a firekeeper's kiln added a ruddy touch. The calls of night birds, the chirping of crickets, the occasional voice of some other city dweller awake long after the day had ended accompanied them as they walked.

It was all as familiar as his own cot or the scent of the seafront, but the boy at his side also changed it. For almost a third of his life, Otah had been in Saraykeht. He knew the shapes of its streets. He knew which firekeepers could be trusted and which could be bought, which teahouses served equally to all its clientele and which saved the better goods for the higher classes. And he knew his place in it. He would no more have thought about it than about breathing. Except for Maati.

The boy made him look at everything again, as if he were seeing it for the first time. The city, the streets, Liat, himself. Especially himself. Now the thing that he had measured his greatest success—the fact that he knew the city deeply and it did not know him—was harder and emptier than it had once been. And odd that it hadn't seemed so before.

And the memories curled and shifted deep in his mind; the unconnected impressions of a childhood he had thought forgotten, of a time before he'd been sent to the school. There was a face with dark hair and beard that might have been his father. A woman he remembered singing and bathing him when his body had been small enough for her to lift with one arm. He didn't know whether she was his mother or a nurse or a sister. But there had been a fire in the grate, and the tub had been worked copper, and he had been young and amazed by it.

And over the days and nights, other half-formed things had joined together in his mind. He remembered his mother handing him a cloth rabbit, sneaking it into his things so that his father wouldn't see it. He remembered an older boy shouting—his brother, perhaps—that it wasn't fair that Otah be sent away, and that he had felt guilty for causing so much anger. He remembered the name Oyin Frey, and an old man with a long white beard playing a drum and singing, but not who the man was or how he had known him.

He couldn't say which of the memories were truth, which were dreams he'd constructed himself. He wondered, if he were to travel back there, far in the north, whether these ghost memories would let him retrace paths he hadn't walked in years—know the ways from nursery to kitchen to the tunnels beneath Machi—or if they would lead him astray, false as bog-lights.

And the school—Tahi-kvo glowering at him, and the whirr of the lacquer rod. He had pushed those things away, pushed away the boy who had suffered those losses and humiliations, and now it was like being haunted. Haunted by who he might be and might have been.

"I think I've upset you, Otah-kvo," Maati said quietly.

Otah turned, taking a questioning pose. Maati's brow furrowed and he looked down.

"You haven't spoken since we left the teahouse," Maati said. "If I've given offense . . ."

Otah laughed, and the sound seemed to reassure Maati. On impulse, Otah put his arm around Maati's shoulder as he might have around a dear friend or a brother.

"I'm sorry. I seem to be doing this to everyone around me these days. No, Maati-kya, I'm not upset. You just make me think about things, and I must be out of practice. I get lost in them. And gods, but I'm tired."

"You could stay at the poet's house if you don't care to walk back to your quarters. There's a perfectly good couch on the lower floor."

"No," Otah said. "If I don't let Muhatia-cha scold me in the morning, he'll get himself into a rage by midday."

Maati took a pose of understanding that also spoke of regret, and put his own arm around Otah's shoulder. They walked together, talking now the same mixture of seriousness and jokes that they'd made yet another evening of. Maati was getting better at navigating the streets, and even when the route he chose wasn't the fastest, Otah let him lead. He wondered, as they approached the monument of the Emperor Atami where three wide streets met, what it would have been like to grow up with a brother.

"Otah?" Maati said, his stride suddenly slowing. "That man there. The one in the cloak."

Otah glanced over. The man was walking away from them, heading to the east, and alone. Maati was right, though. It was the same man who'd been sleeping at the teahouse, or pretending to. Otah stepped away from Maati, freeing his arms in case he needed to fight. It wouldn't have been the first time that someone from the palaces had been followed from a teahouse and assaulted for the copper they carried.

"Come with me," Otah said and walked out to the middle of the wide area where the streets converged. Emperor Atami loomed above them, sad-eyed in the darkness. Otah turned slowly, considering each street, each building.

"Otah-kvo?" Maati said, his voice uncertain. "Was he following us?"

There was no one there, only the too-familiar man retreating to the east. Otah counted twenty breaths, but no one appeared. No shadows moved. The night was empty.

"Perhaps," he said, answering the question. "Probably. I don't know. Let's keep going. And if you see anything, tell me."

The rest of the distance to the palaces, Otah kept them on wide streets where they would see men coming. He would send Maati running for help and buy what time he could. A fine plan unless there were several of them or they had knives. But nothing happened, and Maati safely wished him good night.

By the time Otah reached his own quarters, the fear he'd felt was gone, the bone-weariness taken back over. He fell onto his cot and pulled the netting closed. Exhaustion pressed him to the rough canvas of the cot. The snores and sleeping murmurs of his cohort should have lulled him to sleep. But tired as he was, sleep wouldn't come. In the darkness, his mind turned from problem to problem—they'd been followed by someone who might still be tracking Maati; his indenture was almost over and he would be too weary to work when the dawn came; he had never told Liat of his past. As he turned his mind to one, another distracted him, until he was only chasing his thoughts and being chased by them. He didn't notice when he slipped into dream.

LIAT LEFT MARCHAT WILSIN'S OFFICES WITH HER SPINE STRAIGHT AND RAGE brewing. She walked through the compound to her cell without looking down and without catching anyone's gaze. She closed the door behind her, fastened the shutters so that no one could happen to look in, then sat at her desk and wept.

It was profoundly unfair. She had done everything she could—she'd studied the etiquette, she'd taken the island girl to all the appointments at their appointed times, she'd negotiated with the poet even when he'd made it perfectly clear that he'd be as pleased to have her out of the room—and it was Itani that defeated her. Itani!

She stripped off her outer robe, flinging it to the bed. She wrenched open her wardrobe and looked for another, a better one. One more expressive of wrath.

It's not entirely appropriate, Wilsin-cha still said in her mind. So close to a formal trade it might give the impression that the house was still seeking some advantage after the agreements had been made.

It might, she knew he'd meant, make her look like an idiot sending her lover to try to win favor. And worse, Itani—sweet, gentle, smiling Itani—hadn't even told her. The nights she'd spent working, imagining him with his cohort or in his quarters, waiting for her to complete her task with the sad trade, he'd been out spoiling things for her. Out with the student poet. He hadn't thought of what it would look like, what it would imply about her.

And he hadn't even told her.

She plucked a formal robe, red shot with black, pulled it on over her inner robes, and tied it fast. She braided her hair, pulling back severely. When she was done, she lifted her chin as she imagined Amat Kyaan would have and stalked out into the city.

The streets were still bustling, the business day far from ended. The sun, still eight or nine hands above the horizon, pressed down and the air was wet and stifling and still, and it reeked of the sea. Itani would still be with his cohort, but she wasn't going to wait and risk letting her anger mellow. She would find out what Itani meant by this. She'd have an explanation for Wilsin-cha, and she'd have it now, before the trade was finished. Tomorrow was the only day left to make things right.

At his quarters, she found that he hadn't gone out with the others after all—he'd been out too late and pled illness when Muhatia-cha came to gather them. The club-foot boy who watched the quarters during the working hours assured her with obvious pleasure that Muhatia-cha had been viciously angry.

So whatever it was that Itani was up to, it was worth risking his indenture as well as her standing with Wilsin-cha. Liat thanked the club-foot boy and asked, with a formal pose, where she might find Itani-cha since he was not presently in his quarters. The boy shrugged and rattled off teahouses, bathhouses, and places of ease along the seafront. It was nearly two full hands before Liat tracked him down at a cheap bathhouse near the river, and her temper hadn't calmed.

She stalked into the bath without bothering to remove her robes. The great tiled walls echoed with conversations that quieted as she passed. The men and women in the public baths considered her, but Liat only moved on, ignoring them. Pretending to ignore them. Acting as Amat would have. Itani had taken a private room to one side. She strode down the short corridor of rough, wet stone, paused, breathed deeply twice as if there was something in the thick, salt-scented air that might fortify her, and pushed her way in.

Itani sat in the pool as if at a table, bent slightly forward, his eyes on the surface of the water like a man lost in thought. He looked up as she slammed the door closed behind her, and his eyes spoke of weariness and preparedness. Liat took a pose of query that bordered on accusation.

"I meant to come look for you, love," he said.

"Oh really?" she said.

"Yes."

His eyes returned to the shifting surface of the water. His bare shoulders hunched forward. Liat stepped to the edge of the pool and stared down at him, willing his gaze up to hers. He didn't look.

"There's a conversation we need to have, love," he said. "We should have done before, I suppose, but . . ."

"What are you thinking? Itani? What are you doing? Wilsin-cha just spent half a hand very quietly telling me that you've been making a fool of me before the utkhaiem. What are you doing with the poet's student?"

"Maati," Itani said, distantly. "He's named Maati."

If Liat had had anything to throw, she'd have launched it at Itani's bowed head. Instead, she let out an exasperated cry and stamped her foot. Itani looked up, his vision swimming into focus as if he was waking from a dream. He smiled his charming, open, warm smile.

"Itani. I'm humiliated before the whole court, and you—"

"How?"

"What?"

"How? How is my drinking at a teahouse with Maati humiliating to you?"

"It makes it look as if I were trying to leverage some advantage after the agreements are complete," she snapped.

Itani took a pose that requested clarification.

"Isn't that most of what goes on between the harvest and completing the contracts? I thought Amat Kyaan was always sending you with letters arguing over interpretations of language."

It was true, but it hadn't occurred to her when Wilsin-cha sat been sitting across his table from her with that terrible expression of pity. Playing for advantage had never stopped because a contract had been signed.

"It's not the same," she said. "This is with the Khai. You don't do that with the Khai."

"I'm sorry, then," Itani said. "I didn't know. But I wasn't trying to change your negotiation."

"So what were you doing?"

Itani scooped up a double handful of water and poured it over his head. His long, northern face took on a look of utter calm, and he breathed deeply twice. He nodded to himself, coming to some private decision. When he spoke, his voice was almost conversational.

"I knew Maati when we were boys. We were at the school together."

"What school?"

"The school where the courts send their disowned sons. Where they choose the poets."

Liat frowned. Itani looked up.

"What were you doing there?" Liat asked. "You were a servant? You never told me you were a servant as a child."

"I was the son of the Khai Machi. The sixth son. My name was Otah Machi then. I only started calling myself Itani after I left, so that my family couldn't find me. I left without taking the brand, so it would have been dangerous to go by my true name."

His smile faltered, his gaze shifted. Liat didn't move—couldn't move. It was ridiculous. It was laughable. And yet she wasn't laughing. Her anger was gone like a candle snuffed by a strong wind, and she was only fighting to take in breath. It couldn't be true, but it was. She knew he wasn't lying. Before her and below her, Itani's eyes were brimming with tears. He coughed out something like mirth and wiped his eyes with the back of his bare hand.

"I've never told anyone," he said, "until now. Until you."

"You . . ." Liat began, then had to stop, swallow, begin again. "You're the son of the Khai Machi?"

"I didn't tell you at first because I didn't know you. And then later because I hadn't before. But I love you. And I trust you. I do. And I want you to be with me. Will you forgive me?"

"Is this . . . are you lying to me, Tani?"

"No," he said. "It's truth. You can ask Maati if you'd like. He knows as well."

Liat's throat was too tight to speak. Itani rose and lifted his arms up to her in supplication, the water flowing down his naked chest, fear in his eyes—fear that she would turn away from him. She melted down into the water, into his arms. Her robes, drinking in the water, were heavy as weights, but she didn't care. She pulled him to her, pulled him close, pressed her face against his. There were tears on their cheeks, but she didn't know whether they were hers or his. His arms surrounded her, lifted her, safe and strong and amazing.

"I knew," she said. "I knew you were something. I knew there was something about you. I always knew."

He kissed her then. It was unreal—like something out of an old epic story. She, Liat Chokavi, was the lover of the hidden child of the Khai Machi. He was hers. She pulled back from him, framing his face with her hands, staring at him as if seeing him for the first time.

"I didn't mean to hurt you," he said.

"Am I hurt?" she asked. "I could fly, love. I could fly."

Her held her fiercely then, like a drowning man holding the plank that might save him. And she matched him before pulling off her ruined robes and letting them sink into the bath like water plants at their ankles. Skin to skin they stood, the bath cool around their hips, and Liat let her heart sing with the thought that one day, her lover might take his father's seat and power. One day, he might be Khai.

9

>+< Maati started awake when Heshai-kvo's hand touched his shoulder. The poet drew back, his wide frog-mouth quirking up at the ends. Maati sat up and pushed the netting aside. His head felt stuffed with cotton.

"I have to leave soon," Heshai-kvo said, his voice low and amused. "I didn't want to leave you to sleep through the whole day. Waking at sundown only makes the next day worse."

Maati took a pose of query. It didn't specify a question, but Heshai-kvo took the sense of it.

"It's just past midday," he said.

"Gods," Maati said and pulled himself up. "I apologize, Heshai-kvo. I will be ready in . . ."

Heshai-kvo lumbered to the doorway, waving his protests away. He was already wearing the brown formal robes and his sandals were strapped on.

"Don't. There's nothing going on you need to know. I just didn't want you to feel ill longer than you needed to. There's fruit downstairs, and fresh bread. Sausage if you can stomach it, but I'd start slow if I were you."

Maati took a pose of apology.

"I have failed in my duties, Heshai-kvo. I should not have stayed in the city so long nor slept so late."

Heshai-kvo clapped his hands in mock anger and pointed an accusing hand at Maati.

"Are you the teacher here?"

"No, Heshai-kvo."

"Then I'll decide when you're failing your duties," he said and winked.

When he was gone, Maati lay back on his cot and pressed his palm to his forehead. With his eyes closed, he felt as if the cot was moving, floating down some silent river. He forced his eyes back open, aware as he did that he'd already fallen halfway back to sleep. With a sigh, he forced himself up, stripped off his robes in trade for clean ones, and went down to the breakfast Heshai-kvo had promised.

The afternoon stretched out hot and thick and sultry before him. Maati bathed himself and straightened his belongings—something he hadn't done in days. When the servant came to take away the plates and leavings, Maati asked that a pitcher of limed water be sent up.

By the time it arrived, he'd found the book he wanted, and went out to sit under the shade of trees by the pond. The world smelled rich and green as fresh-cut grass as he arranged himself. With only the buzzing of insects and the occasional wet plop of koi striking the surface, Maati opened the brown leather book and read. The first page began:

Not since the days of the First Empire have poets worked more than one binding in a lifetime. We may look back at the prodigality of those years with longing now, knowing as they did not that the andat unbound would likely not be recovered. But the price of our frugality is this: we as poets have made our first work our last like a carpenter whose apprentice chair must also be the masterwork for which he is remembered. As such it becomes our duty to examine our work closely so that later generations may gain from our subtle failures. It is in this spirit that I, Heshai Antaburi, record the binding I performed as a child of the andat Removing-The-Part-That-Would-Continue along with my notes on how I would have avoided error had I known my heart better.

Heshai-kvo's handwriting was surprisingly beautiful, and the structure of the volume as compelling as an epic. He began with the background of the andat and what he hoped to accomplish by it. Then, in great detail, the work of translating the thought, moving it from abstract to concrete, giving it form and flesh. Then, when the story of the binding was told, Heshai-kvo turned back on it, showing the faults where an ancient grammar allowed an ambiguity, where form clashed with intent. Discords that Maati would never, he thought, have noticed were spread before him with a candor that embarrassed him. Beauty that edged to arrogance, strength that fed willfulness, confidence that was also contempt. And with that, how each error had its root in Heshai's own soul. And while reading these confessions embarrassed him, they also fed a small but growing respect for his teacher and the courage it took to put such things to paper.

The sun had fallen behind the treetops and the cicadas begun their chorus when Maati reached the third section of the book, what Heshai called his corrected version. Maati looked up and found the andat on the bridge, looking back at him. The perfect planes of his cheeks, the amused intelligence in his eyes. Maati's mind was still half within the work that had formed them.

Seedless took a pose of greeting formal and beautiful, and strode across the rest of the span towards him. Maati closed the book.

"You're being studious," Seedless said as he drew near. "Fascinating isn't it? Useless, but fascinating."

"I don't see why it would be useless."

"His corrected version is too near what he did before. I can't be bound the same way twice. You know that. So writing a variation on a complete work makes about as much sense as apologizing to someone you've just killed. You don't mind that I join you."

The andat stretched out on the grass, his dark eyes turned to the south and the palaces and invisible beyond them, the city. The perfect fingers plucked at the grass.

"It lets others see the mistakes he made," Maati said.

"If it showed them the mistakes *they* were making, it would be useful," Seedless said. "Some errors you can only see once you've committed them."

Maati took a pose that could be taken as agreement or mere politeness. Seedless smiled and pitched a blade of grass toward the water.

"Where's Heshai-kvo?"

"Who knows? The soft quarter, most likely. Or some teahouse that rents out rooms by the ships. He's not looking to tomorrow with glee in his heart. And what about you, my boy? You've turned out to be a better study than I'd have guessed. You've already mastered staying out, consorting with men below your station, and missing meetings. It took Heshai years to really get the hang of that."

"Bitter?" Maati said. Seedless laughed and shifted to look at him directly. The beautiful face was rueful and amused.

"I had a bad day," the andat said. "I found something I'd lost, and it turned out not to have been worth finding. And you? Feeling ready for the grand ceremony tomorrow?"

Maati took a pose of affirmation. The andat grinned, and then like a candle melting, his expression turned to something else, something conflicted that Maati couldn't entirely read. The cicadas in their trees went silent suddenly as if they were a single voice. A moment later, they began again.

"Is there . . ." the andat said, and trailed off, taking a pose that asked for silence while Seedless reconsidered his words. Then, "Maati-kya. If there was something you wanted of me. Some favor you would ask of me, even now. Something that I might do or . . . or forbear. Ask, and I'll do it. Whatever it is. For you, I'll do it."

Maati looked at the pale face, the skin that seemed to glow like porcelain in the failing light.

"Why?" Maati asked. "Why would you offer that to me?"

Seedless smiled and shifted with the sound of fine cloth against grass.

"To see what you'd ask," Seedless said.

"What if I asked for something you didn't want to give me?"

"It would be worth it," Seedless said. "It would tell me something about your heart, and knowing that would be justify some very high prices. Anything you want to have started, or anything you want to stop."

Maati felt the beginning of a blush and shifted forward, considering the surface of the pond and the fish—pale and golden—beneath it. When he spoke, his voice was low.

"Tomorrow, when the time comes for the . . . when Heshai-kvo is set to finish the sad trade, don't fight him. I saw the two of you with the cotton when I first came, and I've seen you since. You always make him force you. You always make him struggle to accomplish the thing. Don't do that to him tomorrow."

Seedless nodded, a sad smile on his perfect, soft lips.

"You're a sweet boy. You deserve better than us," the andat said. "I'll do as you ask."

They sat in silence as the sunlight faded—the stars glimmering first a few, then a handful, then thousands upon thousands. The palaces glowed with lanterns, and sometimes Maati caught a thread of distant music.

"I should light the night candle," Maati said.

"If you wish," Seedless said, but Maati found he wasn't rising or returning to the house. Instead, he was staring at the figure before him, a thought turning restlessly in his mind. The subtle weight of the leather book in his sleeve and Seedless' strange, quiet expression mixed and shifted and moved him.

"Seedless-cha. I was wondering if I might ask you a question. Now, while we're still friends."

"Now you're playing on my sentiments," the andat said, amused. Maati took a pose of cheerful agreement and Seedless replied with acceptance. "Ask."

"You and Heshai-kvo are in a sense one thing, true?"

"Sometimes the hand pulls the puppet, sometimes the puppet pulls the hand, but the string runs both ways. Yes."

"And you hate him."

"Yes."

"Mustn't you also hate yourself, then?"

The andat shifted to a crouch and with the air of a man considering a painting, looked up at the poet's house, dark now in the starlight. He was silent for so long that Maati began to wonder if he would answer at all. When he did speak, his voice was little above a whisper.

"Yes," he said. "Always."

Maati waited, but the andat said nothing more. At last, Maati gathered his things and rose to go inside. He paused beside the unmoving andat and touched Seedless' sleeve. The andat didn't move, didn't speak, accepted no more comfort than a stone would. Maati went to the house and lit the night candle and lemon candles to drive away the insects, and prepared himself for sleep.

Heshai returned just before dawn, his robes stained and reeking of cheap wine. Maati helped him prepare for the audience, the sad trade, the ceremony. Fresh robes, washed hair, fresh-shaved chin. The redness of his eyes, Maati could do nothing for. Throughout, Seedless haunted the corners of the room, unusually silent. Heshai drank little, ate less, and as the sun topped the trees, lumbered out and down the path with Maati and Seedless following.

It was a lovely day, clouds building over the sea and to the east, towering white as cotton and taller than mountains. The palaces were alive with servants and slaves and the utkhaiem moving gracefully about their business. And the poets, Maati supposed, moving about theirs.

The party from House Wilsin was at the low hall before them. The pregnant girl stood outside, attended by servants, fidgeting with the skirts that were designed for the day, cut to protect her modesty but not catch the child as it left her. Maati felt the first real qualm pass over him. Heshai-kvo marched past woman and servants and slaves, his bloodshot eyes looking, Maati guessed, for Liat Chokavi who was, after all, overseeing the trade.

They found her inside the hall, pacing and muttering to herself under her breath. She was dressed in white robes shot with blue: mourning colors. Her hair was pulled back to show the softness of her cheek, the curve of her neck. She was beautiful—the sort of woman that Otah-kvo would love and that would love him in return. Her gaze rose as they entered, the three of them, and she took a pose of greeting.

"Can we do this thing?" Heshai-kvo snapped, only now that Maati had known the man longer, he heard the pain underneath the gruffness. The dread.

"The physician will be here shortly," Liat said.

"He's late?"

"We're early, Heshai-kvo," Maati said gently.

The poet glared at him, then shrugged and moved to the far end of the hall to stare sullenly out the window. Seedless, meeting Maati's gaze, pursed his lips, shrugged and walked out into the sunlight. Maati, left alone before the woman, took a pose of formal greeting which she returned.

"Forgive Heshai-kvo," Maati said softly enough to keep his voice from carrying. "He hates the sad trade. It . . . it would be a very long story, and likely not worth the telling. Only don't judge him too harshly from this."

"I won't," Liat said. Her manner was softer, less formal. She seemed, in fact, on the verge of grinning. "Itani told me about it. He mentioned you as well."

"He has been very kind in . . . showing me the city," Maati said, taken by surprise. "I knew very little about Saraykeht before I came here."

Liat smiled and touched his sleeve.

"I should thank you," she said. "If it wasn't for you, I don't know when he would have gotten the courage to tell me about . . . about his family."

"Oh," Maati said. "Then he . . . you know?"

She took a pose of confirmation that implied a complicity Maati found both thrilling and uneasing. The secret was now shared among three. And that was as many as could ever know. In a way, it bound them, he and Liat. Two people who shared some kind of love for Otah-kvo.

"Perhaps we will be able to know each other better, once the trade is completed," Maati said. "The three of us, I mean."

"I would like that," Liat said. She grinned, and Maati found himself grinning back. He wondered what they would look like to someone else—the student poet and the trade house overseer beaming at each other just before the sad trade. He forced himself into a more sober demeanor.

"The woman, Maj," he said. "All went well with her, I hope?"

Liat shrugged and leaned closer to him. She smelled of an expensive perfume, earthy and rich more than floral, like fresh turned soil.

"Keep it between us, but she's been a nightmare," Liat said. "She means well, I suppose, but she's flighty as a child and doesn't seem to remember what I've told her from one day to the next."

"Is she . . . simple?"

"I don't think so. Only . . . unconcerned, I suppose. They have different ways of looking at things on Nippu. Her translator told me about it. They don't think the child's a person until it draws its first breath, so she didn't even want to wear mourning colors."

"Really? I hadn't heard that. I thought the Eastern Islands were . . . stricter, I suppose. If that's the way to say it."

"Apparently not."

"Is he here? The translator?"

"No," Liat said, taking a pose that expressed her impatience. "No, something came up and he had to leave. Wilsin-cha had him teach me all the phrases I need to know for the ceremony. I've been practicing. I can't tell you how pleased I'll be to have this over."

Maati looked over to his teacher. Heshai-kvo stood at the window, still as a statue, his expression bleak. Seedless leaned against the wall near the wide double doors of the entrance, his arms folded, staring at the poet's back. The perfect attention reminded Maati of a feral dog tracking its prey.

The physician arrived at the appointed hour with his retinue. Maj, blushing and pulling at her skirts, was brought inside, and Liat took her post beside her as Maati took his with Heshai-kvo and Seedless. The servants and slaves retreated a respectful distance, and the wide doors were closed. Heshai-kvo seemed bent as if he were carrying a load. He gestured to Liat, and she stepped forward and adopted a pose appropriate to the opening of a formal occasion.

"Heshai-cha," she said. "I come before you as the representative of House Wilsin in this matter. My client has paid the Khai's fee and the accountancy has weighed her payment and found it in accordance with our arrangement. We now ask that you complete your part of the contract."

"Have you asked her if she's sure?" Heshai-kvo asked. His words were not formal, and he took no pose with them. His lips were pressed thin and his face grayish. "Is she certain?"

Liat blinked, startled, Maati thought, by the despair in his teacher's voice. He wished now that he had explained to Liat why this was so hard for Heshai. Or perhaps it didn't matter. Really, it only needed to be finished and behind them.

"Yes," Liat said, also breaking with the formality of the ceremony.

"Ask her again," Heshai said, half demanding, half pleading. "Ask if there isn't another way."

A glimmer of stark terror lit Liat's eyes and vanished. Maati understood. It was not one of the phrases she'd been taught. She had no way to comply. She raised her chin, her eyes narrowing in a way that made her look haughty and condescending, but Maati thought he could see the panic in her.

"Heshai-kvo," he said, softly. "Please, may we finish this thing."

His teacher looked over, first annoyed, then sadly resigned. He took a pose that retracted the request. Liat's eyes shifted to Maati's with a look of gratitude. The physician took his cue and stepped forward, certifying that the woman was in good health, and that the removal of the child posed no great risk to her well-being. Heshai took a pose that thanked him. The physician led Maj to the split-seated stool and sat her in it, then silently placed the silver bowl beneath her.

"I hate this," Heshai murmured, his voice so low that no one could hear him besides Maati and Seedless. Then he took a formal pose and declaimed. "In the name of the Khai Saraykeht and the Dai-kvo, I put myself at your service."

Liat turned to the girl and spoke in liquid syllables. Maj frowned and her wide, pale lips pursed. Then she nodded and said something in return. Liat shifted back to the poet and took a pose of acceptance.

"You're ready?" Heshai asked, his eyes on Maj's. The island girl tilted her head, as if hearing a sound she almost recognized. Heshai raised his eyebrows and sighed. Without any visible bidding, Seedless stepped forward, graceful as a dancer. There was a light in his eyes, something like joy. Maati felt an inexplicable twist in his belly.

"No need to struggle, old friend," Seedless said. "I promised your apprentice that I wouldn't make you fight me for this one. And you see, I can keep my word when it suits me."

The silver bowl chimed like an orange had been dropped in it. Maati looked over, and then away. The thing in the bowl was only settling, he told himself, not moving. Not moving.

And with an audible intake of breath, the island girl began to scream. The pale blue eyes were open so wide, Maati could see the whites all the way around the iris. Her wide lips pulled back until they were thin as string. Maj bent down, and her hands would have touched the thing in the bowl, cradled it, if the physician had not whisked it away. Liat could only hold the woman's hands and look at her, confused, while shriek after shriek echoed in the empty spaces of the hall.

"What?" Heshai-kvo said, his voice fearful and small. "What happened?"

10

>+< Amat Kyaan walked the length of the seafront with the feeling of a woman half-awakened from nightmare. The morning sun made the waters too bright to look at. Ships rested at the docks, taking on cloth or oils or sugar or else putting off brazil blocks and indigo, wheat and rye, wine and Eddensea marble. The thin stalls still barked with commerce, banners shifting in the breeze. The gulls still wheeled and complained. It was like walking into a memory. She had passed this way every day for years. How quickly it had become unfamiliar.

Leaning on her cane, she passed the wide mouth of the Nantan and into the warehouse district. The traffic patterns in the streets had changed—the rhythm of the city had shifted as it did from season to season. The mad rush of harvest was behind them, and though the year's work was still far from ended, the city had a sense of completion. The great trick that made Saraykeht the center of all cotton trade had been performed once more, and now normal men and women would spend their hours and days changing that advantage into power and wealth and prestige.

She could also feel its unease. Something had happened to the poet. Only listening from her window during the evening, she'd heard three or four different stories about what had happened. Every conversation she walked past was the same—something had happened to the poet. Something to do with House Wilsin and the sad trade. Something terrible. The young men and women in the street smiled as they told each other, excited by the sense of crisis and too young or too poor or too ignorant for the news of yesterday's events to sicken them with dread. That was for older people. People who understood.

Amat breathed deeply, catching the scent of the sea, the perfume of grilling meat at the stalls, the unpleasant stench of the dyers' vats that reached even from several streets away. Her city, with its high summer behind it. In her heart, she still found it hard to believe that she had returned to it, that she was not still entombed in the back office of Ovi Niit's comfort house. And as she walked, leaning heavily on her cane, she tried not to wonder what the men and women said about her as she passed.

At the bathhouse, the guards looked at her curiously as they took their poses. She didn't even respond, only walked forward into the tiled rooms with their echoes and the scent of cedar and fresh water. She shrugged off her robes and went past the public baths to Marchat Wilsin's little room at the back, just as she always had.

He looked terrible.

"Too hot," he said as she lowered herself into the water. The lacquer tray danced a little on the waves she stirred, but didn't spill the tea.

"You always say that," Amat Kyaan said. Marchat sighed and looked away. There were bags under his eyes, dark as bruises. His face, scowl-set, held a grayish cast. Amat leaned forward and pulled the tea closer.

"So," she said. "I take it things went well."

"Don't."

Amat sipped tea from her bowl and considered him. Her employer, her friend.

"Then what is there left for us to say?" she asked.

"There's business," Marchat said. "The same as always."

"Business, then. I take it that things went well."

He shot an annoyed glance at her, then looked away.

"Couldn't we start with the contracts with the dyers?"

"If you'd like," Amat said. "Was there something pressing with them?"

Her voice carried the whole load of sarcasm to cover the outrage and anger. And fear. Marchat took a clumsy pose of surrender and acquiescence before reaching over and taking his own bowl of tea from the tray.

"I'm going to a meeting with the Khai and several of the higher utkhaiem. Spend the whole damn time falling on my sword over the sad trade. I've promised a full investigation."

"And what are you going to find?"

"The truth, I imagine. That's the secret of a good lie, you know. Coming to a place where you believe it yourself. I expect our investigation—or anyone else's—will show it was Oshai, the translator. He and his men plotted the whole thing under the direction of the andat Seedless. They found the girl, they brought her to us under false pretenses. I have letters of introduction that I'll turn over to the Khai's men. They'll discover that the letters are forged. House Wilsin will be looked upon as a collection of dupes. At best, it will take us years to recover our reputation."

"It's a small price," Amat said. "What if they find Oshai?"

"They won't."

"You're sure of that?"

"Yes," Wilsin said with a great sigh. "I'm sure."

"And Liat?"

"Still being questioned," Marchat said. "I imagine she'll be out by the end of the day. We'll need to do something for her. To make this right. She's not going to come out of this with a reputation for competence intact. They've already spoken with the island girl. She didn't have anything very coherent to say, I'm afraid. But it's over, Amat. That's really the only bright thing I can say of the whole stinking business. The worst that was going to happen has happened, and now we can get to cleaning up after it and moving on."

"And what's the truth?"

"What I told you," he said. "That's the truth. It's the only truth that matters."

"No. The real truth. Who sent those pearls? And don't tell me the spirit conjured them out of the sea."

"Who knows?" Marchat said. "Oshai told us they were from Nippu, from the girl's family. We had no reason to think otherwise."

Amat slapped the water. She felt the rage pulling her brow together. Marchat met her anger with his. His pale face flushed red, his chin slid forward belligerently like a boy in a play yard.

"I am saving you," he said. "And I am saving the house. I am doing everything I can to kill this thing and bury it, and by all the gods, Amat, I know as well as you that it was rotten, but what do you want me to do about it? Trot up to the Khai and apologize? Where did the pearls come from? Galt, Amat. They came from Acton and Lanniston and Cole.

Who arranged the thing? Galts. And who will pay for this if that story is proved instead of mine? I'll be killed. You'll be exiled if you're lucky. The house will be destroyed. And do you think it'll stop there, Amat? Do you? Because I don't."

"It was evil, Marchat."

"Yes. Yes, it was evil. Yes, it was wrong," he said, motioning so violently that his tea splashed, the red tint of if diffusing quickly in the bath. "But it was decided before anyone consulted us. By the time you or I or any of us were told, it was already too late. It needed doing, and so we've done it.

"Tell me, Amat, what happens if you're the Khai Saraykeht and you find out your pet god's been conspiring with your trade rivals? Do you stop with the tools, because that's all we are. Tools. Or do you teach a lesson to the Galts that they won't soon forget? We haven't got any andat of our own, so there's nothing to restrain you. We can't hit back. Do our crops fail? Do all the women with child in Galt lose their children over this? They're as innocent as that island girl, Amat. They've done as little to deserve that as she has."

"Lower your voice," Amat said. "Someone will hear you."

Marchat leaned back, glancing nervously at the windows, the door. Amat shook her head.

"That was a pretty speech," she said. "Did you practice it?"

"Some, yes."

"And who were you hoping to convince with it? Me, or yourself?"

"Us," he said. "Both of us. It's true, you know. The price would be worse than the crime, and innocent people would suffer."

Amat considered him. He wanted so badly for it to be true, for her to agree. He was like a child, a boy. It made her feel weighted down.

"I suppose it is," she said. "So. Where do we go from here?"

"We clean up. We try to limit the damage. Ah, and one thing. The boy Itani? Do you know why the young poet would call him Otah?"

Amat let herself be distracted. She turned the name over in her mind, searching for some recollection. Nothing came. She put her bowl of tea on the side of the bath and took a pose pleading ignorance.

"It sounds like a northern name," she said. "When did he use it?"

"I had a man follow them. He overheard them speaking."

"It doesn't match anything Liat's told me of him."

"Well. Well, we'll keep a finger on it and see if it moves. Damned strange, but nothing's come from it yet."

"What about Maj?"

"Who? Oh, the girl. Yes. We'll need to keep her close for another week or two. Then I'll have her taken home. There's a trading company making a run to the east at about the right time. If the Khai's men are done with her, I'll pay her passage with them. Otherwise, it may be longer."

"But you'll see her back home safely."

"It's what I can do," Marchat said.

They sat in silence for a long minute. Amat's heart felt like lead in her breast. Marchat was as still as if he'd drunk poison. Poor Wilsin-cha, she thought. He's trying so hard to make this conscionable, but he's too wise to believe his own arguments.

"So, then," she said, softly. "The contracts with the dyers. Where do we stand with them?"

Marchat's gaze met hers, a faint smile on his bushy lips. For almost two hands, he brought her up to date on the small doings of House Wilsin. The agreements they'd negotiated with Old Sanya and the dyers, the problems with the shipments from Obar State, the tax statements under review by the utkhaiem. Amat listened, and without meaning to she moved back into the rhythm of her work. The parts of her mind that held the doings of the house slid back into use, and she pictured all the issues Wilsin-cha brought up and how they would affect each other. She asked questions to confirm that she'd understood and to challenge Marchat to think things through with her. And for a while, she could almost pretend that nothing had happened, that she still felt what she had, that the house she had served so long was still what it had been to her. Almost, but not entirely.

When she left, her fingertips were wrinkled from the baths and her mind was clearer. She had several full days work before her just to put things back in order. And after that the work of the autumn: first House Wilsin's—she felt she owed Marchat that much—and then perhaps also her own.

THE POET'S HOUSE HAD BEEN FULL FOR TWO DAYS NOW, EVER SINCE Heshai had taken to his bed. Utkhaiem and servants of the Khai and representatives from the great trading houses came to call. They came at all hours. They brought food and drink and thinly-veiled curiosity and tacit recrimination. Maati welcomed them as they came, accepted their gifts, saw them to whatever seats were available. He held poses of gratitude until his shoulders ached. He wanted nothing more than to turn them out—all of them.

The first night had been the worst. Maati had stood outside the door of Heshai-kvo's room and pounded and demanded and begged until the night candle was half-burned. And when the door finally scraped open, it was Seedless who had unbarred it.

Heshai had lain on his cot, his eyes fixed on nothing, his skin pale, his lips slack. The white netting around him reminded Maati of a funeral shroud. He had had to touch the poet's shoulder before Heshai's distracted gaze flickered over to him and then away. Maati took a chair beside him, and stayed there until morning.

Through the night, Seedless had paced the room like a cat looking for a way under a woodpile. Sometimes he laughed to himself. Once, when Maati had drifted into an uneasy sleep, he woke to find the andat on the bed, bent over until his pale lips almost brushed Heshai's ear—Seedless whispering fast, sharp syllables too quietly for Maati to make sense of them. The poet's face was contorted as if in pain and flushed bright red. In the long moment before Maati shouted and pushed the andat away, their gazes locked, and Maati saw Seedless smile even as he murmured his poison.

When the morning came, and the first pounding of visitors, Heshai roused himself enough to order Maati down to greet them. The bar had slid home behind him, and the stream of people had hardly slacked since. They stayed until the first quarter of the night candle had burned, and a new wave arrived before dawn.

"I bring greetings from Annan Tiyan of House Tiyan," an older man said loudly as he stood on the threshold. He had to speak up for his words to carry over the conversation behind Maati. "We had heard of the poet's ill health and wished . . ."

Maati took a brief pose of welcome and gratitude that he didn't begin to mean and ushered the man in. The flock of carrion crows gabbled and talked and waited, Maati knew, for news of Heshai. Maati only took the food they'd brought and laid it out for them to eat, poured their gift wine into bowls as hospitality. And upstairs, Heshai . . . It didn't bear thinking about. A regal man in fine silk robes motioned Maati over and asked him gently what he could do to help the poet in his time of need.

The first sign Maati had that something had changed was the sudden silence. All conversations stopped, and Maati rushed to the front of the house to find himself looking into the dark, angry eyes of the Khai Saraykeht.

"Where is your master?" the Khai demanded, and the lack of an accompanying pose made the words seem stark and terrible.

Maati took a pose of welcome and looked away.

"He is resting, most high," he said.

The Khai looked slowly around the room, a single vertical line appearing between his brows. The visitors all took appropriate poses—Maati could hear the shuffle of their robes. The Khai took a pose of query that was directed to Maati, though his gaze remained on the assembled men.

"Who are these?" the Khai asked.

"Well-wishers," Maati said.

The Khai said nothing, and the silence grew more and more excruciatingly uncomfortable. At last, he moved forward, his hand taking Maati by the shoulder and turning him to the stairs. Maati walked before the Khai.

"When I come down," the Khai said in a calm, almost conversational tone, "any man still here forfeits half his wealth."

At the top of the stairs, Maati turned and led the Khai down the short hall to Heshai's door. He tried it, but it was barred. Maati turned with a pose of apology, but the Khai moved him aside without seeming to notice it.

"Heshai," the Khai said, his voice loud and low. "Open the door."

There was a moment's pause, and then soft footsteps. The bar scraped, and the door swung open. Seedless stepped aside as the Khai entered. Maati followed. The andat leaned the bar against the wall, caught Maati's gaze, and took a pose of greeting appropriate to old friends. Maati felt a surge of anger in his chest, but did nothing more than turn away.

The Khai stood at the foot of Heshai's bed. The poet was sitting up, now. Sometime in the last day, he had changed from his brown ceremonial robes to robes of pale mourning cloth. The wide mouth turned down at the corners and his hair was a wild tangle. The Khai reached up and swept the netting aside. It occurred to Maati how much Khai and andat were similar—the grace, the beauty, the presence. The greatest difference was that the Khai Saraykeht showed tiny lines of age at the corners of his eyes and was not so lovely.

"I have spoken with Marchat Wilsin of House Wilsin," the Khai said. "He extends his apologies. There will be an investigation. It has already begun."

Heshai looked down, but took a pose of gratitude. The Khai ignored it.

"We have also spoken with the girl and the overseer for House Wilsin who negotiated the trade. There are . . . questions."

Heshai nodded and then shook his head as if clearing it. He swung his legs over the edge of the bed and took a pose of agreement.

"As you wish, most high," he said. "I will answer anything I can."

"Not you," the Khai said. "All I require is that you compel your creature."

Heshai looked at Maati and then at Seedless. The wide face went gray, the lips pressed thin. Seedless stiffened and then, slowly as a man wading through deep water, moved to the bedside and took a pose of obeisance before the Khai. Maati moved a step forward before he knew he meant to. His impulse to shield someone—Heshai, the Khai, Seedless—was confused by his anger and a deepening dread.

"I think this was your doing. Am I wrong?" the Khai asked, and Seedless smiled and bowed.

"Of course not, most high," he said.

"And you did this to torment the poet."

"I did."

Andat and Khai were glaring at each other, so only Maati saw Heshai's face. The shock of surprise and then a bleak calm more distressing than rage or weeping. Maati's stomach twisted. This was part of it, he realized. Seedless had planned this to hurt Heshai, and this meeting now, this humiliation, was also part of his intention.

"Where may we find the translator Oshai?" the Khai said.

"I don't know. Careless of me, I know. I've always been bad about keeping track of my toys."

"That will do," the Khai said, and strode to the window. Looking down to the grass at the front of the house, the Khai made a gesture. In the distance, Maati heard a man call out, barking an order.

"Heshai," the Khai Saraykeht said, turning back. "I want you to know that I understand the struggles a poet faces. I've read the old romances. But you . . . you must understand that these little shadow plays of yours hurt innocent people. And they hurt my city. In the last day, I have heard six audiences asking that I lower tariffs to compensate for the risk that the andat will find some way to act against you that might hurt the cotton crop. I have had two of the largest trading houses in the city ask me what I plan to do if the andat escapes. How will I maintain trade then? And what was I to tell them? Eh?"

"I don't know," the poet said, his voice low and rough.

"Nor do I," the Khai said.

Men were tramping up the stairway now. Maati could hear them, and the temptation to go and see what they were doing was almost more than his desire to hear when the Khai said next.

"This stops now," the Khai said. "And if I must be the one to stop it, I will."

The footsteps reached the door and two men in workmen's trousers pushed in, a thick, heavy box between them. Maati saw it was fashioned of wood bound with black iron—small enough that a man might fit inside it but too short to stand, too narrow to sit, too shallow to turn around. He had seen drawings of it in books with the Dai-kvo. They had been books about the excesses of the imperial courts, about their punishments. The men placed the box against Heshai-kvo's wall, took poses of abject obeisance to the Khai, and left quickly.

"Most high," Maati said, his voice thick, "You . . . this is . . ."

"Rest yourself, boy," the Khai said as he stepped to the thing and pulled the bar that opened the iron grate. "It isn't for my old friend Heshai. It's only to keep his things in when he isn't using them."

With a clank, the black iron swung open. Maati saw Seedless' eyes widen for a moment, then an amused smile plucked the perfect lips. Heshai looked on in silence.

"But most high," Maati said, his voice growing stronger. "A poet and his work are connected, if you lock a part of Heshai-kvo into a torture box . . ."

The Khai took a sharp pose that required silence, and Maati's words died. The man's gaze held him until Seedless laughed and stepped between them. For a fleeting moment, Maati almost felt that the andat had moved to protect him from the anger in the Khai's expression.

"You forget, my dear," the andat said, "the most high killed two of his brothers to sit in his chair. He knows more of sacrifice than any of us. Or so the story goes."

"Now, Heshai," the Khai said, but Maati saw no effort in Heshai-kvo as Seedless stepped backward into the box, crouching down, knees bent. The Khai shut the grate, barred it, and slid a spike in to hold the bar in place. The pale face of the andat was crossed with shadows and metal. The Khai turned to the bed, standing still until Heshai adopted a pose that accepted the judgement.

"It doesn't roam free," the Khai said. "When it isn't needed, it goes in its place. This is my order."

"Yes, most high," Heshai said, then lay down and turned away, pulling his sheet over him. The Khai snorted with disgust and turned to leave. At the doorway, he paused.

"Boy," he said, taking a pose of command. Maati answered with an appropriate obeisance. "When your turn comes, do better."

After the Khai and his men were gone, Maati stood, shaking. Heshai didn't move or speak. Seedless in his torture box only crouched, fingers laced with the metal grate, the black eyes peering out. Maati pulled the netting back over his master and went downstairs. No one remained—only the remains of the offerings of sympathy and concern half consumed, and an eerie silence.

Otah-kvo, he thought. *Otah-kvo will know what to do. Please, please let Otah-kvo know what to do.*

He hurried, gathering an apple, some bread, and a jug of water, and taking them to the unmoving poet before changing into fresh robes and rushing out through the palace grounds to the street and down into the city. Halfway to the quarters where Otah-kvo's cohort slept, he noticed he was weeping. He couldn't say for certain when he'd begun.

"ITANI!" MUHATIA-CHA BARKED. "GET DOWN HERE!"

Otah, high in the suffocating heat and darkness near the warehouse roof, grabbed the sides of his ladder and slid down. Muhatia-cha stood in the wide double doors that opened to the light and noise of the street. The overseer had a sour expression, but mixed with something—eagerness, perhaps, or curiosity. Otah stood before him with a pose appropriate to the completion of a task.

"You're wanted at the compound. I don't know what good they think you'll do there."

"Yes, Muhatia-cha."

"If this is just your lady love pulling you away from your duties, Itani, I'll find out."

"I won't be able to tell you unless I go," Otah pointed out and smiled his charming smile, thinking as he did that he'd never meant it less. Muhatia-cha's expression softened slightly, and he waved Otah on.

"Hai! Itani!" Kaimati's familiar voice called out. Otah turned. His old friend was pulling a cart to the warehouse door, but had paused, bracing the load against his knees. "Let us know what you find, eh?"

Otah took a pose of agreement and turned away. It was an illusion, he knew, that the people he passed in the streets seemed to stare at him. There was no reason for the city as a whole to see him pass and think anything of him. Another laborer in a city full of men like him. That it wasn't true did nothing to change the feeling. The sad trade had gone wrong. Liat was involved, as was Maati. For two days, he had seen neither. Liat's cell at the compound had been empty, the poet's house too full for him to think of approaching. Otah had made do with the gossip of the street and the bathhouse.

The andat had broken loose and killed the girl as well as her babe; the child had actually been fathered by the poet himself or the Khai or, least probably, the andat Seedless himself; the poet had killed himself or been killed by the Khai or by the andat; the poet was lying sick at heart. Or the woman was. The stories seemed to bloom like blood poured in water—swirling in all directions and filling all mathematical possibilities. Every story that could be told, including—unremarkably among its legion of fellows—the truth, had been whispered in some corner of Saraykeht in the last day. He had slept poorly, and awakened unrefreshed. Now, he walked quickly, the afternoon sun pushing down on his shoulders and sweat pouring off him.

He caught sight of Liat on the street outside the compound of House Wilsin. He recognized the shape of her body before he could see her face, could read the exhaustion in the slope of her shoulders. She wore mourning robes. He didn't know if they were the same that she'd worn to the ceremony or if the grief was fresher than that. When she caught sight of him, she walked to him. Her eyes were sunken, her skin pale, her lips bloodless. She stepped into his embrace without speaking. It was unseemly, of course, a laborer holding an overseer this way—his cheek pressed to her forehead—in the street. It was too hot for the sensation to be pleasant. She held him fiercely, and he felt the deepness of her breath by the way she pressed against him.

"What happened, love?" he asked, but Liat only shook her head. Otah stroked her unbound hair and waited until, with a shuddering sigh, she pulled back. She didn't release his hand, and he didn't try to reclaim it.

"Come to my cell," she said. "We can talk there."

The compound was subdued, men and women passing quickly though their duties as if nothing had happened, except for the air of tension. Liat led the way in silence, pushed open the door of her cell and pulled him into the shadows. A thin form lay on the cot, swathed in brown robes. Maati sat up, blinking sleep out of his eyes.

"Otah-kvo?" the boy asked.

"He came this morning looking for you," Liat said, letting go of Otah's hand at last and sitting at her desk. "I don't think he'd eaten or had anything to drink since it happened. I brought him here, gave him an apple and some water, put him to bed, and sent a runner to Muhatia-cha."

"I'm sorry," Maati said. "I didn't know where to find you, and I thought Liat-cha might . . ."

"It was a fine plan," Otah said. "It worked. But what happened?"

Maati looked down, and Liat spoke. Her voice was hard as slate and as gray. Speaking softly, she told the story: she'd been fooled by the translator Oshai and the andat at the price of Maj and her babe. Maati took the narrative up: the poet was ill, eating little, drinking less, never leaving his bed. And the Khai, in his anger, had locked Seedless away. As detail grew upon detail, problem upon problem, Otah felt his chest grow tighter. Liat wouldn't meet his gaze, and Otah wished Maati were elsewhere, so that he could take her in his arms. But he also knew there was nowhere else that Maati could turn. It was right that he'd come here. When Maati's voice trailed off at last, Otah realized the boy was looking at him, waiting for something. For a decision.

"So he admitted to it," Otah said, thinking as he spoke. "Seedless confessed to the Khai."

Maati took a pose of confirmation.

"Why?" Otah asked. "Did he really think it would break Heshai-kvo's spirit? That he'd be freed?"

"Of course he did," Liat snapped, but Maati took a more thoughtful expression and shook his head.

"Seedless hates Heshai," Maati said. "It was a flaw in the translation. Or else not a flaw but . . . a part of it. He may have only done it because he knew how badly Heshai would be hurt."

"Heshai?" Liat demanded. "How badly *Heshai* would be hurt? What about Maj? She didn't do anything to deserve this. Nothing!"

"Seedless . . . doesn't care about her," Maati said.

"Will Heshai release him?" Otah asked. "Did it work?"

Maati took a pose that both professed ignorance and apologized for it. "He's not well. And I don't know what confining Seedless will do to him—"

"Who cares?" Liat said. Her voice was bitter. "What does it matter whether Heshai suffers? Why shouldn't he? He's the one who controls the andat. If he was so busy whoring and drinking that he couldn't be bothered to do his work, then he ought to be punished."

"That's not the issue, love," Otah said, his gaze still on Maati.

"Yes, it is," she said.

"If the poet wastes away and dies or if this drives him to take his own life, the andat goes free. Unless . . ."

"I'm not ready," Maati said. "I've only just arrived here, really. A student might study under a full poet for years before he's ready to take on the burden. And even then sometimes people just aren't the right ones. I might not be able to hold Seedless at all."

"Would you try?"

It took a long time before Maati answered, and when he did, his voice was small.

"If I failed, I'd pay his price."

"What's his price?" Liat asked.

"I don't know," Maati said. "The only way to find out is to fail. Death, most likely. But . . . I could try. If there was no one else to."

"That's insane," Liat said, looking to Otah for support. "He can't do that. It would be like asking him to jump off a cliff and see if he could learn to fly on the way down."

"There isn't the choice. There aren't very many successful bindings. There aren't many poets who even try them. There may be no replacement for Seedless, and even if there were, it might not work well with the cotton trade," Maati said. He looked pale and ill. "If no one else can take the poet's place, it's my duty—"

"It hasn't come to that. With luck, it won't," Otah said. "Perhaps there's another poet who's better suited for the task. Or some other andat that could take Seedless' place if he escaped—"

"We could send to the Dai-kvo," Liat said. "He'd know."

"I can't go," Maati said. "I can't leave Heshai-kvo here."

"You can write," Liat said. "Send a courier."

"Can you do that?" Otah asked. "Write it all out, everything: the sad trade, Seedless, how the Khai's responded. What you're afraid may happen. All of it."

Maati nodded.

"How long?" Otah asked.

"I could have it tomorrow. In the morning."

Otah closed his eyes. His belly felt heavy with dread, his hands trembling as if he were about to attack a man or else be attacked. Someone had to carry the message, and it couldn't be Maati. It would be him. He would do it himself. The resolve was simply there, like a decision that had been made long before.

Tahi-kvo's face loomed up in his imagination, and with it, the sense of the school—its cold, bruising days and nights, the emptiness and the cruelty and the sense he had had, however briefly, of belonging. The anger rose in him again, as if it had only been banked all these years. Someone would have to go to the Dai-kvo, and Otah was ready to see the man again.

"Bring it here then," he said. "To Liat's cell. There are always ships leaving for Yalakeht this time of year. I'll find a berth on one."

"You're not going," Liat said. "You can't. Your indenture . . ."

Otah opened the door and moved to one side. He walked Maati out to the passage with a pose that was both a thanks and a promise.

"You're sure of this?" Maati asked.

Otah nodded, then turned away again. When they were alone, the cell fell back into twilight.

"You can't go," Liat said. "I need you to stay. I need someone . . . someone by my side. What happened to Maj, what happened to her baby . . . it was my fault. I let that happen."

He moved to her, sitting on her desk, stroking her silk-smooth cheek with his knuckles. She leaned into him, taking his hand in both of hers and pressing it to her chest.

"I have to. Not just for this. My past is up there. It's the right thing."

"She hasn't stopped crying. She sleeps and she wakes up crying. I went to see her when the utkhaiem released me. She was the first person I went to see. And when she looks at me, and I remember what she was like before . . . I thought she was callous. I thought she didn't care. I didn't see it."

Otah slid down, kneeling on the floor, and put his arms around her.

"The reason you're going," Liat whispered. "It isn't because of me, is it? It isn't to get away from me?"

Otah sat, her head cradled against his shoulder. He could feel his mind working just below the level of thought—what he would need to do, the steps he would have to take. He stroked her hair, smooth as water.

"Of course not, love," he said.

"Because you'll be a great man one day. I can tell. And I'm just an idiot girl who can't keep monsters like Oshai from . . . gods. 'Tani. I didn't see it. I didn't *see* it."

She wept, the sobs shaking her as he cooed and rocked her gently. He rested his chin on her bent head, curling her into him. She smelled of musk and tears. He held her until the sobbing quieted, until his arms ached. Her head lay heavy against him and her breath was almost slow as sleep.

"You're exhausted, love," he said. "Come to bed. You need sleep."

"No," she said, rousing. "No, stay with me. You can't go now."

Gently, he lifted her and carried her to her cot. He sat beside her, her hand wrapping his like vine on brick.

"Three weeks to Yalakeht," he said. "Then maybe two weeks upriver and a day or two on foot. Less than that coming back, since the river trip will be going with the water on the way down. I'll be back before winter, love."

In the light pressing in at the shutters and the door, he could see her eyes, bleary with grief and exhaustion, seeking his. Her face was unlined, relaxed, halfway asleep already.

"You're excited to go," she said. "You *want* to."

And, of course, that was the truth. Otah pressed his palm to her lips, closing them. To her eyes. This wasn't a conversation he was ready to have. Or perhaps only not with her.

He kissed her forehead and waited until she was asleep before he quietly opened her door and stepped out into the light.

11

>+< Amat woke in the darkness, her breath fast, her heart pounding. In her dream, Ovi Niit had been kicking in her door, and even when she'd pulled herself up from sleep's dark waters, it took some time for her to feel certain that the booming reports from the dream hadn't been real. Slowly, the panic waned, and she lay back. Above her, the netting glowed like new copper in the light from the night candle and then slowly became brighter and paler as the cool blue light of dawn crept in through the opened windows. The shutters shifted in the sea-scented breeze.

Her desk was piled with papers. Ink bricks hollowed from use stacked one on another at the head of the stairs, waiting to be carried away. The affairs of the house had fallen into near chaos while she was away. She had spent long nights looking over lists and ledgers and telling herself that she cared for them all the way she once had. That House Wilsin and her work for it had not been poisoned.

Amat sighed, sat up, and pushed the netting aside. Her world since her resurrection had been much the same—nightmares until dawn, gray and empty work and messages and meetings until sunset. At one point, seeing the strain on her face at the end of the day, Marchat had offered to send her away for a week to Chaburi-Tan once the season was over. The house could cover the expenses, he said. And she let herself imagine that time—away from Saraykeht and the seafront and her desk and the soft quarter—though the fantasy was washed by melancholy. It could never actually happen, but it would have been nice.

Instead, Amat Kyaan rose from her bed, pulled on clean robes, and walked out, leaning on her cane, to the corner stall where a girl from the low towns sold fresh berries wrapped in sweet frybread. It was good enough as a meal to see her through to midday. She ate it as she walked back to her apartments, trying to order her day in her mind, but finding it hard to concentrate on shifting meetings and duties back and forth. Simply leaving her mind blank and empty was so much easier.

Her time since the sad trade and her banishment had felt like being ill. She'd moved through her days without feeling them, unable to concentrate, uninterested in her work. Something had broken in her, and pretending it back to fixed wasn't working. She'd half known it wouldn't, and her mind had made plans for her almost without her knowing it.

The man waiting at her door was wearing robes of yellow and silver—the colors of House Tiyan. He was young—sixteen, perhaps seventeen summers. Liat's age. An apprentice, then, but the apprentice of someone high in House Tiyan. There was only one errand that could mean. Amat shifted her schedule in her mind and popped the last of the berry-soaked frybread into her mouth. The young man, seeing her, fell into a pose of greeting appropriate for an honored elder. Amat responded.

"Kyaan-cha," the boy said, "I come on behalf of Annan Tiyan . . ."

"Of course you do," she said, opening her door. "Come inside. You have the listings?"

He hesitated behind her for only a moment. Amat went slowly up the stairs. Her hip was much better since she'd returned to her apartments with her stinging ointment and her own bed. She paused at her basin, washing the red stains from her food off her fingertips before she began handling papers. When she reached her desk, she turned and sat. The boy stood before her. He'd taken the paper from his sleeve—the one she'd sent to his master. She held out her hand, and he gave it to her.

The receipt was signed. Amat smiled and tucked the paper into her own sleeve. It would go with her papers later. The papers she was going to take with her, not the ones for House Wilsin. The box was on the desk under a pile of contracts. Amat shifted it out, into her lap. Dark wood banded by iron, and heavy with jewels and lengths of silver. She handed it to the boy.

"My master . . ." the boy began. "That is, Amat Kyaan-cha, I was wondering if . . ."

"Annan wants to know why I'm having him hold the package," she said, "and he wanted you to find out without making it obvious you were asking."

The boy blushed furiously. Amat took a pose that dismissed the issue.

"It's rude of him, but I'd have done the same in his place. You may tell him that I have always followed Imperial form by caching such things with trusted friends. One of the people who had been doing me this favor is leaving the city, though, so it was time to find a new holder. And, of course, if he should ever care to, I would be pleased to return the favor. It's got nothing to do with that poor island girl."

It wasn't true, of course, but it was convenient. This was the fourth such box she'd sent out to men and women in the city to whom she felt she might be able to appeal if circumstances turned against her again. The receipt was only as good as the honor of the people she stowed the boxes with. And there would be a certain amount of theft, she expected—one jewel replaced by another of less value. A few lengths of silver gone despite the locks. It wasn't likely, though, that if she called for them, her boxes would be empty. And in an emergency, that would be very nearly all Amat cared about.

The boy took a pose of acknowledgement and retreated down the stairs. Amat understood what Saraykeht had taught her through Ovi Niit. She wouldn't be caught without her wealth again. That it was a courtesy of the great families of the Empire before it collapsed gave her something like precedent. Annan wouldn't believe that it was unrelated to Maj and the sad trade, but he would understand from her answer that she didn't want him to gossip about it. That would suffice.

For the next hand and a half, she went through the contracts, making notations here and there—one copy for herself, one for the house. So late in the season, there were few changes to be made in the wording. But each contract carried with it two or three letters outlining the completion or modifications of terms and definitions, and these were the sort of things that would sink a trading house if they weren't watched. She went through the motions, checking the translations of the letters in Galtic and the Khaiate, noting discrepancies, or places where a word might have more than one meaning. It was what she'd done for years, and she did it now mechanically and without joy.

When she reached the last one, she checked that the inks were dry, rolled the different documents in tubes tied with cloth ribbons, and packed them into a light satchel—there were too many to fit in her sleeves. She took her cane, then, and walked out into the city, heading north to the Wilsin compound. Away from the soft quarter.

The agents of the utkhaiem were present when she arrived at the wide courtyard of the house. Servants in fine silks lounged at the edge of the fountain, talking among themselves and looking out past the statue of the Galtic Tree to the street. She hesitated when she saw them, fear pricking at her for no reason she could say. She pushed it aside the way she pushed all her feelings aside these recent days, and strode past them toward Marchat Wilsin's meeting room.

Epani Doru, Wilsin-cha's rat-faced, obsequious master of house, sat before the wide wooden doors of the meeting room. When she came close, he rose taking a pose of welcome just respectful enough to pretend he honored her position.

"I've some issues I'd like Wilsin-cha to see," she said, taking an answering pose.

"He's meeting with men from the court," Epani said, his voice an apology.

Amat glanced at the closed doors and sighed. She took a pose that asked for a duration. Epani answered vaguely, but with a sense that she would be lucky to see her employer's face before sundown.

"It can wait, then," Amat said. "It's about the sad trade? Is that what they're picking at him for?"

"I assume so, Amat-cha," Epani said. "I understand from the servants that the Khai wants the whole thing addressed and forgotten as quickly as possible. There have been requests to lower tariffs."

Amat clucked and shook her head.

"Sour trade, this whole issue," she said. "I'm sorry Wilsin-cha ever got involved in it."

Epani took a pose of agreement and mourning, but Amat thought for a moment there was something in the man's expression. He knew, perhaps. Epani Doru might have been someone who Marchat took into his confidence the way he hadn't taken her. An accomplice to the act. Amat noted her suspicion, tucked it away like a paper into a sleeve, and took a pose of query.

"Liat?"

"In the workrooms, I think," Epani said. "The utkhaiem didn't ask to speak with her."

Amat didn't reply. The workrooms of the compound were a bad place for someone of Liat's rank to be. Preparing packets for the archives, copying documents, checking numbers—all the work done at the low slate tables was better suited for a new clerk, someone who had recently come to the house. Amat walked back to the stifling, still air and the smell of cheap lamp oil.

Liat sat at a table by herself, hunched over. Amat paused, considering the girl. The too-round face had misplaced its youth; Amat could see in that moment what Liat would be when her beauty failed her. A woman, then, and not a lovely one. A dreadful weight of sympathy descended on Amat Kyaan, and she stepped forward.

"Amat-cha," Liat said when she looked up. She took a pose of apology. "I didn't know you had need of me. I would have—"

"I didn't know it either," Amat said. "No fault of yours. Now, what are you working on?"

"Shipments from the Westlands. I was just copying the records for the archive."

Amat considered the pages. Liat's handwriting was clean, legible. Amat remembered days in close heat looking over numbers much like these. She felt her smile tighten.

"Wilsin-cha set you to this?" Amat asked.

"No. No one did. Only I ran out of work, and I wanted to be useful. I'm . . . I don't like being idle these days. It just feels . . ."

"Don't carry it," Amat said, still pretending to look at the written numbers. "It isn't yours."

Liat took a questioning pose. Amat handed her back the pages.

"It's nothing you did wrong," Amat said.

"You're kind."

"No. Not really. There was nothing you could have done to prevent this, Liat. You were tricked. The girl was tricked. The poet and the Khai."

"Wilsin-cha was tricked," Liat said, adding to the list.

Or trapped, Amat thought, but said nothing. Liat rallied herself to smile and took a pose of gratitude.

"It helps to hear someone say it," the girl said. "Itani does when he's here, but I can't always believe him. But with him going . . ."

"Going?"

"North," Liat said, startling as if she'd said more than she'd meant. "He's going north to see his sister. And . . . and I already miss him."

"Of course you do. He's your heartmate, after all," Amat said, teasing gently, but the weariness and dread in Liat's gaze deepened. Amat took a deep breath and put a hand on Liat's shoulder.

"Come with me," Amat said. "I have some things I need of you. But someplace cooler, eh?"

Amat led her to a meeting room on the north side of the compound where the windows were in shade and laid the tasks before her. She'd meant to give Liat as little as she could, but seeing her now, she added three or four small things that she'd intended to let rest. Liat needed something now. Work was thin comfort, but it was what she had to offer. Liat listened closely, ferociously.

Amat reluctantly ended her list.

"And before that, I need you to take me to the woman," she said.

Liat froze, then took a pose of acknowledgement.

"I need to speak with her," Amat said, knowing as she said the words precisely how inadequate they were. For a moment, she was tempted to tell the full story, to lighten Liat's burden by whatever measure the truth could manage. But she swallowed it. She put compassion aside for the moment. Along with fear and anger and sorrow.

Liat led her to a private room in the back, not far from Marchat Wilsin's own. Amat knew the place. The delicate inlaid wood of the floor, the Galtic tapestries, the window lattices of carved bone. It was where House Wilsin kept its most honored guests. Amat didn't believe it was where the girl had slept before the crime. That she was here now was a sign of Marchat's pricked conscience.

Maj lay curled on the ledge before the window. Her pale fingers rested on the lattice; the strange dirty gold of her hair spilled down across her shoulders and halfway to the floor. She looked softer. Amat stood behind her and watched the rise and fall of her breath, slow but not so slow as sleep.

"I could stay, if you like," Liat said. "She can . . . I think she is better when there are people around who she knows. Familiar faces."

"No," Amat said, and the island girl shifted at the sound of her voice. The pale eyes looked over her with nothing like real interest. "No, Liat-kya, I think I've put enough on you for today. I can manage from here."

Liat took a pose of acceptance and left, closing the door behind her. Amat pulled a chair of woven cane near the island girl and lowered herself into it. Maj watched her. When Amat was settled, the chair creaking under even her slight weight, Maj spoke.

"You hurt her feelings," she said in the sibilant words of Nippu. "You sent her away, didn't you?"

"I did," Amat said. "I came to speak with you. Not her."

"I've told everything I know. I've told it to a hundred people. I won't do it again."

"I haven't come to ask you anything. I've come to tell."

A slow, mocking smile touched the wide, pale lips. The fair eyebrows rose.

"Have you come to tell me how to save my child?"

"No."

Maj shrugged, asking with motion what else could be worth hearing.

"Wilsin-cha is going to arrange your travel back to Nippu," Amat said. "I think it will happen within the week."

Maj nodded. Her eyes softened, and Amat knew she was seeing herself at home, imagining the things that had happened somehow undone. It seemed almost cruel to go on.

"I don't want you to go," Amat said. "I want you to stay here. In Saraykeht."

The pale eyes narrowed, and Maj lifted herself on one elbow, shifting to face Amat directly. Amat could see the distrust in her face and felt she understood it.

"What happened to you goes deeper than it appears," Amat said. "It was an attack on my city and its trade, and not only by the andat and Oshai. It won't be easy to show this for what it was, and if you leave . . . if you leave, I don't think I can."

"What can't you do?"

"Prove to the Khai that there were more people involved than he knows of now."

"Are you being paid to do this?"

"No."

"Then why?"

Amat drew in a breath, steadied herself, and met the girl's eyes.

"Because it's the right thing," Amat said. It was the first time she'd said the words aloud, and something in her released with them. Since the day she'd left Ovi Niit, she had been two women—the overseer of House Wilsin and also the woman who knew that she would have to have this conversation. Have this conversation and then follow it with all the actions it implied. She laced her fingers around one knee and smiled, a little sadly, at the relief she felt in being only one woman again. "What happened was wrong. They struck at my city. *Mine.* And my house was part of it. Because of that, I was part of it. Doing this will gain me nothing, Maj. I will lose a great deal that I hold dear. And I will do it with you or without you."

"It won't bring me back my child."

"No."

"Will it avenge him?"

"Yes. If I succeed."

"What would he do, your Khai? If you won."

"I don't know," Amat said. "Whatever he deems right. He might fine House Wilsin. Or he might burn it. He might exile Wilsin-cha."

"Or kill him?"

"Or kill him. He might turn Seedless against House Wilsin, or the Galtic Council. Or all of Galt. I don't know. But that's not for me to choose. All I can do is ask for his justice, and trust that the Khai will follow the right road afterward."

Maj turned back to the window, away from Amat. The pale fingers touched the latticework, traced the lines of it as if they were the curves of a beloved face. Amat swallowed to loosen the knot in her throat. Outside, a songbird called twice, then paused, and sang again.

"I should go," Amat said.

Maj didn't turn. Amat rose, the chair creaking and groaning. She took her cane.

"When I call for you, will you come?"

The silence was thick. Amat's impulse was to speak again, to make her case. To beg if she needed to, but her training from years of negotiations was to wait. The silence demanded an answer more eloquently than words could. When Maj spoke, her voice was hard.

"I'll come."

Saraykeht receded. The wide mouth of the seafront thinned; wharves wide enough to hold ten men standing abreast narrowed to twigs. Otah sat at the back rail of the ship, aware of the swell and drop of the water, the rich scent of the spray, but concentrating upon the city falling away behind him. He could take it all in at once: the palaces of the Khai on the top of the northern slope grayed by distance; the tall, white warehouses with their heavy red and gray tiles near the seafront; the calm, respectable morning face of the soft quarter. Coast fishermen resting atop poles outside the city, lines cast into the surf. They passed east. The rivermouth, wide and muddy, and the cane fields. And then over the course of half a hand, the wind pressing the wide, low ship's sails took them around a bend in the land, and Saraykeht was gone. Otah rested his chin on the oily wood of the railing.

They were all back there—Liat and Maati and Kirath and Tuui and Epani who everyone called the cicada behind his back. The streets he'd carted bales of cotton and cloth and barrels of dye and the teahouses he'd sung and drunk in. The garden where he'd first kissed Liat and been surprised and pleased to find her kissing him back. The firekeeper, least of the utkhaiem, who'd taken copper lengths to let him and his cohort roast pigeons over his kiln. He remembered when he'd first come to it, how foreign and frightening it had been. It seemed a lifetime ago.

And before him was a deeper past. He had never been to the villiage of the Dai-kvo, never seen the libraries or heard the songs that were only ever sung there. It was what he might have been, what he had refused. It was what his father had hoped he would be, perhaps. How he might have returned to Machi one day and seen which of his memories were true. He hadn't known, that day marching away from the school, that the price he'd chosen was so dear.

"I hate this part," an unfamiliar voice said.

Otah looked up. The man standing beside him wore robes of deep green. A beard shot with white belied an unlined, youthful face, and the bright, black eyes seemed amused but not unfriendly.

"What do you mean?" Otah asked.

"The first three or four days on shipboard," the man said. "Before your stomach gets the rhythm of it. I have these drops of sugared tar that are supposed to help, but they never seem to. It doesn't seem to bother you, though, eh?"

"Not particularly," Otah said, adopting one of his charming smiles.

"You're lucky. My name's Orai Vaukheter," the man said. "Courier of House Siyanti bound at present from Chaburi-Tan to Machi—longest damn trip in the cities, and timed to put me on muleback in the north just in time for the first snows. And you? I don't think I've met you, and I'd have guessed I knew everyone."

"Itani Noyga," Otah said, the lie still coming naturally to his lips. "Going to Yalakeht to visit my sister."

"Ah. But from Saraykeht?"

Otah took a pose of acknowledgement.

"Rumor has it's difficult times there. Probably a good time to get out."

"Oh, I'll be going back. It's just to see the new baby, and then I'll be going back to finish my indenture."

"And the girl?"

"What girl?"

"The one you were thinking about just now, before I interrupted you."

Otah laughed and took a pose of query.

"And how are you sure I was thinking about a girl?"

The man leaned against the railing and looked out. His smile was quick enough, but his complexion was a little green.

"There's a certain kind of melancholy a man gets the first time he chooses a ship over a woman. It fades with time. It never passes, but it fades."

"Very poetic," Otah said, and changed the subject. "You're going to Machi?"

"Yes. The winter cities. Funny, too. I'm looking forward to it now, because it's all stone and doesn't bob around like a cork in a bath. When I get there, I'll wish I were back here where my piss won't freeze before it hits the ground. Have you been to the north?"

"No," Otah said. "I've spent most my life in Saraykeht. What's it like there?"

"Cold," the man said. "Blasted cold. But it's lovely in a stern way. The mines are how they make their trade. The mines and the metal-workers. And the stonemasons who built the place—gods, there's not another city like Machi in the world. The towers . . . you've heard about the towers?"

"Heard them mentioned," Otah said.

"I was to the top of one once. One of the great ones. It was high as a mountain. You could see for hundreds of miles. I looked down, and I'll swear it, the birds were flying below me and I felt like a few more bricks and I'd have been able to touch clouds."

The water lapped at the boards of the ship below them, the seagulls cried, but Otah didn't hear them. For a moment, he was atop a tower. To his left, dawn was breaking, rose and gold and pale blue of robin's egg. To his right, the land was still dark. And before him, snow covered mountains—dark stone showing the bones of the land. He smelled something—a perfume or a musk that made him think of women. He couldn't say if the vision was dream or memory or something of both, but a powerful sorrow flowed through him that lingered after the images had gone.

"It sounds beautiful," he said.

"I climbed back down as fast as I could," the man said, and shuddered despite the heat of the day. "That high up, even stone sways."

"I'd like to go there one day."

"You'd fit in. You've a northern face."

"So they tell me," Otah said, smiling again though he felt somber. "I'm not sure, though. I've spent quite a few years in the south. I may belong there now."

"It's hard," his companion said, taking a pose of agreement. "I think it's why I keep travelling even though I'm not really suited to it. Whenever I'm in one place, I remember another. So I'll be in Udun and thinking about a black crab stew they serve in Chaburi-Tan. Or in Saraykeht, thinking of the way the rain falls in Utani. If I could take them all—all the best parts of all the cities—and bring them to a single place, I think that would be paradise. But I can't, so I'm doomed. When the time comes I'm too old to do this, I'll have to settle for one place and I truly believe the thought of never seeing the others again will break me."

For a moment, they were silent. Then the courier's distant expression changed, and he turned to look at Otah carefully.

"You're an interesting one, Itani Noyga. I thought I'd come make light with a young man on what looks like his first journey, and I find myself thinking about my final one. Do you always carry that cloud with you?"

Otah grinned and took a pose of light apology, but hands and smile both wilted under the cool gaze. The canvas chuffed and a man in the back of the low, barge-built ship shouted.

"Yes," he surprised himself by saying. "But very few people seem to notice it."

"So the island girl's left," Amat said. "What does it matter? You were about to send her away."

Marchat Wilsin fidgeted, sending little waves across the bath to rebound against the tiles. Amat sipped her tea and feigned disinterest.

"We were sending her *home*. It was arranged. Why would she go?" he asked, as much to the water or himself as to her. Amat put her bowl of tea down in the floating tray and took a pose of query that was by its context a sarcasm.

"Let me see, Wilsin-cha. A young girl who has been deceived, used, humiliated. A girl who believed the stories she'd been told about perfect love and a powerful lover and was taken instead to a slaughterhouse for her own blood. Now why wouldn't she want to go back to the people she'd left? I'm sure they wouldn't think her a credulous idiot. No more than the Khai and the utkhaiem do now. There are jokes about her, you know. At the seafront. Laborers and teahouse servants make them up to tell each other. Did you want to hear some?"

"No," Marchat said and slapped the water. "No, I don't. I don't want it to happen, and if it's going to, I don't want to know about it."

"Shame, Marchat. She left from shame."

"I don't see why she should feel ashamed," he said, a defensiveness in his voice. A defense of himself and, heartbreakingly, of Maj. "She didn't do anything wrong."

Amat released her pose and let her hands slip back under the water. Wilsin-cha's lips worked silently, as if he were in conversation with himself and halfway moved to speaking. Amat waited.

The night before, she had taken Maj out to one of the low towns—a fishing village west of the city. A safe house outside the city would do, Amat thought, until a more suitable arrangement could be made. A week, she hoped, but perhaps more. In the last days, her plans had begun to fall away from House Wilsin's. It wouldn't be long before she and her employer, her old friend, parted company. It was worse, sitting there with him in the bathhouse he'd used for years, because he didn't know. House Wilsin had taken her from a life on knife-edge, and he— Marchat-cha—had chosen her from among the clerks and functionaries. He had promoted her through the ranks. And now they sat as they had for years, but it was nearing the last time.

Despite herself, Amat leaned forward and put her palm on his shoulder. He looked up and forced a smile.

"It's over," he said. "At least it's over."

It was something he'd said often in the last days, repeating it as if saying the words again would make them true. So perhaps some part of him did know that it was far from finished. He took her hand and, to her surprise, kissed it. His whiskers scratched her water-softened skin. Gently and despite him, she pulled away. He was blushing. Gods, the poor man was blushing. It made her want to weep, want to leave, want to shout at him until her echoing fury cracked the tiles. *After all you've done, how dare you make me feel sympathy for you?*

"Wilsin-cha," she said. "The shipping schedule."

"Yes," he said. "Of course. The schedule."

Together, they went through the trivial issues of the day. A small fire in one of the weaver's warehouses meant that they would be three thousand feet of thread short for the ship to Bakta. It was significant enough to warrant holding the ship, but they didn't dare keep it too long—the season was turning. And then there was the issue of a persistent mildew in one of House Wilsin's warehouses that had spoiled two bolts of silk, and had to be addressed before they dared to use the space again.

Amat laid out the options, made her suggestions, answered Wilsin-cha's questions, and accepted his decisions. In the main part of the bathhouse, a man broke out in song, his voice joined—a little off-key—by two more. The warm breeze coming through the cedar trellis at the windows moved the surface of the water. Painful as it was, Amat felt herself grabbing at the details—the pinkness of Marchat's pale skin, the thin crack in the side of the lacquer tray, the just-bitter taste of over-brewed tea. Like a squirrel, she thought, gathering nuts for the winter.

"Amat," he said, when they were through and she started to rise. The hardness in his voice caught her, and she lowered herself back into the water. "There's something . . . You and I, we've worked together for more years than I like to remember. You've always been . . . always been very professional. But I've felt that along with that, we've been friends. I know that I have held you in the highest regard. Gods, that sounds wrong. Highest regard? Gods. I'm doing this badly."

He raised his hands from the water, fingertips wrinkled as raisins, and motioned vaguely. His face was tight and flushed. Amat frowned, confused, and then the realization washed over her like nausea. He was about to declare his love.

She put her head down, pressing a palm to her forehead. She couldn't look up. Laughter that had as much to do with horror as mirth shook her gently. Of all the things she'd faced, of all the evils she'd steeled herself to walk through, this one had taken her blind. Marchat

Wilsin thought he loved her. It was why he'd stood up to Oshai to save her. It was why she was alive. It was ridiculous.

"I'm sorry," he said. "I shouldn't have . . . Forget that. I didn't . . . I sound like a half-wit schoolboy. Here's the thing, Amat. I didn't mean to be involved with this. These last days, I've been feeling a certain distance from you. And I'm afraid that you and I might have . . . lost something between us. Something that . . ."

It had to stop. She had to stop it.

"Wilsin-cha," she said, and forced herself into a formal pose of respect appropriate to a superior in business. "I think perhaps it is too soon. The . . . the wounds are too fresh. Perhaps we might postpone this conversation."

He took a pose of agreement that seemed to carry a relief almost as deep as her own. She shifted to a pose of leave-taking, which he returned. She didn't meet his gaze as she left. In the dressing room, she pulled on her robes, washed her face, and leaned against the great granite basin, her hands clenched white on its rim, until her mind had stilled. With a long, deep, slow breath, she composed herself, then took up her cane and walked out into the streets, as if the world were not a broken place, and her path through it was not twisted.

She strode to the compound, her leg and hip hardly bothering her. She delivered the orders she had to give, made the arrangements she had discussed with Wilsin-cha. Liat, thankfully, was elsewhere. Amat's day was difficult enough without adding the burden of Liat's guilt and pain. And, of course, there was the decision of whether to take the girl with her when Amat left her old life behind.

When Amat had written the last entry in the house logs, she cleaned the nib on its cloth, laid the paper over the half-used inkblock, and walked south, toward the seafront. And not toward her apartments. She passed by the stalls and the ships, the watersellers and firekeepers and carts that sold strips of pork marinated in ginger and cumin. When she reached the wide mouth of the Nantan, she paused, considering the bronze form of the last emperor gazing out over the sea. His face was calm and, she thought, sorrowful. Shian Sho had watched the Empire fall, watched the devastation of war between high councilors who could wield poets and andat. How sad, she thought, to have had so much and been powerless to save it. For the first time in her life, she felt something more than awe or historical curiosity or familiarity with the image of the man eight generations dead. She walked to the base of the statue, reached out and rested her hand on the sun-hot metal of his foot almost painful to touch. When she turned away, her sorrow was not less, but it was accompanied by a strange lifting of her heart. A kinship, perhaps, with those who had struggled before her to save the cities they held dear. She walked toward the river, and the worst parts of the city. Her city. Hers.

The teahouse was rough—its shutters needed painting, the plaster of its walls was scored with the work of vandals cheaply repaired—but not decrepit. Its faults spoke of poverty, not abandonment. A man with the deep blue eyes and red hair of the Westlands leaned out of a window, trying not to seem to stare at her. Amat raised an eyebrow and walked through the blue-painted door and into the murk of the main room.

The smell of roast lamb and Westlands beer and cheap tobacco washed over her. The stone floor was smooth and clean, and the few men and women at their tables seemed to take little notice of her. The dogs under the tables shifted toward her and then away, equally incurious. Amat looked around with an expression that she hoped would be read as confidence and impatience. A dark-haired girl came to her before long, wiping her hands on her robe as she came. She took a pose of greeting which Amat returned.

"We have tables here," the girl said. "Or perhaps you would care for a room in the back? We have a good view of the river, if . . ."

"I'm here to see a man named Torish Wite," Amat said. "I was told that he would expect me."

The girl fell into a pose of understanding without surprise or hesitation, turned, and led Amat back through a short corridor to an open door. Amat took a pose of thanks, and stepped through.

He was a big man, thick hair the color of honey, a rough scar on his chin. He didn't rise as she came in, only watched her with a distant amusement. Amat took a pose appropriate to opening a negotiation.

"No," the man said in the language of the Westlands. "If you want to talk to me, you can use words."

Amat dropped her hands and sat. Torish Wite leaned back in his chair and crossed his arms. The knife he wore at his belt was as long as Amat's forearm. She felt fear tighten her throat. This man was strong, brutal, prone to violence. That was, after all, why she was here.

"I understand you have men for hire," she said.

"Truth," he agreed.

"I want a dozen of them."

"For what?"

"I can't tell you that yet."

"Then you can't have 'em."

"I'm prepared to pay—"

"I don't care what you're prepared to pay. They're my men, and I'm not sending them out unless I know what I'm sending them into. You can't say, then you can't have them."

He looked away, already bored. Amat shook her head, pushing away her emotions. This was the time to think, not feel. The man was a businessman, even if what he traded in was violence. He had nothing to gain by building a reputation of spilling his client's secrets.

"I am about to break with my house," she said. After holding her intentions in silence for so long, it was strange to hear the words spoken. "I am going to be taking up a project that will put me in opposition to my previous employer. If I'm to succeed in it, I will have to secure a large and steady income."

Torish Wite shifted forward, his arms resting on his knees. He was considering her now. He was curious. She had him.

"And how are you going to arrange that?" he asked.

"There is a man named Ovi Niit. He runs a comfort house in the soft quarter. I mean to take it from him."

12

>+<   Maati woke to the sound of driving rain pattering against the shutters. The light that pressed in was cloud softened, with neither direction nor strength to tell him how long he'd slept. The night candle was now only a burnt wick. He pushed away the netting, shuddered, and rose. When he opened the shutters, it was as if the city was gone, vanished in gray. Even the outlines of the palaces were vague, but the surface of the pond was alive and dancing and the leaves of the nearby trees shone with bright wet green just turning to red at the veins. The rain against his face and chest was cool. Autumn was coming to Saraykeht.

The days—nearly two weeks now—since Otah-kvo had left had taken on a rhythm. He would rise in the morning, and go and speak with Heshai-kvo. Some days, the poet would manage three or four exchanges. Others, they would only sit there under the baleful black stare of the andat, silent in his torture box. Maati coaxed his master to eat whatever meal the servants had brought from the palace kitchens: fruit pastries sticky with sugar, or rich, soupy bread puddings, or simple cheese and cut apple. And every morning, Heshai-kvo deigned to eat a mouthful or two, sip a bowl of tea. And then with a grunt, he would turn away, leaving only his wide back as company. Seedless never spoke, but Maati felt the weight of his attention like a hand on the back of his neck.

In the afternoon, he would walk in the gardens or read. And as sunset came, he would repeat the breakfast ritual with an evening meal that excited no more interest in the poet. Then, leaving the night candle lit, Maati would go to his own room, his own cot, light his candle, fasten his netting, and will himself to sleep. It was like a fever dream, repeated again and again, with small variations that seemed only to point out that nothing of substance changed.

He closed the shutters, took a clean robe, washed his face and shaved. There was little enough on his cheek for the razor to take, but it was a ritual. And it comforted him. He would have given anything he had to have Otah-kvo there to talk with.

He went down the stairs to the table where the breakfast had been left for him: honey bread and black tea. He took the tray and went back up and along the corridor to Heshai-kvo's room. It was unbarred, and swung open at the touch of his burdened wrist.

The bed was empty. Netting fine as mist was thrown aside, the bed-clothes in knots and bundles that didn't hide the depression where the poet's body had lain for days. Maati, trembling, put down the tray and walked to the abandoned bed. There was no note, no unfamiliar object, nothing to say what had happened, why his teacher was gone. Sickening images of the poet floating dead in the pond tugged at him, and he turned slowly, dreading to see the torture box empty. Seedless' black eyes met his, and Maati let out the breath he hadn't noticed he was holding.

The andat laughed.

"No such luck, my dear," he said, his voice amused and calm. "The great poet is, to the best of my knowledge, still alive and in something near enough to his right mind not to have set me free."

"Where is he?"

"I don't know. It isn't as if he asked my permission. You know, Maati-kya, it's odd. We never seem to chat anymore."

"Where did he go? What did he say?"

Seedless sighed.

"He didn't say anything. He was just his own pathetic self—all the grace and will of a soiled washcloth—and then just after the last mark of the night candle, he got up like he'd remembered an appointment, pulled on his robes and left."

Maati paced, fighting to slow his breath, to order his thoughts. There had to be something. Some sign that would tell him where Heshai had gone, what he would do.

"Call out the guards," Seedless said, laughter in his voice. "The great poet has slipped his leash."

"Be quiet!" Maati snapped. "I have to think."

"Or you'll do what? Punish me? Gods, Maati, look what they're doing to me already. I can't move. I can't stretch. If I were a man, I'd be
covered in my own shit, and nothing to do but try to push it out with my
toes. What more were you planning to do?"

"Don't. Just . . . don't talk to me."

"Why not, my dear? What did I do to upset you?"

"You killed a baby!" Maati shouted, shocked at his own anger.

In the shadows of his prison, the andat smiled sadly. The pale fingers
wrapped the slats, and the pale flesh shifted an inch.

"The baby doesn't mind," Seedless said. "Ask it, see if it holds a
grudge. What I did, I did to the woman. And to Heshai. And you know
why I've done it."

"You're evil," Maati said.

"I'm a prisoner and a slave held against my will. I'm forced to work
for my captor when what I want is to be free. Free of this box, of this
flesh, of this consciousness. It's no more a moral impulse than you wanting to breathe. You'd sacrifice anyone, Maati, if you were drowning."

Maati turned his back, running his hands down the empty sheets,
looking for something—anything. It was only cloth. He had to go. He
had to alert the Khai. Armsmen. They had to send armsmen out to
search for Heshai and bring him back. Over the drumming of the rain,
he heard the andat shift.

"I told you," Seedless said, "that we wouldn't always be friends."

And from below them another voice called Maati's name. A woman's
voice, tight with distress. Maati rushed down the stairs, three at a stride.
Liat Chokavi stood in the main room. Her robes and hair were rain-
soaked, clinging to her and making her seem younger than she had before. She held her hands tight. When she saw him, she took two steps
forward, and Maati reached out, put his hand on hers.

"What is it," he asked. "What's happened?"

"The poet. Heshai. He's at the compound. He's raving, Maati. We
can't calm him. Epani-cha wanted to send for the utkhaiem, but I told
him I'd come get you. He promised to wait."

"Take me," he said, and together they half-walked, half-ran out,
across the wooden bridge—its timbers rain-slicked and blackened—
through the palace gardens where the water bowed the limbs of trees
and bent the flower blossoms to the ground, and then south, into the
city. Liat kept hold of his hand, pulling him along. The pace was too

fast for speaking, and Maati couldn't imagine what he would say if he'd been able. His mind was too much taken with dread of what he would find when they arrived.

If Otah-kvo had been there, there would have been someone to ask, someone who would have known what to do. It struck Maati as he passed through the darkened streets that he'd had a teacher with him almost his whole life—someone who could guide him when the world got confusing. That was what teachers were supposed to be. Otah-kvo hadn't even accepted the Dai-kvo and he was strong enough to know the right thing. It was monstrously wrong that Heshai was incapable of doing the same.

At the courtyard of the Galtic house, Liat stopped and Maati drew up beside her. The scene was worse than he had thought. The house was two stories built around the courtyard with a walkway on the second level that looked down on the metalwork statue of the Galtic Tree, the fountain overflowing in the downpour, and between them, sitting with his back to the street, his teacher. Around him were the signs of conflict— torn papers, spilled food. A crowd had gathered, robes in the colors of many houses ghosted in the shadows of doorways and on the upper walk, faces blurred by rain.

Maati put his hand on Liat's hip and gently pushed her aside. The stone of the courtyard was an inch underwater, white foam tracing the pattern of drainage from the house out into the streets. Maati walked through it slowly, his sandals squelching.

Heshai looked confused. The rain plastered his long, thinning hair to his neck. His robe was thin—too thin for the weather—and the unhealthy pink of his skin showed through it. Maati squatted beside him, and saw the thick, wide mouth was moving slightly, as if whispering. Drops of water clung like dew to the moth-eaten beard.

"Heshai-kvo," Maati said, taking a pose of entreaty. "Heshai-kvo, we should go back."

The bloodshot eyes with whites the color of old ivory turned to him, narrowed, and then recognition slowly lit the poet's face. He put his thick-fingered hands on Maati's knee, and shook his head.

"She isn't here. She's already gone," Heshai said.

"Who isn't here, Heshai-kvo?"

"The girl," he snapped. "The island girl. The one. I thought if I could find her, you see, if I could explain my error . . ."

Maati fought the urge to shake him—take a handful of robe in each fist and rattle the old man until he came to his senses. Instead, he put his own hand over Heshai's and kept his voice calm and steady.

"We should go."

"If I could have explained, Maati . . . If I could just have explained that it was the andat that did the thing. That I would never have—"

"What good would it do?" Maati said, his anger and embarrassment slipping out, "Heshai-kvo, there aren't any words you know that would apologize for what happened. And sitting here in the rain doesn't help."

Heshai frowned at the words as if confused, then looked down at the flowing water and up to the half-hidden faces. The frog-lips pursed.

"I've made an ass of myself, haven't I?" Heshai asked in a perfectly rational voice.

"Yes," Maati said, unable to bring himself to lie. "You have."

Heshai nodded, and rose to his feet. His robe hung open, exposing his wrinkled breast. He took two unsteady steps before Maati moved close and put his arm around the man. As they passed into the street, Liat went to Heshai's other side, taking his arm over her shoulder, sharing Maati's burden. Maati felt Liat's arm against his own behind Heshai's wide back. Her hand clasped his forearm, and between them, they made a kind of cradle to lead the poet home.

THE ROBE MAATI LENT HER WHEN THEY ARRIVED BACK AT THE POET'S HOUSE was woven cotton and silk, the fabric thicker than her finger and soft as any she'd touched in years. She changed in his small room while he was busy with the poet. Her wet robes, she hung on a stand. She wrung the water out of her hair and braided it idly as she waited.

It was a simple room—cot, desk, and wardrobe, cloth lantern and candle stand. Only the pile of books and scroll and the quality of the furnishings marked it as different from a cell like her own. But then, Maati was only an apprentice. His role was much like her own with Amat. They were even very nearly the same age, though she found she often forgot that.

A murmur of voices reached her—the poet's and Maati's and then the soft, charming, chilling voice of Seedless. The poet barked something she couldn't make out, and then Maati, soothing him. She wanted to leave, to go back to her cell, to be away from the terrible tension in the air of the house. But the rain was growing worse. The pounding of water was joined now with an angry tapping. The wind had turned and allowed her to open Maati's shutters without flooding his room, and when she did, the landscape outside looked like it was covered with spiders' eggs. Tiny hailstones melting as quickly as they fell.

"Liat-cha," Maati said.

She turned, trying to pull the shutters closed and take a pose of apology at the same time, and managing neither.

"No, I'm sorry," Maati said. "I should have kept closer watch on him. But he's never tried to get out of his bed, much less leave the house."

"Is he resting now?"

"Something like it. He's gone to bed at least. Seedless . . . you know about Seedless' box?"

"I'd heard rumor," Liat said.

Maati took a pose of confirmation and looked back over his shoulder, his expression troubled and weary. His brown poet's robes were still dripping at the sleeves.

"I'll go downstairs," she said.

"Why?"

"I thought you'd want some privacy to change," she said slowly, and was rewarded by a fierce blush as Maati took a pose of understanding.

"I'd forgotten . . . I didn't even notice they were wet. Yes, of course, Liat-cha. I'll only be a moment."

She smiled and slapped his shoulder as she'd seen Itani's cohort do. The gesture felt surprisingly natural to her.

"I think we're past calling each other *cha*," she said.

He joined her quickly, changed into a robe of identical brown. They sat in the main room, candles lit to dispel the gloom of weather. He sat across from her on a low wooden divan. His face was calm, but worn and tight about the mouth, even when he smiled. The strain of his master's collapse was written on his brow.

"Have you . . . have you heard from him?" Maati asked.

"No," she said. "It's too early. He won't have reached Yalakeht by now. Soon, but not yet. And then it would take as many weeks as he's been gone to get a message back to us."

Maati took a pose of understanding, but impatience showed in it. She responded with a pose that asked after Maati's wellbeing. In another context, it would have been a formal nicety. Here, it seemed sincere.

"I'll be fine," he said. "It's only difficult not knowing what to do. When Otah-kvo comes back, everything will be all right."

"Will it?" Liat said, looking into the candle flame. "I hope you're right."

"Of course it will. The Dai-kvo knows more than any of us how to proceed. He'll pass it to Otah-kvo, and we'll . . ."

The voice with its forced optimism faded. Liat looked back. Maati was sitting forward, rubbing his eyes with his fingers like an old, weary man.

"We'll do whatever the Dai-kvo tells us," Liat finished.

Maati took a rueful pose of agreement. A gust of wind rattled the great shuttered walls, and Liat pulled her robe tight around her, as if to protect herself from cold, though the room was perfectly warm.

"And you?" Maati asked. "Are things well at House Wilsin?"

"I don't know," Liat said. "Amat Kyaan's come back, and she tries to use me, but there doesn't seem to be as much to do as there once was. I think . . . I think she doesn't trust me. I can't blame her, after what happened. And Wilsin-cha's the same way. They keep me busy, but not with anything serious. No one's actually told me I'm only a clerk again, but for how I've been spending my days, I may as well be."

"I'm sorry. It's wrong, though. It isn't your fault that this happened. You should just be—"

"Itani's going to leave me. Or Otah. Whichever. He's going to leave me," she said. She hadn't meant to, but the words had come out, like vomiting. She stared at her hands and they kept coming. "I don't think he knows it yet, but when he left, there was something in him. In the way he treated me that . . . He isn't my first lover, and I've seen it before. It's just a kind of distance, and then it's something more, and then . . ."

"I'm sure you're wrong," Maati said, and his voice sounded confident for the first time that day. "He won't."

"Everyone else has," she said.

"Not him."

"He went, though. He didn't only have to; he wanted to. He wanted to get away from me, and when he comes back, he'll have had time to think. And then . . ."

"Liat-cha . . . Liat. I know we haven't known each other before this, but Otah-kvo was my first teacher, and sometimes I think he was my best one. He's different from other people. And he loves you. He's told me as much."

"I don't know," Liat said.

"You love him, don't you?"

"I don't know," she said, and the silence after it was worse than walking through the rain. She wiped away a tear with the back of her hand. "I love Itani. I *know* Itani. Otah, though? He's a son of the Khaiem. He's . . . he isn't who I thought he was, and I'm just an apprentice overseer, and not likely to be that for long. How can we stay together when he's what he is, and I'm this?"

"You did when you were an overseer and he was just a laborer. This isn't any different."

"Of course it is," she said. "He always knew he was born to something higher than he was. I'm not. I'm just me."

"Otah-kvo is one of the wisest men I know," Maati said. "He isn't going to walk away from you."

"Why not?"

"Because," Maati said softly, "he's one of the wisest men I know."

She laughed, partly at the sincerity in the boy's voice, partly because she wanted so badly for it to be true, partly because her only other option was weeping. Maati moved to her, put his arm around her. He smelled of the cedar soap than Itani used to shave with. She leaned into his shoulder.

"These next weeks," she said when she'd gathered herself enough to speak. "They aren't going to be easy."

"No," Maati agreed and heaved a sigh. "No, they aren't."

"We can see each other through them, though. Can't we?" Liat said, trying to keep the pleading out of the words. The patter of the rain filled the silence, and Liat closed her eyes. It was Maati, at last, who had the courage to say what she hadn't been able to.

"I think I'm going to need a friend if I'm going to come through this," he said. "Perhaps we're in the same place. If I can help, if a half-ragged student poet who spends most of his days feeling like he's worn thin enough to see through can be of any comfort, I'd welcome the company."

"You don't have to."

"Neither do you, but I hope you will."

The kiss she gave him was brief and meant to be sisterly. If he caught his breath at it, she imagined he was only a little surprised and embarrassed. She smiled, and he did as well.

"We're a sorry pair," she said. "Itani . . . he'll be back soon."

"Yes," Maati said. "And things will be better then."

THE DOOR BURST OPEN, AND A BODY FELL FORWARD ONTO THE MEETING room floor. For a moment, the sounds of the teahouse penetrated—voices, music—and then Torish Wite and two of his men followed the man they'd pushed through and closed the door. Silence returned as if it had never gone. Amat, sitting at the long wooden table, gathered herself. The man beside her wore the simple robes of a firekeeper and the expression of someone deeply amused by a dogfight.

The fallen man rose unsteadily to his knees. A white cloth covered his head, and his thin arms were bound behind him. Torish Wite took him by the shoulder, lifted roughly, and nodded to one of his men. When the cloth was flipped away, Amat swallowed a knot of fear.

"This him?" Torish Wite asked.

"Yes," she said.

Ovi Niit's gaze swam. He had a glazed look that spoke of wine with strange spices as much as fear or anger. It took the space of three long breaths for his eyes to rest on her, for recognition to bloom there. Slowly, he struggled to his feet.

"Niit-cha," Amat said, taking a pose that opened a negotiation. "It has been some time."

The whoremaster answered with a string of obscenities that only stopped with Torish Wite's man stepping forward and striking him across the face. Amat folded her hands in her lap. A drop of blood appeared at the corner of Ovi Niit's mouth, bright as a jewel and distracting to her.

"If you do as I say, Niit-cha," she began again, "this needn't be an unpleasant affair."

He grinned, the blood smearing his crooked teeth. There was no fear in him. He laughed, and the sound itself seemed reckless. Amat wished that they'd found him when he was sober.

"I was never paid, Ovi-cha, for my time with you. I have chosen to take the price in a share of the house. In fact, I've chosen to buy you out." She took a sheaf of papers from her sleeve and placed them on the table. "I'm offering a fair price."

"There isn't enough money in the world," he spat. "I built that house up from three girls in an alley."

The firekeeper shifted in his seat. The distant smile on his lips didn't shift, but his eyes held a curiosity. Amat felt oddly out of her depth. This was a negotiation, after all, and to say she had the upper hand would be gross understatement, and yet she was at sea.

"You're going to kill me, you dust-cunt bitch. Because if you don't, I'll kill you."

"There's no need . . ." she began, then stopped and took a pose of acceptance. Ovi Niit was right. It was only dressed as a negotiation. It was, in point of fact, a murder. For the first time, something like apprehension showed in his expression. His eyes shifted to the side, to Torish Wite.

"Whatever she's paying you, I'll triple it," Ovi Niit said.

"Amat-cha," the firekeeper said. "I appreciate the attempt, but it seems to me unlikely that this gentleman will sign the documents."

Amat sighed and took a pose of concurrence. In the common room someone shrieked with laughter. The sound was made faint by the thick stone walls. Like the call of a ghost.

"You can kill me, but you'll never break me," Ovi Niit said, pulling himself up proud as a pit-cock.

"I'll live with that," Amat said, and nodded. Torish Wite neatly kicked Ovi Niit's knees out, and the two other men stepped forward to hold him while their captain leaned over and looped a knotted cord over his head. An efficient flick of the wrist, and the cord was tight enough to dig into the flesh, buried. The whoremaster's face went deep red and darkening. Amat watched with a sick fascination. It took longer than she'd expected. When the men released it, the body fell like a sack of grain.

The firekeeper reached across the table, picked up the sheaf between his first finger and his thumb, and pulled them before him. As if there wasn't a fresh corpse on the floor, Amat turned to him.

"I suppose you know someone who can do a decent imitation of his chop?" the firekeeper said.

"I'll see it arranged," Amat said.

"Very well. If the watch asks, I'll swear to it that I stood witness at the transaction," the firekeeper said, taking a pen and a small silver inkbox from his sleeve. "You paid Niit-cha his asking price, he accepted, and in fact seemed quite pleased."

"Do you think the watch will ask?"

The inkbox clicked open, the firekeeper's pen touched the inkblock and then the page, scratching with a sound like bird's feet.

"Of course they will," he said, sliding the papers back toward her. "They're the watch. They're paid to. But so long as you pay your share to them, let them sample your wares on occasion, and don't cause them trouble, I doubt they'll ask many. He didn't die in the soft quarter. Their honor isn't at stake."

Amat considered the firekeeper's signature for a moment, then took a small leather sack from her belt and handed it to him. He had the good taste not to count it there at the table, but she saw him weigh it before it disappeared into his sleeve.

"It's odd to hear the term honor associated with any of this," she said.

The firekeeper took a pose of polite correction, appropriate for a master to an apprentice not his own.

"If there were no honor at stake, Torish-cha would have killed *you*."

Torish Wite chuckled, and Amat took a pose of acknowledgement more casual than she felt. The firekeeper shifted to a pose of leave-taking to both Amat and Torish Wite and then, briefly, to the corpse of Ovi Niit. When the door closed behind him, Amat tucked the signed papers into her sleeve and considered the dead man. He was smaller than she remembered, and she wouldn't have said his arms were so thin. Collapsed on the floor, his last breath past him, he seemed oddly vulnerable. Amat wondered for the first time what Ovi Niit had been as a child, and whether he had a mother or a sister who would miss him now that he was gone. She guessed not.

"What do you want done with him?" Torish Wite asked.

"Whatever's convenient, I suppose."

"Do you want him found?"

"I don't care one way or the other," Amat said.

"It'll be easier for the watch to ignore any accusations against you if he vanishes," Torish Wite said, half to Amat, half to his men.

"We'll take care of it," one of the men said; the one who had held Ovi Niit's right arm as he died. Amat took a pose of thanks. The two men hefted the object that had been Ovi Niit between them and carried it out. She assumed they had a wheelbarrow in the alleyway.

"When are you taking the house?" Torish Wite asked when they had gone.

"Soon."

"You'll want protection for that. These soft quarter types aren't going to roll over and show their bellies just because you've got the right chop on the papers."

"Yes, I wanted to speak to you about that," Amat said, vaguely surprised at how distant she felt from the words. "I'm going to need guards for the house. Is that the sort of contract you'd be interested in?"

"Depends," Torish Wite said, but he smiled. It was only a matter of terms. That was a fine thing. Her gaze shifted to the space where Ovi Niit had lain. She told herself the unease was only the normal visceral shock of seeing a man die before her. That she now owned a comfort house—that she was going to make her money from selling the women and boys she'd recently shared table and sleeping quarters with—was nothing to think about. It was, after all, in the cause of justice.

Torish Wite shifted his weight, his movement snapping her back into the moment. He had a broad face and broad shoulders, scars on his chin and arms, and a smile that spoke of easy brutality. His gaze was considering and amused.

"Yes?"

"You're afraid of me, aren't you."

Amat smiled and affected boredom.

"Yes," she said. "But consider what happened to the last man who frightened me."

His expression soured.

"You're in over your head, you know."

She took a pose of acknowledgement, but with a stance that bordered on the defiant. She could see in his face that he understood every nuance. He respected her. It was what she'd hoped. She dropped the pose and leaned against the table.

"When I was very young," she said, "my sister pushed me off a rooftop. A high one. I have never been more certain that I was going to die. And I didn't scream. Because I knew it wouldn't help."

"And your point?"

"What I'm doing now may be harder than I'd wish. But I'm going to do it. Worrying about whether I can manage won't help."

He laughed. It was a low sound, and strangely shallow—like an axe on wood.

"You are a tough bitch," he said, making it a compliment.

No, I'm not, she thought, smiling, *but good that you've misunderstood me.*

13

>+< The ship passed the great island with its white watchtower and into the bay of Yalakeht on a cool, hazy morning. Otah stood at the railing and watched the land turn from outlines of pale hills to the green-gray of pine trees in autumn. The tall, gray buildings of Yalakeht nestled at the edge of the calmest of waters. The noise of their bayfront carried over the water, but muffled by the thick air like a conversation in a nearby room.

They reached land—signaled in by the dock master's torches—just as the sun reached its peak in the sky. Otah had hardly put his feet to the cobbled streets before he heard the news. The bayfront seemed to buzz with it.

The third son the Khai Udun had killed his remaining brother. They had found each other in Chaburi-Tan, and faced each other in a seafront street with knives. Or else the second son—whom Otah had seen in the court of the Khai Saraykeht—had been poisoned after all. Or he had ambushed his younger brother, only to have the fight slip from him. On the docks, on the streets, in the teahouses, the stories ran together and meshed with older, better-known tales, last year's news, and wild imaginings newly formed of what might have happened. Otah found a seat in the back of a teahouse near the bayfront and listened as the stories unfolded. The youngest son would take his father's place—a good sign. When a youngest son took power, it meant the line was vigorous. People said it meant the next Khai Udun would be especially talented and brave.

To Otah, it meant that he had killed two of his brothers, and that the others, younger even than he was, had been cast out. They were wearing brands somewhere even now. Unless they were poets. Unless they were lucky enough to be poets like Heshai of Saraykeht.

"Well, you're looking sour," a familiar voice said.

"Orai," Otah said taking a pose of welcome. The courier sat down across from him, and raised a hand to the serving man. Moments later, two bowls of fish and rice appeared before them along with a pot of smoked tea and two ceramic teabowls of delicate green. Otah took a pose of correction to the serving man, but Orai stopped him.

"It's a tradition of my house. After a journey, we buy our travelling companions a meal."

"Really?"

"No," the courier said, "but I think I have more money than you do, and as it happens the fish here is really quite good."

The serving man hovered, looking uncomfortable, until Otah laughed.

"At least let me pay my half," Otah said, but Orai took a pose of deferment: *next time*.

"So, Itani," he said. "This is the end? Or how far upriver is your sister?"

"A day or so by boat," Otah lied. "Two days walking. Or so she tells me. I've never been."

"A few days more, and you could see the poet's village. You've never been there, have you?"

"No," Otah said.

"It's worth the extra travel, if you can spare it. The houses of the Dai-kvo are actually built into the living rock. They say it's based on the school of the ancients in the old Empire, though I don't suppose there's much left of those ruins to compare. It's a good story."

"I suppose."

The fish was very good—bright with lemon, hot with pepper. Otah realized after a few mouthfuls that he had really been very hungry.

"And now that you're at the end of your first journey over water, what do you think of it?"

"It's strange," Otah said. "The world still feels like it's moving"

"Yes. It does stop after a while. More than that, though. There was a saying when I was young that sea journeys are like women—they change you. And none so much as the first."

"I don't know about that," Otah said. "I seem to be more or less the same man I was in Saraykeht. Ten fingers, ten toes. No flippers."

"Perhaps it's just a saying, then."

Orai poured himself another bowl of tea and held it in his hands, blowing across it to cool it. Otah finished the last of the rice and leaned back to find the courier's gaze on him, considering. He replied with a pose of query that seemed to pull Orai out of a half-dream.

"I have to confess, Itani, it isn't precisely chance that I found you here. The fish really is very good, but I found you by asking after you. I've been working for House Siyanti for eight years, and traveling for five of those. I think it's taught me a few things and I'll flatter myself to say I think I'm a good judge of character. These last weeks, on the ship, you've stuck me as an interesting man. You're smart, but you hide the fact. You're driven, but I don't think you know yet what you're driven toward. And you like travel. You have a gift for it."

"You're just saying that because I didn't get sick the way you did," Otah said, trying to lighten the mood.

"Being able to eat your first day on ship is a gift. Don't underestimate it. But all this time, it's occurred to me that you have the makings of a good courier. And I hold enough influence in the house now, that if you wanted a letter of introduction, I think I might be able to help you with it. You wouldn't be trusted with important work at the start, but that doesn't make seeing the cities any less. It's not an easy life, but it's an interesting one. And it might suit you."

Otah cocked his head and felt a flush rising in him equally gratification and embarrassment. The courier sipped his tea, letting the moment stretch until Otah took a pose that encompassed both gratitude and refusal.

"I belong in Saraykeht," he said. "There are things there I need to see through."

"Your indenture. I understand. But that's going to end before much longer."

"There's more than that, though. I have friends there."

"And the girl," Orai said.

"Yes. Liat. I . . . I don't think she'd enjoy having a lover who was always elsewhere."

Orai took a pose of understanding that seemed to include a reservation, a question on the verge of being formed. When he did speak, it was in fact a question, though perhaps not the one he'd wanted to ask.

"How old are you?"

"Twenty summers."

"And she's . . . ?"

"Seventeen."

"And you love her," Orai said. Otah could hear the almost-covered disappointment in the words. "She's your heartmate."

"I don't know that. But I have to find out, don't I?"

Orai grinned and took a pose that conceded the point, then, hesitating, he plucked something from his sleeve. It was a letter sewn closed and sealed with hard green wax stamped with an ornate seal.

"I took the chance that you'd accept my suggestion," the courier said, passing the letter across the table. "If it turns out this amazing young woman doesn't own your heart after all, consider the offer open."

Otah dropped it into his own sleeve and took a pose of thanks. He felt an unreasonable trust for this man, and an ease that three week's acquaintance—even in the close quarters of a ship—couldn't explain. Perhaps, he thought, it was only the change of his first sea voyage.

"Orai," he said, "have you ever been in love?"

"Yes. Several times, and with some very good women."

"Can you love someone you don't trust?"

"Absolutely," he said. "I have a sister I wouldn't lend two copper lengths if I wanted them back. The problem loving someone you don't trust is finding the right distance."

"The right distance."

"With my sister, we love each other best from different cities. If we had to share a house, it wouldn't go so gracefully."

"But a lover. A heartmate."

Orai shook his head.

"In my experience, you can bed a woman and mistrust her or you can love a woman and mistrust her, but not all three at once."

Otah sipped his tea. It had gone tepid. Orai waited, his boyish face with its graying beard serious. Two men left from another table, and the cold draft from the briefly opened door made Otah shiver. He put down the green bowl and set his hands together on the table. His head felt thick, his mind stuffed with wool.

"Before I left Saraykeht," he said slowly, "I told Liat some things. About my family."

"But not because you trust her?"

"Because I love her and I thought I *ought* to trust her."

He looked up, his gaze meeting Orai's. The courier took a pose of understanding and sympathy. Otah replied with one that surrendered to greater forces—gods or fate or weight of circumstances. There seemed little more to say. Orai rose.

"Keep hold of that letter," he said. "And whatever happens, good luck to you. You've been a good man to travel with, and that's a rare thing."

"Thank you," Otah said.

The courier pulled his robes closed about him and left. Otah finished his bowl of tea before he also quit the teahouse. The bay of Yalakeht was wide and calm and still before him; the port that ended his first journey over the sea. His mind unquiet, he turned to the north and west, walking through the wet, narrow streets to the river gate, and some days beyond that, the Dai-kvo.

"This is shit!" the one-eyed man shouted and threw the papers on the floor. His face was flushed, and the scarring that webbed his cheeks shone white. Amat could feel the others in the room agreeing, though she never took her gaze from this—Ovi Niit's unappointed spokesman. "He would never have done this."

The front room of the comfort house was crowded, though none of the people there were patrons. It was far too early for one thing. The soft quarter wasn't awake in the day. And the watch had closed the house at her request. They were with her still. Big scowling men wearing the colors of the great comfort houses as a symbol of their loyalty to no one house, but the soft quarter itself. The protecting soldiery of vice.

Behind Amat, where she couldn't see them, Torish Wite and his men stood, waiting. And arrayed before her, leaning against walls or sitting on the tables and chairs, were the guards and gambling chiefs and whores of Ovi Niit's house. Amat caught herself, and couldn't entirely stop the smile. Her house. It was a mistake to think of it as the dead man's.

"He did," she said. "If he didn't tell you, perhaps you weren't as close as you'd thought. And you can burn those papers and eat the ashes if you like. It won't change anything."

The one-eyed man turned to the watch captain, taking a pose of imprecation. The captain—a dark-eyed man with a thin, braided beard—took no answering pose.

"They're forged," the one-eyed man said. "They're forged and you know it. If Niit-cha was going to sell out, it wouldn't be to a high town cunt like her."

"I've spoken to the firekeep that signed witness," the captain said.

"Who was it?" a thin, gray-haired man asked. One of the tiles men.

"Marat Golu. Firekeeper for the weaver's quarter."

A murmur ran through the room. Amat felt her belly go tight. That was a detail she would have preferred to leave quiet. The tiles man was clever.

"Gods!" the one-eyed man said. "Him? We have girls that are more expensive."

Amat took a pose that asked clarification. Her hands were steady as stone, her voice pleasant.

"Are you suggesting that one of the utkhaiem is engaging in fraud?"

"Yes I am!" the one-eyed man roared. The tiles man pursed his lips, but stayed silent. "Bhadat Coll was Niit-cha's second now Black Rathvi's gone, and if Niit-cha's dead, the house should be his."

"Niit-cha isn't dead," Amat said. "This house and everyone it have been bought and paid for. You can read the contracts yourselves, if you can read."

"You can roll your contracts up and fuck them," the one-eyed man shouted. There was a fleck of white at the corner of his mouth. The violence in him was just this side of breaking out. Amat rubbed her thumb and finger together, a dry sound. Part of her mind was wrapped in panic, in visceral, animal fear. The other parts of her mind were what had made her the overseer of a great house.

"Gentlemen of the watch," she said. "I'm releasing this man from his indenture. Would you see him to the street."

It had the effect she'd hoped for. The one-eyed man shouted something that might have had words in it, or might only have been rage. A blade appeared in his hand, plucked from his sleeve, and he leaped for her. She forced herself not to flinch as the watchmen cut him down.

The silence that fell was absolute. She surveyed the denizens of her house—*her* house—judging as best she could what they thought, what they felt. Many of these men were watching their lives shatter before them. In the women, the boys, disbelief, confusion, perhaps a sliver of hope. Two of Torish-cha's men gathered up the dying man and hauled him out. The watch wiped their blades, and their captain, fingers pulling thoughtfully at his beard, turned to the survivors.

"Let me make this clear," he said. "The watch recognizes this contract as valid. The house is the lawful property of Amat Kyaan. Any agreements are hers to enforce, and any disagreements that threaten the peace of the quarter, we'll be dealing with."

The tiles man shifted, his brows furrowed, his hands twitching toward some half-formed pose.

"Let's not be stupid about this," the captain said, his eyes, Amat saw, locked on the tiles man. There was a moment of tension, and then it was over. It was rotten as last month's meat, and everyone knew it. And it didn't matter. With the watch behind her, she'd stolen it fairly.

"The house will be closed tonight," Amat announced. "Torish-cha and his men are to be acting as guards. Any of you with weapons will turn them over now. Anyone besides them found with a weapon will be punished. Anyone using a weapon will be blinded and turned out on the street. Remember, you're my property now, until your indentures are complete or I release you. I'm going to ask the watch to stay until a search of the house is complete. Torish-cha?"

From behind her, the men moved forward. The captain moved over to her. His leathers stank.

"You've got yourself a handful of vipers," he said as her thugs and cutthroats disarmed Ovi Niit's thugs and cutthroats. "Are you certain you want this?"

"It's mine now. Good or ill."

"The watch will back you, but they won't like it. Whatever you did, you did outside the quarter, but some people think this kind of thing is poor form. Your troubles aren't over."

"Transitions are always hard," she said, taking a pose of agreement so casual it became a dismissal. The captain shook his head and moved away.

The search went on, moving from room to room with an efficiency that spoke of experience. Amat followed slowly, considering the worn mattresses, the storage chambers in casual disarray. The house was kept no better than its books. That would change. Everything would change. Nothing would be spared.

Sorrow, as powerful as it was unexpected, stung her eyes. She brushed the tears away. This wasn't the time for it. There would never be a time for it. Not in her lifetime.

The search complete, the watch gone, Amat gathered her people—her vipers—in the common room at the back. The speech she'd prepared, rehearsed a thousand times in her mind, seemed suddenly limp;

words that had seemed commanding were petty and weak. Standing at the head of one long table, she drew breath and slowly let it out.

"Well . . ." she said.

In the pause, the voice came from the crowd.

"Grandmother? Is it really you?"

It was a boy of five or six summers. He had been sleeping on a bench one morning, she remembered, when she'd come out of her hellish little cell for a plate of barley gruel and pork. He'd snored.

"Yes," she said. "I've come back."

IN THE DAYS THAT FOLLOWED, HESHAI DIDN'T IMPROVE, BUT NEITHER DID he seem to grow worse. His patchy beard grew fuller, his weight fell for a time and then slowly returned. He would rouse himself now to wander the house, though he didn't leave it, except to lumber down to the pond at night and stare into the black depths. Maati knew—because who else would take the time to care—that Heshai ate less at night than in the mornings, that he changed to clean robes if they were given him, that he might bathe if a bath was drawn, or he might not.

Thankfully the cotton harvest was complete, and there was nothing official the poet had been called on to perform. Physicians came from the Khai, but Heshai refused to see them. Servants who tried to approach the poet soon learned to ask their questions of Maati. Sometimes Maati acted as go between, sometimes, he just made the decisions himself.

For his own life, Maati found himself floating. Unless he was engaged in the daily maintenance of his invalid master, there was no direction for him that he didn't choose, and so he found that his days had grown to follow his emotions. If he felt frightened or overwhelmed, he studied Heshai's brown book, searching for insights that might serve him later if he were called on to hold Seedless. If he felt guilty, he sat by Heshai and tried to coax him into conversation. If he felt lonesome—and he often felt lonesome—he sought out Liat Chokavi. Sometimes he dreamed of her, and of that one brief kiss.

If his feelings for her were complex, it was only because she was beautiful and his friend and Otah-kvo's lover. There was no harm in it, because nothing could come from it. And so, she was his friend, his only friend in the city.

It was because he had become so familiar with her habits and the places where she spent her days that, when the news came—carried by a palace slave with his morning meal—Maati found her so easily. The clearing was west of the seafront and faced a thin stretch of beach she'd shown him one night. Half-leaved trees and the curve of the shore hid the city. Liat sat on a natural bench of stone, leaning against a slab of granite half her height, and looking at the waves without seeing them. Maati moved forward, his feet crackling in the fallen leaves. Liat turned once, and seeing it was him, turned back to the water without speaking. He smoothed a clear spot beside her on the bench and sat.

"It's true then?" he asked. "Amat Kyaan quit the house?"

Liat nodded.

"Wilsin-cha must be furious."

She shrugged. Maati sat forward, his elbows on his knees. The waves gathered and washed the sand, each receding into the rush of the next. Gulls wheeled and screamed to the east and a huge Galtic ship floated at anchor on the horizon. They were the only signs of the city. He stirred the pile of dry leaves below them with his heel, exposing the dark soil beneath them.

"Did you know?"

"She didn't tell me," Liat said, and her voice was calm and blasted and empty. "She just went. Her apartments were empty except for a box of house papers and a letter to Wilsin-cha."

"So it wasn't only you, at least. She hadn't told anyone. Do you know why she left?"

"No," Liat said. "I blame myself for it. If I had done better, if I hadn't embarrassed the house . . ."

"You did what Wilsin-cha asked you to do. If the trade had been what it seemed, they'd be calling your praises for it."

"Perhaps," Liat said. "It hardly matters. She's gone. Wilsin-cha doesn't have any faith in me. I'm an apprentice without a master."

"Well. We're both that, at least."

She coughed out a single laugh.

"I suppose we are," she said, and scooped up his hand, holding it in her own. Maati's heart raced, and something like panic made his mouth taste like copper. Something like panic, only glorious. He didn't move, didn't do anything that might make Liat untwine her fingers from his.

"Where do you think he is?" Maati asked, calling up the spirit of their friend—his master, her heartmate—to show that he understood that this moment, her hand in his, wasn't something inappropriate. It was only friendship.

"He'll have reached Yalakeht. He might even be there by now," Liat said. "Or at least close, if he's not."

"He'll be back soon, then."

"Not for weeks," Liat said.

"It's a long time."

"Heshai-kvo. He's not better?"

"He's not better. He's not worse. He sleeps too much. He eats too little. His beard . . ."

"It's not improving?"

"Longer. Not better. He really ought to shave it off."

Liat shrugged, and Maati felt as if the motion shifted her nearer. So this was friendship with a woman, he told himself. It was pleasant, he told himself, this simple intimacy.

"He seemed better when I came to see him," Liat said.

"He makes an effort I think, when you're there. I don't know why."

"Because I'm a girl."

"Perhaps that, yes," Maati said.

Liat, releasing his hand, stretched and stood. Maati sighed, feeling that a moment had passed—some invisible, exquisite moment in his life. He had heard old epics telling of moments in a man's youth that never truly left the heart—that stayed fresh and sweet and present through all the years and waited on the deathbed to carry him safely into his last sleep. Maati thought that those moments must be like this one. The scent of the sea, the perfect sky, the leaves, the roar of waves, and his hand, cooling where she had touched him.

"I should come by more often, then," Liat said. "If it helps."

"I wouldn't want to impose," he said, rising to stand beside her. "But if you have the time."

"I don't foresee being given any new projects of note. Besides, I like the poet's house. It's a beautiful place."

"It's better when you're there," Maati said.

Liat grinned. Maati took a pose of self-congratulation to which Liat replied with one of query.

"I've made you feel better," he said.

Liat weighed it, looking out to horizon with her eyes narrowed. She nodded, as if he'd pointed out a street she'd never seen, or a pattern in the ways a tree branched. Her smile, when it came again, was softer.

"I suppose you have," she said. "I mean, everything's still a terrible mess."

"I'll try fixing the world later. After dinner. Do you want to go back?"

"I suppose I'd best. There's no call to earn a reputation of being unreliable, incompetent, *and* sulky."

They walked back to the city. It had seemed a longer path when he'd been on it alone, worried for Liat. Now, though they were hardly moving faster than a stroll, the walls of the city seemed to surround them almost immediately. They walked up the street of beads, paused at a stand where a boy of no more then eight summers was selling, with a ferocious seriousness, cakes smothered in fine-powdered sugar, and listened to an old beggar singing in a rough, melodious voice that spoke of long sorrow and moved Maati almost to tears. And still, they reached the crossroads that would lead her to the compound of House Wilsin and him to the oppressive, slow desperation of the poet's house before the sun had reached the top of its arc.

"So," Liat said, taking a pose that asked permission, but so casually that it assumed it granted, "shall I come to the poet's house once I'm done here?"

Maati made a show of consideration then took a pose extending invitation. She accepted, but didn't turn away. Maati felt himself frown, and she took a pose of query that he wasn't entirely sure how to answer.

"Liat-cha," he began.

"Cha?"

He raised his hands, palm out. Not a real pose, but expressive nonetheless. *Let me go on.*

"Liat-cha, I know it's only because things went so wrong that Otahkvo had to leave. And I wouldn't ever have chosen what happened with Seedless. But coming to know you better has been very important to me, and I wanted you to know how much I appreciate your being my friend."

Liat considered him, her expression unreadable but not at all upset.

"Did you rehearse that?" she asked.

"No. I didn't really know what I was going to say until I'd already said it."

She smiled briefly, and then her gaze clouded, as if he'd touched some private pain. He felt his heart sink. Liat met his eyes and she smiled.

"There's something I think you should see, Maati-kya. Come with me."

He followed her to her cell in silence. With each step, Maati felt his anxiety grow. The people they passed in the courtyard and walkway nodded to them both, but seemed unsurprised, undisturbed. Maati tried to seem to be there on business. When Liat closed the door of her cell, he took a pose of apology.

"Liat-cha," he said. "If I've done anything that would . . ."

She batted his hands, and he released the pose. To his surprise, he found she had moved forward, moved against him. He found that her lips had gently pressed his. He found that the air had all gone from the room. She pulled back from the kiss. Her expression was soft and sorrowful and gentle. Her fingers touched his hair.

"Go. I'll come to the poet's house tonight."

"Yes," was all he could think to say.

He stopped in the gardens of the low palaces, sat on the grass, and pressed his fingertips to his mouth, as if making sure his lips were still there; that they were real. The world seemed suddenly uprooted, dreamlike. She kissed him—truly kissed him. She had touched his hair. It was impossible. It was terrible. It was like walking along a familiar path and suddenly falling off a cliff.

And it was also like flying.

14

>+< The raft was big enough to carry eight people. It was pulled against the current by a team of four oxen, moving slowly but implacably along paths worn in the shore by generations of such passage. Otah slept in the back, wrapped in his cloak and in the rough wool blankets the boatman and his daughter provided. In the mornings, the daughter—a child of no more then nine summers—lit a brazier and cooked sweet rice with almond milk and cinnamon. At night, after they tied up, her father made a meal—most often a chicken and barley soup.

In the days spent in this routine, Otah had little to do besides watch the slow progress of trees moving past them, listen to the voices of the water and the oxen, and try to win over the daughter by telling jokes and singing with her or the boatman by asking him about life on the river and listening to his answers. By the time they reached the end of the last full day's journey, both boatman and child were comfortable with him. The boatman shared a bowl of plum wine with him after the other passengers had gone to sleep. They never mentioned the girl's mother, and Otah never asked.

The river journey ended at a low town larger than any Otah had seen since Yalakeht. It had wide, paved streets and houses as high as three stories that looked out across the river or into the branches of the pine forest that surrounded it. The wealth of the place was clear in its food, its buildings, the faces of its people. It was as if some nameless quarter of the cities of the Khaiem had been struck off and moved here, into the wilderness.

That the road to the Dai-kvo's village was well kept and broad didn't surprise him, but the discovery that—for a price higher than he wished to pay—he could hire a litter that would carry him the full day's steep, uphill journey and set him down at the door of the Dai-kvo's palaces did. He passed men in fine robes of wool and fur, envoys from the courts of the Khaiem or trading houses or other places, further away. Food stands at the roadside offered sumptuous fare at high prices for the great men who passed by or wheat gruel and chicken for the lower orders like himself.

Despite the wealth and luxury of the road, the first sight of the Dai-kvo's village took Otah's breath away. Carved into the stone of the mountain, the village was something half belonging to the world of men, half to the ocean and the sun and the great forces of the world. He stopped in the road and looked up at the glittering windows and streets, stairways and garrets and towers. A thin golden ribbon of a waterfall lay just within the structures, and warm light of the coming sunset made the stone around it glow like bronze. Chimes light as birdsong and deep as bells rang when the breeze stirred them. If the view had been designed to humble those who came to it, the designer could rest well. Maati, he realized, had lived in this place, studied in it. And he, Otah, had refused it. He wondered what it would have been like, coming down this road as a boy coming to his reward; what it would have been like to see this grandeur set out before him as if it were his right.

The path to the grand offices was easily found, and well peopled. Firekeepers—not members of the utkhaiem, but servants only of the Dai-kvo—kept kilns at the crossroads and teahouses and offered the promise of warmth and comfort in the falling night. Otah didn't pause at them.

He reached the grand offices: a high, arched hall open to the west so that the sunset set the white stone walls ablaze. Men—only men, Otah noted—paced through the hall on one errand or another, passing from one corridor to another, through doors of worked rosewood and oak. Otah had to stop a servant who was lighting lanterns to find the way to the Dai-kvo's overseer.

He was an old man with a kind face in the brown robes of a poet. When Otah approached his table, the overseer took a pose that was both welcome and query with a flowing grace that he had seen only in the Khai Saraykeht or the andat. Otah replied with a pose of greeting, and for an instant, he was a boy again in the cold, empty hallways of the school.

"I've come with a letter for the Dai-kvo," he said, pushing the memory aside. "From Maati Vaupathi in Saraykeht."

"Ah?" the overseer said, "Excellent. I will see that he gets it immediately."

The beautiful, old hand reached to him, open to accept the packet still in Otah's sleeve. Otah considered the withered fingers like carved wood, a sudden alarm growing in him.

"I had hoped to see the Dai-kvo myself," he said, and the overseer's expression changed to one of sympathy.

"The Dai-kvo is very busy, my friend. He hardly has time to speak to me, and I'm set to schedule his days. Give the letter to me, and I will see that he knows of it."

Otah pulled the letter out and handed it over, a profound disappointment blooming in his breast. It was obvious, of course, that the Dai-kvo wouldn't meet with simple couriers, however sensitive the letters they bore. He shouldn't have expected him to. Otah took a pose of gratitude.

"Will you be staying to carry a reply?"

"Yes," Otah said. "If there is one."

"I will send word tomorrow whether the most high intends to respond. Where will I find you?"

Otah took a pose of apology and explained that he had not taken rooms and didn't know the village. The overseer gave him a recommendation, directions, and the patience Otah imagined a grandfather might have for a well-loved but rather slow grandchild. It was twilight— the distant skyline glorious with the gold and purple of the just-set sun—when Otah returned to the street, his errand complete.

On the way back down, there was time to see the village more closely, though the light around him was fading. It struck him for the first time that he had seen no women since he had left the road. The firekeeper's kilns, the food carts and stalls, the inn to which he'd been directed—all were overseen by men. None of the people passing him in the steep, dim street had a woman's face.

And as he looked more closely, he found other signs, subtler ones, that the life of the Dai-kvo's village was unlike that of the ones he had known. The streets had none of the grime and dust of Saraykeht—no small plants or grasses pushed at the joints of the paving stones, no moss stained the corners of the walls. Even more than its singularity of gender, the unnatural perfection of the place made it seem foreign and unsettling and sterile.

He ate his dinner—venison and wine and fresh black bread—sitting alone at a low table with his back to the fire. A dark mood had descended on him. Visions of Liat and some small house, some simple work, bread cooked in his own kiln, meat roasted in his own kitchens seemed both ludicrous and powerful. He had done what he said he'd set out for. The letter was in the Dai-kvo's hands, or would be shortly.

But he had come for his own reasons too. He was Otah, the sixth son of the Khai Machi, who had walked away from the greatest power in all the nations. He had been offered the chance to control the andat and refused. For the first time, here in this false village, he imagined what that must be to his brothers, his teachers, the boys who had taken the offer gladly when it had been given. To men like Maati.

And so who was this Itani Noyga, this simple laborer with simple dreams? He had come halfway across the lands of the Khaiem, he realized, to answer that question, and instead he had handed an old man a packet of papers. He remembered, setting out from Saraykeht, that it had seemed an important adventure, not only to Heshai and Seedless, the Khai Machi and Saraykeht, but to himself personally. Now, he wasn't sure why he'd thought delivering a letter would mean more than delivering a letter.

He was given a small room, hardly large enough for the stretched-canvas cot and the candle on the table beside it. The blankets were warm and thick and soft. The mattress was clean and free of lice or fleas. The room smelled of cut cedar, and not rat piss or unbathed humanity. Small as it was, it was also perfect.

The candle was snuffed, and Otah more than half asleep when his door opened. A small man, bald as an egg, stepped in, a lantern held high. His round face was marked by two bushy eyebrows—black shot with white. Otah met his gaze, at first bleary, and then an instant later awake and alert. He took the pose of greeting he'd learned as a boy, he smiled sweetly and without sincerity.

"I am honored by your presence, most high Dai-kvo."

Tahi-kvo scowled and moved closer. He held the lantern close to Otah's face until the brightness of the flame made old teacher shadowy. Otah didn't look away.

"It *is* you."

"Yes."

"Show me your hands," his old teacher said. Otah complied, and the lantern shifted, Tahi-kvo leaning close, examining the callused palms. He bent so close, Otah could feel the breath on his fingertips. The old man's eyes were going.

"It's true then," Tahi-kvo said. "You're a laborer."

Otah closed his hands. The words were no surprise, but the sting of them was. He would have thought he was beyond caring what opinion Tahi-kvo held. He smiled his charming smile like a mask and kept his voice mild and amused.

"I've picked my own path," he said.

"It was a poor choice."

"It was mine to make."

The old man—Tahi-kvo, the Dai-kvo, the most powerful man in world—stood, shaking his head in disgust. His robes whispered as he moved—silk upon silk. He tilted his head like a malefic bird.

"I have consultations to make concerning the message you brought. It may take some days before I draft my reply."

Otah waited for the stab of words or the remembered whir of the lacquer rod, but Tahi only stood waiting. At length Otah took a pose of acceptance.

"I will wait for it," he said.

For a moment, something glittered in Tahi-kvo's eyes that might have been sorrow or impatience, and then without farewell, he was gone, the door closed behind him, and Otah lay back in his bed. The darkness was silent, except for the slowly retreating footsteps. They were long vanished before Otah's heart and breath slowed, before the heat in his blood cooled.

THE DAYS THAT FOLLOWED WERE AMONG THE MOST DIFFICULT OF AMAT Kyaan's life. The comfort house was in disarray, and her coup only added to the chaos. Each individual person—whores, guards, the men at the tables, the men who sold wine, all of them—were testing her. Three times, fights had broken out. It seemed once a day that she was

called on to stop some small liberty, and always with the plaintive explanation that Ovi Niit had allowed it. To hear it told now, he had been
the most selfless and open-handed of men. Death had improved him. It
was to be expected.

If that had been all, it might not have kept her awake in the nights.
But also there was the transfer of Maj into the house. No one else
spoke Nippu, and Maj hadn't picked up enough of the Khaiate
tongue to make herself understood easily. Since she'd come, Amat
had been interrupted for her needs, whatever they were, whenever
they came.

Torish Wite, thankfully, had proved capable in more ways than she'd
hoped. When she asked him, he had agreed to spread the word at the
seafront that Amat Kyaan in the soft quarter was looking for information
about shipments of pearls from Galt. Building the case against House
Wilsin would be like leading a second life. The comfort house would
fund it, once she had the place in order, but the time was more a burden
than the money. She was not so young as she had been.

These early stages, at least, she could leave to the mercenary, though
some nights, she would remember conversations she'd had with traders
from the Westlands and the implications for trading with a freehold or
ward that relied on paid soldiery. As long as she was in a position to offer these men girls and money, they would likely stay. If they ever became indispensable, she was doomed.

Her room, once Ovi Niit's, was spacious and wide and covered—
desk, bed, and floor—with records and papers and plans. The morning
sun sloped through windows whose thick, tight-fit shutters were meant
to let her sleep until evening. She sipped from a bowl of tea while Mitat, her closest advisor in the things specifically of the house, paced the
length of the room. The papers in her hands hissed as she shifted from
one to another and back.

"It's too much," Mitat said. "I honestly never thought I'd say it, but
you're giving them too much freedom. To choose which men they take?
Amat-cha, with all respect, you're a whoremonger. When a man comes
in with the silver, it's your place to give him a girl. Or a boy. Or three
girls and a chicken, if that's what he's paid for. If the girls can refuse a
client . . ."

"They take back less money," Amat said, her voice reasonable and
calm, though she already knew that Mitat was right. "Those who work

most, get most. And with that kind of liberty and the chance to earn more, we'll attract women who want to work in a good house."

Mitat stopped walking. She didn't speak, but her guarded expression was enough. Amat closed her eyes and leaned back in her seat.

"Don't beat them without cause," Mitat said. "Don't let anyone cut them where it would scar. Give them what they're owed. That's all you can do now, grandmother. In a year—two, perhaps—you could try something like this, but to do it now would be a sign of weakness."

"Yes. I suppose it would. Thank you, Mitat-cha."

When she opened her eyes again, the woman had taken a pose of concern. Amat answered with one of reassurance.

"You seem tired, grandmother."

"It's nothing."

Mitat hesitated visibly, then handed back the papers. Before Amat could ask what was troubling her, steps came up the stairs and a polite knock interrupted them. Torish Wite stepped in, his expression guarded.

"There's someone here to see you," he said to Amat.

"Who?"

"Marchat Wilsin."

Her belly went tight, but she only took in a deep breath.

"Is anyone with him?"

"No. He stinks a little of wine, but he's unarmed and he's come alone."

"Where's Maj?" she asked.

"Asleep. We've made your old cell a sleeping chamber for her."

"Set a guard on her room. No one's to go in, and she's not to come out. I don't want him knowing that we have her here."

"You're going to see him?" Mitat asked, her voice incredulous.

"He was my employer for decades," Amat said, as if it were an answer to the question. "Torish-cha. I'll want a man outside the door. If I call out, I want him in here immediately. If I don't, I want privacy. We'll finish our conversation later, Mitat."

The pair retreated, closing the door behind them. Amat rose, taking up her cane and walking to the doors that opened onto the private deck. It had rained in the night, and the air was still thick with it. It was that, Amat told herself, that made it hard to breathe. The door opened behind her, then closed again. She didn't turn at once. Across the deck, the soft quarter flowed street upon street, alley upon alley. Banners flew and beggars sang. It was a lovely city, even this part. This was why she was doing what she'd done. For this and for the girl Maj and the babe she'd lost. She steeled herself.

Marchat Wilsin stood at the doorway in a robe of green so deep and rich it seemed shot with black. His face was grayish, his eyes bloodshot. He looked frightened and lost, like a mouse surrounded by cats. He broke her heart.

"Hello, old friend," she said. "Who'd have thought we'd end here, eh?"

"Why are you doing this, Amat?"

The pain in his voice almost cracked it. She felt the urge to go to him, comfort him. She wanted badly to touch his hand and tell him that everything would end well, in part because she knew that it wouldn't. It occurred to her distantly that if she had let him profess love for her, she might not have been able to leave House Wilsin.

"What happened to the poet. To the girl. It was an attack," she said. "You know it, and I do. You attacked Saraykeht."

He walked forward, his hands out, palms up before him.

"*I* didn't," he said. "Amat, you have to see that this wasn't my doing."

"Can I offer you tea?" she asked.

Bewildered, he sank onto a divan and ran his hands through his hair in wordless distress. She remembered the man she'd first met—his dark hair, his foreign manners. He'd had an easy laugh back then, and power in his gaze. She poured a bowl of tea for him. When he didn't take it from her hand, she left it on the low table at his knee and went back to her own desk.

"It didn't work, Amat. It failed. The poet's alive, the andat's still held. They see that it can't work, and so it won't happen again, if you'll only let this go."

"I can't," she said.

"Why not?"

"Because of what you did to Maj. She wanted that child. And because Saraykeht is my home. And because you betrayed me."

Marchat flushed red and took a pose so sloppy it might have meant anything.

"Betrayed you? How did I betray you? I did everything to keep you clear of this. I warned you that Oshai was waiting for you. And when you came back I was the one who argued for keeping you alive. I risked my life for yours."

"You made me part of this," Amat said, surprised to hear the anger in her own voice, to feel the warmth in her face. "You did this and you put me in a position where I have to sacrifice everything—*everything*—in order to redeem myself. If I had known in time, I would have stopped it. You knew that when you asked me to find you a bodyguard. You hoped I'd find a way out."

"I wasn't thinking clearly then. I am now."

"Are you? How can I do anything besides this, Marchat-kya? If I keep silent, it's as much as saying I approve of the crime. And I don't."

His eyes shifted, his gaze going hard. Slowly, he lifted the bowl of tea to his lips and drank it down in one long draw. When he put the bowl down—ceramic clicking against the wooden table—he was once again the man she'd known. He had put his heart aside, she knew, and entered the negotiation that might save his life, his house. Might, if he could convince her, even save her from the path she'd chosen. She felt a half-smile touch her lips. A part of her hoped he might win.

"Granted, something wrong was done," he said. "Granted, I had some part—though I didn't have a choice in it. But put aside that I was coerced. Put aside that it was none of it my plan. Let me ask you this— what justice do you expect?"

"I don't know," she said. "That's for the Khai and his men to choose."

He took a pose that showed his impatience with her.

"You know quite well the mercy he'll show me and House Wilsin. And Galt as a whole. And it won't be for Maj. It'll be for himself."

"It will be for his city."

"And how much is a city worth, Amat? Even in the name of justice. If the Khai chooses to kill a thousand Galtic babies out of their mothers, is that a fair price for a city? If they starve because our croplands go sterile, is that a fair price? You want justice, Amat. I know that. But the end of this road is only vengeance."

A breeze thick with the smell of the sea shifted the window cloths. The doors to the private deck shifted closed with a clack, and the room went dim.

"You're thinking with your heart," he continued. "What happened was terrible. I don't deny it. We were caught up in something huge and grotesque and evil. But be clear of the cost. One child. How many women miscarry in a single year? How many lose their children from being beaten by their men, or from falling, or from illness? I can think of six in the last five months. What happened was wrong, Amat, and I swear to you I will do what I can to make it right again. But not at the cost of making things worse."

He leaned forward. Her retort was finding its shape in her mind, but not quickly.

"They see now that it can't work," he said. "They weren't able to be rid of Seedless when he was *conspiring* with them. They can see now that they'd never be able to coordinate freeing all of them at once. The experiment *failed*. Sure they may try something again someday, but not anytime soon. They'll turn their efforts back to the Westlands, or maybe to the south, or the islands for the time being. The war won't come here. Not unless they find some way to do it safely."

Amat's blood went cold, and she looked at her hands to avoid letting the shock show in her eyes. Trade, she had thought. With Seedless gone, trade would shift. Her city would suffer, and other cotton markets would flourish. She'd been thinking too small. Eight generations without war. Eight generations of the wealth that the andat commanded, the protection they gave. This was not trade. This was the first step toward invasion, and he thought she'd known it.

She forced herself to smile, to look up. Without the andat, the cities would fall. The wealth of the Khaiem would go to pay for what mercenaries they could hire. But faced with the soldiery of Galt, Amat doubted many companies would choose to fight for a clearly losing side, or would keep their contracts with the Khaiem if they made them.

Everything she knew would end.

"Come back to the house," Marchat said. "It's almost time for the end of season negotiations, and I need you there. I need you back."

She called out sharply, and the guard was in the room. Marchat—her old friend, her employer, the hard-headed, funny, thoughtful man whose house had saved her from the streets, the man who loved her and had never had the courage to say it—looked lost. Amat took a pose of farewell appropriate to the beginning of a long absence. She was fairly sure he wouldn't catch the nuance of permanence in it, but perhaps it was more for herself than him anyway.

"The past was a beautiful place, Marchat-kya," she said. "I miss it already."

And then, to the guard.

"See him out."

HESHAI'S IMPROVEMENT, WHEN IT CAME, WAS SUDDEN AS A CHANGE IN THE weather. Liat was in the main room of the poet's house peeling an orange. Maati had gone up to his room for something, telling her to wait there. The steps that descended behind her were slow and heavy, as if Maati were bearing a large and awkward burden. She turned, and instead found Heshai washed and shaved and wrapped in a formal robe.

Liat started to her feet and took a pose of greeting appropriate to one of a much higher station. On the seat where she'd been, the long golden length of peel still clung to the white flesh of the orange. The poet sketched a brief pose of welcome and moved over to her, his gaze on the fruit. His smile, when it came, was unsure, a configuration unfamiliar to the wide lips. Liat wondered whether she had ever seen the man laugh.

"I don't suppose there's enough of that to share with an old man?" he said. He seemed almost shy.

"Of course," she said, picking up the orange and splitting off a section. He accepted it from her with a pose of thanks and popped it in his mouth. His skin was pale as the belly of a fish, and there were dark sacks under his eyes. He had grown thinner in the weeks since the sad trade had gone wrong. Still, when he grinned at her, his smile finding its confidence, she found herself smiling back. For a moment, she could see clearly what he had looked like as a child.

"You seem much better," she said.

"Tired of moping around, I suppose," he said. "I thought I might go out. I haven't been to a good teahouse in some time."

The lighter footsteps she knew came down the stairs behind them and stopped. Maati had forgotten the book in his hand. His mouth was open.

"Come down," Heshai said. "It isn't a private conversation. We were only sharing a bite. There's enough for you too, I imagine."

"Heshai-kvo . . ."

"I was just telling Liat-kya here that I've decided to stretch my legs this evening. I've been too much within myself. And tomorrow, there are things we should do. It's past time we began your education in earnest, eh?"

Maati took a pose of agreement made clumsy by the volume in his hand, but Liat could see that he was hardly aware of it. She caught his gaze, encouraging him silently to be pleased, or if he wasn't, to act as if he were.

"I will be ready, Heshai-kvo," he said. If there was an edge to his voice, Heshai seemed not to hear it. He only took a pose of farewell to Liat more formal than her rank called for, and a subtler pose of congratulation to Maati that she was fairly certain she had not been meant to see, and then he was off. They sat on the steps up to the house and watched him striding over the bridge and along the path until it turned. Maati, beside her, was trembling with rage.

"I thought this was what we wanted," Liat said, gently.

He snapped his head, her words pulling him back to the world.

"Not like this," he said.

"He's out of his bed. He's going into the city."

"It's like nothing happened," Maati said. "He's acting like nothing happened. All these weeks, just vanished . . ."

Liat smoothed his neck with her palm. For a moment, Maati went tight, then, slowly, she felt him relax. He turned to her.

"You wanted an apology," she said. "Or some recognition for what you did for him all this time."

Maati put down the book on the step beside him and pulled his robe closer around him. For a long time, they didn't speak. The trees were turning, the first fallen leaves covering the grounds. It wasn't winter, but autumn had reached its center.

"It's wrong of me," Maati said, his voice thick with shame and anger. "I should accept that he's improving and be pleased. But . . ."

"This may be the best he can do," Liat said. "Give him time."

Maati nodded and took her hand in his, their fingers laced. With her other hand, she reached across him and took up the book. It was old, and heavy for its size, bound in copper and leather.

"Read me that poem you were talking about," she said.

Much later, the darkness fallen, Liat lay with Maati on his cot and listened to his breath. The breeze that stirred the netting raised gooseflesh on her arms, but he was soft and warm as a cat against her. She stroked his hair. She felt safe and content and sick with guilt. She had never been unfaithful to a lover before this. She had always imagined it would be difficult, that people would stare at her in the streets and talk of her in scandalized whispers. In the event, it seemed no one cared. The isolation that had come after Seedless and the baby—from Amat, from Wilsin-cha, from the people of the house, and worst from Itani—was easier to bear with Maati. And he could listen when she spoke about her part, her failings, the way she'd let the child die.

The night candle fluttered, and three slow moths beat at the walls of its glass lantern. Liat shifted and Maati murmured in his sleep and turned away from her. She parted the netting and stood naked, letting the cool of night wash over her. Their coupling had left her feeling sticky. She thought of going to a bathhouse, but the long walk through the city after dark and the prospect of leaving Maati behind failed to appeal. It would be better, she thought, to stay near, even if it meant being cold. She deserved, she supposed, a little discomfort for her sins. She pulled on her robe, but didn't tie the fastenings.

In the darkness, stars spilled across the sky. The distant lights of the palaces, of the city, might almost not have been. Liat considered the crescent moon, its shining curve of light cupping a darkness of blotted stars. Frogs and crickets sang and the manicured grass at the side of the koi pond tickled the bottom of her feet. She looked around carefully before shrugging out of her robe. The water of the pond was no worse than she might find in the cold pool of a bathhouse. The fish darted away from her and then slowly returned. Reeds at the water's edge rubbed against each other with a sound like hands on skin, disturbed by the waves of her movements.

Floating on her back, her legs kicking slowly, she thought of Itani. She didn't feel as if she were betraying him, though she knew that she was. Maati and Itani—Otah—seemed to inhabit entirely different places in her heart. The one seemed so little related to the other. Itani was her heartmate, the man she'd shared her bed with for months. Maati was her friend, her confidant, her only support in a world empty even of the other man. For hours at a time and especially in his company, she could forget the guilt and the dread. She didn't know how it could be like this: so easy and so difficult both.

The chill touched her bones, and she turned, swimming easily to the shore. The rich mud squelched between her toes. Against wet flesh, the air was much colder than the water had been. By the time she found her robe, she was shivering. The night around her was silent, the insects and night birds gone still.

"There must be some etiquette to address situations like this," Seedless said from the darkness, "but I'm sure I don't know what it is."

The andat's face seemed hung in the air, the pale lips quirked in a smile both amused and grim. He moved forward as she pulled on her robe. His cloak—black shot with blue—seemed to weave in and out of the darkness. He pulled something bulky from a sleeve and held it out to her. A hair cloth.

"I brought this for you," he said. "Once I understood what you were doing I thought you'd want it."

Liat took it, falling into a pose of gratitude by reflex. The andat returned it dismissively, squatted on the grassy slope and, his arms resting on his knees, looked out over the pond.

"You got out of the torture box."

"One of them. Heshai-kvo let me out. He's been doing it for several days now on the condition that I promise to stay within sight of the house. I've sworn a sacred oath, though I imagine I'll break it eventually. It's why he's improving. Locking away a part of yourself—especially a shameful one—gives that part power over all the rest. It's the danger of splitting yourself in two, don't you find?"

"I don't know what you mean," Liat said.

Seedless smiled in genuine amusement.

"Dry your hair," he said. "I'm not judging you, my dear. I'm a babykiller. You're a girl of seventeen summers who's taken a second lover. It hardly gives me the high ground."

Liat wrapped her hair in the cloth and turned to leave, dry leaves stirring at her ankles. The words that stopped her were so soft, she might almost have imagined them.

"I know about Otah."

She paused. As if on cue, the chorus of crickets began again.

"What do you know?" she asked.

"Enough."

"How?"

"I'm clever. What do you intend to do when he comes back?"

Liat didn't answer. The andat turned to consider her. He took a pose that unasked the question. Anger flashed in Liat's breast.

"I love him. He's my heartmate."

"And Maati?"

"I love him, too."

"But he isn't your heartmate."

Liat didn't reply. In the dim light of moon and star, the andat smiled sadly and took a pose that expressed understanding and sympathy and acceptance.

"Maati and I . . . we need each other. We're alone otherwise. Both of us are very, very alone."

"Well, at least that won't last. He'll be back very soon," Seedless said. "Tomorrow, perhaps. Or the day after."

"Who?"

"Otah."

Liat felt her breath go shallow. It was a sensation quite like fear.

"No, he won't. He can't."

"I think he can," the andat replied.

"It's a full three weeks just to Yalakeht. Even if he took a fast boat up the river, he'd only just be arriving now."

"You're sure of that?"

"Of course I am."

"Then I suppose I must be mistaken," the andat said so mildly that Liat had no answer. Seedless laughed then and put his head in his hands.

"What?" Liat asked.

"I've been an idiot. Otah is the Otah-kvo that Maati told me of. He doesn't wear a brand and he's not a poet, so I never connected them. But if Maati's sent him to see the Dai-kvo . . . Yes. He must be."

"I thought you knew all about Otah," Liat said, her heart falling.

"That may have been an exaggeration. Otah-kvo. A black robe who didn't take the brand or become a poet. I think . . . I think I heard a story like that once. Well, a few questions of Heshai, and I'm sure I can dredge it up."

The horror of what she'd done flooded her. Liat didn't sit so much as give way. The leaves crackled under her weight. The andat looked over to her, alarmed.

"You tricked me," she whispered.

Seedless tilted his head with an odd, sensual smile as much pity as wonderment. He took a pose offering comfort.

"It wasn't you, Liat-kya. Maati told me all about it before he even knew who I was. If you've betrayed your heartmate tonight—and, really, I think there's a strong argument that you have—it wasn't with me. And whether you believe it or not, the secret's safe."

"I don't. I don't believe you."

The andat smiled, and for a moment the sincerity in his face reminded her of Heshai-kvo.

"Having a secret is like sitting at a roof's edge with a rock, Liat. As long as you have the rock, you have the power of life and death over anyone below you. Drop the rock, and you've just got a nice view. I won't spread your secret unless it brings me something, and as it stands, there's no advantage to me. Unless things change, I won't be telling any of your several secrets."

Liat took a pose of challenge.

"Swear it," she said.

"To whom are you talking? How likely am I to be bound by an oath to you?"

Liat let her arms fall to her sides.

"I won't betray you," Seedless said, "because there's no reason to, and because it would hurt Maati."

"Maati?"

Seedless shrugged.

"I'm fond of him. He's . . . he's young and he hasn't lived in the world for very long, perhaps. But he has the talent and charm to escape this if he's wise."

"You sound like Heshai when you say that."

"Of course I do."

"Do you . . . I mean, you don't *really* care about Maati. Do you?"

Seedless stood. He moved with the grace and ease of a thrown stone. His robe hung from him, darker than the night. His face was the perfect white of a carnival mask, smooth as eggshell and as expressionless. The crickets increased their chirping songs until they were so loud, Liat was surprised that she could hear Seedless' voice, speaking softly over them.

"In ten years time, Liat-kya, look back at this—at what you and I said here, tonight. And when you do, ask yourself which of us was kinder to him."

15

>+< The days passed with an exquisite discomfort in the village of the Dai-kvo. The clear air, the cold stone of the streets, the perfection, the maleness and austerity and beauty were like a dream. Otah moved through the alleyways and loitered with other men by the fire-keepers' kilns, listening to gossip and the choir of windchimes. Messengers infested the village like moths, fluttering here and there. Speakers from every city, dressed in sumptuous robes and cloaks, appeared every day and vanished again. The water tasted strange from influence, the air smelled of power.

While Otah had been lifting bales of cotton all day and pulling ticks out of his arms in the evenings, Maati had lived in these spaces. Otah went to his rooms each night, sick with waiting, and wondering who he would have been, had he taken the old Dai-kvo's offer. And then, he would remember the school—the cruelty, the malice, the cold-hearted lessons and beatings and the laughter of the strong at the weak—and he wondered instead how Maati had brought himself to accept.

In the afternoon of his fifth day, a man in the white robes of a high servant found him on the wide wooden deck of a teahouse.

"You are the courier for Maati Vaupathai?" the servant asked, taking a pose both respectful and querying. Otah responded with an affirming pose. "The most high wishes to speak with you. Please come with me."

The library was worked in marble; tall shelves filled with scrolls and bound volumes lined the walls, and sunlight shone through banks of clerestory windows with glass clear as air. Tahi-kvo—the Dai-kvo—sat at long table of carved blackwood. An iron brazier warmed the room, smelling of white smoke and hot metal and incense. He looked up as the servant took a pose of completion and readiness so abjectly humble as to approach the ludicrous. Otah took no pose.

"Go," the Dai-kvo said, and the white-robed servant left, pulling the wide doors closed behind him. Otah stood as Tahi-kvo considered him from under frowning brows then pushed a sewn letter across the table. Otah stepped forward and took it, tucking it into his sleeve. They stood for a moment in silence.

"You were stupid to come," Tahi-kvo said, his tone matter-of-fact. "If your brothers find you're alive they'll stop eyeing each other and work in concert to kill you."

"I suppose they might. Will you tell them?"

"No." Tahi-kvo rose and stalked to a bookshelf, speaking over his shoulder as he went. "My master died, you know. The season after you left."

"I'm sorry," Otah said.

"Why did you come? Why *you*?"

"Maati is a friend. And there was no one else who could be trusted." The other reasons weren't ones he would share with Tahi-kvo. They were his own.

Tahi-kvo ran his fingers across the spines of the books. Even turned almost away, Otah could see the bitterness in his smile.

"And he trusts you? He trusts Otah Machi? Well, he's young. Perhaps he doesn't know you so well as I do. Do you want to know what's in this letter I'm sending with you?"

"If he cares to tell me," Otah said.

The volume Tahi-kvo pulled down was ancient—bound in wood with clasps of metal and thick as a hand spread wide. He hefted it back and laid it on the table before he answered.

"It says he mustn't let Heshai lose control of his andat. It says there isn't a replacement for it, and that there isn't the prospect of one. If Seedless escapes, I have nothing to send, and Saraykeht becomes an oversized low town. That's what it says."

Tahi-kvo's eyebrows rose, challenging. Otah took a pose that accepted the lesson from a teacher—a pose he'd taken before, when he'd been a boy.

"Every generation, it's become more difficult," Tahi-kvo said, angry, it seemed, at speaking the words. "There are fewer men who take up the mantle. The andat that escape are more and more difficult to recapture. Even the fourth-water ones like Seedless and Unstung. The time will come—not for me, I think, but for my successor or his—when the andat may fail us entirely. The Khaiem will be overrun by Galts and Westerman. Do you understand what I'm telling you?"

"Yes," Otah said. "But not why."

"Because you had promise," Tahi-kvo said bitterly. "And because I don't like you. But I have to ask this. Otah Machi, have you come here with this letter because you've regretted your refusal? Was it an excuse to speak to me because you're seeking the robes of a poet?"

Otah didn't laugh, though the questions seemed absurd. Absurd and—as they mixed in his mind with the sights and scents of the village—more than half sad. And beneath all that, perhaps he had. Perhaps he had needed to come here and see the path he had chosen to know as a man whether he still believed in the choices he had made as a boy.

"No," he said.

Tahi-kvo nodded, undid the clasps on the great book and opened it. It was in no script Otah had ever seen. The poet looked up at him, his gaze direct and unpleasant.

"I thought not," he said. "Go then. And don't come back unless you decide you're man enough to take on the work. I don't have time to coddle children."

Otah took a pose of leave-taking, then hesitated.

"I'm sorry, Tahi-kvo," he said. "That your master died. That you had to live this way. All of it. I'm sorry the world's the way it is."

"Blame the sun for setting," the Dai-kvo said, not looking at him, not looking up.

Otah turned and walked out. The magnificence of the palaces was amazing, rich even past the Khai Saraykeht. The wide avenues outside it were crowded in the late afternoon with men going about business of the highest importance, dressed in silks and woven linen and leather supple as skin. Otah took in the majesty of it and understood for the first time since he'd come the hollowness that lay beneath it. It was the same, he thought, as the emptiness in Heshai-kvo's eyes. The one was truly a child of the other.

He was surprised, as he walked down to the edge of the village, to find himself moved to sorrow. The few tears that escaped him might have been shed for Maati or Heshai, Tahi-kvo or the boys of his cohort scattered now into the world, the vanity of power or himself. The question that had carried him here—whether he was truly Otah Machi or

Itani Noyga; son of the Khaiem or seafront laborer—was unresolved, but it was also answered.

Either one, but never this.

"WHEN?" MAJ DEMANDED, HER ARMS CROSSED. HER CHEEKS WERE RED AND flushed, her breath smelled of wine. "I've been weeks living with whores and you, their pimp. You told me that the men who killed my child would be brought to justice. Now tell me *when*."

The island girl moved quickly, scooping up a vase from Amat's desk and throwing it against the far wall. The pottery shattered, flowers falling broken to the floor. The wet mark on the wall dripped and streaked. The guard was in the room almost before Amat could move, a knife the length of his forearm at the ready. Amat rose and pushed him back out despite his protests, closing the door behind him. Her hip ached badly. It had been getting worse these last weeks, and it added to everything else that made her irritable. Still, she held herself tall as she turned back to her sometime ally, sometime charge. The girl was breathing fast now, her chin jutting out, her arms pulled back. She looked like a little boy, daring someone to strike him. Amat smiled sweetly, took two slow strides, and slapped her smartly across the mouth.

"I am working from before the sun comes up to half through the night for you," Amat said. "I am keeping this filthy house so that I have the money we need to prosecute your case. I have ruined my life for you. And I haven't asked thanks, have I? Only cooperation."

There were tears brimming in Maj's pale eyes, streaking down her ruddy cheek. The anger that filled Amat's chest like a fire lessened. Moving more slowly, she walked to the mess against the far wall and, slowly, painfully, knelt.

"What I'm doing isn't simple," Amat said, not looking as she gathered the shards and broken flowers. "Wilsin-cha didn't keep records that would tie him directly to the trade, and the ones that do exist are plausible whether he knew of the treachery or not. I have to show that he did. Otherwise, you may as well go home."

The floor creaked with Maj's steps, but Amat didn't look up. Amat made a sack from the hem of her robe, dropped in the shattered vase and laid in the soft petals afterwards. The flowers, though destroyed, smelled lovely. She found herself reluctant to crush them. Maj crouched down beside her and helped clean.

"We've made progress," Amat said, her voice softer now. She could hear the exhaustion in her own words. "I have records of all the transactions. The pearls that paid the Khai came on a Galtic ship, but I have to find which one."

"That will be enough?"

"That will be a start," Amat said. "But there will be more. Torish-cha has had men on the seafront, offering payment for information. Nothing's come from it yet, but it will. These things take time."

Maj leaned close, placing a handful of debris into Amat's makeshift bag. She meant well, Amat knew, but she buried the flowers all the same. Amat met her gaze. Maj tried to smile.

"You're drunk," Amat said gently. "You should go and sleep. Things will look better in the morning."

"And worse again when night comes," Maj said and shook her head, then lurched forward and kissed Amat's mouth. As she left—awkward phrases in civilized languages passing between her and the guard at the door—Amat dropped the ruined vase into the small crate she kept beside her desk. Her flesh felt heavy, but there were books to be gone over, orders to place for the house and audits to be made.

She was doing the work, she knew, of three women. Had she seen forty fewer summers, it might have been possible. Instead, each day seemed to bring collapse nearer. She woke in the morning to a list of things that had to be completed—for the comfort house and for the case she was building inch by inch against House Wilsin—and fell asleep every night with three or four items still undone and the creeping sense that she was forgetting something important.

And the house, while it provided her the income she needed to pay for investigations and bribes and rewards, was just the pit of vipers that she'd been warned it would be. Mitat was her savior there—she knew the politics of the staff and had somehow won the trust of Torish Wite. Still, it seemed as if every decision had to be brought to Amat eventually. Whose indenture to end, whose to hold. What discipline to mete out against the women whose bodies were the produce she sold, what against the men who staffed the gambling tables and provided the wine and drugs. How to balance rule from respect and rule from fear. And Mitat, after all, had stolen from the house before. . . .

The night candle—visibly longer now and made of harder wax than the ones that measured the short nights of summer—was near its halfway mark when Amat put down her pen. Three times she added a column of numbers, and three times had found different sums. She shrugged out of her robes and pulled the netting closed around the bed, asleep instantly, but troubled by dreams in which she recalled something critical a hand's breadth too late.

She woke to a polite scratch at her door. When she called out her permission, Mitat entered bearing a tray. Two thick slices of black bread and a bowl of bitter tea. Amat sat up, pulled the netting aside, and took a pose of gratitude as the red-haired woman put the tray on the bed beside her.

"You're looking nicely put together this morning," Amat said.

It was true. Mitat wore a formal robe of pale yellow that went nicely with her eyes. She looked well-rested, which Amat supposed also helped.

"We have the payment to make to the watch," Mitat said. "I was hoping you might let me join you."

Amat closed her eyes. The watch monies. Of course. It would have been very poor form to forget that, but she nearly had. The darkness behind her eyelids was comfortable, and she stayed there for a moment, wishing that she might crawl back to sleep.

"Grandmother?"

"Of course," Amat said, opening her eyes again and reaching for the bowl of tea. "I could do with the company. But you'll understand if I handle the money."

Mitat grinned.

"You're never going to let me forget that, are you?"

"Likely not. Get me a good robe, will you. There's a blue with gray trim, I think, that should do for the occasion."

The streets of the soft quarter were quiet. Amat, her sleeve weighted by the boxed lengths of silver, leaned on her cane. The night's rain had washed the air, and sunlight, pale as fresh butter, shone on the pavements and made the banners of the great comfort houses shimmer. The baker's kilns filled the air with the scent of bread and smoke. Mitat walked beside her, acting as if the slow pace were the one she'd have chosen if she had been alone, avoiding the puddles of standing water where the street dipped, or where alleyways still disgorged a brown trickle of foul runoff. In the height of summer, the mixture of heat and damp would have been unbearable. Autumn's forgiving cool made the morning nearly pleasant.

Mitat filled in Amat Kyaan on the news of the house. Chiyan thought she might be pregnant. Torish-cha's men resented that they were expected to pay for the use of the girls—other houses in the quarter included such services as part of the compensation. Two weavers were cheating at tiles, but no one had caught them at it as yet.

"When we do, bring them to me," Amat said. "If they aren't willing to negotiate compensation with me, we'll call the watch, but I'd rather have it stay private."

"Yes, grandmother."

"And send for Urrat from the street of beads. She'll know if Chiyan's carrying by looking at her, and she has some teas that'll cure it if she is."

Mitat took a pose of agreement, but something in her expression—a softness, an amusement—made Amat respond with a query.

"Ovi Niit would have taken her out back and kicked her until she bled," Mitat said. "He would have said it was cheaper. I don't think you know how much you're respected, grandmother. The men, except Torish-cha and his, would still as soon see you hanged as not. But the girls all thank the gods that you came back."

"I haven't made the place any better."

"Yes," Mitat said, her voice accepting no denial. "You have. You don't see how the—"

The man lurched from the mouth of the alley and into Amat before she had time to respond. Her cane slipped as the drunkard staggered against her, and she stumbled. Pain shrieked from her knee to her hip, but her first impulse was to clutch the payment in her sleeve. The man, however, wasn't a thief. The silver for the watch was still where it had been and the drunk was in a pose of profound apology.

"What do you think you're doing?" Mitat demanded. Her chin was jutting out; her eyes burned. "It's hardly mid-day. What kind of man is already drunk?"

The thick man in the stained brown robe shook his head and bowed, his pose elegant and abasing.

"It is my fault," he said, his words slurred. "Entirely my fault. I've made an ass of myself."

Amat clutched Mitat's arm, silencing her, and stepped forward despite the raging ache in her leg. The drunkard bowed lower, shaking his head. Amat almost reached out to touch him—making certain that this wasn't a dream, that she wasn't back in her bed still waiting for her bread and tea.

"Heshai-cha?"

The poet looked up. His eyes were bloodshot and weary. The whites were yellow. He stank of wine and something worse. He seemed slowly to focus on her, and then, a heartbeat later, to recognize her face. He went gray.

"I'm fine, Heshai-cha. No damage done. But what brings—"

"I know you. You work for House Wilsin. You . . . you knew that girl?"

"Maj," Amat said. "Her name is Maj. She's being well taken care of, but you and I need to speak. What happened wasn't all it seemed. The andat had other parties who—"

"No! No, I was entirely to blame! It was my failing!"

The shutters of a window across the street opened with a clack and a curious face appeared. Heshai took a pose of regret spoiled only by his slight wavering, like a willow in a breeze. His lips hardened, and his eyes, when he opened them, were black. He looked at her as if she'd insulted him, and in that moment, Amat could see that the andat Seedless with his beautiful face and perfect voice had indeed been drawn from this man.

"I am making an ass of myself," he said. He bowed stiffly to her and to Mitat, turned, and strode unsteadily away.

"Gods!" Mitat said, looking after the wide, retreating back. "What was that?"

"The poet of Saraykeht," Amat said. She turned to consider the alley from which he'd emerged. It was thin—hardly more than a slit between buildings—unpaved, muddy and stinking of garbage.

"What's down there?" Amat asked.

"I don't know."

Amat hesitated, dreading what she knew she had to do next. If the mud was as foul as it smelled, the hems of her robe would be unsavable.

"Come," she said.

The apartment wasn't hard to find. The poet's unsteady footsteps had left fresh, sliding marks. The doorway was fitted with an iron lock, the shutters over the thin window beside it were barred from the inside. Amat, her curiosity too roused to stop now, rapped on the closed door and called, but no one came.

"Sometimes, if they don't want to be seen in the houses, men take rooms," Mitat said.

"Like this?"

"Better, usually," Mitat allowed. "None of the girls I know would want to follow a man down an alley like this one. If the payment was high enough, perhaps . . ."

Amat pressed her hand against the door. The wood was solid, sound. The lock, she imagined, could be forced, if she could find the right tools. If there was something in this sad secret place that was worth knowing. Something like dread touched her throat.

"Grandmother. We should go."

Amat took a pose of agreement, turning back toward the street. Curiosity balanced relief at being away from the private room of the poet of Saraykeht. She found herself wondering, as they walked to the offices of the watch, what lay behind that door, how it might relate to her quiet war, and whether she wanted to discover it.

WINTER CAME TO THE SUMMER CITIES. THE LAST LEAVES FELL, LEAVING bare trees to sleep through the long nights. Cold mists rose, filling the streets with air turned to milk. Maati wore heavier robes—silk and combed wool. But not his heaviest. Even the depths of a Saraykeht winter were milder than a chilly spring in the north. Some nights Maati walked through the streets with Liat, his arm around her, and both of them hunched against the cold, but it was a rare thing to see his own breath in the air. In Pathai as a child, at the school, then with the Dai-kvo, Maati had spent most of his life colder than this, but the constant heat of the high seasons of Saraykeht had thinned his blood. He felt the cold more deeply now than he remembered it.

Heshai-kvo's return to health seemed to have ended the affair of the dead child in the minds of the utkhaiem. Over the weeks—the terribly short weeks—Heshai had taken him to private dinners and public feasts, had presented him to high families, and made it clear through word and action that Liat was welcome—was *always* welcome—at the poet's house. That Seedless had been given a kind of freedom seemed to displease the Khai Saraykeht and his nearest men, but no words were said and no action taken. So long as the poet was well enough to assuage the general unease, all was close enough to well.

The teahouse they had retreated to, he and Liat, was near the edge of the city proper. Buildings and streets ran further out, north along the river, but it was in this quarter that the original city touched the newer buildings. Newer buildings, Maati reflected, older than his grandfather's grandfather. And still they took the name.

They'd taken a private room hardly larger than a closet, with a small table and a bench against the wall that they both shared. Light and music and the scent of roast pork drifted though carved wood lacework, and a small brazier hung above them, radiating heat like a black iron sun.

Liat poured hot tea into her bowl, and then without asking, into his. Maati took a pose of thanks, and lifted the fine porcelain to his lips. The steam smelled rich and smoky, and Liat leaned against him, the familiar weight of her body comforting as blankets.

"He'll be back soon," Maati said.

Liat didn't stiffen, but stilled. He sipped his tea, burning his lips a little. He felt her shrug as much as seeing it.

"Let's not talk of it," she said.

"I can't keep on with this once he's come back. Half the time I feel like I've killed something as it stands. When he's here . . ."

"When he's here we'll have him with us," Liat said softly. "We both will. I'll have him as a lover, you'll have him as a friend. We'll none of us be alone."

"I'm not entirely hoping for it," Maati said.

"Parts will be difficult. Let's not talk about it. It'll come soon enough without borrowing it now." Maati took a pose of agreement, but a moment later Liat sighed and took his arm.

"I didn't mean to be cruel. . . ."

"You haven't been," Maati said.

"You're kind to say so."

In the front of the house a woman or a child began singing—the voice high and sweet and pure. The talking voices stilled and gave the song their silence. It was one that Maati had heard before many times, a traditional ballad of love found and lost that dated back to the days when the Empire still stood. Maati sat back, his spine pressing into the wall behind him, and laid his arm across Liat's shoulders. His head swam with emotions that he could only partly name. He closed his eyes and let the ancient words and old grammars wash over him. He felt Liat shudder. When he looked, her face was flushed, her mouth drawn tight. Tears glistened in her eyes.

"Let's go home," he said, and she nodded. He took six lengths of copper from a pouch in his sleeve and left them in a row on the table—it would more than cover the charges. Together, they rose, pushed aside the door and slipped out. The song continued on as they stepped out into the darkness. The moon was just past new, and the streets were dark except for the torches at crossroads where large streets met, and, elsewhere, lit by the kilns of the firekeepers. They walked arm in arm, heading north.

"Why do they call you poets?" Liat asked. "You don't really declaim poetry. Or, I mean, we have, but not as what you do for the Khai."

"There are other terms," Maati said. "You could also call us shapers or makers. Thought-weavers. It's from the binding."

"The andat. They're poems?"

"They're like poems. They're translations of an idea into a form that includes volition. When you take a letter in the Khaiate tongue and translate it into Galtic, there are different ways you could word it, to get the right meaning. The binding is like translating a letter perfectly from one language to another. You make it clear, and the parts that aren't there—if there isn't quite the right word in Galtic, for instance—you create them so that the whole thing holds together. The old grammars are very good for that work."

"What do you do with it? With the description?"

"You hold it in your mind. Forever."

The words lapsed. They walked. The high walls of the warehouse district stopped and the lower buildings of the weavers took up. The palaces at the top of the city glittered with lanterns and torches, like the field of stars pulled down and overlapping the earth until they were obscured again by high walls, now of the homes of merchants and lesser trading houses.

"Have you ever been in the summer cities for Candles Night?" Liat asked.

"No," Maati said. "I've seen the Dai-kvo's village, though. It was beautiful there. All the streets were lined with people, and the light made the whole mountain feel like a temple."

"You'll like it here," Liat said. "There's likely more wine involved than with the Dai-kvo."

Maati smiled in the darkness and pulled her small, warm body closer to him.

"I imagine so," he said. "At the school, we didn't—"

The blow was so sudden, Maati didn't really have time to feel it. He was on the ground. The stones of the street were rough against his skinned palms, and he was consumed by a sense of urgency whose object he could not immediately identify. Liat lay unmoving beside him. A roof tile—six hands square and three fingers deep of baked red clay—rested between them like an abandoned pillow. A scraping sound like rats in plaster walls caught Maati's crippled attention and another tile fell, missing them both, detonating on the street at Liat's side. Maati's panic found its focus. He lurched toward her. Blood soaked her robe at the shoulder. Her eyes were closed.

"Liat! Wake up! The tiles are loose!"

She didn't answer. Maati looked up, his hands shaking though he wasn't aware of the fear, only of the terrible need to act immediately trapped against his uncertainty of what action to take. No other tile moved, but something—a bird, a squirrel, a man's head?—ducked back over the roof's lip. Maati put his hand on Liat's body and willed his mind into something nearer to order. They were in danger here. They had to move away from the wall. And Liat couldn't.

Carefully he took her by the shoulders and dragged her. Each step made his ribs shriek, but he took her as far as the middle of the street before the pain was too much. Kneeling over her, fighting to breathe, Maati's fear turned at last to panic. For a long airless moment, Maati convinced himself that she wasn't breathing. A shifting of her bloody robe showed him otherwise. Help. They needed help.

Maati stood and staggered. The street was empty, but a wide ironwork gate opened to rising marble steps and a pair of wide wooden doors. Maati pushed himself toward it, feeling as if he was at one remove from his own muscles, as if his body was a puppet he didn't have the skill to use well. It seemed to him, hammering on the wide doors, that no one would ever come. He wiped the sweat from his brow only to discover it was blood.

He was trying to decide whether he had the strength to go looking for another door, a firekeeper, a busier street, when the door swung open. An old man, thin as sticks, looked out at him. Maati took a pose that begged.

"You have to help her," he said. "She's hurt."

"Gods!" the man said, moving forward, supporting Maati as he slid down to the steps. "Don't move, my boy. Don't move. Chiyan! Out here! Hurry! There's children hurt!"

Tell Otah-kvo, Maati thought, but was too weak to say. *Find Otah-kvo and tell him. He'll know what to do.*

He found himself in a well-lit parlor without recalling how he'd come there. A younger man was prodding at his head with something painful. He tried to push the man's arm away, but he was nearly too weak to move. The man said something that Maati acknowledged and then immediately forgot. Someone helped him to drink a thin, bitter tea, and the world faded.

16

>+< Marchat Wilsin woke from an uneasy sleep, soft footsteps in the corridor enough to disturb him. When the knock came, he was already sitting up. Epani pushed the door open and stepped in, his face drawn in the flickering light of the night candle.

"Wilsin-cha . . ."

"It's him, isn't it?"

Epani took a pose of affirmation, and Marchat felt the dread that had troubled his sleep knot itself in his chest. He put on a brave show, pushing aside the netting with a sigh, pulling on a thick wool robe. Epani didn't speak. Amat, Marchat thought, would have said something.

He walked alone to his private hall. The door of it stood open, lantern light spilling out into the corridor. A black form passed in front of it, pacing, agitated, blocking out the light. The knot in Marchat Wilsin's chest grew solid—a stone in his belly. He drew himself up and walked in.

Seedless paced, his pale face as focused as a hunting cat's. His robe— black shot with red—blended with the darkness until he seemed a creature half of shadow. Marchat took a pose of welcome which the andat ignored except for the distant smile that touched his perfect lips.

"It was an accident," Marchat said. "They didn't know it was him. They were only supposed to kill the girl."

Seedless stopped. His face was perfectly calm, his eyes cool. Anger radiated from him like a fire.

"You hurt my boy," he said.

"Blame Amat, if you have to blame anyone," Wilsin said. "It's her vendetta that's driving this. She's trying to expose us. She's dedicating her life to it, so don't treat this like it's something I chose."

Seedless narrowed his eyes. Marchat forced himself not to look away.

"She's close," he said. "She's looking at shipments of pearls from Galtic ports and tying them to the payment. With the money she's offering, it's a matter of time before she gets what she's looking for. Leaving Liat be would have been . . . The girl could damage us. If it came before the Khai, she might damage us."

"And yet your old overseer hasn't taken her apprentice into confidence?"

"Would you? Liat's a decent girl, but I wouldn't trust her with my laundry."

"You think she's incompetent?"

"No, I think she's *young.*"

And that, oddly, seemed to touch something. The andat's anger shifted, lost its edge. Marchat took a free breath for the first time that night.

"So you chose to remove her from the field of play," Seedless said. "An accident of roof tiles."

"I didn't specify the tiles. Only that it should be plausible."

"You didn't tell them to avoid Maati?"

"I did. But gods! Those two are connected at the hip these days. The men . . . grew impatient. They thought they could do the job without damaging the poet boy."

"They were wrong."

"I know. It won't happen again."

The andat flowed forward, lifting himself up to sit on the meeting table beside the lantern. Marchat took a step back before he knew he had done it. The andat's pale fingers laced together and it smiled, an expression of such malice and beauty that it could never have been mistaken for human.

"If Maati had died," Seedless said, its voice low as distant thunder, "every crop in Galt would fail. Every cow and ewe would go barren. Your people would die. Do you understand that? There wouldn't have been a bargain struck or threats made. It would simply have happened, and no one might ever have known why. That boy is precious to you, because while he lives, your people live."

"You can't mean that," Marchat said, but sickeningly, he knew the andat was quite serious. He shook his head and adopted a pose of acknowledgement that he prayed would move the conversation elsewhere, onto some subject that didn't dance so near the cliff edge. "We need a plan. What to do if Amat makes her case to the Khai. If we don't have our defense prepared, she may convince him. She's good that way."

"Yes. She's always impressed me."

"So," Marchat said, sitting, looking up at the dark form above him. "What are we going to do? If she finds the truth and the proof of it, what then?"

"Then I do as I'm told. I'm a slave. It works that way with me. And you? You get your head and your sex shipped back to the Galtic High Council as an explanation for why a generation of Galtic babies are dropping out of their mother's wombs. That's only a guess, of course. The Khai might be lenient," Seedless grinned, "and stones may float on water, but I wouldn't want to rely on it."

"It's not so bad as that," Marchat said. "If you say that Oshai and his men—"

"I won't do that," the andat said, dismissing him as casually as an unwanted drink. "If it comes before the Khai Saraykeht and they ask me, I'll tell them what they want to know."

Marchat laughed. He couldn't help it, but even as he did, he felt the blood rushing away from his face. Seedless tilted his head like a bird.

"You can't," Marchat said. "You're as deep in this as I am."

"Of course I'm not, Wilsin-kya. What are they going to do to me, eh? I'm the blood their city lives on. If our little conspiracy comes to light, you'll pay the price of it, not me. What we've done, you and I, was lovely. The look on Heshai's face when that baby hit the bowl was worth all the weeks and months it took to arrange it. Really, it was brilliantly done. But don't think because we did something together once that we're brothers now. I'm playing new games, with other players. And this time, you don't signify."

"You don't mean that," Marchat said. The andat stood, its arms crossed, and considered the lantern flame.

"It would be interesting, destroying a nation," Seedless said, more than half, it seemed, to himself. "I'm not certain how Heshai would take it. But . . ."

The andat sighed and turned, stepping to Wilsin's chair and kneeling beside it. It seemed to Marchat that the andat smelled of incense and ashes. The pale hand pressed his knee and the vicious smile was like a blade held casually at his throat.

". . . but, Wilsin-kya, don't make the mistake again of thinking that you or your people matter to me. Our paths have split. Do you understand me?"

"You can't," Wilsin said. "We've been in this together from the start—you and the Council both. Haven't we done everything that you asked?"

"Yes. I suppose you have."

"You owe us something," Wilsin said, ashamed at the desperation he heard in his own voice.

The andat considered this, then slowly stood and took a pose of thanks that carried nuances of both dismissal and mockery.

"Then take my thanks," the andat said. "Wilsin-cha, you have been insincere, selfish, and short-sighted as a flea, but you were the perfect tool for the work, and for that, I thank you. Hurt Maati again, and your nation dies. Interfere with my plans, and I'll tell Amat Kyaan the full story and save her her troubles. This game's moved past you, little man. It's too big. Stay out if it."

THE DREAM, IF IT WAS A DREAM, WAS PAINFUL AND DISJOINTED. LIAT thought she heard someone crying, and thought it must be from the pain. But the pain was hers, and the weeping wasn't, so that could hardly be. She found herself in a rainstorm outside the temple, all the doors locked against her. She called and called, but no one opened the doors, and the patter of rain turned to the clicking of hail and the hailstones grew and grew until they were the size of a baby's fist, and all she could do was curl tight and let the ice strike her neck and the back of her head.

She woke—if the slow swimming up to lucidity was truly waking—with her head throbbing in pain. She lay on an unfamiliar bed—worked wood and brass—in a lavish room. A breeze came though the opened shutters and stirred the fine silk netting with the scent of rain. The rough cough and the clearing of a throat made her turn too quickly, and pain shot from her neck to her belly. She closed her eyes, overcome by it, and opened them to find the poet Heshai at the bedside in a pose of apology.

"I didn't see you were awake," he said, his wide mouth in a sheepish smile. "I'd have warned you I was here. You're in the Second Palace. I'd have taken you to the poet's house, but the physicians are nearer."

Liat tried to take a pose of casual forgiveness, but found that her right arm was strapped. She tried for the first time to understand where she was and how she'd come there. There had been something—a teahouse and Maati, and then . . . something. She pressed her left palm to her eyes, willing the pain to stop and give her room to think. She heard the rustle of cloth pulled aside, and the mattress dipped to her left where the poet sat beside her.

"Maati?" she asked.

"Fine," the poet said. "You took the worst of it. He had his brain rattled around a bit for him, and a shard cut his scalp above the ear. The physician says it's not such a bad thing for a boy to bleed a little when he's young, though."

"What happened?"

"Gods. Of course. You wouldn't know. Loose tiles, two of them. The utkhaiem are fining the owner of the compound for not keeping his roof better repaired. Your shoulder and arm—no, don't move them. They're strapped like that for good cause. The first tile broke some bones rather badly. Once they found who Maati was, they brought you both to the Khai's palaces. The Khai's own physicians have been watching over you for the last three days. I asked for them myself."

Her mind seemed foggy. Simple as his explanation was, the details of the poet's words swam close, darted away. She took hold of one.

"Three days?" Liat asked. "I've been asleep for three days?"

"Not so much asleep," the poet admitted. "We've been giving you poppy milk for the pain. Maati's been here most of the time. I sent him off to rest this morning. I promised him I'd watch over you while he was gone. I have some tea, if you'd like it?"

Liat began to take a pose of thanks and the pain sang in her neck and shoulder. She paled and nodded. The poet stood slowly, trying, she could tell, not to jostle her. He was back in a moment, helping her to sip from a bowl of lemon tea, sweet with honey. Her stomach twisted at the intrusion, but her mouth and throat felt like the desert in a rainstorm. When he pulled the bowl back and helped her ease back down, Liat saw an odd expression on the poet's face—tenderness, she thought. She had always thought of Heshai as an ugly man, but in that light, at that moment, the wide lips and thinning hair seemed to transcend normal ideas of beauty. He looked strong and gentle. His movements were protective as a mother's and as fierce. Liat wondered why she'd never seen it before.

"I should thank you, in a way," he said. "You've given me a chance to give back part of what Maati's done for me. Not that we talk of it in those terms, of course."

"I don't understand."

The frog mouth spread into a rueful smile. "I know how much it cost him, caring for me while I was ill. It isn't the sort of thing you discuss, of course, but I can tell. It isn't easy watching the man who is supposed to be your master fall apart. And it isn't a simple thing to stand beside him while he pulls himself back together. Would you like more tea? The physician said you could have as much as you wanted, but that we'd want to go slowly with heavier foods."

"No. No more. Thank you. But I still don't see . . ."

"You've made Maati happy these last few weeks," Heshai said, his voice softer. "That he let me take part in caring for you pays back a part of the time he cared for me."

"I didn't think you'd noticed how much it took from him," Liat said. The poet took a querying pose. "You seemed . . . too busy with other things, I suppose. I'm sorry. It isn't my place to judge what you—"

"No, it's quite all right. I . . . Maati and I haven't quite found our right level. I imagine there are some opinions you both hold of me. They're my fault. I earned them."

Liat closed her eyes, marshalling her thoughts, and when she opened them again, it was night, and she was alone.

She didn't remember falling asleep, but the night candle, burning steady in a glass lantern at her bedside, was past its halfway point, and heavy blankets covered her. Despite the pain, she pulled herself up, found and used the night pot, and crawled back to bed, exhausted. Sleep, however didn't return so easily. Her mind was clear, and her body, while aching and bruised at best and pain-bright at worst, at least felt very much her own. She lay in the dim light of the candle and listened to the small sounds of the night—wind sighing at the shutters, the occasional clicking of the walls as they cooled. The room smelled of mint and mulled wine. Someone had been drinking, she thought, or else the physicians had thought that being in air that smelled so pleasant would help her body heal. The first distant pangs of hunger were shifting in her belly.

As the candle burned lower, the night passing, Liat grew clearer, and more awake. She tested how much she could move without the pain coming on, and even walked around the room. Her arm and shoulder were still bound, and her ribs ached to touch, but she could breathe deeply with only an ache. She could bring herself to sitting, and then stand. Walking was simple so long as she didn't bump into anything. She imagined Maati watching over her while she slept, ignoring his own wounds. And Heshai—more like a friend or father—sharing that burden. It was more, she knew, than the two had ever shared before, and she found herself both embarrassed and oddly proud of being the occasion of it.

A thick winter robe hung on a stand by the door, and Liat put it on, wrapping the cloth around her bandages and tying it one-handed. It took longer than she'd expected, but she managed it and was soon sitting in the chair that Maati and Heshai must have used in their vigil. When a servant girl arrived, Liat instructed her not to tell anyone that she'd risen. She wanted Maati to be surprised when he came. The girl took a pose of acknowledgement that held such respect and formality, Liat wondered whether Heshai had told them who she was, or if they were under the impression that she was some foreign princess.

When Maati came, he was alone. His robes were wrinkled and his hair unkempt. He came in quietly, stopping dead when he saw her bed empty, his chair inhabited. She rose as gracefully as she could and held out her good hand. He stepped forward and took it in his own, but didn't pull her close. His eyes were bloodshot and bright, and he released her hand before she let go of his. She smiled a question.

"Liat-cha," he said, and his voice was thick with distress. "I'm pleased you're feeling better."

"What's happened?"

"Good news. Otah-kvo's come back. He arrived last night with a letter from the Dai-kvo himself. It appears there is no andat to replace Seedless, so I'm to do anything necessary to support Heshai-kvo's wellbeing. But since he's already feeling so much better, I don't see that it amounts to much. It seems there's no one ready to take Heshai's place, and may not be for several years, you see, and so it's very important that . . ."

He trailed off into silence, a smile on his lips and something entirely different in his eyes. Liat felt her heart die a little. She swallowed and nodded.

"Where is he?" Liat asked. "Where's Itani?"

"With Heshai-kvo. He came straight there when his ship arrived. It was very late, and he was tired. He wanted to come to you immediately, but I thought you would be asleep. He'll come later, when he wakes. Liat, I hope . . . I mean, I didn't . . ."

He looked down, shaking his head. When he looked up, his smile was rueful and raw, and tears streaked his face.

"We knew, didn't we, that it would be hard?" he said.

Liat walked forward, feeling as if something outside of her was moving her. Her hand cupped Maati's neck, and she leaned in, the crown of her head touching his. She could smell his tears, warm and salty and intimate. Her throat was too tight for speech.

"Heshai was very . . ." Maati began, and she killed the words with kissing him. His lips, familiar now, responded. She could feel when they twisted into a grimace of pain against her. His mouth closed, and he stepped back. She wanted to hold him, to be held by him, the way a dropped stone wants to fall, but his expression forbade her. The boy was gone, and someone—a man with his face and his expression, but with something deep and painful and new in his eyes—was in his place.

"Liat-cha," he said. "Otah's *back*."

Liat took a breath and slowly let it out.

"Thank you, Maati-cha," she said, the honorific like ashes in her mouth. "Perhaps . . . perhaps if I could join you all later in the day. I find I'm more tired than I thought."

"Of course," Maati said. "I'll send someone in to help you with your robe."

With her good hand, she took a pose of thanks. Maati replied with a simple response. Their eyes met, the gaze holding all the things they were not speaking. Her need, and his. His resolve. Morning rain tapped at the shutters like time passing behind them. Maati turned and left her, his back straight, his bearing formal and controlled.

For the space of a breath, she wanted to call him back. Pull him into the room, into the bed. She wanted to feel the warmth of him against her one last time. It wasn't fair that their bodies hadn't had the chance to say their farewells. And she would have, she thought, even with Itani . . . even with Otah returned and sleeping in the poet's house that she knew now so well. She would have called, except that it would have broken her soul when Maati refused her. And she saw now that he would have.

Instead, she lay in the bed by herself, her flesh mending and her spirit ill. She had expected to feel torn between the two of them, but instead she was only shut out. The bond between Maati and Otah—the relationship of her two lovers—was deeper than what she had with either. She was losing each of them to the other, and the knowledge was like a stone in her throat.

MAATI SAT AT THE TOP OF THE BRIDGE, THE POND BELOW HIM DARK AS TEA. His belly was heavy, his chest so tight his shoulders shifted forward in a hunch. The breeze smelled of rain, though the sky was clear. The world seemed a dark, deadened place.

He had known, of course, that Liat wasn't truly his lover. What they had been to each other for those few, precious weeks was comfort and friendship. That was all. And with Otah back, everything could return to the way it had been—the way it should have been. Only Maati hadn't ached before the way he did now. The memory of Liat's body against him, her lips against his, hadn't haunted him. And Otah's long, thoughtful face hadn't made Maati sick with guilt.

And so, he thought, nothing would be what it had been. The idea that it could had been an illusion.

"You've done it, then?"

Maati turned to his left, back toward the palaces. Seedless stepped onto the bridge, dark robes shifting as he walked. The andat's expression was unreadable.

"I don't know what you mean," Maati said.

"You've broken it off with the darling Liat. Returned her from whence she came, now that her laborer's back from his errand."

"I don't know what you mean," Maati repeated, turning back to stare that the cold, dark water. Seedless settled beside him. Their two faces reflected on the pond's surface, wavering and pale. Maati wished he had a stone to drop, something that would break the image.

"Bad answer," the andat said. "I'm not a fool. I can smell love when I'm up to my knees in it. It's hard, losing her."

"I haven't lost anything. It's only changed a bit. I knew it would."

"Well then," Seedless said gently. "That makes it easy, doesn't it. He's still resting, is he?"

"I don't know. I haven't gone to see him yet today."

"Gone to see him? It's your couch he's sleeping on."

"Still," Maati said with a shrug. "I'm not ready to see him again. To-night, perhaps. Only not yet."

They were silent for a long moment. Crows barked from the treetops, hopping on twig-thin legs, their black wings outstretched. Somewhere in the water, koi shifted sluggishly, sending thin ripples to the surface.

"Would it help to say I'm sorry for it?" Seedless asked.

"Not particularly."

"Well, all the same."

"It's hard to think that you care, Seedless-cha. I'd have thought you'd be pleased."

"No. Not really. On the one hand, whether you think it or not, I don't have any deep love of your pain. Not yet, at least. Once you take Heshai's burden . . . well, we'll neither of us have any choices then. And then, for my own selfish nature, all this brings you one step nearer to being like him. The woman you've loved and lost. The pain you carry with you. It's part of what drives him, and you're coming to know it now yourself."

"So when you say you're sorry for it, you mean that you think it might help me do my task?"

"Makes you wonder if the task's worth doing, doesn't it?" Seedless said, a smile in his voice more than his expression. "I doubt the Dai-kvo would share our concerns, though, eh?"

"No," Maati sighed. "No, he at least is certain of what's the right thing."

"Still, we're clever," Seedless said. "Well, you're not. You're busy being lovesick, but I'm clever. Perhaps I'll think of something."

Maati turned to look at the andat, but the smooth, pale face revealed nothing more than a distant amusement.

"Something in particular?" Maati asked, but Seedless didn't answer.

OTAH WOKE FROM A DEEP SLEEP TO LIGHT SLANTING THROUGH HALF-opened shutters. For a moment, he forgot he had landed, his body still shifting from memory of the sea beneath him. Then the blond wood and incense, the scrolls and books, the scent and sound of winter rain recalled him to himself, and he stood. The wall-long shutters were closed, a fire burned low in its grate. Heshai and Maati were gone, but a plate of dried fruit and fresh bread sat on a table beside the letter from the Dai-kvo, its pages unsewn and spread. He sat alone and ate.

The journey back had been easy. The river bore him to Yalakeht and then a tradeship with a load of furs meant for Eddensea. He'd taken a position on the ship—passage in return for his work, and he'd done well enough by the captain and crew. Otah imagined they were now in the soft quarter spending what money they had. Indulging themselves before they began the weeks-long journey across the sea.

Heshai had seemed better, alert and attentive. It even seemed that Maati and his teacher had grown closer since Otah had left—brought together, perhaps, by the difficulties they had weathered. It might have been the bad news of Liat's injury or Otah's own weariness and sense of displacement, but there had seemed something more as well. A weariness in Maati's eyes that Otah recognized, but couldn't explain.

The first thing he needed, of course, was a bath. And then to see Liat. And then . . . and then he wasn't sure. He had gone on his journey to the Dai-kvo, he had come back bearing news that seemed out of date when it arrived. According to Maati, Heshai-kvo had bested his illness without the aid of the Dai-kvo. The tragedy of the dead child was fading from the city's memory, replaced by other scandals—diseased cotton in the northern fields; a dyer who killed himself after losing a year's wages gambling; Liat's old overseer Amat Kyaan breaking with her house in favor of a business of her own in the soft quarter. The petty life-and-death battles of the sons of the Khaiem.

And so what had seemed of critical importance at the time, proved empty now that it was done. And his own personal journey had achieved little more. He could go, if he chose, to speak to Muhatia-cha this afternoon. Perhaps House Wilsin would take him back on to complete his indenture. Or there were other places in the city, work he could do that would pay for his food and shelter. The world was open before him. He could even have taken the letter from Orai Vaukheter and taken work as a courier if it weren't for Liat, and for Maati, and the life he'd built as Itani Noyga.

He ate strips of dried apple and plum, chewing the sweet flesh slowly as he thought and noticing the subtlety of the flavors as they changed. It wasn't so bad a life, Itani Noyga's. His work was simple, straightforward. He was good at it. With only a little more effort, he could find a position with a trading house, or the seafront authority, or any of a hundred places that would take a man with numbers and letters and an easy smile. And half a year ago, he would have thought it enough. Otah or Itani. It was still the question.

"You're up," a soft voice said. "And the men of the house are still out. That's good. We have things to talk about, you and I."

Seedless leaned against a bookshelf, his arms crossed and his dark eyes considering. Otah popped the last sliver of plum into his mouth and took a pose of greeting appropriate for someone of low station to a member of the utkhaiem. There was, so far as he knew, no etiquette appropriate for a common laborer to an andat. Seedless waved the pose away and flowed forward, his robes—blue and black—hissing cloth against cloth.

"Otah Machi," the andat said. "Otah Unbranded. The man too wise to be a poet and too stupid to take the brand. And here you are."

Otah met the glittering black gaze and felt the flush in his face. His words were ready, his hands already halfway to a pose of denial. Something in the perfect pale mask of a face stopped him. He lowered his arms.

"Good," Seedless said, "I was hoping we might dispense with that part. We're a little short of time just now."

"How did you find out?"

"I listened. I lied. The normal things anyone would do who wanted to know something hidden. You've seen Liat?"

"Not yet, no."

"You know what happened to her, though? The tiles?"

"Maati told me."

"It wasn't an accident," the andat said. "They were thrown."

Otah frowned, aware that Seedless was peering at him, reading his expressions and movement. He forced himself to remain casual.

"Was it you?"

"Me? Gods, no," Seedless said, sitting on a couch, his legs tucked up beneath him like they were old friends chatting. "In the first place I wouldn't have done it. In the second, I wouldn't have missed. No, it was Marchat Wilsin and his men."

Otah leaned forward, letting the smile he felt show on his face. The andat didn't move, even to breathe.

"You know there's no sane reason that I should believe anything you say."

"True," the andat said. "But hear me out first, and then you can disbelieve my little story entirely instead of just one bit at a time."

"There's no reason Wilsin-cha would want to hurt Liat."

"Yes, there is. His sins are creeping back to kill him, you see. That little incident with the island girl and her dead get? It was more than it seemed. Listen carefully when I say this. It's the kind of thing men are killed for knowing, so it's worth paying attention. The High Council of Galt arranged that little mess. Wilsin-cha helped. Amat Kyaan—his overseer—found out and is dedicating what's left of her life to prying the whole sordid thing open like it was shellfish. Wilsin-cha in his profoundly finite wisdom is cleaning up anything that might be of use to Amat-cha. Including Liat."

Otah took a pose of impatience and stood, looking for his cloak.

"I've had enough of this . . ."

"I know who you are, boy. Sit back down or I'll end all your choices for you, and you can spend the rest of your life running from your brothers over a chair you don't even want to sit in."

Otah paused and then sat.

"Good. The Galtic Council had a plan to ally themselves with the andat. We poor suffering spirits get our freedom. The Galts kick out the supports that keep the cities of the Khaiem above the rest of the world. Then they roll over you like you were just another Westlands warden, only with more gold and fewer soldiers. It's a terrible plan."

"Is it?"

"Yes. Andat aren't predictable. That's what makes us the same, you and I. Ah, relax, Otah-cha. You look like I have a knife at your belly."

"I think you do," Otah said.

The andat leaned back, gesturing at the empty house around them—the crackling fire, the falling rain.

"There's no one to hear us. Anything we say to each other, you and I, is between us unless we choose otherwise."

"And I should trust you to keep quiet?"

"Of course not. Don't be an ass. But the less you say, the less I can repeat to others, eh? Right. Amat's near getting what she needs. And she won't stop. She's a pit hound at heart. Do you know what happens when she does?"

"She'll take it to the Khai."

"Yes!" the andat said, clapping his hands together once as if it were a festival game and Otah had earned a prize. "And what would he do?"

"I don't know."

"No? You disappoint me. He'd do something bloody and gaudy and out of all proportion. Something that sounded like a plague from the old epics. My guess—it's only my opinion, of course, but I consider myself fairly expert on the subject of unrestrained power—he'll turn me and Heshai against whatever Galtic women are carrying babes when he learns of it. It will be like pulling seeds out of a cotton bale. A thousand, maybe. More. Who can say?"

"It would break Heshai," Otah said. "Doing that."

"No. It wouldn't. It would bend him double, but it wouldn't break him. Seeing the one child die in front of him didn't do it, and tragedy fades with distance. Put it close enough to your eye, and a thumb can blot out a mountain. A few thousand dead Galt babies will hurt him, but he won't have to watch it happen. A few bottles of cheap wine, a few black months. And then he'll train Maati. Maati will have all the loneliness, all the self-hatred, all the pain of holding me in check for all the rest of his life. That's already happening. Heshai fell in love and lost her, and he's been chewed by guilt ever since. Maati will do the same."

"No, he won't," Otah said.

Seedless laughed.

"More the fool, you. But let it go. Let it go and look at the near term. Here's my promise, Otah of Machi. Amat will make her case. Liat may be killed before it comes before the Khai, or she may not, but Amat *will* make her case. Innocent blood *will* wash Galt. Maati *will* suffer to the end of his days. Oh, and I'll betray you to your family, though I think it's really very small of you to be concerned about that. Your problems don't amount to much, you know." Seedless paused. "Do you understand me?"

"Yes."

"Then you see why we have to act."

"We?"

"You and I, Otah. We can stop it. Together we can save them all. It's why I've come to you."

The andat's face was perfectly grave now, his hands floating up into a plea. Slowly, Otah took a pose that was a query. Wind rattled the shutters and a chill touched the back of Otah's neck.

"We can spare the people we love. Saraykeht will fall, but there's no helping that. The city will fall, and we will save Liat and Maati and all those babies and mothers who had nothing to do with this. All you have to do is kill a man who—and I swear this—would walk onto the blade if you only held it steady. You have to kill me."

"Kill you, or Heshai?"

"There isn't a difference."

Otah stood, and Seedless rose with him. The perfect face looked pained, and the pose of supplication Seedless took was profound.

"Please," he said. "I can tell you where he goes, how long he stays, how long it takes him to drink himself to sleep. All you'll need is—"

"No," Otah said. "Kill someone? On your word? No. I won't."

Seedless dropped his hands to his sides and shook his head in disappointment and disgust.

"Then you can watch everyone you care for suffer and die, and see if you prefer that. But if you're going to change your mind, do it quickly, my dear. Amat's closer than she knows. There isn't much time."

17

"Something has to be done," Torish Wite said. "She went into the street yesterday. If she'd been mistaken for a whore, there's no knowing how she'd have responded. And given the restraint she's managed so far, we could have had the watch coming down our throats. We can't have that."

Her rooms were dark, the windows and wide doors covered with tapestries that held in the heat as well as blocking the light. Downstairs, the girls and the children were all sleeping—even Mitat, even Maj. Only not Amat or Torish. She ached to rest, only not quite yet.

"I'm aware of what we can and cannot have," Amat said. "I'll see to it."

The thug, the murderer, the captain of her personal guard shook his head. His expression was grim.

"All respect, grandmother," he said. "But you've sung that song before. The island girl's trouble. Another stern talking to isn't going to do more than the last one did."

Amat drew herself up, anger filling her chest partly because she knew what he said was true. She took a pose of query.

"I had not known this was your house to run," she said.

Torish shook his wide, bear-like head again, his eyes cast down in something like regret or shame.

"It's your house," he said. "But they're my men. If you're going to be putting them on the wrong side of the watch, there isn't enough silver in the soft quarter to keep them here. I'm sorry."

"You'd break contracts?"

"No. But I won't renew. Not on those terms. This is one of the best contracts we've had, but I won't take a fight I know we can't win. You put that girl on a leash, or we can't stay with you. And—truly, all respect—you need us."

"She lost a child last summer," Amat said.

"Bad things happen," Torish Wite said, his voice surprisingly gentle. "You move past them."

He was right, of course, and that was the galling thing. In his position, she would have done the same. Amat took a pose of acceptance.

"I understand your position, Torish-cha. I'll see to it that Maj doesn't endanger your men or your contract with me. Give me a day or so, and I'll see it done."

He nodded, turned, left her rooms. He had the grace not to ask what it was she intended. She wouldn't have been able to say. Amat rose, took her cane, and walked out the doors to her deck. The rain had stopped, the whole great bowl of the sky white as bleached cotton. Seagulls screamed to one another, wheeling over the rooftops. She took a deep breath and let herself weep. The tears were as much about exhaustion as anything else, and they brought her no relief.

Between the late hour of the morning and the rain that had fallen all the last day and through the night, the streets of the soft quarter were near deserted. The two boys, then, who came around the corner together caught her attention. The older was broad across the shoulders—a sailor or a laborer—with a long, northern face and a robe of formal cut. The younger boy at his side—smaller, softer—wore the brown robes of a poet. Amat knew as they stepped into the street that there would even now be no rest for her. She watched them until they came too near the comfort house to see without leaning over into the street, then went inside and composed herself. It took longer than she'd expected for the guard to come and announce them. Perhaps Torish-cha had seen how tired she felt.

The older boy proved to be Itani Noyga, Liat's vanished lover. The younger, of course, was the young poet Maati. Amat, seated at her desk, took a pose of welcome and gestured to chairs she'd had brought in for them. Both boys sat. It was an interesting contrast, the pair or them. Both were clearly in earnest, both wore expressions of perfect seriousness, but Itani's eyes reminded her more of her own—focused out, on her, on the room, searching, it seemed, for something. The poet boy was like his master—brooding, turned inward. Like his master, or like Marchat Wilsin. Amat put her hand on her knees and leaned a degree forward.

"And what business brings you young gentlemen?" she asked. Her tone was light and pleasant and gave nothing away. Her subtlety was lost on them, though. The older boy, Itani, clearly wasn't looking to finesse an advantage.

"Amat-cha," he said. "I'm told you hope to prove that the High Council of Galt conspired with the andat Seedless when he killed the child out of the island girl last summer."

"I'm investigating the matter," Amat said, "and I've broken with House Wilsin, but I don't know that it's fair to say the Galtic Council must therefore be . . ."

"Amat-cha," the poet boy, Maati, broke in. "Someone tried to kill Liat Chokavi. Marchat Wilsin is keeping it quiet, but I was there. And . . . Itani thinks it was something to do with you and House Wilsin."

Amat felt her breath catch. Marchat, the old idiot, was panicking. Liat Chokavi was his best defense, if he could trust her to say the right things before the Khai. Except that he wouldn't. She was too young, and too unskilled at these games. It was why he had used her in the first place. Something like nausea swept through her.

"It may have been," Amat said. "How is she?"

"Recovering in the Khai's palaces," Itani said. "But she's doing well. She'll be able to go back to her house tomorrow. Wilsin-cha will expect her."

"No," Amat said. "She can't go back there."

"It's true, then," Itani said, his voice somber. Perhaps he had a talent for finesse after all. Amat took a pose of acknowledgement.

"I wasn't able to stop the crime against Maj from happening, but yes. House Wilsin knew of the deceit. I believe that the Galtic Council did as well, though I can't prove that as yet. That *I* think it is hardly a great secret, though. Anyone might guess as much. That I'm right in thinking it . . . is more difficult."

"Protect Liat," Maati said, "and whatever we can do for you, we will."

"Itani-cha? Are those your terms as well?"

"Yes," the boy said.

"It may mean speaking before the Khai. Telling him where you went the night you acted as Wilsin-cha's bodyguard."

Itani hesitated, then took a pose of acceptance.

Amat sat back, one hand up, requesting a moment to herself. This wasn't something she'd foreseen, but it might be what she'd needed. If the young poet could influence Heshai or find some scrap of memory from the negotiations that showed Marchat Wilsin knew that all wasn't what it seemed . . . But there was something more in this—she could feel it as sure as the tide. One piece here didn't fit.

"Itani-cha's presence I understand," Amat said. "What is the poet's interest in Liat Chokavi."

"She's my friend," Maati said, his chin lifted a fraction higher than before. His eyes seemed to defy her.

Ah! she thought. *So that's how it is.* She wondered how far that had gone and whether Itani knew. Not that it made any difference to her or to what was called for next.

Liat. It had always been a mess, of course, what to do with Liat. On the one hand, she might have been able to help Amat's case, add some telling detail that would show Marchat had known of the translator Oshai's duplicity. On the other hand, pulling the girl into it was doing her no favors. Amat had thought about it since she'd come to the house, but without coming to any conclusions. Now the decision was forced on her.

Liat could room with Maj, Amat supposed, except that the arrangement had the ring of disaster. But she couldn't put her out with the whores. Perhaps a cot in her own rooms, or an apartment in one of the low towns. With a guard, of course. . . .

Later. That could all come later. Amat rose. The boys stood.

"Bring her here," she said. "Tonight. Don't let Wilsin-cha know what you're doing. Don't tell her until you have to. I'll see her safe from there. You can trust me to it."

"Thank you, Amat-cha," Itani said. "But if this business is going to continue . . . I don't want to burden you with this if it's something you don't want to carry forever. This investigation might go on for years, no?"

"Gods, I hope not," Amat said. "But I promise you, even if it does, I'll see it finished. Whatever it costs, I *will* bring this to light."

"I believe you," Itani said.

Amat paused, there was a weight to the boy's tone that made her think he'd expected to hear that. She had confirmed something he already suspected, and she wondered what precisely it had been. She had no way to know.

She called in Torish-cha, introduced the boys and let them speak until the plans had been made clear. The girl would come that night, just after sundown, to the rear of the house. Two of Torish's men would meet them at the edge of the palace grounds to be sure nothing odd happened along the way. Itani would go along as well, and explain the situation. Amat sent them away just before midday, easing herself into bed after they left, and letting her eyes close at last. Any fear she had that the day's troubles would keep her awake was unfounded—sleep rolled over her like a wave. She woke hours later, the falling sun shining into her eyes through a gap where one of her tapestries had slipped.

She called Mitat up for the briefing that opened the day. The red-haired woman came bearing a bowl of stewed beef and rice and a flask of good red wine. Amat sat at her desk and ate while Mitat spoke—the tiles man thought he knew how the table was being cheated and should know for certain by the end of the night, Little Namya had a rash on his back that needed to be looked at by a physician but Chiyan was recovering well from her visit to the street of beads and would be back to work within a few more days. Two of the girls had apparently run off, and Mitat was preparing to hire on replacements. Amat listened to each piece, fitting it into the vast complexity that her life had become.

"Torish-cha sent his men out to recover the girl you discussed with him this morning," Mitat went on. "They should be back soon."

"I'll need a cot for her," Amat said. "You can put it in my rooms, against the wall there."

Mitat took a pose of acknowledgement. There was something else in it, though, a nuance that Amat caught as much from a hint of a smile as the pose itself. And then she saw Mitat realize that she'd noticed something, and the red-haired woman broke into a grin.

"What?" Amat asked.

"The other business," Mitat said. "About Maj and the Galts? I had a man come by from a hired laborers' house asking if you were only paying for information about this island girl, or if you wanted to know about the other one too."

Amat stopped chewing.

"The other one?" Amat asked.

"The one Oshai brought in last year."

Amat took a moment, sitting back, as the words took time to make sense. In the darkness of her exhaustion, hope flickered. Hope and relief.

"There was *another* one?"

"I thought you might find that interesting," Mitat said.

MAATI SAT ON THE WOODEN STEPS OF THE POET'S HOUSE, STARING OUT AT trees black and bare as sticks, at the dark water of the pond, at the ornate palaces of the Khai with lanterns glittering like fireflies. Night had fallen, but the last rays of sunlight still lingered in the west. His face and hands were cold, his body hunched forward, pulled into itself. But he didn't go into the warmth of the house behind him. He had no use for comfort.

Otah and Liat had left just before sunset. They might, he supposed, be in the soft quarter by now. He imagined them walking briskly through the narrow streets, Otah's arm across her shoulder protectively. Otah-kvo would be able to keep her safe. Maati's own presence would have been redundant, unneeded.

Behind him, the small door scraped open. Maati didn't turn. The slow, lumbering footsteps were enough for him to know it was his teacher and not Seedless.

"There's chicken left," Heshai-kvo said. "And the bread's good."

"Thank you. Perhaps later," Maati said.

Grunting with the effort, the poet lowered himself onto the step beside Maati, looking out with him over the bare landscape as it fell into darkness. Maati could hear the old poet's wheezing breath over the calling of crows.

"Is she doing well?" Heshai asked.

"I suppose so."

"She'll be going back to her house soon. Wilsin-cha . . ."

"She's not going back to him," Maati said. "The old overseer—Amat Kyaan—is taking her up."

"So House Wilsin loses another good woman. He won't like that," Heshai said, then shrugged. "Serves the old bastard right for not treating them better, I'd guess."

"I suppose."

"I see your friend the laborer's back."

Maati didn't answer. He was only cold, inside and out. Heshai glanced over at him and sighed. His thick-fingered hand patted Maati's knee the way his father's might have had the world been something other than it was. Maati felt tears welling unbidden in his eyes.

"Come inside, my boy," the poet said. "I'll warm us up a little wine."

Maati let himself be coaxed back in. With Heshai-kvo recovered, the house was slipping back into the mess it had been when he'd first come. Books and scrolls lay open on the tables and the floor beside the couches. An inkblock hollowed with use stained the desk where it sat directly on the wood. Maati squatted by the fire, looking into the flames as he had the darkness, and to much the same effect.

Behind him, Heshai moved through the house, and soon the rich scent of wine and mulling spices began to fill the place. Maati's belly rumbled, and he forced himself up, walking over to the table where the remains of the evening meal waited for him. He pulled a greasy drumstick from the chicken carcass and considered it. Heshai sat across from him and handed him a thick slice of black bread. Maati sketched a pose of gratitude. Heshai filled a thick earthenware cup with wine and passed it to him. The wine, when he drank it, was clean and rich and warmed his throat.

"Full week coming," Heshai-kvo said. "There's a dinner with the envoys of Cetani and Udun tomorrow I thought we should attend. And then a religious scholar's talking down at the temple the day after that. If you wanted to . . ."

"If you'd like, Heshai-kvo," Maati said.

"I wouldn't really," the poet said. "I've always thought religious scholars were idiots."

The old poet's face was touched by mischief, a little bit delighted with his own irreverence. Maati could see just a hint of what Heshai-kvo had looked like as a young man, and he couldn't help smiling back, if only slightly. Heshai-kvo clapped a hand on the table.

"There!" he said. "I knew you weren't beyond reach."

Maati shook his head, taking a pose of thanks more intimate and sincere than he'd used to accept the offered food. Heshai-kvo replied with one that an uncle might offer to a nephew. Maati stirred himself. This was as good a time as any, and likely better than most.

"Is Seedless here?" Maati asked.

"What? No. No, I suppose he's out somewhere showing everyone how clever he is," Heshai-kvo said bitterly. "I know I ought to keep him closer, but that torture box . . . ."

"No, that's good. There was something I needed to speak with you about, but I didn't want him nearby."

The poet frowned, but nodded Maati on.

"It's about the island girl and what happened to her. I think . . . Heshai, that wasn't only what it seemed. Marchat Wilsin knew about it. He arranged it because the Galtic High Council told him to. And Amat Kyaan—the one Liat's gone to stay with—she's getting the proof of it together to take before the Khai."

The poet's face went white and then flushed red. The wide froglips pursed, and he shook his wide head. He seemed both angry and resigned.

"That's what she says?" he asked. "This overseer?"

"Not only her," Maati said.

"Well, she's wrong," the poet said. "That isn't how it happened."

"Heshai-kvo, I think it is."

"It's not," the poet said and stood. His expression was closed. He walked to the fire, warming his hands with his back to Maati. The burning wood crackled and spat. Maati, putting down the still-uneaten bread, turned to him.

"Amat Kyaan isn't the only—"

"They're all wrong, then. Think about it for a moment, Maati. Just think. If it had been the High Council of Galt behind the blasted thing, what would happen? If the Khai saw it proved? He'd punish them. And how'd you think he'd do it?"

"The Khai would use you and Seedless against them," Maati said.

"Yes, and what good would come of that?"

Maati took a pose of query, but Heshai didn't turn to see it. After a moment, he let his hands fall. The firelight danced and flickered, making the poet seem almost as if he were part of the flame. Maati walked toward him.

"It's the truth," he said.

"Doesn't matter if it is," Heshai-kvo said. "There are punishments worse than the crimes. What happened, happened. There's nothing to be gotten by holding onto it now."

"You don't believe that," Maati said, and his voice was harder than he'd expected it to be. Heshai-kvo shifted, turned. His eyes were dry and calm.

"There's nothing that will put life back into that child," Heshai-kvo said. "What could possibly be gained by trying?"

"There's justice," Maati said, and Heshai laughed. It was a disturbing sound, more anger than mirth. Heshai-kvo stood and moved toward him. Without thinking Maati stepped back.

"Justice? Gods, boy, you want *justice*? We have larger problems than that, you and I. Getting through another year without one of these small gods flooding a city or setting the world on fire. That's important. Keeping the city safe. Playing court politics so that the Khaiem never decide to take each other's toys and women by force. And you want to add justice to all that? I've sacrificed my life to a world that wouldn't care less about me as a man if you paid it. You and I, both of us were cut off from our brothers and sisters. That boy from Udun who we saw in the court was slaughtered by his own brother and we all applauded him for doing it. Am I supposed to punish him too?"

"You're supposed to do what's right," Maati said.

Heshai-kvo took a dismissive pose.

"What we do is bigger than right and wrong," he said. "If the Dai-kvo didn't make that clear to you, consider it your best lesson from me."

"I can't think that," Maati said. "If we don't push for justice . . ."

Heshai-kvo's expression darkened. He took a pose appropriate to asking guidance from the holy, his stance a sarcasm. Maati swallowed, but held his ground.

"You love justice?" Heshai asked. "It's harder than stone, boy. Love it if you want. It won't love you."

"I can't think that—"

"Tell me you're never transgressed," Heshai interrupted, his voice harsh. "Never stolen food from the kitchens, never lied to a teacher. Tell me you've never bedded another man's woman."

Maati felt something shift in him, profound as a bone breaking, but painless. His ears hummed with something like bees. He took the corner of the table and lifted. Food, wine, papers, books all spilled together to the ground. He took a chair and tossed it aside, scooped up the winebowl with a puddle of redness still swirling in its curve and threw it against the wall. It shattered with a loud, satisfying pop. The poet looked at him, mouth gaping as if Maati had just grown wings.

And then, quickly as it had come, the rage was gone, and Maati sank to his knees like a puppet with its strings cut. Sobs wracked him, as violent as being sick. Maati was only half-aware of the poet's footsteps as he came near, as he bent down. The thick arms cradled him, and Maati held Heshai-kvo's wide frame and cried into the brown folds of his cloak while the poet rocked him and whispered *I'm sorry, I'm sorry, I'm sorry.*

It felt like it would go on forever, like the river of pain could run and run and run and never go dry. It wasn't true—in time exhaustion as much as anything else stilled him. Maati sat beside his master, the overturned table beside them. The fire had burned low while he wasn't watching it—embers glowed red and gold among ashes still arched in the shapes of the wood they'd once been.

"Well," Maati said at last, his voice thick, "I've just made an ass of myself, haven't I?"

Heshai-kvo chuckled, recognizing the words. Maati, despite himself, smiled.

"A decent first effort, at least," Heshai-kvo said. "You'll get better with time. I didn't mean to do that to you, you know. It was unfair bringing Liat-kya into it. It's only that . . . the island girl . . . if I'd done better work when I first fashioned Seedless, it wouldn't have happened. I just don't want things getting worse. I want it over with."

"I know," Maati said.

They were silent for a time. The embers cooled a shade, the ashes crumbled.

"They say there's two women you don't get past," Heshai-kvo said. "Your first love and your first sex. And then, if it turns out to be the same girl . . ."

"It is," Maati said.

"Yes," Heshai said. "It was the same for me. Her name was Ariat Miu. She had the most beautiful voice I've ever heard. I don't know where she is now."

Maati leaned over and put his arm around Heshai as if they were drinking companions. Heshai nodded as if Maati had spoken. He took a deep breath and let it out slowly.

"Well, we'd best get this cleaned up before the servants see it. Stoke the fire, would you? I'll get some candles burning. Night's coming on too early these days."

"Yes, Heshai-kvo," Maati said.

"And Maati? You know I won't tell anyone about this, don't you?"

Maati took a pose of acknowledgement. In the dim light he couldn't be sure that Heshai had seen it, so he let his hands fall and spoke.

"Thank you," he said into the dark.

THEY WALKED SLOWLY, HAMPERED BY LIAT'S WOUNDS. THE TWO MERCE-naries walked one before and one behind, and Otah walked at her side. At first, near the palaces, he had put his arm around her waist, thinking that it would be a comfort. Her body told him, though, that it wasn't. Her shoulder, her arm, her ribs—they were too tender to be touched and Otah found himself oddly glad. It freed him to watch the doorways and alleys, rooftops and food carts and firekeepers' kilns more closely.

The air smelled of wood smoke from a hundred hearths. A cool, thick mist too dense to be fog, too insubstantial to be rain, slicked the stones of the road and the walls of the houses. In her oversized woolen cloak, Liat might have been anyone. Otah found himself half-consciously flexing his hands, as if preparing for an attack that never came.

When they reached the edge of the soft quarter, passing by the door of Amat Kyaan's now-empty apartments, Liat motioned to stop. The two men looked to Otah and then each other, their expressions professional and impatient, but they paused.

"Are you all right?" Otah asked, his head bent close to the deep cowl of Liat's cloak. "I could get you water . . ."

"No," she said. Then, a moment later. "'Tani, I don't want to go there."

"Where?" he asked, his fingertips touching her bound arm.

"To Amat Kyaan. I've done everything so badly. And I can't think she really wants me there. And . . ."

"Sweet," Otah said. "She'll keep you safe. Until we know what's . . ."

Liat looked at him directly. Her shadowed face showed her impatience and her fear.

"I didn't say I wouldn't," she said. "Only that I don't want it."

Otah leaned close, kissing her gently on the lips. Her good hand held him close.

"Don't leave me," she said, hardly more than a whisper.

"Where would I go," he said, his tone gentle to hide that his answer was also a question. She smiled, slight and brave, and nodded. Liat held his hand in hers for the rest of the way.

The soft quarter never knew a truly quiet night. The lanterns lit the streets with the dancing shadows of a permanent fire. Music came from the opened doors of the houses: drums and flutes, horns and voices. Twice they passed houses with balconies that overlooked the street with small groups of underdressed, chilly whores leaning over the rails like carcasses at a butcher's. The wealth of Saraykeht, richest and most powerful of the southern cities, eddied and swirled around them. Otah found himself neither aroused nor disturbed, though he thought perhaps he should be.

They reached the comfort house, going through an ironbound doorway in a tall stone wall, through a sad little garden that separated the kitchens from the main house, and then into the common room. It was alive with activity. The red-haired woman, Mitat, and Amat had covered the long common tables with papers and scrolls. The island girl, Maj, paced behind them, gnawing impatiently at a thumbnail. As the two guards who'd accompanied them moved deeper into the house greeting other men similarly armed and armored, Otah noticed two young boys, one in the colors of House Yanaani, the other wearing the badge of the seafront's custom house, waiting impatiently. Messengers. Something had happened.

Amat's closer than she knows. There isn't much time.

"Liat-kya," Amat said, raising one hand in a casual greeting. "Come here. I've something I want you ask you."

Liat walked forward, and Otah followed her. There was a light in Amat's eyes—something like triumph. Amat embraced Liat gently, and Otah saw the tears in Liat's eyes as she held her old master with one uninjured arm.

"I'm sorry," Amat said. "I though you'd be safe. And there was so much that needed doing, that . . . I didn't understand the situation deeply enough. I should have warned you."

"Honored teacher," Liat said, and then had no more words. Amat's smile was warm as summer sunlight.

"You know Maj, of course. This is Mitat, and that brute against that wall is Torish Wite, my master of guard."

When Maj spoke, she spoke the Khaiate tongue. Her accent was thick but not so much that Otah couldn't catch her words.

"I didn't think I was to be seeing you again."

Liat's smile went thin.

"You speak very well, Maj-cha."

"I am waiting for weeks here," Maj said, coolly. "What else do I do?"

Amat looked over. Otah saw the woman called Mitat glance up at her, then at the island girl, then away. Tension quieted the room, and for a moment, even the messengers stopped fidgeting and stared.

"She's come to help," Amat said.

"She is come because you called her," Maj said. "Because she needs you."

"We need each other," Amat said, command in her voice. She drew herself to her full height, and even leaning on her cane, she seemed to fill the room. "She's come because I wanted her to come. We have almost everything we need. Without her, we aren't ready."

Maj stared at Amat, then slowly turned and took a pose of greeting as awkward as a child's. Otah saw the flush in the pale cheeks, the brightness of her eyes, and understood. Maj was drunk. Amat gathered Liat close to the table, peppering her with questions about dates and shipping orders, and what exactly Oshai and Wilsin-cha had said and when. Otah sat at the table, near enough to hear, near enough to watch, but not a part of the interrogation.

For a moment, he felt invisible. The intensity and excitement, desperation and controlled violence around him became like an epic on a stage. He saw it all from outside. When, unconsciously, he met the island girl's gaze, she smiled at him and nodded—a wordless, informal, unmistakable gesture; a recognition between strangers. She, with her imperfect knowledge of language and custom, couldn't truly be a part of the conspiracy now coming near to full bloom before them. He, by contrast, could not because still heard Seedless laying the consequences of Amat's success before him—*Liat may be killed, innocent blood will wash Galt, Maati will suffer to the end of his days, I will betray you to your family*—and that private knowledge was like an infection. Every step that Amat made brought them one step nearer that end.

And to his unease, Otah found that his refusal of the andat was not so certain a thing as he had though it.

For nearly a quarter candle, Amat and Mitat, Liat and sometimes even Torish Wite chewed and argued. The messengers were questioned, the letters they bore added to the growing stacks, and they were sent away with Amat's replies tucked in their sleeves. Otah listened and watched as the arguments to be presented before the Khai Saraykeht became clearer. Proofs of billing, testimonies, collisions of dates and letters from Galt, and Maj—witness and centerpiece—to stand as the symbol of it all. And then the whole web of coincidence repeated a year earlier with some other girl who had taken fright, the story said, and escaped. There was no proof—no evidence which in itself showed anything. But like tile chips in a mosaic, the facts related to one another in a way that demanded a grim interpretation.

And only so much proof, of course, was required. Amat's evidence need only capture the imagination of the court, and the avalanche would begin. What she said was true, and once the full powers of the court were involved, Heshai-kvo would be brought before it, and Seedless. And the andat, when forced, would have to speak the truth. He might even be pleased to, bringing in another wave of disaster as a second-best to his own release.

As the night passed—the moon moving unseen overhead—Liat began to flag. Amat noticed it and met Otah's gaze.

"Liat-kya, I'm being terrible," Amat said, taking a pose of apology. "You're hurt and tired and I've been keeping you awake."

Liat made some small protest, but its weakness was enough to show Amat's argument valid. Otah moved to her and helped her to her feet, and Liat, sighing, leaned into him.

"There's a cot made up upstairs," Mitat said. "In Amat-cha's rooms."

"But where will 'Tani sleep?"

"I'm fine, love," he said before Amat—clearly surprised by the question—could think to offer hospitality. "I've a place with some of my old cohort. If I didn't come back, they'd worry."

It wasn't true, but that hardly mattered. The prospect of staying at the comfort house while Amat's plans reached fruition held no appeal. Only the sleepy distress in Liat's eyes made him wish to stay, and then for her more than himself.

"I'll stay until you're asleep," he said. It seemed to comfort her. They gave their goodnights and walked up the thick wooden stairs, moving slowly for Liat's benefit. Otah heard the conversation begin again behind him, the plan moving forward.

He closed the door of Amat's rooms behind him. The shutters were fast but the dull orange of torchlight from the street glowed at their seams. The night candle on Amat's desk was past its half-mark. Its flame guttered as they passed. The cot was thick canvas stretched over wood with a mattress three fingers thick and netting strung over it even though there were few insects flying so late in the winter. With his arm still around Liat's thin frame, their single shadow flickered against the wall.

"She hates me, I think," Liat said, her voice low and calm.

"What are you talking about. Amat-cha was perfectly . . ."

"Not her. Maj."

Otah was silent. He wanted to deny that too—to tell Liat that no one thought ill of her, that everything would be fine if only she'd let it. But he didn't know it was true, or even if it would be wise to think it. They had thought no particular ill of Wilsin-cha, and Liat could have died for that. He felt his silence spread like cold. Liat shrugged him away and pulled at the ties of her cloak.

"Let me," Otah said. Liat held still as he undid her cloak, folded it on the floor under her cot.

"My robe too?" she asked. In the near darkness, Otah felt her gaze as much as saw it. An illusion, perhaps. It might only have been something in the tone of her voice, an inflection recognized after months of being her lover, sharing her bed and her body. Otah hesitated for more reasons than one.

"Please," Liat said.

"You're hurt, love. It was hard enough even walking upstairs . . ."

"Itani."

"It's Amat-cha's room. She could come up."

"She won't be up for hours. Help me with my robe. Please."

Objections pushed for position, but Otah moved forward, drawn by her need and his own. Carefully, he untied the stays of her robes and drew them from her until she stood naked but for her straps and bandages. Even in the dim light, he could see where the bruises marked her skin. She took his hand and kissed it, then reached for the stays of his own robe. He did not stop her. It would have been cruel, and even if it hadn't, he did not want to.

They made love slowly, carefully, and he thought as much in sorrow as in lust. Her skin was the color of dark honey in the candlelight, her hair black as crows. When they were both spent, Otah lay with his back to the chill wall, giving Liat as much room on the cot as she needed to be comfortable. Her eyes were only half-open, the corners of her mouth turned down. When she shivered, he half rose and pulled her blanket over her. He did not climb beneath it himself, though the warmth would have been welcome.

"You were gone for so long," Liat said. "There were days I wondered if you were coming back."

"Here I am."

"Yes," she said. "Here you are. What was it like? Tell me everything."

And so he told her about the ship and the feeling of wood swaying underfoot, the creaking of rope and the constant noise of water. He told her about the courier with his jokes and stories of travelling, and the way Orai had known at once that he'd left a woman behind. About Yalakeht with its tall gray buildings and the thin lanes with iron gates at the mouth that could lock whole streets up for the night like a single apartment.

And he could have gone on—the road to the Dai-kvo's village, the mountain, the town of only men, the Dai-kvo himself, the odd half-offer to take him back. He might even have gone as far as Seedless' threats, and the realization he was still struggling with—that Itani Noyga would be exposed as the son of the Khai Machi. That if Seedless lived, Itani Noyga would have to die. But Liat's breath was heavy, deep, and regular. When he lifted himself over her, she murmured something and curled herself deeper into the bedding. Otah pulled on his robes. The night candle was past the three-quarter mark, the darkness moving closer and closer to dawn. For the first time, he noticed the fatigue in his limbs. He would need to find someplace to sleep. A room, perhaps, or one of the sailor's bunks down by the seafront where he'd be sharing a brazier with nine men who'd drunk themselves asleep the night before.

In the buttery light of the common room, the conversation was still going on, but to his surprise, the focus had shifted. Maj, an observer before like himself, was seated across from Amat Kyaan, stabbing at the tabletop with a finger and letting loose a long string of syllables with no clear break between them. Her face was flushed, and he could hear the anger in her voice without knowing the words. Anger and wine. Amat looked up at he descended the stairs. She looked older than usual.

Maj followed the old woman's gaze, glanced up at the closed door behind him, and said something else. Amat replied in the same language, her voice calm but not placating. Maj stood, rattling the bench, and strode to Otah.

"Your woman sleeps?" Maj said.

"She's asleep. Yes."

"I have questions. Wake her," Maj said, taking a pose that made the words a command. Her breath was a drunk's. Over her shoulder, he saw Amat shake her head no. Otah took a pose of apology. The refusal seemed to break something in Maj, and tears brimmed in her eyes, streaked her cheeks.

"Weeks," she said, her tone pleading. "I am waiting for weeks, and for nothing. There is no justice here. You people you have *no* justice."

Mitat approached them and put her hand on the island girl's arm. Maj pulled away and went to a different door, wiping her eyes on the back of her hand. As the door closed behind her, Otah took a pose of query.

"She didn't understand that the Khai Saraykeht might make his own investigation," Mitat said. "She thought he'd act immediately. When she heard that there'd be another delay . . ."

"It isn't entirely her fault," Amat said. "This can't have been easy for her, any of it." The master of guard—a huge bear of a man—coughed. The way he and Amat considered each other was enough to tell Otah this wasn't the first time the girl had been the subject of conversation. Amat continued, "It will all be finished soon enough. Or our part, at least. As long as she's here to make the case before the Khai, we'll have started the thing. If she goes home after that, she goes home."

"And if she leaves before that?" Mitat asked, sitting on the table.

"She won't," Amat said. "She's not well, but she won't leave before someone answers for her child. And Liat. She's resting?"

"Yes, Amat-cha," Otah said, taking a pose of thanks. "She's asleep."

"Wilsin-cha will know by now that she's not going back to his house," Amat said. "She'll need to stay inside until this is over."

"Another one? And how long's that going to be, grandmother?" Torish Wite asked.

Amat rested her head in her hands. She seemed smaller than she had been, diminished by fatigue and years, but not broken. Weary to her bones perhaps, but unbroken. In that moment, he found that he admired Liat's old teacher very much.

"I'll send a runner in the morning," she said. "This time of year, it might take a week before we get an audience."

"But we aren't ready!" Mitat said. "We don't even know where the first girl was kept or where she's gone. We won't have time to find her!"

"We have all the pieces," Amat said. "And what we don't have, the utkhaiem will find when the Khai looks into it. It isn't all I'd hoped, but it will do. It will have to."

18

>+< Marchat Wilsin had seen wildfires spread more slowly than the news. Amat Kyaan's petition had reached the servants of the Master of Tides—an idiot title for an overfed secretary, he thought—just before dawn. By the time the sun had risen the width of two hands together, a messenger from the compound had come to the bathhouse with a message from Epani. The panicky twig of a man had scratched out the basic information from the petition, his letters so hasty they were hardly legible. Not that it mattered. The word of Amat Kyaan and her petition were enough. It was happening.

Epani's letter floated now on the surface of the water. It was a warm bath, now that the half-hearted winter was upon them, and steam rose in wisps from the drowned paper. The ink had washed away as he'd watched it, threads of darkness like shadows fading into the clear water. It was over. There was nothing he could do now that would put the world back in its right shape, and in a strange way it was a relief. Night after night since Seedless, that miserable Khaiate god-ghost, had come to his apartments, Marchat had lain awake. He'd had a damn fine mind, once. But in the dark hours, he'd found nothing, no plan of action, no finessed stroke that would avoid the thing that had now come. And since there was no halting it, he could at least stop looking. He closed his eyes and let his head sink for a moment under the tiny lapping waves. Yes, it was a relief that at least now he wouldn't have to try.

He lay underwater until his lungs began to burn, and then even a little longer, not wanting to leave this little moment of peace behind. But time and breath being what they were, he rose and tramped up out of the bath. The water streamed off his body leaving gooseflesh behind it, and he dried himself quickly as he walked into the changing room. The heat from a wide, black brazier combined with the vapors from the baths to make the air thick. Any chill at all would freeze these people. The summer cities couldn't imagine cold, and after so many years here, perhaps he couldn't either. As he pulled on his thick woolen robes, it struck Marchat that he didn't remember the last time he'd seen snow. Whenever it had been, he hadn't known it was the last time he ever would, or he'd have paid it more attention.

A pair of men came in together, round-faced, black-haired, speaking as much in gesture as with words. The same as all the others in Saraykeht. He was the one—pale skin, kinky hair, ridiculously full beard—who stood out. He'd lived here since he'd been a young man, and he'd never really become of the place. He'd always been waiting for the day when he'd be called back to Galt. It was a bitter thought. When the pair noticed him, they took poses of greeting which he returned without thinking. His hands simply knew what to do.

He walked back to the compound slowly. Not because of the dread, though the gods knew he wasn't looking forward, but instead because his failure seemed to have washed his eyes. The sounds and scents of the city were fresh, unfamiliar. When he had been traveling as a young man, it had been like this coming home. The streets his family lived among had carried the same weight of familiarity and strangeness that Saraykeht now bore. At the time, he'd thought it was only that he had been away, but now he thought it was more that the travels he'd made back then had changed him, as the letter from Epani had changed him again just now. The city was the same, but he was a new man seeing it: The ancient stonework; the vines that rose on the walls and were pulled back every year only to crawl up again; the mixture of languages from all across the world that came to the seafront; the songs of the beggars and cry of birdcall.

Too soon, he was back at his own compound where the Galtic Tree stood as it always had in the main courtyard, the fountain splashing behind it. He wondered who would take the place once he'd gone. Some other poor bastard whom the family wanted rid of. Some boy desperate to prove his worth in the wealthiest, most isolated position in the house. If they didn't tear the place down stone by stone and burn the rubble. That was another distinct possibility.

Epani waited in his private chambers, wringing his hands in distress. Marchat couldn't bring himself to feel anything more than a mild annoyance at the man.

"Wilsin-cha, I've just heard. The audience was granted. Six days. It's going to come in six days!"

Marchat put up his hand, palm out, and the cicada stopped whining.

"Send a runner to the palaces. One of the higher clerks. Or go yourself. Tell the Khai's people that we expect Amat Kyaan's audience to touch upon the private business of the house, and we want them to postpone her audience until we can be present with our response."

"Yes, Wilsin-cha."

"And bring me paper and a fresh inkblock," Marchat said. "I have some letters to write."

There must have been something in his tone—a certain gravity, perhaps—that reassured the overseer, because Epani dropped into a pose of acknowledgement and scurried out with a sense of relief that was almost palpable. Marchat followed him far enough to find a servant who could fetch him some mulled wine, then returned to his desk and prepared himself. The tiny flask in the thin drawer at his knee was made of silver, the stopper sealed with green wax. When he shook it, in clinked like some little piece of metal was hidden in it, and not a liquid at all. It was a distillation of the same drugs comfort houses in the soft quarter used to make exotic wines. But it was, of course, much too potent. This thumbfull in his palm was enough to make a man sleep forever. He closed his fingers over it.

This wasn't how he'd wanted it. But it would do.

He put the flask back in its place as Epani-cha arrived, paper and inkblock and fresh pens in his hands. Marchat thanked him and sent him away, then turned to the blank page.

I am Marchat Wilsin of House Wilsin of Galt, he began then scraped his pen tip over the ink. *I write this to confess my crimes and to explain them. I and I alone* . . .

He paused. I and I alone. It was what he could do, of course. He could eat the sin and save those less innocent than himself from punishment. He might save Galt from the wrath of the Khaiem. For the first time since he'd read Epani's scratched, fear-filled words, Marchat felt a pang of sorrow. It was a bad time, this, to be alone.

The servant arrived with his wine, and Marchat drank it slowly, looking at the few words he'd written. He'd invented the whole tale, of course. How he'd hoped to shift the balance of trade away from Saraykeht and so end his exile. How he had fed himself on foolish hopes and dreams and let his own evil nature carry him away. Then he'd apologize to the Khai for his sins, confess his cowardice, and commend his fortune to the island girl Maj who he had wronged and to Amat Kyaan whose loyalty to him had led her to suspect those in Galt who could command him, since she would not believe the sickness of the plan to be his own.

The last part was, he thought, a nice touch. Recasting Amat as a woman so loyal to him, so in love with him, that she didn't see the truth clearly. He felt sure she'd appreciate the irony.

I and I alone.

He took the barely-started confession, blew on it to cure the ink, and set it aside for a time. There was no hurry. Any time in the next six days would suit as well perhaps more if the Khai let him stall Amat and cheat the world out of a few more sunsets. And there were other letters to write. Something to the family back in Galt, for instance. An apology to the High Council for his evil plans that the utkhaiem might intercept. Or something more personal. Something, perhaps, real.

He drew his pen across the ink, and set the metal nib to a fresh sheet.

Amat, my dear old friend. You see what I'm like? Even now, at this last stop on the trail, I'm too much the coward to use the right words. Amat, my love. Amat, who I never did tell my heart to for fear she'd laugh or, worse, be polite. Who ever would have thought we'd come to this?

OTAH WOKE LATE IN THE AFTERNOON FROM A HEAVY, TROUBLED SLEEP. THE room was empty—the inhabitants of the other bunks having gone their ways. The brazier was cool, but the sun glowed against a window covering of thin-stretched leather. He gathered his things from the thin space between himself and the wall where someone would have had to reach over his sleeping body to steal them. Even so he checked. What money he'd had before, he had now. He dressed slowly, waiting for half-remembered dreams to dissolve and fade. There had been something about a flood, and feral dogs drowning in it.

The streets of the seafront were busy, even in winter. Ships arrived and departed by the spare handful, heading mostly south for other warm ports. The journey to Yalakeht would have been profoundly unpleasant, even now. At one of the tall, thin tables by the wharves, he bought a small sack of baked apple slices covered in butter and black sugar, tossing it from one hand to the other as the heat slapped his palms. He thought of Orai in Machi and the deep-biting cold of the far north. It would, he thought, make apples taste even better.

The scandal in every teahouse, around every firekeeper's kiln, on the corners and in the streets, was the petition of Amat Kyaan to speak before the Khai. The petition to speak against House Wilsin. Otah listened and smiled his charming smile without ever once meaning it. She was going to disclose how the house had been evading taxes, one version said. Another had it that the sad trade that had gone wrong was more than just the work of the andat—a rival house had arranged it to discredit Wilsin, and Amat was now continuing the vendetta still in the pay of some unknown villain. Another that Amat would show that the island girl's child had truly been Marchat Wilsin's. Or the Khai Saraykeht's. Or the get of some other Khai killed so that the Khaiem wouldn't have to suffer the possibility of a half-Nippu poet.

It was no more or less than any of the other thousand scandals and occasions of gossip that stirred the slow blood of the city. Even when he came across people he knew, faces he recognized, Otah kept his own counsel. It was coming soon enough, he thought.

The sun was falling in the west, vanishing into the low hills and cane fields, when Otah took himself up the wide streets toward the palaces of the Khai and through those high gardens to the poet's house. Set off from the grandeur of the halls of the Khai and the utkhaiem, the poet's house seemed small and close and curiously genuine in the failing light. Otah left the bare trees behind and walked over the wooden bridge, koi popping sluggishly at the water as he passed. Nothing ever froze here.

Before he'd reached the doors, Maati opened them. The waft of air that came with him was warm and scented with smoke and mulled wine. Maati took a pose of greeting appropriate for a student to an honored teacher, and Otah laughed and pushed his hands aside. It was only when Maati didn't laugh in return that he saw the pose had been sincere. He took one of apology, but Maati only shook his head and gestured him inside.

The rooms were more cluttered than usual—books, papers, a pair of old boots, half the morning's breakfast still uneaten. A small fire burned, and Maati sat down in one of the two chairs that faced it. Otah took the other.

"You stayed with her last night?" Maati asked.

"Most of it," Otah said, leaning forward. "I rented a bunk by the seafront. I didn't want to stay in the comfort house. You heard that Amat Kyaan . . ."

"Yes. I think they brought word to Heshai-kvo before they told the Khai."

"How did he take it?"

"He's gone off to the soft quarter. I doubt he'll come back soon."

"He's going to Amat Kyaan?"

"I doubt it. He seemed less like someone solving a problem than participating in it."

"Does he know? I mean, did you tell him what she was going to say?"

Maati made a sound half laugh, half groan.

"Yes. He didn't believe it. Or he did, but he wouldn't admit to it. He said that justice wasn't worth the price."

"I can't think that's true," Otah said. Then, "But maybe there's no justice to be had."

There was a long pause. There was a deep cup of wine, Otah saw, near the fire. A deep cup, but very little wine in it.

"And how did you take the news?" he asked.

Maati shrugged. He looked tired, unwell. His skin had a gray cast to it, and the bags under his eyes might have been from too much sleep or too little. Now that he thought to look for it, Maati's head was shifting slightly, back and forth with the beating of his heart. He was drunk.

"What's the matter, Maati?" he asked.

"You should stay here," the boy said. "You shouldn't sleep at the seafront or the comfort house. You're welcome here."

"Thank you, but I think people would find it a little odd that—"

"People," Maati said angrily, then became quiet. Otah stood, found the pot of wine warming over a small brazier, and pushed away the papers that lay too close to the glowing coals before he poured himself a bowl. Maati was looking up at him, sheepish, when he returned to the chair.

"I should have gotten that."

"It hardly matters. I've got it now. Are you well, Maati? You seem . . . bothered?"

"I was thinking the same thing about you. Ever since you got back from the Dai-kvo, it's seemed . . . difficult between us. Don't you think?"

"I suppose so," Otah said and sipped the wine. It was hot enough to blow across before he drank it, but it hadn't been cooking so long that the spirit had been burned out of it. The warmth of it in his throat was comfortable. "It's my fault. There are things I've been trying not to look at too closely. Orai said that sea travel changes you. Changes who you are."

"It may not be only that," Maati said softly.

"No?"

Maati sat forward, his elbows on his knees, and looked into the fire as he spoke. His voice was hard as slate.

"There's something I promised not to speak of. And I'm going to break that promise. I've done something terrible, Otah-kvo. I didn't mean to, and if I could undo it, I swear by all the gods I would. While you were away, Liat and I . . . there was no one else for us to speak with. We were the only two who knew all the truth. And so we spent time in each other's company . . ."

I need you to stay, Liat had said before he'd left for the Dai-kvo. *I need someone by my side.*

And Seedless when he'd returned: *Heshai fell in love and lost her, and he's been chewed by guilt ever since. Maati will do the same.*

Otah sat back, his chair creaking under his shifting weight. With a rush like water poured from a spout, he knew what he was seeing, what had happened. He put down his bowl of wine. Maati was silent, shaking his head back and forth slowly. His face was flushed and although there was no thickness in his voice, no hidden sob in his breath, still a single tear hung from the tip of his nose. It would have been comical if it had been someone else.

"She's a wonderful woman," Otah said, carefully. "Sometimes maybe a little difficult to trust, but still a good woman."

Maati nodded.

"Perhaps I should go," Otah said softly.

"I'm so sorry," Maati whispered to the fire. "Otah-kvo, I am so very, very sorry."

"You didn't do anything that hasn't been done a thousand times before by a thousand different people."

"But I did it to you. I betrayed *you*. You love her."

"But I don't trust her," Otah said softly.

"Or me. Not any longer," Maati said.

"Or you," Otah agreed, and pulling his robes close around him, he walked out of the poet's house and into the darkness. He closed the door, paused, and then hit it hard enough to bloody his knuckle.

The pain in his chest was real, and the rage behind it. And also, strangely, an amusement and a sense of relief. He walked slowly down to the edge of the pond, wishing more than anything that the courier Orai had been on his way to Saraykeht instead of Machi. But the world was as it was. Maati and Liat had become lovers, and it was devouring Maati just as some other tragedy had broken his teacher. Amat Kyaan was pursuing her suit before the Khai Saraykeht in a matter of days. Everything Seedless had said to him appeared to be true. And so he stood in the chill by the koi pond, and he waited, throwing stones into the dark water, hearing them strike and sink and be forgotten. He knew the andat would come to him if he were only patient. It wasn't more than half a hand.

"He's told you, then," Seedless said.

The pale face hovered in the night air, a rueful smile on the perfect, sensual lips.

"You knew?"

"Gods. The world and everyone knew," the andat said, stepping up beside him to look out over the black water. "They were about as discreet as rutting elk. I was only hoping you wouldn't hear of it until you'd done me that little favor. It's a pity, really. But I think I bear up quite well under failure, don't you?"

Otah took a deep breath, and let it out slowly. He thought perhaps his could see just the wisps of it in the cold. Beside him the andat didn't breathe because whatever it looked like, it was not a man.

"And . . . I have failed," Seedless said, his tone suddenly careful, probing. "Haven't I? I can spill your secrets, but that's hardly worth murder. And I can't expect you to kill a man in order to protect your faithless lover and the dear friend who bedded her, now can I?"

Otah saw again Maati's angry, self-loathing, empty expression and felt something twist in his belly. An impulse born in him as a child in a bare garden of half-turned earth, half a life ago. It didn't undo the hurt or the anger, but it complicated them.

"Someone told me once that you can love someone and not trust them, or you can bed someone and not trust them, but never both."

"I wouldn't know," the andat said. "My experience of love is actually fairly limited."

"Tell me what I need to know."

In the moonlight, pale hands took a pose that asked for clarification.

"You said you knew where he would be. How long it would take him to drink himself to sleep. Tell me."

"And you'll do what I asked?"

"Tell me what I need to know," Otah said, "and find out."

THE MORNING AFTER LIAT'S ARRIVAL AT THE COMFORT HOUSE—TWO DAYS ago now—she'd awakened to the small sounds of Amat Kyaan sleeping. Only the faintest edge of daylight came through the shutters— these were the rooms of an owl. The faintest scent of Itani had still haunted her bedding then. When she rose, aching and awkward and half-sorry for the sex she'd insisted on in the night, Amat woke and took her downstairs. The workings of the house were simple enough— the sleeping chambers where the whores were shelved like scrolls in their boxes, cheap cloth over the bunks instead of netting; the kitchens in the back; the wide bath used for washing clothes and bodies during the day, then refilled and scented with oils before the clients came at night. The front parts of the house Amat explained were forbidden to her. Until the case against House Wilsin was made, she wasn't to leave the comfort house, and she wasn't to be seen by the clients. The stakes were too high, and Wilsin-cha had resorted to violence once already.

Since then, Liat had slept, eaten, washed herself, sat at Amat-cha's desk listening to musicians on the street below, but no word had come from Itani or from Maati. On her second night, Liat had sent out a message to the barracks where Itani's cohort slept. It had come back in the morning with a response from Muhatia-cha. Itani Noyga had left, breaking his indenture in violation of contract; he was not with the men of the house, nor was he welcome. Liat read the words with a sense of dread that approached illness. When she took it to Amat Kyaan, her old master had frowned and tucked the letter into her sleeve.

"What if Wilsin-cha's killed him?" Liat said, trying to keep the panic she felt from her voice.

Amat Kyaan, sitting at her desk, took a reassuring pose.

"He wouldn't. I have you and Maj to say what he would have said. Killing him would make our suit stronger, not weaker. And even then, I have the impression that your boy is able to take care of himself," Amat said, but seeing how little the assurances comforted her, she went on. "Still I can have Torish-cha's men ask after him."

"He'd have come back if things were well."

"Things aren't well," Amat said, her eyes hard and bright and tired. "But that doesn't mean he's in danger. Still, perhaps I should have had him stay as well. Have you sent to the poet's boy? Perhaps Maati's heard of him. He might even be staying there."

Amat took her cane and rose, gesturing at the desk. Fresh paper and ink.

"I have some things to attend to," she said. "Use what you need and we'll send him a runner."

Liat took a pose of gratitude and sat, but when she took up the pen, her hand trembled. The nib hovered just over the page, waiting, it seemed, to see which name she would write. In the end, it was Maati's name on the outside leaf. She wanted to be sure that someone would read it.

With the runner gone, Liat found there was little to do but pace. At first, she walked the length of Amat's rooms, then, as the day moved past its midpoint, her anxiety drove her downstairs. The common room smelled of roast pork and wine, and platters of bones still sat on the tables waiting to be cleared away. The whores were asleep, the men who worked the front rooms either sleeping in bunks as well or gone off to apartments away from the house. The soft quarter ran on a different day than the world Liat knew; daylight here meant rest and sleep. That Amat was awake and out of the house with Mitat and an armed escort meant that her old teacher was missing sleep. There were only five days until the case was to be made before the Khai Saraykeht.

Liat walked through the empty common room, stopping to scratch an old black dog behind the ears. It would be easy to step out the back as if going to the kitchens, and then out to the street. She imagined herself finding Itani, bringing him back to the safety of the comfort house. It was a bad idea, of course, and she wouldn't go, but the dream of it was powerful. The dream that she could somehow make everything come out right.

It was a small sound—hardly more than a sigh—that caught her attention. It had come from the long alcove in the back, from among the sewing benches and piles of cloth and leather where, according to Amat Kyaan, the costumes and stage props of the house were created. Liat moved toward it, walking softly. Behind the unruly heaps of cloth and thread, she found Maj sitting cross-legged, her hair pulled back. Her hands worked with something in her lap, and her expression was of such focus that Liat was almost afraid to interrupt. When Maj's hands shifted, she caught a glimpse of a tiny loom and black cloth.

"What is it?" Liat asked, pushed to speak by curiosity and her own buzzing, unfocused energy.

"Mourning cloth," Maj said without looking up. Her accent was so thick, Liat wasn't entirely sure she'd understood her until Maj continued. "For the dead child."

Liat came closer. The cloth was thin and sheer, black worked with tiny beads of clear glass in a pattern of surprising subtlety. Folds of it rested beside Maj's leg.

"It's beautiful," Liat said.

Maj shrugged. "It fills time. I am working on it for weeks now."

Liat knelt. The pale eyes looked up at her, questioning—maybe challenging—then returned to the small loom. Liat watched Maj's hands shifting thread and beads in near silence. It was very fine thread, the sort that might not make more than two or three hand-spans of cloth in a whole day's work. Liat reached out and ran her fingers along the folds of finished cloth. It was as wide as her two hands together and long, she guessed, as Maj was tall.

"How long do you make it?"

"Until you finish," Maj said. "Usually is something to make while the pain is fresh. When done with day's work, make cloth. When wake up in the middle night, make cloth. When time comes you want to go sing with friends or swim in quarry pond and not make cloth, is time to stop weaving."

"You've made these before. Mourning cloths."

"For mother, for brother. I am much younger then," Maj said, her voice heavy and tired. "Their cloth smaller."

Liat sat, watching as Maj threaded beads and worked them into the black patterns, the loom quiet as breathing. Neither spoke for a long time.

"I'm sorry," Liat said at last. "For what happened."

"Was your plan?"

"No, I didn't know anything about what was really happening."

"So, why sorry?"

"I should have," Liat said. "I should have known and I didn't."

Maj looked up and put the loom aside.

"And why did you not know?" she said, her gaze steady and accusing.

"I trusted Wilsin-cha," Liat said. "I thought he was doing what you wanted. I thought I was helping."

"And is this Wilsin who does this to you?" Maj asked, gesturing at the bandages and straps on Liat's shoulder.

"His men. Or that's what Amat-cha says."

"And you trust her?"

"Of course. Don't you?"

"I am here for a season, more than a season. At home, when a man does something evil, the *kiopia* pass judgement and like this . . ." Maj clapped her hands ". . . he is punished. Here, it is weeks living in a little room and waiting. Listening to nothing happen and waiting. And now, they say that the Khai, he may take his weeks to punish who killed my baby. Why wait except he doesn't trust Amat Kyaan? And if he doesn't why do I stay? Why am I waiting, if not for justice done?"

"It's complicated," Liat said. "It's all complicated."

Maj snorted with anger and impatience.

"Is simple," she said. "I thought before perhaps you know back then, perhaps you come now to keep the thing from happening, but instead I think you are just stupid, selfish, weak girl. Go away. I am weaving."

Liat stood, stung. She opened her mouth as if to speak, but there was nothing she could think to say. Maj spat casually on the floor at her feet.

Liat spent the next hours upstairs, out on the deck that overlooked the street, letting her rage cool. The winter sun was strong enough to warm her as long as the air was still. The slightest breeze was enough to chill her. High clouds traced scratch marks on the sky. Her heart was troubled, but she couldn't tell any longer if it was Maj's accusation, Itani and Maati, or the case about to go before the Khai that bothered her. Twice, she turned, prepared to go back down to Maj and demand an apology or else offer another of her own. Both times, she stopped before she had passed Amat Kyaan's desk, swamped by her own uncertainties. She was still troubled, probing her thoughts in search of some little clarity, when a figure in the street caught her eye. The brown robe fluttered as Maati ran toward the house. His face was flushed. She felt her heart flutter in sudden dread. Something had happened.

She took the wide, wooden stairs three at a time, rushing down into the common room. She heard Maati's voice outside the rear door, raised and arguing. Unbolting the door and pulling it open, she found one of the guards barring Maati's way. Maati was in a pose of command, demanding that he be let in. When he saw her, he went silent, and his face paled. Liat touched the guard's arm.

"Please," she said. "He's here for me."

"The old woman didn't say anything about him," the guard said.

"She didn't know. Please. She'd want him to come through."

The guard scowled, but stood aside. Maati came in. He looked ill— eyes glassy and bloodshot, skin gray. His robes were creased and wrinkled, as if they'd been slept in. Liat took his hand in her own without thinking.

"I got your message," Maati said. "I came as soon as I could. He isn't here?"

"No," Liat said. "I thought, since he stayed with you after he came back from the Dai-kvo, maybe he'd come to you and . . ."

"He did," Maati said, and sat down. "After he brought you here, he took a bunk at the seafront. He came to see me last night."

"He didn't stay?"

Maati pressed his lips thin and looked away. She was aware of Maj, standing in the alcove, watching them, but the shame in Maati's face was too profound for her to care what the islander made of this. Liat swallowed, trying to ease the tightness in her throat. Maati carefully, intentionally, released her hand from his. She let it drop to her side.

"He found out?" Liat asked, her voice small. "He knows what happened?"

"I told him," Maati said. "I had to. I thought he would come back here, that he'd be with you."

"No. He never did."

"Do you think . . . if Wilsin found him . . ."

"Amat doesn't think Wilsin would do anything against him. There's nothing to gain from it. More likely, he only doesn't want to see us."

Maati sank to a bench, his head in his hands. Liat sat beside him, her unwounded arm around his shoulders. Itani was gone, lost to her. She knew it like her own name. She rested her head against Maati, and closed her eyes, half-desperate with the fear that he would go as well.

"Give him time," she murmured. "He needs time to think. That's all. Everything is going to be fine."

"It isn't," Maati said. His tone wasn't despairing or angry, only matter-of-fact. "Everything is going to be broken, and there's nothing I can do about it."

She closed her eyes, felt the rise and fall of his breath like waves coming to shore. Felt him shift as he turned to her and put his arms around her. Her wounds ached with the force of his embrace, but she would have bitten her tongue bloody before she complained. Instead she stroked his hair and wept.

"Don't leave me," she said. "I couldn't stand to lose you both."

"I'll stop breathing first," Maati said. "I swear I'll stop breathing before I leave you. But I have to find Otah-kvo."

The painful, wonderful arms unwrapped, and Maati stood. His face was serious to the point of grave. He took her hand.

"If Otah-kvo . . . if the two of you cannot reconcile . . . Liat, I would be less than whole without you. My life isn't entirely my own—I have duties to the Dai-kvo and the Khaiem—but what is mine to choose, I'd have you be part of."

Liat blinked back tears.

"You would choose me over him?"

The words shook him, she could see that. For a moment, she wanted more than anything to unsay them, but time only moved forward. Maati met her gaze again.

"I can't lose either of you," he said. "What peace Otah-kvo and I make, if we can make any, is between the two of us. What I feel for you, Liat . . . I could sink my life on those rocks. You've become that much to me. If you stay with him, I will be your friend forever."

It was like pouring cool water on a burn. Liat felt herself sink back.

"Go, then. Find him if you can and tell him how sorry I am. And whether you do or not, come back to me, Maati. Promise you'll come back."

It was still some minutes before Maati tore himself away and headed out into the streets of the city. Liat, after he had gone, sat on the bench, her eyes closed, observing the roiling emotions in her breast. Guilt, yes, but also joy. Fear, but also relief. She loved Maati, she saw that now. As she had loved Itani once, when they had only just begun. It was because of this confusion that she didn't notice for a long time that she was being watched.

Maj stood in the alcove, one hand pressed to her lips, her eyes shining with tears. Liat stood slowly, and took a pose that was a query. Maj strode across the room to her, put her hands on Liat's neck and—unnervingly—kissed her on the lips.

"Poor rabbit," Maj said. "Poor stupid rabbit. Am very sorry. The boy and you together. It makes me think of the man who I was . . . of the father. Before, I call you stupid and selfish and weak because I am forgetting what it is to be young. I am young once, too, and I am not my best mind now. What I say to hurt you, I take back, yes?"

Liat nodded, recognizing the apology in the words, if not the whole sense of them. Maj responded with a string of Nippu that Liat couldn't follow, but she caught the words for *knowledge* and for *pain*. Maj patted Liat's cheek gently and stepped away.

19

>+< "Does it bother you, grandmother?" Mitat asked as they walked down the street. She spoke softly, so that the words stayed between the two of them, and not so far forward as the two mercenary guards before them or so far back as the two behind.

"I can think of a half dozen things you might mean," Amat said.

"Speaking against Wilsin."

"Of course it does," Amat said. "But it isn't something I chose."

"It's only that House Wilsin was good to you for so long . . . it was like family, wasn't it? To make your own way now . . ."

Amat narrowed her eyes. Mitat flushed and took a pose of apology which she ignored.

"This isn't a conversation about me, is it?" Amat asked.

"Not entirely," Mitat said.

The breeze blowing in from the sea chilled her, and the sun, already falling to the horizon, did nothing more than stretch the shadows and redden the light. The banners over the watch house fluttered, the mutter of cloth like voices in another room. Her guards opened the door, nodded to the watchmen inside and gestured Amat and her aide, her friend, her first real ally in the whole sour business, through. Amat paused.

"If you're thinking of leaving, you and your man, I want two things of you. First, wait until the suit is presented. Second, let me make an offer for your time. If we can't negotiate something, you can go with my blessings."

"The terms of my indenture were harsh, and you could . . ."

"Oh don't be an ass," Amat said. "That was between you and Ovi Niit. This is between us. Not the same thing at all."

Mitat smiled—a little sadly, Amat thought—and took a pose that sealed an agreement. In the watch house, Amat paid her dues, signed and countersigned the documents, and took her copy for the records of the house. For another turn through the moon's phases, she and her house were citizens in good standing of the soft quarter. She walked back to the house with her five companions, and yet also very much alone.

The scent of garlic sausages tempted her as they passed an old man and his cart, and Amat wished powerfully that she could stop, send away the men and their knives, and sit with Mitat talking as friends might. She could find what price the woman wanted to stay—whatever it was Amat expected she'd be willing to pay it. But the guards wouldn't let them pause or be alone. Mitat wouldn't have had it. Amat herself knew it would have been unwise—somewhere in the city, Marchat Wilsin had to be in a fever of desperation, and he'd proven willing to kill before this. Leaving the comfort house at all was a risk. And still, something like an ordinary life beckoned more seductively than any whore ever had.

One step at a time, Amat moved forward. There would be time later, she told herself, for all that. Later, when the Galts were revealed and her burden was passed on to someone else. When the child's death was avenged and her city was safe and her conscience was clean. Then she could be herself again, if there was anything left of that woman. Or create herself again if there wasn't.

The messenger waited for them at the front entrance of the house. He was a young man, not older than Liat, but he wore the colors of a high servant. A message, Amat knew with a sinking heart, from the Khai Saraykeht.

"You," she said. "You're looking for Amat Kyaan?"

The messenger—a young boy with narrow-set eyes and a thin nose—took a pose of acknowledgement and respect. It was a courtly pose.

"You've found her," Amat said.

The boy plucked a letter from his sleeve sealed with the mark of the Khai Saraykeht. Amat tore it open there in the street. The script was as beautiful as any message from the palaces—calligraphy so ornate as to approach illegibility. Still, Amat had the practice to make it out. She sighed and took a pose of thanks and dismissal.

"I understand," she said. "There's no reply."

"What happened?" Mitat asked as they walked into the house. "Something bad?"

"No," Amat said. "Only the usual delays. The Khai is putting the audience back four days. Another party wishes to be present."

"Wilsin?"

"I assume so. It serves us as much as him, really. We can use a few more days to prepare."

Amat paused in the front room of the house, tapping the folded paper against the edge of a dice table. The sound of a young girl laughing came from the back, from the place where her whores waited to be chosen by one client or another. It was an odd thing to hear. Any hint of joy, it seemed, had become an odd thing to hear. If she were Marchat Wilsin, she'd try one last gesture—throw one last dart at the sky and hope for a miracle.

"Get Torish-cha," Amat said. "I want to discuss security again. And have we had word from Liat's boy? Itani?"

"Nothing yet," the guard by the front door said. "The other one came by before."

"If either of them arrive, send them to see me."

She walked through to the back, Mitat beside her.

"It's likely only a delay," Amat said, "but if he's winning time for a reason, I want to be ready for it."

"Grandmother?"

They had reached the common room—full now with women and boys in the costumes they wore, with the men who ran the games and wine, with the smell of fresh bread and roast lamb and with voices. Mitat stood at the door, her arms crossed. Amat took a querying pose.

"Someone has to tell Maj," she said.

Amat closed her eyes. Of course. As if all the rest wasn't enough, someone would have to tell Maj. She would. If there was going to be a screaming fight, at least they could have it in Nippu. Amat took two long breaths and opened her eyes again. Mitat's expression had softened into a rueful amusement.

"I could have been a dancer," Amat said. "I was very graceful as a girl. I could have been a dancer, and then I would never have had to march through any of this piss."

"I can do it if you want," Mitat said. Amat only smiled, shook her head, and walked toward the door to the little room of Maj's and the storm that was inescapably to be suffered.

OTAH MACHI, THE SIXTH SON OF THE KHAI MACHI, SAT AT THE END OF THE wharf and looked out over the ocean. The fading twilight left only the light of a half moon dancing on the tops of the waves. Behind him, the work of the seafront was finished for the day, and the amusements of night time—almost as loud—had begun. He ignored the activity, ate slices of hot ginger chicken from the thick paper cone he'd bought at a stand, and thought about nothing.

He had two lengths of copper left to him. Years of work, years of making a life for himself in this city, and he had come to that—two lengths of copper. Enough to buy a bowl of wine, if he kept his standards low. Everything else, spent or lost or thrown away. But he was, at least, prepared. Below him, the tide was rising. It would fall again before the dawn came.

The time had come.

He walked the length of the seafront, throwing the spent paper soaked in grease and spices into a firekeeper's kiln where it flared and blackened, lighting for a moment the faces of the men and women warming themselves at the fire. The warehouses were dark and closed, the wide Nantan empty. Outside a teahouse, a woman sang piteously over a begging box with three times more money in it than Otah had in the world. He tossed in one of his copper lengths for luck.

The soft quarter was much the same as any night. He was the one who was different. The drum and flute from the comfort houses, the smell of incense and stranger smokes, the melancholy eyes of women selling themselves from low parapets and high windows. It was as if he had come to the place for the first time—a traveler from a foreign land. There was time, he supposed, to turn aside. Even now, he could walk away from it all as he had from the school all those years before. He could walk away now and call it strength or purity. Or the calm of stone. He could call it that, but he would know the truth of it.

The alley was where Seedless had said it would be, hidden almost in the shadows of the buildings that lined it. He paused there for a time. Far down in the darkness, a lantern glowed without illuminating anything but itself. A showfighter lumbered past, blood flowing from his scalp. Two sailors across the street pointed at the wounded man, laughing. Otah stepped into darkness.

Mud and filth slid under his boots like a riverbed. The lantern grew nearer, but he reached the door the andat had described before he reached the light. He pressed his hand to it. The wood was solid, the lock was black iron. The light glimmering through at the edges of the shutters showed that a fire was burning within. The poet in his private apartments, the place where he hid from the beauty of the palaces and the house that had come with his burden. Otah tried the door gently, but it was locked. He scratched at it and then rapped, but no one came. With a knife, he could have forced the lock, unhinged the door—a man drunk enough might even have slept through it, but he would have had to come much later. The andat had told him not to go to the hidden apartment until well past the night candle's middle mark, and it wasn't to the first quarter yet.

"Heshai-kvo," he said, not shouting, but his voice loud enough to ring against the stonework around him. "Open the door."

For a long moment, he thought no one would come. But then the line of light that haloed the shutters went dark, a bolt shot with a solid click, and the door creaked open. The poet stood silhouetted. His robes were disheveled as his hair. His wide mouth was turned down in a heavy scowl.

"What do you think you're doing here?"

"We need to talk," Otah said.

"No we don't," the poet said, stepping back and starting to pull the door closed. "Go away."

Otah pushed in, first squaring his shoulder against the door, and then leaning in with his back and legs. The poet fell back with a surprised huff of breath. The rooms were small, dirty, squalid. A cot of stretched canvas was pulled too close to a fireplace, and empty bottles littered the floor by it. Streaks of dark mold ran down the walls from the sagging beams of the ceiling. The smell was like a swamp in summer. Otah closed the door behind him.

"Wh- what do you want?" the poet said, his face pale and fearful.

"We need to talk," Otah said again. "Seedless told me where to find you. He sent me here to kill you."

"Kill me?" Heshai repeated, and then chuckled. The fear seemed to drain away, and a bleak amusement took its place. "Kill me. Gods."

Shaking his head, the poet lumbered to the cot and sat. The canvas groaned against its wooden frame. Otah stood between the fire and the doorway, ready to block Heshai if he bolted. He didn't.

"So. You've come to finish me off, eh? Well, you're a big, strong boy. I'm old and fat and more than half drunk. I doubt you'll have a problem."

"Seedless told me that you'd welcome it," Otah said. "I suspect he overstated his case, eh? Anyway, I'm not his puppet."

The poet scowled, his bloodshot eyes narrowing in the firelight. Otah stepped forward, knelt as he had as a boy at the school and took a pose appropriate to a student addressing a teacher.

"You know what's happening. Amat Kyaan's audience before the Khai Saraykeht. You have to know what would happen."

Slowly, grudgingly, Heshai took an acknowledging pose.

"Seedless hoped that I would kill you in order to prevent it. But I find I'm not a murderer," Otah said. "The stakes here, the price that innocent people will pay . . . and the price Maati will pay. It's too high. I can't let it happen."

"I see," Heshai said. He was silent for a long moment, the ticking of the fire the only sound. Thoughtfully, he reached down and lifted a half-full bottle from the floor. Otah watched the old man drink, the thick throat working as he gulped the wine down. Then, "And how do you plan to reconcile these two issues, eh?"

"Let the andat go," Otah said. "I've come to ask you to set Seedless free."

"That simple, eh?"

"Yes."

"I can't do it."

"I think that you can," Otah said.

"I don't mean it can't be done. Gods, nothing would be easier. I'd only have to . . ." He opened one hand in a gesture of release. "That isn't what I meant. It's that *I* can't do it. It's not . . . it isn't in me. I'm sorry, boy. I know it looks simple from where you are. It isn't. I'm the poet of Saraykeht, and that isn't something you stop being just because you get tired. Just because it eats you. Just because it kills children. Look, if you had the choice of grabbing a live coal and holding it in your fist or destroying a city of innocent people, you'd do everything you could to stand the pain. You wouldn't be a decent man if you didn't at least try."

"And you would be a decent man if you let the Khai Saraykeht take his vengeance?"

"No, I'd be a poet," Heshai said, and his smile was as much melancholy as humor. "You're too young to understand. I've been holding this coal in my hand since before you were born. I can't stop now because

I *can't*. Who I am is too much curled around this. If I stopped—just *stopped*—I wouldn't be anyone anymore."

"I think you're wrong."

"Yes. Yes, I see you think that, but your opinion on it doesn't matter. And that doesn't surprise you, does it?"

The sick dread in Otah's belly suddenly felt as heavy as if he'd swallowed stone. He took a pose of acknowledgement. The poet leaned forward and put his wide, thick hand gently over Otah's.

"You knew I wouldn't agree," he said.

"I . . . hoped . . ."

"You had to try," Heshai said, his tone approving. "It speaks well of you. You had to try. Don't blame yourself. I haven't been strong enough to end this, and I've been up to my hips in it for decades. Wine?"

Otah accepted the offered bottle. It was strong—mixed with something that left a taste of herb at the back of his throat. He handed it back. Warmth bloomed in his belly. Heshai, seeing his surprise, laughed.

"I should have warned you. It's a little more than they serve with lamb cuts, but I like it. It lets me sleep. So, if you don't mind my asking, what made our mutual acquaintance think you'd do his killing for him?"

Otah found himself telling the tale—his own secret and Wilsin's, the source of Liat's wounds and the prospect of Maati's. Throughout, Heshai listened, his face clouded, nodding from time to time or asking questions that made Otah clarify himself. When the secret of Otah's identity came out, the poet's eyes widened, but he made no other comment. Twice, he passed the bottle of wine over, and Otah drank from it. It was strange, hearing it all spoken, hearing the thoughts he'd only half-formed made real by the words he found to express them. His own fate, the fate of others—justice and betrayal, loyalty and the changes worked by the sea. The wine and the fear and the pain and dread in Otah's guts turned the old man into his confessor, his confidant, his friend even if only for the moment.

The night candle was close to the halfway mark when he finished it all—his thoughts and fears, secrets and failures. Or almost all. There was one left that he wasn't ready to mention—the ship he'd booked two passages on with the last of his silver, ready to sail south before the dawn—a small Westlands ship, desperate enough to ply winter trade

where the waters never froze. An escape ship for a murderer and his accomplice. That he held still to himself.

"Hard," the poet said. "Hard. Maati's a good boy. Despite it all, he is
good. Only young."

"Please, Heshai-kvo," Otah said. "Stop this thing."

"It's out of my hands. And really, even if I were to let the beast slip,
your whoremonger sounds like she's good enough to tell a strong story.
The next andat the Dai-kvo sends might be just as terrible. Or another
Khai could be pressed into service, meting out vengeance on behalf of
all the cities together. Killing me might spare Maati and keep your secrets, but Liat . . . the Galts . . ."

"I'd thought of that."

"Anyway, it's too late for me. Shifting names, changing who you are,
putting lives on and off like fine robes—that's a young man's game.
There's too many years loaded on the back of my cart. The weight
makes turning tricky. How would you have done it, if you did?"

"Do what?"

"Kill me?"

"Seedless told me to come just before dawn," Otah said. "He said a
cord around the throat, pulled tight, would keep you from crying out."

Heshai chuckled, but the sound was grim. He swallowed down the
last dregs of the wine, leaving a smear of black leaves on the side of the
bottle. He fumbled for a moment in the chaos under his cot, pulled out
a fresh bottle and opened it roughly, throwing the cork into the fire.

"He's an optimist," Heshai said. "The way I drink, I'll be senseless
as stones by the three quarters."

Otah frowned, and then the import of the words came over him like
cold water. The dread in his belly became a knot, but he didn't speak.
The poet looked into the fire, the low, dying flames cast shadows on his
wide, miserable features. The urge to take the old man in his arms and
embrace or else shake him came over Otah and passed—a wave against
the shore. When the old man's gaze shifted, Otah saw his own darkness
mirrored there.

"I've always done what I was told to, my boy. The rewards aren't
what you'd expect. You aren't a killer. I'm a poet. If we're going to stop
this thing, one of us has to change."

"I should go," Otah said, drawing himself up to his feet.

Heshai-kvo took a pose of farewell, intimate as family. Otah replied with something very much the same. There were tears, he saw, on Heshai's cheeks to match his own.

"You should lock the door behind me," Otah said.

"Later," Heshai said. "I'll do it later if I remember to."

The fetid, chill air of the alley was like waking from a dream—or half-waking. Overhead, the half-moon slipped through wisps and fingers of clouds, insubstantial as veils. He walked with his head held high, but though he was ashamed of them, he couldn't stanch the tears. From outside himself, he could observe the sorrow and the black tarry dread, different from fear because of its perfect certainty. He was becoming a murderer. He wondered how his brothers would manage this, when the time came for them to turn on one another, how they would bring themselves with cool, clear minds, to end another man's life.

The comfort house of Amat Kyaan glowed in the night as the others of its species did—music and voices, the laughter of whores and the cursing of men at the tables. The wealth of the city poured through places like this in a tiny city in itself, given over entirely to pleasure and money. It wouldn't always be so, he knew. He stood in the street and drank in the sight, the smell, the golden light and brightly colored banners, the joy and the sorrow of it. Tomorrow, it would be part of a different city.

The guard outside the back door recognized him.

"Grandmother wants to see you," the man said.

Otah watched himself take a pose of acknowledgement and smile his charming smile.

"Do you know where I could find her?"

"Up in her rooms with Wilsin's girl."

Otah gave his thanks and walked in. The common room wasn't empty—a handful of women sat at the tables, eating and talking among themselves. A black-haired girl, nearly naked, stood in the alcove, cupping her breasts in diaphanous silk with the air of a fish seller wrapping cod. Otah considered the wide, rough-hewn stairs that led to Amat Kyaan's apartments, to Liat. The door at the top landing was closed. He turned away, scratching lightly on the door of the other room—the one he had seen Maj retreat to the one night he had been there, the one time they had spoken.

The door pulled open just wide enough for the islander's face to appear. Her pale skin was flushed, her eyes bright and bloodshot. Otah leaned close.

"Please," he said. "I need to speak with you."

Maj's eyes narrowed, but a breath later, she stepped back, and Otah pushed into the room, closing the door behind him. Maj stood, arms pulled back, chin jutting like a child ready for a fight. A single lantern sat on a desk showing the cot, the hand-loom, the heap of robes waiting for the launderer. An empty winebowl lay canted in the corner of wall and floor. She was drunk. Otah calculated that quickly, and found that it was likely a good thing.

"Maj-cha," Otah said. "Forgive me, but I need your help. And I think I may be of service to you."

"I am living here," she said. "Not working. I am not one of these girls. Get out."

"No," Otah said, "that isn't what I mean. Maj, I can give you your vengeance now—tonight. The man who wields the andat. The one who actually took the child from you. I can take you to him now."

Maj frowned and shook her head slowly, her gaze locked on Otah. He spoke quickly, and low, using simple words with as few poses as he could manage. He explained that the Galts had been Seedless' tools, that Heshai controlled Seedless, that Otah could take her to him if they left now, right now. He thought he saw her soften, something like hope in her expression.

"But afterwards," he said, "you have to let me take you home. I have a ship ready to take us. It leaves before dawn."

"I ask grandmother," Maj said, and moved toward the door. Otah shifted to block her.

"No. She can't know. She wants to stop the Galts, not the poet. If you tell her, you have to go the way she goes. You have to put it before the Khai and wait to see what he chooses to do. I can give it to you now—tonight. But you have to leave Amat before you see the Khai. It's my price."

"You think I am stupid? Why should I trust you? Why are you doing this?"

"You aren't stupid. You should trust me because I have what you want—certainty, an end to waiting, vengeance, and a way back home. I'm doing this because I don't want to see any more women suffer what you've suffered, and because it takes the thing that did this out of the world forever."

Because it saves Maati and Liat. Because it saves Heshai. Because it is a terrible thing, and it is right. And because I have to get you away from this house.

A half smile pulled at her thick, pale mouth.

"You are man?" Maj asked. "Or you are ghost?"

Otah took a pose of query. Maj reached out and touched him, pressing his shoulder gently with her fingertips, as if making sure his flesh had substance.

"If you are man, then I am tired of being tricked. You lie to me and I will kill you with my teeth. If you are ghost, then you are maybe the one I am praying for."

"If you were praying for this," Otah said, "then I'm the answer to it. But get your things quickly. We have to go now, and we can't come back."

For a moment she wavered, and then the anger he had seen in her before, the desperation, shone in her eyes. It was what he had known was there, what he had counted on. She looked around at the tiny room, gathered up what looked like a half-knitted cloth and deliberately spat on the ground.

"Is nothing more I want here," Maj said. "You take me now. You show me. If is not as you say, I kill you. You doubt that?"

"No," he said. "I believe you."

It was a simple enough thing to distract the guard, to send him up to speak with Amat Kyaan—her security was done with attack in mind, not escape. Leading Maj out the back took the space of four breaths, perhaps five. Another dozen, and they were gone, vanished into the maze of streets and alleys that made up the soft quarter.

Maj stayed close to him as they went, and when they passed torches or street lanterns, he caught glimpses of her face, wild with release and the heat of fury. The alley, when he reached it, was empty. The door, when he tried it, was unlocked.

MAATI STEPPED INTO THE POET'S HOUSE, HIS FEET SORE, HIS HEAD BUZZING like a hive. The house was silent, dark, and cold. Only the single, steady flame of a night candle stood watch in a lantern of glass. It had burned down past the half mark, the night more than half over. He dropped to a tapestry-draped divan and pulled the heavy cloth over

him. He had visited every teahouse he knew of, had asked everyone he
recognized. Otah-kvo had vanished—stepped into the thin mists of the
seafront like a memory. And every step had been a journey, every
fingers-width of the moon in its nightly arc had encompassed a lifetime.
He'd expected, huddled under the heavy cloth, for sleep to come
quickly and yet the dim glow of the candle distracted him, pulled his
eyes open just when he had told himself that finally, finally he was letting the day fall away from him. He shifted, his robes bunching uncomfortably under his arm, at his ribs. It seemed half a night before he gave
up and sat, letting his makeshift blankets fall away. The night candle
was still well before the three-quarter mark.

"Wine might help," the familiar voice said from the darkness of the
stairway. "It has the advantage of tradition. Many's the night our noble
poet's slept beside a pool of his own puke, stinking of half-digested
grapes."

"Be quiet," Maati said, but there was no force to his voice, no reserve
left to fend off the attentions of the andat. Slowly, the perfect face and
hands descended. He wore a robe of white, pale as his skin. A mourning
robe. His demeanor when he sat on the second stair, stretching out his
legs and smiling, was the same as ever—amused and scheming and un-
trustworthy and sad. But perhaps there was something else, an underly-
ing energy that Maati didn't understand.

"I only mean that a hard night can be ended, if only you have the will
to do it. And don't mind paying the price, when it comes."

"Leave me alone," Maati said. "I don't want to talk to you."

"Not even if your little friend came by, the seafront laborer?"

Maati's breath stopped, his blood suddenly with a separate life from
his own. He took an interrogative pose. Seedless laughed.

"Oh, he didn't," the andat said. "I was just wondering about your
terms. If you didn't want to speak to me under any conditions, or if perhaps there might be exceptions to your rule. Purely hypothetical."

Maati felt the flush in his face, as much anger as embarrassment, and
picked up the nearest thing to throw at Seedless. It was a beaded cushion, and it bounced off the andat's folded knees. Seedless took a pose of
contrition, rose, and carried the cushion back to its place.

"I don't mean to hurt you, my dear. But you look like someone's just
stolen your puppy, and I thought a joke might brighten things. I'm sorry
if I was wrong."

"Where's Heshai?"

The andat paused, looking out, as if the black eyes could see through the walls, through the trees, any distance to consider the poet where he lay. A thin smile curled its lips.

"Away," Seedless said. "In his torture box. The same as always, I suppose."

"He isn't here, though."

"No," Seedless said, simply.

"I need to speak to him."

Seedless sat on the couch beside him, considering him in silence, his expression distant as the moon. The mourning robe wasn't new though it clearly hadn't seen great use. The cut was simple, the cloth coarse and unsoftened by pounding. From the way it sagged, it was clearly intended for a wider frame than Seedless'—it was clearly meant for Heshai. Seedless seemed to see him notice all this, and looked down, as if aware of his own robes for the first time.

"He had these made when his mother died," the andat said. "He was with the Dai-kvo at the time. He didn't see her pyre, but the news reached him. He keeps it around, I suppose, so that he won't have to buy another one should anybody else die."

"And what makes you wear it?"

Seedless shrugged, grinned, gestured with wide-spread hands that indicated everything and nothing.

"Respect for the dead," Seedless said, "Why else?"

"Everything's a joke to you," Maati said. The fatigue made his tongue thick, but if anything, he was farther from rest than before he'd come back to the house. The combination of exhaustion and restlessness felt like an illness. "Nothing matters."

"Not true," the andat said. "Just because something's a game, doesn't mean it isn't serious."

"Gods. Is there something in the way Heshai-kvo made you that keeps you from making sense? You're like talking to smoke."

"I can speak to the point if you'd like," Seedless said. "Ask me what you want."

"I don't have anything to ask you, and you don't have anything to teach me," Maati said, rising. "I'm going to sleep. Tomorrow can't be worse than today was."

"Possibility is a wide field, dear. *Can't* is a word for small imaginations." Seedless said from behind him, but Maati didn't turn back.

His room was colder than the main room. He lit a small fire in the brazier before he pulled back the woolen blankets, pulled off his shoes, and tried again to sleep. The errands of the day ran through his mind, unstoppable and chaotic: Liat's distress and the warmth of her flesh, Otah-kvo's last words to him and the searing remorse that they held. If only he could find him, if only he could speak with him again.

Half-awake, Maati began to catalog for himself the places he had been in the night, searching for a corner he knew of, but might have overlooked. And, as he pictured the night streets of Saraykeht, he found himself moving down them, knowing as he did that he was dreaming. Street and alley, square and court, until he was in places that were nowhere real in the city, searching for teahouses that didn't truly exist other than within his own frustration and despair, and aware all the time that this was a dream, but was not sleep.

He kicked off the blankets, desperate for some sense of freedom. But the little brazier wasn't equal to its work, and the cold soon brought him swimming back up into his full mind. He lay in the darkness and wept. When that brought no relief, he rose changed into fresh robes, and stalked down the stairs.

Seedless had started a fire in the grate. A copper pot of wine was warming over it, filling the room with its rich scent. The andat sat in a wooden chair, a book open in his lap. The brown, leather-bound volume that told of his own creation and its errors. He didn't look up when Maati came in and walked over to the fire, warming his feet by the flames. When he spoke, he sounded weary.

"The spirit's burned out of it. You can drink as much as you'd like and not impair yourself."

"What's the point, then?" Maati asked.

"Comfort. It may taste a little strong, though. I thought you'd come down sooner, and it gets thick if it boils too long."

Maati turned his back to the andat and used an old copper ladle to fill his winebowl. When his took a sip, it tasted rich and hot and red. And, perversely, comforting.

"It's fine," he said.

He heard the hush of paper upon paper as, behind him, Seedless closed the book. The silence afterward went on so long that he looked back over his shoulder. The andat sat motionless as a statue; not even breath stirred the folds of his robe and his face betrayed nothing. His ribs shifted an inch, taking in air, and he spoke.

"What would you have said, if you'd found him?"

Maati shifted, sitting with his legs crossed, the warm bowl in his hands. He blew across it to cool it before he answered.

"I'd have asked his forgiveness."

"Would you have deserved it, do you think?"

"I don't know. Possibly not. What I did was wrong."

Seedless chuckled and leaned forward, lacing his long graceful fingers together.

"Of course it was," Seedless said. "Why would anyone ask forgiveness for something they'd done that was right? But tell me, since we're on the subject of judgment and clemency, why would you ask for something you don't deserve?"

"You sound like Heshai-kvo."

"Of course I do, you're evading. If you don't like that question, leave it aside and answer me this instead. Would you forgive me? What I did was wrong, and I know it. Would you do for me what you'd ask of him?"

"Would you want me to?"

"Yes," Seedless said, and his voice was strangely plaintive. It wasn't an emotion Maati had ever seen in the andat before now. "Yes, I want to be forgiven."

Maati sipped the wine, then shook his head.

"You'd do it again, wouldn't you? If you could, you'd sacrifice anyone or anything to hurt Heshai-kvo."

"You think that?"

"Yes."

Seedless bowed his head until his hair tipped over his hands.

"I suppose you're right," he said. "Fine, then this. Would you forgive Heshai-kvo for his failings? As a teacher to you, as a poet in making something so dangerously flawed as myself. Really, pick anything—there's no end of ways in which he's wanting. Does he deserve mercy?"

"Perhaps," Maati said. "He didn't mean to do what he did."

"Ah! And because I planned, and he blundered, the child is more my wrong than his?"

"Yes."

"Then you've forgotten again what we are to each other, he and I. But let that be. If your laborer friend—you called him Otah-kvo, by the way. You should be more careful of that. If Otah-kvo did something wrong, if he committed some crime or helped someone else commit one, could you let that go?"

"You know . . . how did you . . ."

"I've known for weeks, dear. Don't let it worry you. I haven't told anyone. Answer the question; would you hold his crimes against him as you hold mine against me?"

"No, I don't think I would. Who told you that Otah was . . ."

Seedless leaned back and took a pose of triumph.

"And what's the difference between us, laborer and andat that you'll brush his sins aside and not my own?"

Maati smiled.

"You aren't him," he said.

"And you love him."

Maati took a pose of affirmation.

"And love is more important than justice," Seedless said.

"Sometimes. Yes."

Seedless smiled and nodded.

"What a terrible thought," he said. "That love and injustice should be married."

Maati shifted to a dismissive pose, and in reply the andat took the brown book back up, leafing through the handwritten pages as if looking for his place. Maati closed his eyes and breathed in the fumes of the wine. He felt profoundly comfortable, like sleep—true sleep—coming on. He felt himself rocking slowly, involuntarily shifting in time with his pulse. A sense of disquiet roused him and without opening his eyes again, he spoke.

"You mustn't tell anyone about Otah-kvo. If his family finds him . . ."

"They won't," Seedless said. "At least not through me."

"I don't believe you."

"This time, you can. Heshai-kvo did his best by you. Do you know that? For all his failings, and for all of mine, to the degree that our private war allowed it, we have taken care of you and . . ."

The andat broke off. Maati opened his eyes. The andat wasn't looking at him or the book, but out, to the south. It was as if his sight penetrated the walls, the trees, the distance, and took in some spectacle that held him. Maati couldn't help following his gaze, but there was nothing but the rooms of the house. When he glanced back, the andat's expression was exultant.

"What is it?" Maati asked, a cold dread at his back.

"It's Otah-kvo," Seedless said. "He's forgiven you."

THE SINGLE CANDLE BURNED, MARKING THE HOURS OF THE NIGHT. ON THE cot where Otah had left him, the poet slept, all color leached from his face by the dim light. The poet's mouth was open, his breath deep and regular. Maj, at his side, knelt, considering the sleeping man's face. Otah shut the door.

"Is him," Maj said, her voice low and tense. "Is the one who does this to me. To my baby."

Otah moved forward, careful not to rattle the bottles on the floor, not to make any sound that would wake the sleeper.

"Yes," he said. "It is."

Silently, Maj pulled a knife from her sleeve. It was a thin blade, long as her hand but thinner than a finger. Otah touched her wrist and shook his head.

"Quiet," he said. "It has to be quiet."

"So how?" she asked.

Otah fumbled for a moment in his own sleeve and drew out the cord. It was braided bamboo, thin and supple, but so strong it would have borne Otah's weight without snapping. Wooden grips at each end fit his fingers to keep it from cutting into his flesh when he pulled it tight. It was a thug's weapon. Otah saw it in his own hands as if from a distance. The dread in his belly had suffused through his body, through the world, and disconnected him from everything. He felt like a puppet, pulled by invisible strings.

"I hold him," Maj said. "You do this."

Otah looked at the sleeping man. There was no rage in him to carry him through, no hatred to justify it. For a moment, he thought of turning away, of rousing the man or calling out for the watch. It would be so simple, even now, to turn back. Maj seemed to read his thoughts. Her eyes, unnatural and pale, met his.

"You do this," she said again.

He would walk onto the blade . . .

"His legs," Otah said. "I'll worry about his arms, but you keep him from kicking free."

Maj moved in so close to the cot, she seemed almost ready to crawl onto it with Heshai. Her hands flexed in the space above the bend of the poet's knees. Otah looped the cord, ready to drop it over the poet's head, his fingers in the curves that were made for them. He stepped forward. His foot brushed a bottle, the sound of glass rolling over stone louder than thunder in the silence. The poet lurched, lifted himself, less than half awake, up on his elbow.

As if his body had been expecting it, Otah dropped the cord into place and pulled. He was dimly aware of the soft sounds of Maj struggling, pulling, holding the poet down. The poet's hands were at his throat now, fingers digging for the cord that had vanished, almost, into the flesh. Otah's hands and arms ached, and the broad muscles across his shoulders burned as he drew the cord as tight as his strength allowed. The poet's face was dark with blood, his wide lips black. Otah closed his eyes, but didn't loose his grip. The struggle grew weaker. The flailing arms and clawing fingers became the soft slaps of a child, and then stopped. In the darkness behind his eyes, Otah still pulled, afraid that if he stopped too soon it would all have to be done again. There was a wet sound, and the smell of shit. His back knotted between his shoulder blades, but he counted a dozen breaths, and then a half dozen more, before he looked up.

Maj stood at the foot of the cot. Her robes were disarranged and a bad bruise was already blooming on her cheek. Her expression was serene as a statue's. Otah released the cord, his fingers stiff. He kept his gaze high, not wanting to see the body. Not at any price.

"It's done," he said, his voice shaky. "We should go."

Maj said something, not to him but to the corpse between them. Her words were flowing and lovely and he didn't know what they meant. She turned and walked solemn and regal out of the room, leaving Otah to follow her. He hesitated at the doorway, caught between wanting to look back and not, between the horror of the thing he had done and the relief that it was over. Perversely, he felt guilty leaving Heshai like this without giving some farewell; it seemed rude.

"Thank you, Heshai-kvo," he said at last, and took a pose appropriate for a pupil to an honored teacher. After a moment, he dropped his hands, stepped out, and closed the door.

The air of the alleyway was sharp and cold, rich with the threat of rain. For a brief, frightened moment, he thought he was alone, that Maj had gone, but the sound of her retching gave her away. He found her doubled over in the mud, weeping and being sick. He placed a hand on her back, reassuring and gentle, until the worst had passed. When she rose, he brushed off what he could of the mess and, his arm around her, led her out from the alleyway, to the west and down, towards the seafront and away at last from Saraykeht.

"WHAT DO YOU MEAN?" MAATI ASKED. "HOW HAS OTAH-KVO . . ."

And then he stopped because, with a sound like a sigh and a scent like rain, Seedless had vanished, and only the mourning robes remained.

20

>+< Morning seemed like any other for nearly an hour, and then the news came. When Liat heard it humming through the comfort house—Maj gone, the poet killed—she ran to the palaces. She forgot her own safety, if there was safety to be had anywhere. When she finally crossed the wooden bridge over water tea-brown with dead leaves, her sides ached, her wounded shoulder throbbed with her heartbeat.

She didn't know what she would say. She didn't know how she would tell him.

When she opened the door, she knew there was no need.

The comfortable, finely appointed furniture was cast to the walls, the carpets pulled back. A wide stretch of pale wooden flooring lay bare and empty as a clearing. The air smelled of rain and smoke. Maati, dressed in formal robes poorly tied, knelt in the center of the space. His skin was ashen, his hair half-wild. A book lay open before him, bound in leather, its pages covered in beautiful script. He was chanting, a soft sillibant flow that seemed to echo against the walls and move back into itself, complex as music. Liat watched, fascinated, as Maati shifted back and forth his lips moving, his hands restless. Something like a wind pressed against her without disturbing the folds of her robes. A sense of profound presence, like standing before the Khai only a thousand times as intense and a thousand times less humane.

"Stop this!" she screamed even, it seemed, as she understood. "*Stop!*"

She rushed forward, pushing through the thick presence, the air oppressive as a furnace, but with something besides heat. Maati seemed to hear her voice distantly. His head turned, his eyes opened, and he lost the thread of the chant. Echoes fell out of phase with each other, their rhythms collapsing like a crowd that had been clapping time falling into mere applause. And then the room was silent and empty again except for the two of them.

"You can't," she said. "You said that it was too near what Heshai had done before. You said that it couldn't work. You *said* so, Maati."

"I have to try," he said. The words were so simple they left her empty. She simply folded beside him, her legs tucked beneath her. Maati blinked like he was only half-awake. "I have to try. I think, perhaps, if I don't wait . . . if I do it now, maybe Seedless isn't all the way gone . . . I can pull him back before Heshai's work has entirely . . ."

It was what she needed, hearing the poet's name. It gave her something to speak to. Liat took his hand in hers. He winced a little, and she relaxed her grip, but not enough to let him go.

"Heshai's dead, Maati. He's gone. And whether he's dead for an hour or a year, he's just as dead. Seedless . . . Seedless is gone. They're both gone."

Maati shook his head.

"I can't believe that," he said. "I understand Heshai better than anyone else. I know Seedless. It's early, and there isn't much time, but if I can only . . ."

"It's too late. It's too late, and if you do this, it's no better than sinking yourself in the river. You'll die, Maati. You told me that. *You* did. If a poet fails to capture the andat, he dies. And this . . ." she nodded to the open book written in a dead man's hand. "It won't work. *You're* the one who said so."

"It's different," he said.

"How?"

"Because I have to try. I'm a poet, love. It's what I am. And you know as well as I do that if Seedless escapes, there's nothing. There's nothing to take his place."

"So there's nothing," she said.

"Saraykeht . . ."

"Saraykeht is a city, Maati. It's roads and walls and people and warehouses and statues. It doesn't know you. It doesn't love you. It's me who does that. I love you. Please, Maati, do not do this."

Slowly, carefully, Maati took his hand from hers. When he smiled, it was as much sorrow as fondness.

"You should go," he said. "I have something I need to do. If it works out as I hope, I'll find you."

Liat rose. The room was hazy with tears, but sorrow wasn't what warmed her chest and burned her skin. It was rage, rage fueled by pain.

"You can kill yourself if you like," she said. "You can do this thing now and die, and they may even talk about you like a hero. But I'll know better."

She turned and walked out, her heart straining. On the steps, she stopped. The sun shone cool over the bare trees. She closed her eyes, waiting to hear the grim, unnatural chant begin again behind her. Crows hopped from branch to branch, and then as if at a signal, rose together and streamed off to the south. She stood for almost half a hand, the chill air pressing into her flesh.

She wondered how long she could wait there. She wondered where Itani was now, and if he knew what had happened. If he would ever forgive her for loving more than one man. She chewed at the inside of her cheek until it hurt.

Behind her, the door scraped open. Maati looked defeated. He was tucking the leather bound book into his sleeve as he stepped out to her.

"Well," he said. "I'll have to go back to the Dai-kvo and tell him I've failed."

She stepped close to him, resting her head against his shoulder. He was warm, or the day had cooled her even more than she'd thought. For a moment, she remembered the feeling of Itani's broad arms and the scent of his skin.

"Thank you," she said.

IT WAS THREE WEEKS NOW SINCE THE POET HAD DIED. THREE WEEKS WAS TOO long, Amat knew, for a city to hold its breath. The tension was still there—the uncertainty, the fear. It showed in the faces of the men and women in the street and in the way they held their bodies. Amat heard it in the too-loud laughter, and angry words of drunkards in the soft quarter streets. But the initial shock was fading. Time, suspended by the sudden change of losing the andat, was moving forward again. And that, as much as anything, drew her out, away from the protection of the comfort house and into the city. Her city.

In the gray of winter fog, the streets were like memories—here a familiar fountain emerged, took shape, and form and weight. The dark green of the stone glistened in the carvings of ship and fish, eagle and archer. And then as she passed, they faded, becoming at last a darkness behind her, and nothing more. She stopped at a stand by the seafront to buy a paper sack of roasted almonds, fresh from the cookfire and covered with raw sugar. The woman to whom Amat handed her length of copper took a pose of gratitude, and Amat moved to the water's edge, considering the half-hidden waves, the thousand smells of the seafront—salt and spiced foods, sewage and incense. She blew sharply through pursed lips to cool the sweets before she bit into them, as she had when she was a girl, and she prepared herself for the last meeting. When the sack was empty, she crumpled it and let it drop into the sea.

House Wilsin was among the first to make its position on the future known by its actions. Even as she walked up the streets to the north, moving steadily toward the compound, carts passed her, heading the other way. The warehouses were being cleared, the offices packed into crates bound for Galt and the Westlands. When she reached the familiar courtyard, the lines of men made her think of ants on sugarcane. She paused at the bronze Galtic Tree, considering it with distaste and, to her surprise, amusement. Three weeks was too long, apparently, for her to hold her breath either.

"Amat-cha?"

She shifted. Epani, her thin-faced, weak-spirited replacement, stood in a pose of welcome belied by the discomfort on his face. She answered it with a pose of her own, more graceful and appropriate.

"Tell him I'd like to speak with him, will you?"

"He isn't . . . that is . . ."

"Epani-cha. Go, tell him I'm here and I want to speak with him. I won't burn the place down while you do it."

Perhaps it was the dig that set him moving. Whatever did it, Epani retreated into the dark recesses of the compound. Amat walked to the fountain, listening to the play of the water as though it was the voice of an old friend. Someone had dredged it, she saw, for the copper lengths thrown in for luck. House Wilsin wasn't leaving anything behind.

Epani returned and without a word led her back through the corridors she knew to the private meeting rooms. The room was as dark as she remembered it. Marchat Wilsin himself sat at the table, lit by the diffuse cool light from the small window, the warm, orange flame of a lantern. With one color on either cheek, he might almost have been two different men. Amat took a pose of greeting and gratitude. Moving as if unsure of himself, Marchat responded with one of welcome.

"I didn't expect to see you again," he said, and his voice was careful.

"And yet, here I am. I see House Wilsin is fleeing, just as everyone said it was. Bad for business, Marchat-cha. It looks like a failure of nerve."

"It is," he said. There was no apology in his voice. They might have been discussing dye prices. "Being in Saraykeht's too risky now. My uncle's calling me back home. I think he must have been possessed by some passing moment of sanity, and what he saw scared him. What we can't ship out by spring, we're selling at a loss. It'll take years for the house to recover. And, of course, I'm scheduled on the last boat out. So. Have you come to tell me you're ready to bring your suit to the Khai?"

Amat took a pose, more casual than she'd intended, that requested clarification. It was an irony, and Marchat's sheepish grin showed that he knew it.

"My position isn't as strong as it was before the victim best placed to stir the heart of the utkahiem killed the poet and destroyed the city. I lost a certain credibility."

"Was it really her, then?"

"I don't know for certain. It appears it was."

"I'd say I was sorry, but . . ."

Amat didn't count the years she'd spent talking to this man across tables like this, or in the cool waters of the bathhouse, or walking together in the streets. She felt them, habits worn into her joints. She sat with a heavy sigh and shook her head.

"I did what I could," she said. "Now . . . now who would believe me, and what would it matter?"

"Someone might still. One of the other Khaiem."

"If you thought that was true, you'd have me killed."

Wilsin's face clouded, something like pain in the wrinkles at the corners of his eyes. Something like sorrow.

"I wouldn't enjoy it," he said at last.

Despite the truth of it, Amat laughed. Or perhaps because of it.

"Is Liat Chokavi still with you?" Marchat asked, then took a pose that offered reassurance. "It's just that I have a box of her things. Mostly her things. Some others may have found their way into it. I won't call it apology, but . . ."

"Unfortunately, no," Amat said. "I offered her a place. The gods all know I could use competent help keeping my books. But she's left with the poet boy. It seems they're heartmates."

Marchat chuckled.

"Oh, *that'll* end well," he said with surprisingly gentle sarcasm.

"Tell Epani to bring us a pot of tea," Amat said. "He can at least do something useful. Then there's business we need to talk through."

Marchat did as she asked, and minutes later, she cupped a small, lovely tea bowl in her hands, blowing across the steaming surface. Marchat poured a bowl for himself, but didn't drink it. Instead, he folded his hands together and rested his great, whiskered chin in them. The silence wasn't a ploy on his part; she could see that. He didn't know what to say. It made the game hers to start.

"There's something I want of you," she said.

"I'll do what I can," he said.

"The warehouses on the Nantan. I want to rent them from House Wilsin."

He leaned back now, his head tilted like a dog hearing an unfamiliar sound. He took an interrogative pose. Amat sipped her tea, but it was still too hot. She put the bowl on the table.

"With the andat lost, I'm gathering investment in a combers hall. I've found ten men who worked as combers when Petals-Falling-Open was still the andat in Saraykeht. They're willing to act as foremen. The initial outlay and the first contracts are difficult. I have people who might be willing to invest if I can find space. They're worried that my relationship with my last employer ended poorly. Rent me the space, and I can address both issues at once."

"But, Amat . . ."

"I lost," she said. "I know it. You know it. I did what I could do, and it got past me. Now I can either press the suit forward despite it all, raise what suspicions against Galt I can in the quarters who will listen to me at the cost of what credibility I have left, or else I can do this. Recreate myself as a legitimate business, organize the city, bind the wounds that can be bound. Forge connections between people who think they're rivals. But I can't do both. I can't have people saying I'm an old woman frightened of shadows while I'm trying to make weavers and rope-makers who've been undercutting each other for the last three generations shake hands."

Marchat Wilsin's eyebrows rose. She watched him consider her. The guilt and horror, the betrayals and threats fell away for a moment, and they were the players in the game of get and give that they had been at their best. It made Amat's heart feel bruised, but she kept it out of her face as he kept his feelings from his. The lantern flame spat, shuddered, and stood back to true.

"It won't work," he said at last. "They'll hold to all their traditional prejudices and alliances. They'll find ways to bite each other while they're shaking hands. Making them all feel loyal to each other and to the city? In the Westlands or Galt or the islands, you might have a chance. But among the Khaiem? It's doomed."

"I'll accept failure when I've failed," Amat said.

"Just remember I warned you. What's your offer for the warehouses?"

"Sixty lengths of silver a year and five hundredths of the profit."

"That's insultingly low, and you know it."

"You haven't figured in that it will keep me from telling the world what the Galtic Council attempted in allying with Seedless against his poet. That by itself is a fair price, but we should keep up appearances, don't you think?"

He thought about it. The tiny upturn of his lips, the barest of smiles, told her what she wanted to know.

"And you really think you can make a going project of this? Combing raw cotton for its seeds isn't a pleasant job."

"I have a steady stream of women looking to retire from one less pleasant than that," she said. "I think the two concerns will work quite nicely together."

"And if I agree to this," Marchat said, his voice suddenly softer, the game suddenly sliding out from its deep-worn track, "does that mean you'll forgive me?"

"I think we're past things like forgiveness," she said. "We're the servants of what we have to do. That's all."

"I can live with that answer. All right, then. I'll have Epani draw up contracts. Should we take them to that whorehouse of yours?"

"Yes," Amat said. "That will do nicely. Thank you, Marchat-cha."

"It's the least I could do," he said and drank at last from the bowl of cooling tea at his elbow. "And also likely the most I can. I don't imagine my uncle will understand it right off. Galtic business doesn't have quite the same subtlety you find with the Khaiem."

"It's because your culture hasn't finished licking off its caul," Amat said. "Once you've had a thousand years of Empire, things may be different."

Marchat's expression soured and he poured himself more tea. Amat pushed her own bowl toward him, and he leaned forward to fill it. The steaming tea clinked against the porcelain.

"There will be a war," Amat said at last. "Between your people and mine. Eventually, there will be a war."

"Galt's a strange place. It's so long since I've been there, I don't know how well I'll fit once I'm back. We've done well by war. In the last generation, we've almost doubled our farmlands. There are places that rival the cities of the Khaiem, if you'll believe that. Only we do it with ruthlessness and bloody-minded determination. You'd have to be there, really, to understand it. It isn't what you people have here."

Amat took an insinstent pose, demanding an answer to her question. Marchat sighed; a long, slow sound.

"Yes, someday. Someday there will be a war, but not in our lifetimes."

She shifted to a pose that was both acknowledgement and thanks. Marchat toyed with his teabowl.

"Amat, before . . . before you go, there's a letter I wrote you. When it looked like the suit was going to go to the Khai and sweet hell was going to rain down on Galt in general and me in particular. I want you to have it."

His face was legible as a boy's. Amat wondered at how he could be so closed and careful with business and so clumsy with his own heart and hers. If she let it continue, he'd be offering her work in Galt next. And a part of her, despite it all, would be sorry to refuse.

"Keep it for now," she said. "I'll take it from you later."

"When?" he asked as she rose.

She answered gently, making the words not an insult, but a moment of shared sorrow. There were, after all, ten thousand things that had been lost in this. And each one of them real, even this.

"After the war, perhaps. Give it to me then."

DREAMING, OTAH FOUND HIMSELF IN A PUBLIC PLACE, PART STREET CORNER, part bathhouse, part warehouse. People milled about, at ease, their conversations a pleasant murmur. With a shock, Otah glimpsed Heshai-kvo in the crowd, moving as if alive, speaking as if alive, but still dead. In the logic of sleep, that fleeting glimpse carried a weight of panic.

Gasping for breath, Otah sat up, his eyes open and confused by the darkness. Only as his heart slowed and his breath grew steady, did the creaking of the ship and rocking of waves remind him where he was. He pressed his palms into his closed eyes until pale lights appeared. Below him, Maj murmured in her sleep.

The cabin was tiny—too short to stand fully upright and hardly long enough to hang two hammocks one above the other. If he put his arms out, he could press his palms against the oiled wood of each wall. There was no room for a brazier, so they slept in their robes. Carefully, he lifted himself down and without touching or disturbing the sleeper, left the close, nightmare-haunted coffin for the deck and the moon and a fresh breeze.

The three men of the watch greeted him as he emerged. Otah smiled and ambled over despite wanting more than anything a moment of solitude. The moment's conversation, the shared drink, the coarse joke— they were a small price to pay for the good will of the men to whom he had entrusted his fate. It was over quickly, and he could retreat to a quiet place by the rail and look out toward an invisible horizon where haze blurred the distinction between sea and sky. Otah sat, resting his arms on the worn wood, and waited for the wisps of dream to fade. As he had every night. As he expected he would for some time still to come. The changing of watch at the half candle brought another handful of men, another moment of sociability. The curious glances and concern that Otah had seen during his first nights on deck were gone. The men had become accustomed to him.

Otah would have guessed the night candle had nearly reached its three quarters mark when she came out to join him, though the night sea sometimes did strange things to time. He might also have been staring at the dark ripples and broken moonlight for sunless weeks.

Maj seemed almost to glow in the moonlight, her skin picking up the blue and the cold. She looked at the landless expanse of water with an almost proprietary air, unimpressed by vastness. Otah watched her find him, watched her walk to where he sat. Though Otah knew that at least one of the sailors on watch spoke Nippu, no one tried to speak with her. Maj lowered herself to the deck beside him, her legs crossed, her pale eyes almost colorless.

"The dreams," she said.

Otah took a pose of acknowledgement.

"If we had hand loom, you should weave," she said. "Put your mind to something real. Is unreal things that eat you."

"I'll be fine," he said.

"You are homesick. I know. I see it."

"I suppose," Otah said. "And I wonder now if we did the right thing."

"You think no?"

Otah turned his gaze back to the water. Something burst up from the surface and vanished again into the darkness, too quickly for Otah to see what shape it was.

"Not really," he said. "That's to say I think we did the best that we could. But that doing that thing was right . . ."

"Killing him," Maj said. "Call it what it is. Not *that thing*. Killing him. Hiding names give them power."

"That killing him was right . . . bothers me. At night, it bothers me."

"And if you can go back—make other choice—do you?"

"No. No, I'd do the same. And that disturbs me, too."

"You live too long in cities," Maj said. "Is better for you to leave."

Otah disagreed but said nothing. The night moved on. It was another week at least before they would reach Quian, southernmost of the eastern islands. The hold, filled now with the fine cloths and ropes of Saraykeht, the spices and metalworks of the cities of the Khaiem, would trade first for pearls and shells, the pelts of strange island animals, and the plumes of their birds. Only as the weeks moved on would they begin taking on fish and dried fruits, trees and salt timber and slaves. And only in the first days of spring—weeks away still and ten island ports at least—would they reach as far north as Nippu.

Years of work on the seafront, all the gifts and assistance Maati had given him for the journey to the Dai-kvo, everything he had, he had poured into two seasons of travel. He wondered what he would do, once he reached Nippu, once Maj was home and safe and with the people she knew. Back from her long nightmare with only the space where a child should have been at her side.

He could work on ships, he thought. He knew enough already to take on the simple, odious tasks like coiling rope and scrubbing decks. He might at least make his way back to the cities of the Khaiem . . . or perhaps not. The world was full of possibility, because he had nothing and no one. The unreal crowded in on him, as Maj had said, because he had abandoned the real.

"You think of her," Maj said.

"What? Ah, Liat? No, not really. Not just now."

"You leave her behind, the girl you love. You are angry because of her and the boy."

A prick of annoyance troubled him but he answered calmly enough.

"It hurt me that they did what they did, and I miss him. I miss them. But . . ."

"But it also frees you," Maj said. "It is for me, too. The baby. I am scared, when I first go to the cities. I think I am never fit in, never belong. I am never be a good mother without my own *itiru* to tell me how she is caring for me when I am young. All this worry I make. And is nothing. To lose everything is not the worst can happen."

"It's starting again, from nothing, with nothing," Otah said.

"Is exactly this," Maj agreed, then a moment later. "Starting again, and doing better."

The still-hidden sun lightened water and sky as they watched it in silence. The milky, lacework haze burned off as the fire rose from the sea and the full crew hauled up sails, singing, shouting, tramping their bare feet. Otah rose, his back aching from sitting so long without moving, and Maj brushed her robes and stood also. As the work of the day entered its full activity, he descended behind her into the darkness of their cabin where he hoped he might cheat his conscience of a few hours sleep. His thoughts still turned on the empty, open future before him and on Saraykeht behind him, a city still waking to the fact that it had fallen.

ABOUT THE AUTHOR

Daniel Abraham has had stories published in the *Vanishing Acts*, *Bones of the World*, and *The Dark* anthologies, and has been included in Gardner Dozois's *Year's Best Science Fiction* anthology as well. *A Shadow in Summer* is his first published novel.

He is currently working on the Long Price Quartet, the second volume of which, *Winter Cities*, will be published in 2007. He lives in New Mexico with his wife.